THICKER THAN WATER

Also by Bethan Darwin and available from Honno

Back Home
Two Times Twenty

THICKER
THAN WATER

by
Bethan Darwin

Tynnwyd o'r stoc
Withdrawn

HONNO MODERN FICTION

First published by Honno Press in 2016. 'Ailsa Craig', Heol y Cawl, Dinas
Powys, South Glamorgan, Wales, CF64 4AH
1 2 3 4 5 6 7 8 9 10
Copyright: Bethan Darwin © 2016

A catalogue record for this book is available from the British Library.

Published with the financial support of the Welsh Books Council.

ISBN 978-1-909983-46-5 (paperback)
ISBN 978-1-909983-47-2 (ebook)

Cover design: Graham Preston
Cover image: © Shutterstock, Inc
Text design: Elaine Sharples
Printed in Wales by Gomer Press

For the Gaskell, Darwin,
Davies and Hopkins families.

This book is fiction and the characters whose stories are told are made up. However, my family's history did give me the idea for the story and some markers around which to drape it.

My grandmother's twin brother from Shevington, Wigan, agreed to accompany his sister on the ship to Canada to join her husband who had gone on ahead. He was meant to return to Shevington having safely dropped his sister off but, having fallen in love with a Scottish lady on the ship on the way over, he stayed in Canada for good. I have been to Oshawa many times to visit my lovely family who still live in the city. My great grandfather Idris was a miner in the Rhondda and decided when registering my grandmother's birth that he would drop one letter from his own name and call her Iris. It was a privilege to have them all keep me company while I was writing.

The historical events that are the backdrop to the story are correct and a few of the characters are also real – members of the British royal family, UK and Canadian politicians, and the McLaughlin family. Parkwood, the McLaughlin family home, is now a National Historic Site, popular for weddings and as a film location. The Parkwood website and that of the Oshawa Historical Society were both hugely helpful when writing this book.

Mr and Mrs Dunington-Grubb, the landscape designers who worked on the gardens at Parkwood, moved to Canada from the UK in 1911 and set up one of Canada's first landscape gardening businesses, called Sheridan Nurseries, which is still in operation today. When researching the Dunington-Grubbs and the Parkwood gardens I found a reference in a local Oshawa newspaper article to a head gardener at Parkwood called Mr Wragg. I hope he would not have minded his namesake having a part in this story.

The 1926 General Strike paralysed Britain between 3 and 11 May, 1926, when other workers came out on strike in support of the miners who were faced with a cut in pay by mine owners. On

12 May, 1926, the TUC announced the end of the General Strike as terms had been agreed with Stanley Baldwin's government. The Miners Union rejected the agreement, and continued striking. The strike caused great hardship with many families dependent on public soup kitchens. Faced with starvation and many miners having already returned to work, the strike finally ended on 19 November, 1926. Between 1921 and 1931 there was a decrease of 21,371 in Rhondda's population, as many families left the valleys to seek employment elsewhere, escaping from the General Strike, and I found many Welsh names in the passenger lists of people emigrating to Canada during this period. The website of the Canadian Museum of Immigration at Pier 21 provided useful detail about what it was like for people arriving in Canada around this time.

Between 1869 and the late 1930s it is estimated that 100,000 children were sent to Canada, Australia, South Africa and New Zealand from Britain as part of the child migration scheme. Churches and philanthropic organizations such as Barnado's, the Salvation Army and the Quarriers believed that the British Home Children as they became known would have a better chance in the the New World.

Some became members of the family but others were used as a cheap form of labour and overworked and neglected. Others were subjected to the stigma attached to being a Home Child – scum from the slums, as Jean is told in this story – and as a result often concealed their origins. In 1987 British social worker Margaret Humphreys brought public attention to the Home Children, leading to the creation of the Child Migrant Trust whose purpose is to help Home Children re-establish their identity and reconnect with relatives.

Over 10 per cent of Canada's population is estimated to be descended from Home Children.

I grew up in Clydach Vale in the Rhondda and my primary school was Ysgol Gynradd Gymraeg Ynyswen. The Polikoff's clothing factory was very near the school and most people knew somebody who worked there. Production at the factory had started in 1939 and in its first three months the workforce increased to nearly 1,000. In the 1970s the factory became known as the Burberry factory, latterly making Burberry polo shirts. When the factory was closed in 2007 around 300 jobs were lost. It would make me very happy if there was a real life Perfect somewhere out there willing to open a factory in the Rhondda.

My thanks go to Caroline Oakley, Honno's editor, whose gentle prodding helped get this book written round and about my full time job as solicitor; to my sister Anwen Darwin who did a final proofread and found the typos I'd missed; and to my husband and business partner David Thompson for the male perspective he brings to proofreading and for the many weekends and evenings he did all of the cooking and the homework supervising so that I could write.

Chapter 1

Gareth wakes early and with a crick in his neck. This always happens when he has to sleep in his daughter's bed. It's too narrow for him, on account of the many soft toys that Nora insists share her bed with her. The dollies got ditched when she hit eight but the soft toys are hanging on and she keeps them lined up along her bed in a special, secret order. It is more than Gareth's life is worth to sling them out of the small single bed to make more room for his long frame. Even last night, as he rescued Nora from a bad dream, scooping her up sobbing and sweaty and delivering her to the safety of his side of the bed, when he put her down gently next to her mother, she'd whispered to him urgently "Don't mess my Beanie Boos up Dad."

He sits up sleepily and rubs his sore neck. It is early, 5.45am or so he reckons. July sunshine falls through the thin material of Nora's bedroom curtains and makes pink puddles on the floor. He realises that what has woken him is Jake crying. He gets out of bed gingerly so as not to disturb the long line of soft toys staring at him dolefully with big, round, unblinking eyes.

Gareth finds Jake standing upright in his cot, gripping the bars and howling fit to burst. He stops crying immediately he sees his father and beams instead. Tears glisten, silver on the edges of his smile.

"How do you do that fella?" Gareth asks as he picks him up. "Go from sad to happy in a heartbeat? The wonders of being one."

Downstairs in the kitchen, with Jake settled comfortably on his hip, Gareth lets the dog out and opens the fridge. It's still a pleasant surprise that he doesn't have to make up formula, can just pour ordinary milk from the fridge into a bottle and shove it in the microwave for 40 seconds. He is well aware that Rachel is trying to move Jake away from a bottle and onto a cup, but Jake much prefers a bottle and it's much less hassle to give him what he wants. Anyway, Rachel is still asleep and is not around to see what Gareth is doing. While Jake necks his bottle, Gareth changes his nappy. No poo – result! – but the nappy is round and tight as a bomb, swollen with night-time wee. Another fifteen minutes and Gareth figures it could well have exploded. He has witnessed one or two exploded nappies in his time and he counts his lucky stars that this morning is not being spent scooping absorbent gel beads out of every corner of Jake and his babygro.

Gareth rummages around in his sports bag in the hall, finds tracksuit bottoms and a t-shirt, some smelly sports socks that will do again rather than risk waking Rachel and Nora fetching clean ones. He stashes Jake into his pram, finds the dog's lead and off the three of them go for an early morning run.

There are many joys of living in Penarth, a Victorian seaside town just outside Cardiff. For Gareth, the main one is being able to see the sea from his home. Running along a wide, cliff top coastal path before most people are up and about comes a close second. Jake loves it the faster Gareth runs and giggles whenever Gareth swerves the pram around in big circles. The dog, a ten year old Border Terrier called Oscar, finds the pace hard to keep up. He lives in a house with four children and there are always food scraps on the floor to hoover up. Oscar suffers from middle age spread.

Gareth passes very few people on his run. One other runner, female, slim and fit with her hair in a bouncing pony tail, faces straight ahead and does not make eye contact. A couple of other dog walkers, to whom he nods companionably, maintain the etiquette required of dog owners. We own dogs. We therefore have a bond. We will acknowledge each other despite being strangers. Just like people with campervans and Fiat 500s do.

He runs as far as Lavernock Point, where Marconi sent the first wireless signals over the open sea from Flat Holm in 1897. The first message, in Morse code, was "Are you ready?" Gareth never fails to think of this message when he reaches Lavernock Point. He thinks that if he were going to send a historical message, something that would end up in the national museum, he would have come up with something more lyrical, more memorable. Something more like Neil Armstrong's one small step. Or failing that, something funnier. *I can see your house from here.*

Lavernock Point is where Gareth turns round. Jake and Oscar both know this marks the return leg of the journey but they also know what comes next. Oscar pulls up at the first bench they reach, flops to the ground, panting. Gareth sits down and fishes around under Jake's push chair, retrieving a bottle of water for himself and a box of apple juice for Jake. He swerves Jake's pushchair around so that he is facing away from him, looking out over the Bristol Channel. Then he pops open the iPhone carrier strapped to his right arm which does not contain an iPhone at all but a pack of ten fags, a lighter and a box of Tic Tacs. He lights up and pulls deeply on his cigarette while Jake slurps his juice. When they are both done Gareth gargles with Tic Tacs and gets up ready to go but Oscar refuses to budge, stares expectantly at Gareth.

"Sorry mate, I forgot," says Gareth, pulling out the buggy board from under the pram. Oscar hops on and off they go again. Gareth puts on a faster turn of speed for the way back. It will be 7am soon and his family will be waking.

When he arrives home, breathing more heavily than he would like, Nora is sitting on the stairs waiting for him. She looks at him accusingly as he manoeuvres the pushchair into their hallway, which still has the original Victorian tiled floor. These tiles are just one of the reasons Rachel fell in love with this house, but they are rarely visible under the sea of shoes and coats and school bags that everyone dumps there.

"I didn't touch your teddies Nora. Honestly."

"They're Beanie Boos, not teddies. And yes you did. Coconut and Stripes had switched places."

"Well they must have done that by themselves to wind you up when I was sleeping because I didn't touch them, honestly."

"Yeah, right Dad! Anyway I put them back in the right order now. Will you make me pancakes for breakfast?"

"Not on your nelly, Nora. I only make pancakes for birthdays and holidays. And sometimes when we've run out of bread. Come on, I'll make you all some toast. Go wake up Iris and Eloise. Keep the noise down though – let your mother sleep a bit longer."

"Do I really have to wake up Eloise? She shouts at me."

"She shouts at us all love, it's an intrinsic part of your job when you're seventeen."

Thirty minutes later Gareth is showered and suited and booted, ready for work. He takes Rachel a cup of tea. He has timed it to perfection. Her alarm goes off just as he puts the tea down on her bedside table, shoving aside books and face creams to make enough room. She opens one sleepy eye and smiles at him. Despite having on his best suit, a navy pin stripe, he throws himself down on the bed next to her and puts his head on the pillow next to hers.

"Morning beautiful," he says, reaching over and gently brushing her auburn hair out of her eyes. "Nice bed head."

"Morning handsome."

Gareth always looks good straight from the shower, his dark hair damp and slightly curling. Rachel knows it's shallow but not a day goes past that she doesn't feel grateful that her husband still has hair. Lots of thick hair. Not even the slightest threat of one of those bald patches on the crown that always remind her of medieval monks. Streaked with a lot of grey at the temples now but Rachel thinks the grey suits him.

She pulls him towards her and kisses him hard. He kisses her back.

4

"Wow! If only we had more time and fewer kids." He sighs.

"Have we not got any KitKats?"

After Eloise was born, Rachel and Gareth perfected the art of the KitKat quickie. They can have sex in the time it takes a child to consume one.

"I don't think even chocolate would be enough of a distraction today Rachel. "

She raises an eyebrow. Gareth is not one for turning down even the remotest possibility of sex.

"Jake is sitting in the mother of all stinky nappies which, of course, I could not change, being in my suit and all."

Rachel raises an eyebrow even further, swats him gently on the arm.

"Give me a hug instead then."

He pulls her tight towards him and she breathes in deeply.

"Ah," she says. "Good old Imperial Leather."

He pulls away, pretending to be annoyed. "I don't know why you have such a downer on Imperial Leather. I've told you before. I like it. No matter how many fancy grapefruit or fig soaps you buy me. I want to smell clean, not like a fruit salad. You should be glad of Imperial Leather. The only other soap I like is Wright's Coal Tar. Smells like my dad."

Rachel props herself up on one elbow, reaches for her tea. "OK, OK. I give in. I hate Coal Tar. From now I shall embrace the scent of Imperial Leather as being eau de Gareth. No more verbena I promise. Where's Nora? I didn't hear her get up?"

"All four of your children are downstairs eating breakfast. Cereal and toast all round. Eloise is in charge, under sufferance because she has pressing diary commitments to attend to before school such as checking Facebook and putting on too much eyeliner but I've told her to suck it up or she won't be getting any more driving lessons. Dishwasher is on. Packed lunches are made. Only Jake's stinky nappy for you to sort out. Oh, and Iris can't find any clean school trousers and is kicking off at the horrible prospect of having to wear a skirt. And now I am going to work. I've got an agreement to finish drafting that I should have got out yesterday and I've got a client lunch I could really do without."

"Gosh Gareth, all this getting up early and going running and making breakfast. I could get used to this. You're a changed man since you gave up smoking."

"I do my best. Don't forget I'm playing squash straight after work but I'll be done in time to fetch Iris from Scouts."

Gareth shuts the door behind him and Rachel flops back onto her pillow. She needs to get up. Karen the nanny will be here shortly and she likes to be dressed before she arrives. Rachel feels that being in her bathrobe when Karen arrives is like admitting that she has not got her house and her children and herself under control. Which she absolutely does not but there is no need for Karen to know that. But instead of getting up she takes another sip of her tea, putting off changing Jake's nappy for just a little while longer.

She often wonders what possessed her to have another baby aged 42. What was she thinking? She already had three girls aged between 15 and 6. She had finally got equity partnership at her law firm, ten years after Gareth had become a partner at his firm. The inequality of this had smarted. Still smarted. She was every bit as good a corporate lawyer as him. Better even.

They'd been competitive from the moment they'd met as post graduates studying the Legal Practice Course in London. They happened to sit next to each other on the first day and sat next to each other every day after that. Rachel had teased Gareth about his accent and had recited *Under Milk Wood* at him. It had been a set text for her English A level, and she knew great chunks of it by heart. It amused Gareth to hear her recite it in a passable Welsh accent, particularly given how very posh her natural Buckinghamshire accent was. Not that Gareth teased her about her accent at that time because he was trying to get her into bed. This involved prising her away from her university boyfriend, a process which took a little while but which eventually he pulled off. From that point on, they not only vied with each other during the day for the best grades but during the night had what now seems to be unfeasible amounts of cinematic quality sex.

Rachel had been the first to land a training contract at a top City firm but Gareth was selected by a similarly high profile firm just weeks later. They were both poised at the start of highflying legal careers and destined for great things.

Getting pregnant with Eloise when she had only just qualified as a solicitor and had landed her dream job in the corporate department had not been on Rachel's career plan at all. She was just 25 and had been ignoring Gareth's hints that they should get married. They hadn't even discussed children very much. And then somehow, within a year of the second blue line appearing on the pregnancy test, she was married, had had a baby, (in that order but only just) and was going back to work.

Rachel had found it relatively easy to leave Eloise at childcare, handing her over to cheerful women dressed in primary coloured tunics whose names she did not know and rushing off to work. Gareth however could not bear it.

"It's not right Rachel. She's half asleep when we put her in there in the morning and half asleep when we pick her up again at night."

"You make it sound like something from a Charles Dickens novel. They don't dose the babies with laudanum in there to keep them quiet you know! It's a highly recommended nursery with a price tag to match. They take better care of her in there than we would. She's fine Gareth."

"Well she may be fine but I'm not. Let's move home to Wales, Rachel. Mam has offered to help out with Eloise some days. We can get jobs at a firm in Cardiff, have less of a commute into work. Hire a nanny for the other days."

"Wales isn't my home though is it? It's yours. And who's to say my mother wouldn't help out with Eloise if we asked?"

"Your mother, that's who! She spends most of the year out in France doing up her git." Gareth knew very well it was pronounced "gîte". He enjoyed dumbing up to annoy Rachel from time to time.

"There's no way I'm moving to the Valleys, Gareth. Sorry. I don't wish to be rude."

"You are being rude, but I'm not suggesting we live in the Valleys, Rachel. Cardiff. I'm suggesting Cardiff. Metropolitan city. Lots going on. Mam will come down on the train to help with Eloise. Plenty of opportunities for good lawyers."

"But I like being a good lawyer right here in London, thank you very much."

In the end it was the house that Gareth found that persuaded Rachel to move to Wales. A semi-detached Victorian villa on three floors, with views over the Bristol Channel from the front and a long garden at the back with a dilapidated greenhouse and some ancient apple trees. With four bedrooms it was bigger than they needed and required a ton of work – a new roof, re-wiring, redecorating throughout – which they did not have the money for. But it had high ceilings and lots of original features including the tiled floor in the hallway, draughty sash windows and fireplaces in every room. When Rachel put her hand flat against the red brick walls of the house, she could feel the warmth of the sun and of happy families who'd previously lived in it. She managed to contain herself until they'd said goodbye to the estate agent and then had flung her arms around Gareth and muttered fiercely into his neck,

"We'll be able to lie in bed and listen to the sea. I couldn't possibly live anywhere else now other than that house."

"No pressure then," he'd said, smiling at her.

Thanks to a surge in London prices, the sale of their second floor flat in Kentish Town just about put the purchase price of the house within their budget.

They both got jobs at good Cardiff firms relatively easily,

although having a baby seemed to adversely impact on Rachel's career while have no bearing on Gareth's whatsoever. However many late nights she worked, however many early mornings she spent at her computer in her bathrobe while Gareth and Eloise slept, the view of her firm was that Rachel did not have the same commitment to her career as a man simply because she had a child. But then when Iris came along and she went back to work after just three months she was surprised to find that her dedication to her job made her bosses distrustful of her. As if she were some sort of she-wolf who would eat her own children if they got in the way of her job.

When she became pregnant with Nora, thoroughly hacked off with not being able to win either way and thinking this would be her last baby, Rachel had figuratively stuck two fingers up at her bosses and taken a full year off.

The rest of the family remember this year with fondness. So does Rachel, up to a point. Nora had been an easy baby who slept well, and it was the only time the house had ever run smoothly – when they ate dinner together every night, something Rachel had cooked rather than takeaway or pizza; when there was always clean school uniform and bedtime stories every night and Play-Doh was no longer banned because it was just too much work and caused far too much mess.

Rachel had enjoyed the time with her daughters and new baby, walking to and from school pushing a buggy, the slow rhythm of days that involved going to the park or taking the girls swimming while casseroles simmered in the oven ready for when Gareth got home from work. It had reminded Rachel of the feeling she'd had as a child during the long school holidays – lots of lovely time stretching ahead. But as each day of sweet domesticity slid past, she also felt herself diminish a little more. She missed being a lawyer; the cut and thrust of negotiations, the juggling of client demands and billing targets. She didn't enjoy not earning her own money. And she hated the fact that almost from the very outset of that year, Gareth stopped talking to her about his day at work or asking her opinion on legal issues and instead asked her only how her day had been and what had she and the girls been up to.

When her year was up, Rachel had been glad to go back to work. Putting on her suit on her first morning back felt like being whole again. Like an important part of herself had been hung away in the cupboard and neglected for a year.

Finally, after years of being passed over for partnership, and after two consecutive years of being the firm's biggest biller, she got equity partnership. And with her career finally back on track she'd been suddenly hijacked by hormones. Swept off her feet by broodiness. All she wanted was another baby. Now. Right now. This minute. Before it was too late.

Gareth had not taken any persuading. Though he had never said anything, Rachel had always suspected that he would like a son. And anyway, Rachel reasoned with herself, at her age she probably had only a slim chance of getting pregnant again so there was nothing to lose by giving it a go.

But, being a girl with focus and dedication, Rachel gave it more than a go. Three months of sex every other night and bingo. And the baby had arrived safe and sound and with a willy at that and she loved Jake, she really loved him. But she had felt compelled by her equity partnership to go back to work after just twelve weeks and she had forgotten how much hard work babies involved and just how early they woke up. And what lame excuses Gareth could come up with to avoid changing nappies.

Chapter 2

Eloise doesn't like changing nappies any more than her father does. She barges into her parents' bedroom, her arms rigid in front of her, holding Jake as far away from her as is physically possible without actually dropping him.

"You have got to do something about this, Mum. Now! He smells disgusting! And he's been wriggling about in it for so long it's starting to ooze out the top of his nappy. Gross!"

Rachel surveys her first born. Sixth formers are still required to wear school uniform at Eloise's school but Eloise's interpretation of it is part goth, part tart. Her black skirt is so short it barely covers her bottom and she has a run in her black tights that Rachel is fairly certain will have been intentionally made, earlier that morning when Eloise put the tights on fresh from the packet. All of Rachel's children have red hair of some hue, even Jake who barely has any hair at all is clearly going to be ginger, but Eloise is the most red of all, a deep copper colour that Gareth says reminds him of a red setter. Eloise hates it which is why she dyes it jet black and then crimps it to within an inch of its life. It makes her blue eyes, heavily lined with black eyeliner, seem even bluer. She wears black Dr. Marten lace up boots, three silver hoops in each ear and her arms jangle with dozens of shiny, silver bangles. To Rachel she looks like a very pissed off, very beautiful, baby crow.

She reaches out to relieve Eloise of Jake. When Eloise was a baby she'd had a special changing table and plastic mat, with a colourful mobile hanging from the ceiling to keep Eloise amused during nappy changing. Rachel had used floral scented nappy sacs and had a special bin for dirty nappies. Now she just lays Jake straight on her bed and with just a few wet wipes he is done. She expertly tucks the nappy into itself and plops it straight into the bathroom bin. Even as vile a nappy as this is no challenge for a mother of four. She scoops Jake up off the bed and cuddles him.

"Didn't think to be nice to your brother and change him yourself Eloise? Not much more work than bringing him up to me."

"Oh please Mother. It's bad enough that people think I'm his teenage mum every time you force me to take him out. Bad enough that he is living proof that my parents are still having actual sex. I'm not changing his bum too. Ew."

"You should count yourself lucky my girl. Felix is living proof that *my* mother is still having sex."

After many lonely years of being a widow, Rachel's mother Francesca has in the past few years taken up with a Frenchman and moved permanently to her place in France to be near him.

"Gross Mum! Please don't make me think about Granny and Felix having sex as well."

Rachel laughs. "What's the difference between actual sex and non-actual sex anyway?" she asks.

Eloise just stares at her.

"I'm not being clever. I'm just wondering."

Eloise thinks for a moment, probably taking her time to come up with the answer she judges most likely to irk her mother.

"You can get pregnant from actual sex. With non-actual sex you can have a lot of fun but not get pregnant. I'm going to my room now."

Jake has long since got bored of cuddling and struggles in Rachel's arms. She puts him down on the bed and plays peekaboo with him for a while, listening to Eloise striding around her room above in her heavy boots.

In the early days of living in this house, it had seemed

enormous to Rachel and Gareth. Far too much house for the number of people they were and for the amount of furniture they owned. They had set up one entire bedroom devoted to ironing, where they could leave the ironing board up on a permanent basis. They never imagined that one day all the rooms would be full and they would need an attic conversion to provide a bedroom for their eldest daughter because they were pushing her out of her existing bedroom to make room for her brand new baby brother. About the only thing that Eloise likes about the arrival of Jake is the fact she got a spanking brand new bedroom out of it, complete with her own shower and toilet.

*

Gareth likes getting to work early. It avoids the final mad panic of his family's morning routine – the really stressful bit after the nanny arrives and she and Rachel are doing a pincer movement to get everyone out the door. There is always someone crying and someone shouting and someone who can't find their shoes/sports kit/homework (delete as appropriate). Gareth will gladly stack any number of dishwashers and pack endless school lunches to avoid this bit of the day.

His drive to work is short – he could walk it in forty minutes – but he has dedicated parking under his office and he likes the drive to Cardiff Bay, past clinking sailing boats and the sun shining on the water, accompanied by a cheerful blast of Radio 2. Even though it's been over fifteen years since they lived in London, he still congratulates himself for having escaped daily commuting by tube; the misery of being squashed in an overfull, overwarm, carriage on sunny days like this one; sweaty shirts and salty lips.

Just four years ago, his journey to work was slightly longer, right into the centre of Cardiff. He worked for a huge law firm then, a global one with offices all over the UK and the rest of the world. The building he worked in had been fifteen floors high, stuffed to the gills with lawyers and support staff and gleamingly full of glass and chrome and money. It had been a good place to work – top quality clients and high level work, and as good as anything to be had in the City of London. Even though Gareth's lawyer friends working in the City of London looked down their noses when he said this.

"Yes, but it's not the City is it, Gareth," they said, smugly.

"Er, no, it's not. Which is precisely the point. It's Cardiff. In Wales."

"QED, Gareth. Quod Erat Demonstrandum. The very thing it was meant to have shown."

VSK, Gareth thought. Vos Sunt Knobs. He decided not to invite these friends to visit him and Rachel in Penarth again. They seemed not to notice.

Gareth had liked his firm and the people who worked there. And it wasn't that he was a wage slave or anything, he'd been made a partner quickly, earned well and was given a great deal of autonomy as to how he did his work. But he was only one small cog in a very large wheel. The firm was run by a management team, mostly based in London and the partners themselves had very little say in decision making. What Gareth really wanted was to be his own boss.

Finally the right time came for him to achieve that. Their family was complete – or so he thought – Nora had started school and Rachel had got partnership. With some careful budgeting they could cover the essential family finances on her earnings alone if absolutely required. It was a big risk but if he didn't do it then, Gareth figured he never would.

His old firm's managing partner had not taken the news kindly and had made immediate threats of restrictive covenants and injunctions and damages.

"Whoa, hold your horses!" Gareth had said to him, calmly. "I don't want to fall out with you or anyone else. I've enjoyed

14

working here. You've been good to me. And I've been good to you too. I've been one of the best billers in the corporate department across the whole of the UK for the past ten years. Let's not get heavy handed here. Sure, some of the clients may want to follow me. My secretary definitely will. Contractually you can stop that from happening, if you really want to take that step. But when the covenants have expired, the clients will come then anyway and we will have fallen out for good and I won't be recommending my clients come to you for all the services I can't offer. So let's be grown up shall we and talk about the ways in which we are going to work together in the future, rather than you flinging court action at me."

In the end, his old firm had been persuaded to be sensible about things. Just a few months later and with a blessing of sorts, Gareth had opened his own small office in what had once been Tiger Bay and is now known as Cardiff Bay.

Gareth enjoys being based here rather than in Cardiff City centre. He likes the faded glamour of the old, Grade I and Grade II listed Georgian-style commercial buildings built in the heyday of Tiger Bay, when top quality coal from the South Wales valleys where Gareth grew up would arrive here before being exported by steamship all over the world. He likes the echo of that time that he sees in the faces of many of the people who still live here, the mix of nationalities that arrived from the 1830s onwards for work – Irish, Somali, Yemeni, Norwegian. And he likes the view from his office over the wide body of freshwater created by damming the tidal waters of the rivers Ely and Taff to regenerate the area. Tiger Bay started to decline after the 1926 general strike and was derelict within a few years of the end of the Second World War. In the late 1980s, the Cardiff Bay Development Corporation was set up to regenerate the area. Now, the past and the future stand shoulder to shoulder here, the legacy of old industrial businesses that first made Cardiff wealthy and the establishment and growth of new businesses, like Gareth's law firm, helping make the city successful again. Coal dug out of the ground by men like his grandfather and his great-grandfather is what used to be exported from here. Now Gareth exports his legal services – via the internet – to large and small companies in Wales and all across the UK.

His firm, Maddox Legal, has grown a little but he has purposefully kept it small. There are now five partners and seven assistants. This is about right as far as Gareth is concerned – enough people to be profitable, not enough to divert the partners away from being lawyers and into being managers and rainmakers. They deal only in corporate law – transactions involving buying and selling companies and businesses. The firm has a fearsome reputation for being excellent, not only in Cardiff but in London too. Gareth is particularly well known not just for his legal skills but for how good he is at negotiating and solving the commercial angles, not just legal issues. He is known amongst the legal fraternity as Gareth Fly Half because of his deal conversion rates.

At the office he makes himself a quick cup of coffee, checks his diary and gets on with drafting the agreement. At 11am his PA, Celia, brings him another cup of coffee. She has been at work since 8.45am sharp but she knows better than to disturb him before then if he is in drafting mode.

"There you go Gareth," she says, putting the coffee at his elbow. "Black, hot, two sweeteners." She says this in a fresh, perky way, as if it is not something she has said most mornings for the past fifteen years. "Ready for me to work on the document now?"

"Just about. I think I've saved it in the right place. Half an hour and it's all yours."

Gareth does most of his typing himself. He hasn't dictated for years. But he remains useless at formatting. Page breaks, indents, headings and the like are beyond him. This is where Celia comes in. Celia is 60 this year but she loves technology. She has thrown her arms around the digital revolution and given it a big kiss. There is nothing she cannot do on a computer but Gareth is always rather proud when he asks her to accompany him to meetings because she can also take the meeting notes in shorthand. She eats nothing but four kiwi fruits for lunch most days and is a keen line dancer because "she likes to keep trim." Gareth has never seen her wear a pair of trousers or anything less than a 2.5 inch heel in her life. Next to his family, Celia is the most important woman in Gareth's life.

"Don't forget you've got a lunch. New prospect. I've booked the Park Plaza for you, usual table, 12.30pm."

"I haven't forgotten but I could really do without it."

"Very important meeting at 5.30pm?" Celia smiled.

"Yep, very important." Gareth has a very important meeting every Tuesday and Thursday evening with his squash club ladder. "Have you done the research for me?"

Celia's research on new client prospects is legendary. Gareth attributes a large part of the success of his firm to the competitive edge that Celia's research can give him.

"Of course. Just emailed it to you now. Want the executive summary?"

"Got to love an executive summary. Shoot."

"Cassandra Taylor is a Canadian businesswoman and one of the two majority shareholders of a clothing company called Perfect, specialising in business shirts for men and women. She is the CEO. The other majority shareholder, Beverley Allen, founded the business in 1995 and is a director too but far lower profile than Taylor. She personally designs most of Perfect's highly regarded shirt ranges but she likes to keep out of the limelight.

"Perfect is based in Toronto but manufactures mostly from Chinese factories. It has won numerous Canadian industry prizes for being a fast track company, consistently increasing profits and turnover, but has won just as many design and fashion awards. It has considerable online business but in the UK also supplies Liberty, Selfridges, John Lewis and a number of high-end independent retailers.

"They pride themselves on their corporate social responsibility policies. They are considering a manufacturing base in the South Wales Valleys, tapping into our low cost labour market. They are keen to access Welsh government funding and other European grant funding for this initiative. Various areas of England are wooing Perfect to set up in their regions instead. Cassandra Taylor is in the UK for a couple of weeks attending numerous meetings to consider Perfect's options. She was given some recommendations for lawyers and corporate finance advisors in Cardiff by the inward investment guys in the Welsh government and you are one of the lawyers recommended. Your mate Adrian Matthews of Stratagem Corporate Finance was also recommended by the inward investment department and he, too, will be at your lunch with Ms Taylor today, as will representatives from the Welsh Government. "

"I don't really need to read the research document now, do I Celia?"

"Not really, no. If you get a wriggle on, you can have that agreement done before you need to leave."

*

Gareth hates people who are late and he hates being late himself. Despite this, since he also hates wasting time by arriving anywhere too early and having to wait around, he is very often *almost* late. He finds himself jogging at a fair old pace for the second time that day to be on time for his lunch meeting. He arrives with five minutes to spare.

It seems Ms Taylor has a similar attitude towards lateness. She is already seated at the table when Gareth arrives. He greets her warmly as he greets every new client prospect.

"Hello Ms Taylor, I'm Gareth Maddox. Pleased to meet you."

She stands up to shake his outstretched hand. "Pleased to meet you too, Gareth. Please, call me Cassandra."

"In that case, welcome to Wales, Cassandra. *Croeso.*"

"*Diolch yn fawr.*"

She has shoulder length, curly blonde hair and a wide smile showing very straight, very white North American teeth. She is wearing a tailored cherry red dress with a V neckline that looks very smart and professional whilst also showing, Gareth can't help noticing, just a hint of cleavage. He focuses on eye contact instead – she has brown eyes, very cheerful and sparkly.

"That was rather good pronunciation, have you been studying Welsh?"

"Not really, no, I've just got that one phrase ready to use off the bat at every possible opportunity. Oh and I've learned how to pronounce Rhondda too." She says it perfectly.

"That was very well done. Impressive."

"It was easy once it was explained to me that the double d is pronounced like 'th' at the beginning of 'the'."

"I could reciprocate for your excellent Welsh pronunciation with my rendition of the Canadian anthem if you like. We were required to learn it for a school rugby trip to Toronto a lifetime ago. Trouble is, I only remember the bit about 'standing on guard for thee'."

"I think I'll pass on that then, if you don't mind." Cassandra smiles… "So did you enjoy your trip to Toronto?"

"I was twelve. I can't remember a great deal about it to be honest. We played a lot of rugby and discovered Canadians were far better at it than we had been led to believe. I had my first ever hot dog, from one of those silver hot dog stands, which I thought was exceptionally cool. I remember I missed my mother more than a twelve year old was prepared to admit to. And that I was disappointed when the other teams sang the 'standing on guard for thee' bit that they weren't wearing fencing masks and flourishing pointy swords."

Cassandra Taylor throws back her head and laughs. She has a loud laugh, infectious, and people at the other tables turn their heads to smile at her. A lady with blonde curly hair and a bright red dress having a really good laugh.

"You've ruined our national anthem for me, now. Have you been back to Toronto since?"

Gareth shakes his head, "No sadly. I've not dared miss my mother that much again. Seriously, I'd love to visit. I hear great things about Toronto and my grandfather tells me that an uncle of his emigrated there years ago. Unfortunately, my wife and I seem to have been having babies for the past seventeen years or so. Makes getting anywhere further than west Wales a challenge."

Gareth spots Adrian making his way to the table, the Welsh government representatives in tow. "Ah, here the others are now," he says.

"Shame." Cassandra smiles at him.

For a moment Gareth is put off his stride. It's not as if other women have never flirted with him. At parties or weddings, Rachel enjoys pointing out women who have been eyeing him up and there was an assistant solicitor he worked with once who used to stare at him with a look of hero worship in her eyes that he found very uncomfortable. But Cassandra Taylor isn't eyeing him up. She is just smiling at him. Isn't she? Or maybe she'd caught him noticing her hint of cleavage and has got the wrong idea?

Chapter 3

Before Gareth is able to get his focus back, he has missed the representatives from the Welsh government introducing themselves. He thinks they said their names are Alun Griffiths and Griffith Alun but suspects he can't possibly have heard that properly.

Adrian has taken no time at all in clocking Cassandra's cherry red cleavage. He instantly turns on the famous Matthews charm, clasping Cassandra's hand in both his rather than just a handshake, flashing his full beam smile, looking her straight in the eyes and holding the gaze. Gareth has been doing deals and playing squash with Adrian for a long time now and he has seen this opening gambit dozens of times. It is rare that when Adrian sets out to charm he does not succeed. He is 6'4", generous with his cash and his attention, and women seem to really fall for him even though his longest standing relationship is with his personal trainer, a burly ex-boxer called Ed, whom he sees at least three times a week, far more time than he will ever give anyone he is dating.

Adrian is wearing a beautifully cut charcoal grey business suit and a white, open necked shirt that shows off Ed's hard work. His head, as always, is shaved although he has a full head of hair and baldness for Adrian is optional. The shirt exhibits the exact right amount of open neck. Not so low that he is showing too much chest, not so high that he looks like he's just got home from school and taken his tie off. Gareth wishes he could carry off this open necked shirt look. Ever since dress codes everywhere were relaxed and no ties became the norm Gareth has felt a little unsure of his clothing choices. He knew where he stood with ties. No tie still feels strange, like wearing brogues without socks. But Adrian doesn't look strange at all and it crosses Gareth's mind for the first time that maybe open necked shirts are a different type of shirt altogether, and not at all the same as wearing the shirts you already own, just without a tie.

Cassandra takes charge of the meeting.

"Thank you gentlemen, for taking the time to meet with me. I appreciate it. It's a privilege to meet with you. I've never before had the honour of lunch with four Welsh men."

"Actually, I'm Irish," says Adrian. "A Cork man. The accent's a bit of a giveaway Been here in Wales a long time but still can't ditch it."

"My apologies. I'm from Canada. I won't insult any of you Celts by telling you how many people back home have asked me where exactly in England Wales is situated."

"Ach, Cassandra, it takes an awful lot more than that to insult me," Adrian smiles. He's really hamming it up now, Gareth thinks, exaggerating his Irish accent, and grinning like a leprechaun. A really tall one.

Cassandra seems not to notice, signals to a waiter who immediately comes to their table.

"Right gentlemen. I'm going to order quickly so we can get on with our discussion. I'll just have a main course please, a rare steak and a salad, no fries. Tap water to drink with ice and lemon – please bring a jug and we can all share. And it would be really appreciated if you could serve us quickly as I'm due back in London later this afternoon."

She looks expectantly at her fellow diners, signalling to them to order quickly.

"Oh, I'll have the same but with chips for me please," says Adrian. "Been to the gym this morning and I'm starving."

"Me too," said Alun hurriedly. "And me," says Griffith.

Gareth hesitates for all of about three seconds. "Sounds good. Me too."

"Excellent," Cassandra smiles at the men seated around her, hanging on her every word. "So, as you know the reason we're here today is to discuss Perfect's proposals to set up a shirt factory here in the UK. Up until now, we have manufactured in China. We've been responsible employers, paying above average wages to our Chinese workers, providing decent living accommodation and other benefits such as funding schooling for their children. Being fair is at the heart of our company ethos. However, recent continued wage increases in China and a steep rise in transportation costs have led to us doing an analysis of the figures. And we think the costs of moving some of our manufacturing to the UK, and to Wales in particular, could be on the brink of being competitive. We are not going to move everything from China – we would not do that to our Chinese employees who rely on us. But we are looking at moving the manufacture of one of our most successful ranges to the UK.

That range is our Sharp Shirt range which is a top end range of shirts for both men and women. Double cuff, pearl buttons, top quality cotton. If I'm not mistaken Adrian, I think you are modelling one of our range today."

"Well spotted Cassandra. Always like to do my research before a meeting."

He winks at her. An actual wink. Gareth stifles an internal groan.

"If we do move production to the UK, we also hope to source our cloth from UK textiles factories and to expand our women's range, develop our cut so that it fits ladies of *all* sizes." With this last bit, Cassandra glances down very quickly at her own capacious frontage and smiles ruefully.

"Why the UK? Why not Canada given you are a Canadian company?" asks Alun. Or possibly Griffith.

"Good question. The south east of England and London in

particular is one of our busiest areas of demand so having the shirts made here reduces cost and decreases waiting time. It also allows us to get new designs to market faster. But I'd be lying if I said that possible funding from Welsh government to help create those jobs is not a significant factor. But more significantly, and the reason we are particularly interested in setting up in the Rhondda, is our interest in the Burberry factory that closed a number of years ago."

"Are Perfect and Burberry considering some sort of joint venture or merger?" Adrian asks, thinking of the fees he could make on a deal like that.

"Not at all. Perfect only grows organically not via merger. What we are interested in is harnessing the sewing skills of the ex-employees of Burberry. Our research suggests there will be a pool of talented and experienced labour that we can tap into for Perfect."

Their food arrives and there is silence for a while as everyone cuts into their steaks.

Gareth is the first one to speak. "As someone who grew up in the Rhondda, this sounds a very worthwhile proposal. But the Burberry factory closed down back in 2007. Some of the employees will have long since retired or become unwell, died even, or retrained and got jobs elsewhere. I'm not certain that any pool of experienced labour will be a particularly large one."

"We know these people are going to be rusty, we know they will need some re-training and we are going to have to train some people from scratch. This is not a problem for us. We aren't unduly concerned about that. So long as we can identify a few key people who can help us train others, that will suffice. We think we will need up to 300 employees eventually. And if we choose the Valleys for our location, we believe the story behind the people who make our shirts here in the UK is going to be a selling point for us, and help Mr Matthews raise the funding we need."

"And, of course, there is some funding to assist potentially available via the Welsh Government," says Griffith.

"So there is," Cassandra smiles at him.

"You'll need a good business plan," Adrian comments.

Cassandra looks annoyed and pointedly puts down her knife and fork before responding curtly. "Mr Matthews, Perfect has been in business for over twenty years. Do you really think we don't already have an exceptional business plan?"

Gareth steps in to fill the awkward silence that follows. "I can think of a number of the people I grew up with who left Wales a long time ago, and have been very successful in business, who might be persuaded to put some money into this venture. Partly for sentimental reasons but mostly because of that exceptional business plan you refer to. With Adrian's help, the investment could be structured in a very tax efficient way."

"And the Welsh government is extremely interested in helping in every way possible to bring those jobs to Wales," added Alun.

"Excellent news gentlemen. I shall email you some further details later this evening when I am back in London. I need to wrap this lunch up, now, I'm afraid."

Mr Alun and Mr Griffith set about finishing their steak and chips with vigour.

"Gareth, would you mind giving me just a little more of your time. I would like to discuss with you my suggestions for how this business will be structured and get your initial feedback. Perhaps you'll come to the bar and have a coffee with me there and everyone else can finish their lunch at their leisure."

With that, Cassandra rises gracefully from the table, shakes hands with the other three and in a swirl of red leads the way to the bar.

"Let me guess what coffee you'll have," she says, choosing a table tucked away in the far end of the bar, well out of view of the restaurant. "Double espresso? How did I do?"

"Spot on. Good guess."

"Not really, you don't look like the kind of man who drinks a cappuccino or latte. Too mild and milky. "

"Two double espressos," she calls to the barman, who nods. Gareth comes to this restaurant a lot and in his experience requests for coffee from the barman result in a curt statement that they should order from the waitress. But the barman appears to be under the same spell as the lunch guests had been and does what Cassandra requires and does it straight away.

Cassandra looks at Gareth and grins cheekily.

"The structure is going to be a wholly owned UK subsidiary of the Canadian company."

"Right. So…"

"It wasn't really necessary to whisk you away into the bar to talk about structure but Alun was eating with his mouth open and I couldn't take it a moment longer."

"Can't say I noticed myself."

"Well I wish I hadn't. It was like a cement mixer in there. Look, we haven't made a final decision on location yet. The Rhondda is definitely on our shortlist but there are others. However, wherever Perfect locates its UK factory we would like you to represent us. Are you willing to do that? Even if we don't choose your home town?"

"The Rhondda's not exactly a town."

"You know what I mean," Cassandra says, rolling her eyes.

"I'd love to."

"Excellent!"

She takes a little sip of her coffee and smiles at him over the rim of her cup. Gareth is still not certain whether she is flirting with him. He thinks she might be and the fact that he thinks she might be makes him more conscious of her sparkly eyes and big smile and her curves under that red dress. He twists his wedding ring nervously.

"So Gareth, what is your initial view on our UK factory idea?" His name sounds entirely different in her mouth, alien and somehow more interesting.

"I think it's great. You are a very successful company already. You've got all the marketing skills and contacts. You already have a proven market and loyal customers for this particular clothing range. Provided the quality is maintained, that customer base will be very glad to buy British and that USP can feature in your marketing campaigns. Speaking personally, I really do hope you choose the Valleys as this is exactly the sort of thing needed. New jobs, new skills, new focus. But I can assure you that my personal opinions will not impact on my service to you as your lawyer."

"Good to hear it. Some of the feedback we've had suggests we may struggle to find the work ethic we require in the Valleys. We're told that there are people living in the Rhondda who are now third generation unemployed and not in the habit of working for a living."

Gareth winces. "I'm afraid that is true in some cases. But not all – a very long way from all."

"You know, in Canada people are still arriving from other countries, and our new citizens can't wait to work hard, build something new, make something of themselves. We're a young country and we still have a strong pioneering spirit."

"The Rhondda's heritage is pioneer spirit. People arriving from all over to work in the coal mining industry. A company like Perfect will be able to find that spirit."

"If we just dig deep enough?" Cassandra teases.

"Something like that. So where did this idea of setting up in the Valleys come from? Did your family come from Wales originally?"

"No, although that would have been neat wouldn't it? Girl with Welsh roots rides back into town with a high falutin' business plan to help her kinsmen and women back into work. Like something out of the movies. I'm actually Ukrainian originally. My parents were both very young when their families arrived in Hamilton, which is a big steel town, a city now, in fact, about an hour's drive east of Toronto. There are lots of Ukrainian Canadians all over

Canada and we have a history of marrying within our community. One of my grandfathers ran a small dry-cleaning shop – he did minor clothing alternations too – and did pretty well at it, even though he never really fully mastered English. In his eighties, before he died, he forgot whatever English he'd had and reverted to speaking only Ukrainian. He was lucky there is such a strong Ukrainian community – there were plenty of people who could speak to him."

"Can you speak Ukrainian?"

"Very little, just enough to communicate with a grandfather suffering from dementia. Just enough to feel desperately sorry about Ukraine's current political situation. I am glad for my grandfather that he is not around to have to see it."

"Is Taylor your married name? Doesn't sound very Ukrainian?"

"I've never been married. Not yet anyway. My family name is Sukmonowski. After 18 years of Fuckmonowski and Suckmycockski jokes I legally changed my name. Taylor was the name of the girl who bullied me most at High School. That really Fuckmonowski'd her off, I can tell you."

Gareth giggles, a little nervously.

"There you go," Cassandra throws up her arms in mock indignation. "My old name makes even fully grown lawyers titter. Anyway, I have no idea why I'm telling you all this. It's not something I usually share with people I've just met."

"Don't worry," Gareth smiles, "legal privilege. I promise not to tell anyone your deep dark secret."

She summons the bill from the waiter.

"Let me get it," Gareth offers.

"Not at all. You were all my guests. It's my shout, I insist."

As she keys in her credit card number, she asks the waiter to organise a taxi to the station. They finish their coffee, promising each other heads of terms and fee quotes within the next 24 hours. When she leaves, she does not shake his hand but reaches her face to his cheek and instinctively he turns his face towards her and her kiss lands gently on the corner of his mouth. She breathes in sharply. They pull away, both a little startled. And then she's gone.

Gareth has to sit down suddenly then. He is not used to feeling this way at all. It is something he has not felt for almost twenty years. Attraction to someone other than his wife.

Chapter 4

August 1926

Idris Maddox is at the top of Clydach Vale mountain, checking his rabbit traps. He doesn't bother to look down at the pit heads standing idle or further away at the Institute, full of men sitting around reading books and newspapers or doing even more choir or band practice because there is nothing else to do.

He focuses solely on his rabbit traps. He has them set up in a dozen or more places, spread far and wide over the mountain, carefully hidden behind tussocks of grass. He moves them often because rabbits aren't as stupid as they look and eventually get wise, and also because men who stumble upon the location of his traps won't think twice about taking his kill home to their hungry families.

The first four traps he checks are empty but then he has a spate of good luck and by the time he has checked them all, he has seven fat rabbits to take home. His Mam will use some of them to make stews, with onions, potatoes and herbs from her garden. Some she will use to barter with the neighbours for eggs or a stringy chicken too old to lay. And some she will give away to families with nothing to put on their tables.

It's good he's managed to trap as many rabbits as he has. It will put his mother in a better mood when he tells her his news. She's not going to like what he has done but he's made up his mind now and there's no going back. He's been delaying telling the family, knows they will be upset and angry with him, but he can't put it off any longer. There are lots of things he has to do before he goes, not least of which is teaching his twin brother Tommy how to trap rabbits. That's going to take some time. Tommy hates killing anything. Doesn't mind eating it though.

The sun is starting to sink down into the valley by the time Idris turns into the terraced street where he and his parents live, the bag of rabbits over his shoulder getting heavy and uncomfortable. He enters the very last house in a row of identical houses, slings the bag on the kitchen table, and walks straight out the back where he knows he will find his mother, Gwen, tending to her garden.

He stands by the back gate for a while and watches her work, crouched down next to a bed of carrots, weeding with great determination. The garden is narrow, like all the other gardens in the street, but this particular street backs onto the mountain and over the years his mother has stealthily extended her garden beyond its fences and over onto the mountain itself. Every available inch of space is used to grow food. There are pots everywhere stacked carefully to provide greater growing space and beans and peas are planted along the fences. In the stolen mountain sections of her garden Gwen grows potatoes, carrots and onions.

The only flowers she grows are round the privy, five or six different colours of rose that she has trained to grow right over the roof. Gwen says it's the only place she ever gets five minutes sit down to herself so it might as well look pretty and smell as good as it can.

She senses she is being watched, straightens up and turns to smile at him, her hand immediately going to the small of her back to knead her tired muscles.

"How did you get on?"

"Seven big 'uns waiting for you on the kitchen table. You'll be making stew all day tomorrow."

Gwen smiles in pleasure and relief.

"Good boy. Will you help me with this weeding?"

Idris groans. "Mam! You know how much I hate gardening."

31

"Of course. You tell me on a daily basis. But someone's got to do it. Come on now – hard work never killed anyone."

For once, Idris doesn't complain further and kneels down next to his mother.

"What are you trying to do boy? Climb into my lap? Go and work over there a bit, I've done most of this."

"I need to talk to you, Mam."

Gwen goes immediately still, steels herself for a few seconds, then asks, "What have you done?"

"I haven't done anything Mam. For once. No soapboxes, no fighting, and no chance of getting drunk when no one's had any money since the strike to eat, let alone go drinking."

"So what is it then?"

"I'm moving away."

"What do you mean moving away? Where is there to move to? You moving in with Tommy and Maggie? "

"Canada, Mam. I'm going to Canada."

"You're teasing me now, aren't you? This is some sort of joke – isn't it?"

"No Mam, I'm dead serious. I'm leaving as soon as I can – in a couple of weeks. Canadian department of colonisation says it needs people to move to Canada. Farmers, miners, domestic workers – as many people as possible. It's a big country to fill and not many people in it. Chap from the Canadian government says there's plenty of work for everyone."

"And how are you planning on paying your fare?"

"Something called the Empire Settlement Act means I'll get over half of it paid for me, rest I've just about got saved. So long as I leave as soon as possible."

There are tears in Gwen's eyes as it starts to sink in that her son is not teasing. Not teasing at all.

"Have you told Tommy? Or your Dad?"

"No, Mam, just you so far."

"Why do you want to go Idris? What is there in Canada for

you that you can't get here?" Gwen knows the answer to this question but asks it anyway.

"Mam, the strike achieved nothing. Absolutely nothing. A general strike that lasted all of a fortnight. Took just 10 days for the TUC to sell us miners down the river. You know as well as I do that just about every family in these valleys has been starved to breaking point. No one wants to have to rely on soup kitchens any more. The miners have no choice but to go back to work – for less money and longer hours. They've started going back already. They'll all be back before Christmas, I wager. I don't blame them for that but I can't do it. I won't. I refuse to work for the owners again and I can't live here and watch Tommy and Dada go back to work neither. I don't have any choice."

Gwen's head is bent now, tears dripping into her lap, her shoulders shaking slightly. She knows her son, better than he knows himself. She knows he is telling the truth and that he can't go back to work and she also knows that the trickle of miners returning to work will soon be a flood. She wipes her tears away fiercely, lifts her head high to face her boy.

"You'll tell your father tonight then?"

"That's the plan."

"And Tommy?"

"Going to tell them both at the same time. Maggie too. They come here for their tea on Wednesdays.

"It's going to break your brother's heart, you know?"

"Tommy'll be fine. He's got Maggie. They'll be starting a family of their own any time soon. He's not going to be lonely."

*

As anticipated, Thomas Maddox grows angry when his son tells him his news.

"How dare you Idris! How dare you! Make a decision of this sort without regard to me and your mother."

33

"Dada, I'm 21. Tommy's been married over a year. I'm not a boy anymore."

His father doesn't have a lot to say to that. At 21 he'd been married himself, with Idris and Tommy on the way.

"Cambrian miners don't run away from our battles, son. We stand together, shoulder to shoulder. That's what we did in 1910, even after Churchill sent the troops in, and that's what we'll do now."

"The miners went back to work in 1911 Dada and that's what they'll do this time too."

"But we're your family, Idris. You know no one in Canada. Nobody."

"Just like you knew nobody when you set out from north Wales and walked all the way south to find work in the pits. You've been telling us that story since we were tiny – how you walked thirty miles or more a day, knocking on doors on the way, offering to milk cows or patch fences in return for a meal and a bed for the night. And you did find work, and you met Mam, had me and Tommy, made a life. I'm going to do what you did. Put one foot in front of the other till they lead me somewhere."

Thomas Maddox says nothing for a while. Eventually, in a tired voice, he says, "We're going to struggle without the rabbits."

"I'm going to teach Tommy how to do it. It's not difficult."

"Tommy, try and talk some sense into your brother will you? He can't desert his family like this."

"He's not deserting anyone. He's making a choice. He's a grown man. I'm going to miss him every day he's gone but I'm not going to stop him from leaving. I respect his decisions." Tommy's voice is wobbly with emotion. He doesn't want his brother to go, but he also knows things will be easier when he has gone. And it won't be so difficult going back to work if Idris isn't here to see.

*

34

Idris knows that Maggie will find a way to talk to him alone. He doesn't expect that it will be at the top of the mountain, even though she knows all his favourite places up there. He had expected it to be somewhere safe, probably at his mother's house. Her creeping out to sit next to him while he has a cigarette after tea, some excuse about putting peelings in the compost or putting ash from the fire in the ash bins. But here she is, broad as daylight, striding towards him over the tussocky grass of Clydach Vale mountain. He enjoys watching her walk, her long strides, tall and strong legged. Tommy and he were fifteen before they grew taller than Maggie. Before they could beat her in an arm wrestle.

"You don't have to go," is the first thing she says to him. She's angry with him and Idris can feel it, like heat rising from her body. Her cheeks are pink from the climb and her dark brown hair is loose around her shoulders.

"I do Maggie. I do. "

"Not because of me you don't."

"I'm not going because of you."

"That's how it feels."

"You are one of the few things that could keep me here. Despite being married to my brother. Despite having to see you every day playing happy families."

"We are a happy family. I wouldn't have married him if that wasn't the case."

"Really Mags, when you couldn't choose between us for the longest time? When you can't tell us apart in the dark."

"I can tell you apart. Eyes open or eyes shut I can tell you apart. You might look exactly the same but you smell differently and you think differently and you kiss differently."

"Kiss differently? Is that what we're calling it now?"

"There's no need to be uncouth, Idris. Since I married Tommy there's not even been kissing with you."

"And don't I know it. Not with you and not with anyone else either. You know what Maggie? I'm starting to think it was a good

35

thing this strike was a failure because it's giving me the kick up the arse I needed to move thousands of miles away. Where no one knows I've been in love with my brother's wife since I was a little boy."

"Come sit down with me, Idris."

Without discussing it, they walk across to a spot they used to go to a lot when they were younger. A heap of rocks, some of them flat. The rocks provide protection from the wind and some privacy. They sit down next to each other, close enough to touch.

First Maggie lets her knee rest against his and then she reaches over and rests her hand on the back of Idris' neck. He tries to move away at first but eventually relaxes. After a little while, she starts to rub his neck ever so gently.

"Can you be persuaded to stay?'

"No."

"Please, I really don't want you to go. Nothing will ever be the same again without you."

"I don't *want* things to be the same."

"Then in that case, I have a favour to ask. A big one."

Idris says nothing, waits for her to continue.

"Tommy can't make babies."

"Don't talk rubbish. How can you know that? You've not been married long. Give the man a chance."

"He can't Idris." She pauses, not wanting to hurt Idris with the detail but needing to say it anyway. "We've been trying hard – ever since the wedding – and nothing has happened."

Idris flinches. "And what has this got to do with me?"

"I need you to lie with me Idris. I want a baby. But that's not going to happen with Tommy and a baby from you will look just like a baby from him."

"Are you insane Maggie! I can't do that to Tommy! He's my brother."

"That's precisely why I am asking you. Please Idris. For me and Tommy. And your Mam and Dad. In a couple of weeks you'll be

36

gone. It's now or never. No one will ever know. It's not as if it's something you've not done before."

"I don't know Maggie. It was different before you married Tommy. Before then we knew you went with both of us but we never talked about it, never even mentioned it. I told you if you married him all of that between you and me would have to stop. And it did. You're my sister-in-law now, Maggie, and it's just wrong."

Maggie gets up and kneels in front of Idris, holding his hands in both hers so that he can't get up and stride away.

"Do you know how hard it was to choose between you?" she asks.

"Wouldn't know," Idris says gruffly. "I didn't get to do the choosing. You were the one got to do that."

"I didn't want to have to choose. I loved you both. You were the one that turned it into a contest."

"I didn't turn it into any contest, Maggie, and you know it. I said you needed to pick one of us. So that the other one could try and find someone else and have a proper life. It was fine for you, of course, you always had one of us at your side. But it wasn't fine for whichever one of us wasn't with you. We didn't have you and we didn't have each other either. We might not have talked about it, but it was killing us both. And you picked Tommy – the nicer, gentler, one – not me, and there it is."

"It wasn't as simple as that, Idris Maddox, and you know it. Tommy didn't give me an ultimatum and tell me I needed to pick – he said he loved me and worshipped me and asked me to marry him so that he could look after me till the day he died. And I knew he meant every word of it and that I'd always be top of the list as far as Tommy is concerned. I picked the one who *asked* me to marry him rather than *tell* me I needed to make a choice between you. You have an anger in you Idris, a restlessness, that appeals to me because I recognise a little of it in myself. It's that fire in your belly that has made you so forceful in your support for this strike. It's what drives you out of the house to traipse around this mountain all hours of the day and night. But it doesn't make for a calm marriage. Tommy's steady and he'll keep me steady too."

"Then you picked the right one for you, didn't you Maggie? And the brother you picked should be the father of your babies."

"I did make the right choice Idris but I miss you so much it can floor me sometimes, like I've been barged over with longing for you. I sleep every night next to someone who looks just like you, is every bit as beautiful as you, but he doesn't do things like you did them and that just makes me miss you more."

Idris looks at Maggie kneeling in front of him, holding on tightly to his hands. He misses her and he wants her and he hates her all at the same time.

"What makes you think that if Tommy can't make babies, I can?"

"I just know you can. Just like I know that it's Tommy not me that can't make babies. I can feel it."

She lifts one of his hands to her lips, kisses his fingers gently. She knows he will kiss her. She knows how hard it has been for him not to kiss her every day since she chose Tommy. She knows this because at times it has been every bit as hard for her not to kiss him.

Idris sighs and sinks to his knees next to her, pulls her towards him and holds her tight.

*

His last weeks in Wales go past in a blur. Gwen is close to tears a lot of the time but desperately trying to hide it. The only thing that seems to calm her is if Idris stands next to her in the garden and just lets her talk about what she plants where and when and what care everything needs. He makes Gwen a lot of tea and he lets her talk of seeds and pricking out and the importance of manure. Her words wash over him in a sea of tannin and tears.

His father acts as if Idris is not going anywhere; will not actually see his plans through. He will only talk about the upcoming Catty and Doggy tournament that is to be played on the Oval in Tonypandy, a few days before Idris is due to leave. The game, popular with children and played in the streets, involves a team of four to six men hitting a short stick called the Catty into the air and then hitting it again as far as possible with a longer stick, usually fashioned from a pick axe handle, called the Doggy. The distance the Catty travels is measured, with each length of the Doggy counting as a run. Like cricket, if the Catty is caught the player is out. The Maddox men are all very good at the game and will play for the same team.

"I don't know, Dada," Idris says, "maybe with me leaving so soon afterwards, it would be better if I didn't play, and let someone else take my place."

"Don't talk nonsense, son. Why would you want to let us all down like that?"

On the day of the tournament, Idris is surprised to see just how many have turned out to watch. Always well attended, even more men have turned out to watch the tournament than usual, to relieve the boredom of the General Strike. Rows of men, all dressed very similarly in the uniform of miners when not at work – dark trousers, dark waistcoats, white shirts and caps – lining the sides of the ground and all along the fences.

Dada, the oldest player in their team, plays like he is fighting in a contest far more important than a game of Catty and Doggy. Idris thinks he has never seen him hit the Catty so hard or field so energetically, catching half a dozen men out with no regard to the sting in the palms caused by a piece of wood travelling at speed. Their team win the tournament easily.

There is no trophy to win but Idris and Tommy and the other men in their team hoist Dada on to their shoulders to accept the applause. They walk home grinning, three abreast, striding up the hill with purpose, in the same way they used to walk home from the pit together at the end of a shift. Without taking his eyes off the road ahead, Dada asks quietly, "Why would you want to leave us all behind, Idris?"

Idris doesn't answer.

Idris shows Tommy how to set the rabbit traps, where to place them so as to get the best results, how to skin the rabbits ready for Gwen to cook. Tommy listens, even takes notes, but Idris suspects Tommy will never actually set a trap once he has gone.

Every late afternoon is spent with Maggie. Neither of them offers Tommy an explanation for these absences and he does not ask for one. Some of the time they just sit together, leaning against the other, looking out over the valley, watching summer turn gently towards the arms of early autumn. Some of the time they talk – about things they did when they were children, about the strike that is collapsing fast, about what Idris can expect to find when he arrives in Canada. But most of the time they spend trying to make a baby.

Chapter 5

Back at the office, Gareth finds it difficult to concentrate on his work. He blames it on the onion rings that came as a side with his steak at lunch. He knew they would give him indigestion but he ate them anyway.

At 4.30pm he decides to call it a day and to drive over to the squash club early. Calling it a squash club makes the place sound grand and exclusive, when actually it is four scruffy, smelly courts and an equally scruffy, smelly bar presided over by a stewardess called Valmai with dyed orange hair who serves good clean beer and makes a mean corned beef and pickled onion sandwich. Despite this, the club is very popular with professionals and Gareth has landed a lot of work through his squash ladder.

He rings Adrian Matthews from the car on the way over.

"I've finished work a bit early. Wondering if you fancied knocking a few balls around the court before the matches later. I could do with a warm up."

"That's a coincidence! I'm just walking through the door. Valmai's waving at me, making her beer eyes. See you when you get here."

The club is where Gareth had first met Adrian, not long after he and Rachel arrived from London. Adrian had come to Cardiff to go to University and although he had vague plans to move to London for work they had somehow never materialised. He and Gareth had found they were a good match in terms of skill on the squash court – competent, competitive, often having to cancel games due to work commitments. From playing squash they'd evolved to drinking Valmai's beer together. By now, Gareth counts Adrian as a good friend and Adrian has put a lot of work Gareth's way over the years.

Gareth changes into his kit and finds Adrian waiting for him in the furthest court, doing stretches.

"Gareth! My main man. Do you just want a knock about or do you fancy a quick match, let me batter you again like I did last week?"

"You did not batter me Adrian, you won. Only just. I haven't got time for a proper match, I'm playing Nathan Bayliss in half an hour and he's top of the league right now."

"Knock about it is. Hey, what did you think of that Cassandra Taylor?"

"I thought she was a very focussed, very driven woman."

"Wasn't she just! I fancy the arse off of her. I've already emailed her, made up some story about being in London on business next week and inviting her to dinner to discuss the deal."

Gareth is flooded with hot, irrational jealousy. "Oh yeah, what did she say?"

"Hasn't replied yet."

"How do you know she doesn't have a husband or boyfriend?"

"Didn't see any ring. And no mention of a fella which is what most women do when I turn on the full beams and they want to let me know politely they are not available. Anyway, she lives in Canada. Who cares if she has a husband or boyfriend, so long as he's not over here with her."

"Don't you think that's a bit unprofessional?"

"It's all right for you. You're happily married to someone you still fancy after hundreds of years of marriage. Me, I'm still looking and it's not often a woman that hot crosses my path."

"She's a hot client not just a hot woman."

"So you agree with me she's hot then?"

Gareth frowns. "You know exactly what I mean Matthews. She's a client, an important one, not some bird you picked up on Beaujolais Nouveau Day."

"Get over yourself Gazza. It's not as if I've invited her to join me for a bit of bondage in a dungeon party. I've said I'm in London anyway and would she care to join me for dinner, that's all. If she doesn't want to, she'll just say she's not available and we can both pretend it was a serious business invitation and carry on working on the deal together. No blood, no foul. If she says yes, I'll assess the situation and analyse the risk at the time. Hey do you think she's as bossy in bed as she is when it comes to business? Maybe she'll be the one suggesting a bit of bondage."

"Shut up Adrian and just play squash, will you?"

"I thought you only wanted a knock about?"

"Changed my mind, first to fifteen points wins. My serve." Gareth hits the ball so hard, Adrian has no chance of returning it.

*

Rachel sits at her desk, panicking a little. She has had the kind of day where she has not had time to pee, let alone eat lunch. She is working on a deal that is due to complete tomorrow. It is not the biggest of deals nor the most sexy. Her client, Cole Lapthorne Engineering, is selling its fabricating and welding business to another fabricating and welding business in Cardiff. The difference between fabricators and welders has been explained to her more than once but she appears incapable of retaining this information. They both involve metal, that much she does know.

She has spent much of the day sitting in an overheated office suspended above a workshop. The office had MDF wooden cladded walls and was decorated with framed rugby shirts. Its end wall had open windows overlooking the workshop so that Mr Cole and Mr Lapthorne could keep an eye on the men in navy blue overalls below, bashing things loudly with spanners and listening to Planet Rock at full volume. The din meant that explaining to Mr Cole and Mr Lapthorne about warranties and indemnities in a sale agreement was even more difficult.

"Why do we have to have all this blessed paperwork?" Mr Cole had complained bitterly. In the old days we'd have done it on a handshake and everyone would have been happy and there would be no enormous lawyer's bills to pay." Mr Cole drives a Jaguar XJS and has a huge house overlooking Roath Lake but the very idea of lawyers making money makes him evil.

Mr Lapthorne had tried to help him understand. "People just don't do business like that anymore Morgan. We need this paperwork. All Rachel is trying to do is protect us."

"Fleece us, more like, Bruce. Fleece us is what she's doing."

Rachel is used to getting hassle from the other side on deals but getting it from your own client is a tough one. Made tougher by the fact that at the same time as being rude about her, and not really listening as she explained the terms of the agreement she had worked hard on drafting so as to protect his interests, Mr Cole also managed to spend a lot of time staring openly at Rachel's legs.

The meeting had taken far longer than it should have and now it has gone 5pm already and Rachel has a phone call to return, which will take a good twenty minutes, and three emails she needs to get out which will take longer. But Karen's shift ends at 6pm and whilst Karen is a great nanny she takes great exception at working so much as five minutes beyond her allotted hours. It will take at least thirty minutes for Rachel to get home at this time of the day. There is nothing in the house for dinner and Iris got some new badges at Scouts last week which Rachel has been meaning to sew on her uniform but somehow she has not done it and now all of a sudden it's Scouts again tonight.

It wouldn't be so bad if this low point, or another just like it, didn't roll round pretty much every day. Too much to do and not enough time to do it in.

Rachel drops her head into her hands, breathes deeply for a moment or two like she was taught at yoga the three times in her life she ever managed to actually make it to a yoga class, and prioritises her list. Then she leaves the office.

She makes the phone call from the car driving home. She manages to bring the call to an end just as she pulls up outside the Spar. She buys sausages – pale pink, flabby fingers, neither organic nor free range but the kids will love them – a bag of pasta, some tins of tomatoes, onions and a bag of frozen broccoli which they won't love but will at least be one of their five a day. And a bottle of Oxford Landing Sauvignon Blanc, a very long way from being her favourite Sauvignon Blanc but nevertheless still wine.

She figures she can sew the badges on while the sausage pasta is cooking and that she'll send the emails later that night after Jake and Nora are in bed. With a glass of Sauvignon at her elbow.

She arrives home at 6pm precisely but it is not a clock watching Karen she finds sitting in her kitchen but her friend Jenny, whose son Daniel is in the same class as Nora at school. Jake is sat in his high chair and Jenny is feeding him yoghurt. Or more precisely letting Jake feed himself which means that most of the yoghurt is outside Jake not inside him.

"What's happened? Is something wrong? Are the girls OK?"

"Keep your hair on lawyer lady. Nothing's happened. Nora asked if Daniel could come round for his tea after school. I arrived five minutes ago to collect him. Karen asked me if I could watch Jake till you got home so she could get off a bit early and I said fine."

Rachel's shoulders descend from where they had shot up around her ears in fear.

"Thank goodness for that. Now excuse me I need to go to the loo. Not been all day today."

When she emerges from the small toilet next to the kitchen, Jenny is laughing to herself.

"You pissed like a horse then Rachel. It's not healthy keeping that in all day."

Rachel blushes a little. "I had a busy day."

"You have a busy day every day. Is that a bottle of wine you've got in that bag?

"Yes, do you want some? It's not very cold."

"Crack it open girl. You must have one of those icy straitjacket things for bottles in the freezer somewhere. Or some ice cubes?" Jenny is already reaching in the cupboard for a couple of wine glasses.

"OK, but I'll just have a small one. I've got to sew on some Scout badges, then make tea, then send some emails."

Jenny laughs. "Why do you bother, Rachel, with this mummy career juggle thing you do. Really? It's beyond me. You're run ragged looking after all these kids that you chose to have, doing this big job you chose to have. Why do you live at such a fast pace? You should embrace the slow movement like I do – slow walking, slow food, slow job."

Jenny's not kidding about the slow movement. She really does live life in slo-mo. Daniel is her only child and she has a part-time job in the local library, three days a week till 3pm. She didn't really want either of these things but her husband Alastair insisted. Jenny's delighted that Alastair insisted on a child, although continues to be grumpy about the part-time job.

Rachel has located the icy coat thing for wine bottles in the back of the freezer. She hands it to Jenny together with a half-full tray of ice cubes. Jenny slides it over the wine bottle, pops a couple of ice cubes into each glass, then without waiting opens the wine.

"I do enjoy a twist cap, don't you? There you go," she says, handing a glass to Rachel. "Get your chops round that."

Rachel takes a sip. "I do the mummy career juggle thing, Jenny, because I enjoy my job and I'm good at it – and I love my family," she says frostily. "It's not too much to ask to do both is it?"

"It's way too much to ask of me. You know how I am Rachel. I don't want a big job like you. I just want to hang around the house in my pyjamas reading and listening to the radio, bake cakes for when Daniel gets home from school. Go for a slow walk on the beach at the weekend. I don't understand why you and everyone else are in such a rush all the time. Like they want to get through life as fast as they can. What exactly are you people expecting to find on the other side? Is there some sort of league table? Someone at the Pearly Gates keeping count of who rushed around the most? But hey – to each their own. "

Jenny is ordinarily the antidote to Rachel's frenetic pace of life. Short and plump Jenny has a stillness about her that Rachel finds soothing. She admires Jenny's calm dedication to doing exactly what Jenny wants to do and nothing else and not feeling in the slightest bit bad about that. After Daniel has gone to school, if Jenny is not working, she will spend her mornings sitting in an armchair in her kitchen reading a book. She doesn't worry about the dishes in the sink or the fact that it might get sunny later so best put a wash on now. She'll get round to those things eventually – or maybe she won't – but for now she'll enjoy the moment and nothing is going to hurry her.

Usually, Rachel finds Jenny's approach to life refreshing but this evening her dig at Rachel's choices in life have annoyed her. "You think your focus on doing very little is worthy, Jenny, like you're the Dalai Lama and have found some higher pursuit in life. Truth is you're just plain idle. It's a miracle you keep your job when you spend most of your working day reading."

"It's a library! Libraries are all about reading. They can't sack me for doing my job. Anyway, I wouldn't care if I did get sacked. I don't want the bloomin' job anyway. I only do it because Alastair makes me. It's not as if we need the money. He says he makes me do the job because if I didn't have to get up in the morning to go to work, I'd never leave the house, just lie around taking root, with books sprouting up in great piles around me until there is no room left for Daniel or him. And he's right Rachel and so are you. I *am* plain idle. What I don't understand is why other people don't want to be plain idle too. More wine?"

"I have to sew Iris' Scout badges on ready for Scouts tonight and then send some emails."

"Do you *have* to? Do you really? Does Iris care if her Scout badges don't get sewn on for another week?"

Rachel stops to think. "No she doesn't. It's me that wants to sew them on for her. Because I said I would."

"But will Iris notice if you don't sew them on?'

"No."

"And these emails you've got to send. Are the people you are sending them to sitting at their desks right now, waiting for your emails? Their entire lives on hold until they hear from you?"

"Er, no."

"So you could send them tomorrow?"

"I suppose so, yes."

"So here's the deal Rachel. We're going to spring matey boy here from his high chair prison, maybe wipe him down a bit with a flannel first, and we are all going to go sit in the garden together. Nora and Daniel have already gone feral out there, digging in the dirt, but I won't tell Social Services if you don't. We're going to finish this bottle of wine together and put those disgusting looking sausages you've bought on your state of the art gas barbecue to keep the kids going. You'll text your husband and tell him to pick up a couple of pizzas and some more wine on the way home and I'll get Alastair to do the same. Then we'll all get a bit pissed on a school night but not so pissed you can't do your emails in the morning. You can tell that overdeveloped conscience of yours that it's all my fault for leading you astray. Agreed?"

Rachel is too tired to argue with Jenny. "Agreed."

"Lovely. You high powered career women wouldn't know what to do with yourselves if you didn't have plain idle cows like me around to make you feel better about yourselves."

Chapter 6

The furthest Idris Maddox has been away from home before is Barry Island and that was just a day trip to the seaside with the Miners' Welfare club.

They had arrived at Barry in two crammed coach loads, miners and their families, swarming out from the buses buzzing with excitement. They'd gone on the rides at White Brothers' Funfair until their money ran out and then made their way to the beach to go paddle in the sea. Idris remembers the faint shock he'd felt as colliers he had worked many shifts alongside suddenly abandoned their shoes and rolled up their trousers, revealing bits of themselves Idris had not seen before. Puffs of greying chest hair, knobbly ankles and feet pale as milk. Vulnerable, intimate flesh.

The coaches had returned home to the Rhondda full of happy people, their faces tinted pink by their day of fun and sunshine and the salty tang of the sea on their lips.

The port of Liverpool is far busier than Barry Island, busier than ten Barry Islands. Idris lets the rush and bustle of the place wash over him, allows himself to share in the excitement of the hundreds of people who like him are emigrating to a New World and a better life. He concentrates on this rather than thinking of leaving the Rhondda that morning. How his father and brother had set their faces tight and hard so as not to show any emotion but how when he'd embraced his mother a noise of such sadness had seeped out of her that he had wondered whether he could leave after all. How Tommy had made some excuse about Maggie feeling a little under the weather and not being able to come and say goodbye but that she sent her best wishes. Best wishes is all he will ever get from Maggie and that made the leaving not only possible but necessary.

All these people at the port of Liverpool, pushing and jostling their way to new opportunities, carry Idris along on their tide of high spirits and expectation. They sweep him onto the SS Montroyal, bound for Quebec, which will be his home for the next six days.

Being a third class passenger isn't half bad in Idris' estimation. There is food – plenty of it – with a main meal in the middle of the day and beef tea and sandwiches at teatime. Sleeping accommodation is shared and cramped but that does not bother a miner who is used to being in close proximity to other men. Idris has smelled far worse. People are kind to each other, bound together in their shared adventure, and there is always someone to chat to if chat is what you are looking for.

Idris himself is not very good at small talk and prefers to spend as much time as possible out walking on the deck. He is lucky not to suffer from seasickness and he enjoys the rise and swell of the sea, even enjoys the lurch in his stomach which reminds him of the rides at White Brothers' fun fair. He soon recognises the other people who like being outside on the decks too. There aren't many of them. A couple in their fifties, who are outside every bit as much as Idris but who always walk very gingerly, holding tight onto each other, as if scared that a puff of wind will suddenly sweep one of them up and blow them overboard. A dad and three sons, who sit companionably together on a bench, looking out across the sea, saying very little. Two girls in their early teens, sisters most likely but close in age, who lean over the rails and into the wind, wearing summer dresses too thin to keep them warm. They let the wind whip their hair around their faces. Both have long, pale blonde hair; mostly all Idris sees on this ship are women in hats. The hats look like bells and under the hats the women have chin length bobs, sometimes straight, sometimes tightly waved. It's as if the women mould their bobs under their hats, easing their hairstyles out, like cakes from tins.

The girls giggle as their hair flies around their faces and Idris likes the carefree sound of their laughter; their carefree hair. The clear bond between them makes him feel a sharp pang of loss for Tommy.

On the third day of the voyage only one of the young girls is out on the deck, the slightly older one. Idris surprises himself by talking to her when she walks past him.

"Only you today?"

"Yes, my sister is not feeling very well. I'm fine though."

"That's good to hear. I am fine too."

"I'm pleased to hear it."

The pleasantries are over and really Idris should move on, but he stays where he is. He can think of nothing else to say, the girl is much younger than him and it is not attraction to her that is keeping him there, but she is alone and so is Idris, so he stays.

"Would you like to walk with me a little?" he asks awkwardly, for he is far from certain he actually wants her to take a walk with him.

She hesitates.

"I'm perfectly safe, I assure you. My name is Idris. I'm from the Rhondda Valleys in Wales."

"Is being from the Rhondda Valleys a guarantee of being an upstanding, decent sort of person?"

"Of course."

"In that case I'll come for a walk with you. I'm called Jean. From Edinburgh."

They do four circuits of the ship in total. Jean explains that she is almost 15 and her sister Janet is 13. They are travelling with a group of girls from the Orphan Homes of Scotland – more than 50 girls in total – who are emigrating. Many of the children, Jean and Janet included, are orphans. But there are some whose parents have had to hand over their children so as to secure them a better life.

51

"Some of them are tiny – four or five – and they cry all the time, missing their mams. It doesn't matter whether they are dead or alive. Their mams are not on this ship with them either way. It's pitiful. That's why Janet and I come up here so often. There's only so much cuddling we can manage before it sets the two of us off weeping. Our mother died when we were babies and neither of us can remember her and you can't miss what you never had but it was only January we lost our dad and we've had a rough road since then. Got kicked out of our house within a few days of his going and ended up taking ourselves off to the Quarriers. It was pretty there – out in the countryside – but the Dominion needs us so that's where we're going to live now. We're part of the golden bridge across the Atlantic. Dad would have liked that – me and Janet being part of something golden."

"What's going to happen to you when we arrive?"

"We all go to a home first, in a place called Brockville in Ontario. From there the Quarriers will arrange for us to be taken in by a family and get trained up as servants. We've asked for a big house where there's room for both me and Janet so we can stay together. A place that needs hard workers like us."

"What about the little ones?"

"They'll be adopted by families in Canada, farmers and the like. They'll have good homes, open countryside and plenty of food. And what are you hoping to find in Canada?"

"Work and a fresh start. I'm a collier, came out on the general strike, but only us miners stayed out. The rest of the TUC are cowards and gave in after ten days. I'm told there's work in Canada for experienced miners and plenty of coalmines in Nova Scotia. Alberta too. Going to see where my feet lead me when we land."

"New beginning for us all then…"

Janet's health doesn't improve and for the next few days Jean and Idris walk the decks together. Being so much younger than him, he figures she must understand that the time he spends with her is offered in friendship – like an older brother – much the same way as she cares for the younger children in her group.

Friendship is all that Idris has to offer. He is too taken up with how he feels about Maggie for anything else. His mind boils with the memory of the time he spent with her before he left Wales – at night, he can feel and taste her as if she were lying in the bunk next to him, her hand on his thigh and her breath warm in his ear. He yearns for Maggie but that is nothing new. He has yearned for her for years, every second she spent with his brother and not him. Yearning for Maggie was part of his life long before she actually married Tommy. But now as well as yearning he also feels guilt for betraying his brother.

He dreams of Maggie every night. They are on Clydach Vale mountain making love. Maggie's legs are wrapped tight around him and he has one hand up her blouse, resting on her breast, the other cradling her head. He is kissing her. Long, deep kisses. The dream is vivid and exciting. Idris breaks away from the kiss so he can look at Maggie's pretty face. Her big brown eyes with such long eyelashes, the soft colour in her cheeks, the curve of her beautiful lips. Suddenly he becomes aware that someone is watching them; that it is in fact Tommy who is watching them. The look on Tommy's face – the disgust, the hatred, the sorrow – it is this look that always wakes Idris up. He wakes with a shock – glad to be awake and free from the dream – but with a fading erection which just makes him feel even more guilty.

Talking with Jean – the easy, companionable way she talks – takes his mind off Maggie. He likes to listen to her strong Scots accent and after so many tours of the ship's deck he no longer struggles to understand her. She is thrilled with the wooden trunk given to each girl by the Quarriers for their journey and the abundance of clothes within – including three nightgowns, three chemises, two summer frocks, two winter frocks, every item and the trunk itself clearly marked with their names. A straw hat in a box for Sunday. A Bible and the prayer book.

She is a good storyteller and recounts the funny things the Quarrier children say to make Idris laugh. She describes life in Edinburgh – the good bits before her father died and the sad bits afterwards – and she tells him, quietly confident, of the happiness she expects to find in Canada. Jean is brimful of hope and Idris stands close to her so that some of this hope might leak into him.

*

"Am I allowed to recover from this mystery illness of mine today," Janet asks her sister. "It's very boring being cooped up down here all day. If I don't get some air soon I am going to end up a genuine invalid. Is your ploy working?"

"I don't know, Janet. He likes me, I know he likes me. But I believe he considers me still a child."

"He wouldn't if he could hear you talking about him. All that stuff about his wide shoulders and his lovely brown hair and how when he speaks it sounds like singing. Strewth – he'd work out soon enough if he heard you prattle on about him non-stop that you're no child."

"There's only one day left Janet. We'll be arriving in Quebec tomorrow. Can you carry on being ill a bit longer?"

"No, I can't. It smells down here. Today I am making a recovery. I promise not to be well enough to join you as you walk round the ship for hours but I will be feeling some cool air on my face. You'll just have to find a way of getting a forwarding address to him. With any luck he'll come visit."

"Have you any idea just how big Canada is Janet?

"I know, it's enormous. But you and me, we deserve a bit of luck, Jeanie."

*

54

As soon as the SS Montroyal is within sight of the Canadian coast the passengers start making preparations to disembark. It takes the best part of a day for the ship to make its way along the St Lawrence river and the buzz of excitement from the passengers rises steadily until they arrive at Quebec City.

Idris threads through the crowd of passengers. Finally, he finds what he is looking for. The gaggle of Quarrier children. They look so little, so weary and lost. Pity for them thumps Idris in the chest. Janet and Jean are easy to spot as there are very few teenagers in the group. Tall and slim, their blonde hair loose to their shoulders, they move amongst the younger girls, instructing them to hold onto each other's hands, to step carefully down the ramp. Jean places her hand gently on top of one child's head, wipes another's nose. Idris doesn't know why but he feels compelled to stay close to the children. He wants to protect them – all of them – although he doesn't know what it is they might need protecting from.

Jean has been watching out for him too. Idris sees the smile that floods her face when she spots him, realises for the first time two things that should have been obvious to him for some days. That she is very pretty and that she is sweet on him. She twists and turns through the crowd of children to reach him.

"Idris. I'm so glad to see you." Her voice is wavering with emotion. "I was frightened I'd miss you and not get the chance to give you this." She hands him a piece of paper. "It's the address of the children's home in Brockville that we are all going to first. We'll be allocated new homes from there. If you write to me at this address, I will get your letter eventually."

Idris doesn't say anything. He looks briefly at the piece of paper, sees that Janet and Jean are destined for the Distributing Home for Scotch Children and Canadian Orphan Home.

"Promise you'll write to me Idris? When you have an address. I'll write back to let you know where Janet and I end up. The minute I get your letter I'll write back. "

He hesitates, but when he sees the look of disappointment in her eyes he relents. He folds the piece of paper and puts it in his pocket.

"I promise to write to you Jean."

"Cross your heart and hope to die?"

Idris draws the shape of a cross across his chest with his finger.

"Cross my heart and hope to die."

*

Idris has not given much thought to what he would do when he got off the boat. His focus has been on the process of leaving the Rhondda and of getting to Canada, not on what would happen once he was actually there. He had told Jean he would let his feet lead him when they landed. Only now that he's here, his feet seem unwilling to choose a destination. He wasn't exactly expecting to see mine owners queuing up on the dock to greet him, holding big placards aloft advertising vacancies for Welsh miners, but maybe on reflection that was precisely what he had been expecting. He certainly had not been expecting the other passengers of the SS Montroyal to disappear so quickly. Off to take the train or the bus or simply walk to their new lives in the New World.

He and Maggie had talked a little about what it would be like when he arrived in Quebec. How strange it would be to finally arrive in a new country and how everyone would be speaking French. But they'd had other things to do beyond talking and the conversations had never got further than arriving at this dock.

On the form he'd had to fill in for Canadian immigration there was a question about what trade or occupation he'd followed in his own country and what trade or occupation he intended to follow in Canada. His answer to both had been miner which was true. He'd also had to state the address to which he was going in Canada and having nowhere lined up he'd lied and given an address in Toronto he'd overheard one of the passengers talking about. He knows that where he will find coalmines is in Nova Scotia and Alberta. Alberta involves a long journey west across Canada. Nova Scotia makes the most sense, being closer to Quebec City. Only he finds, now he thinks about it, he doesn't much want to go to either. Nor does he want to waste any of his small amount of money on overnight lodgings in Quebec. Finally his feet make a decision and he starts walking to the train station. He will take the train that so many of the passengers on SS Montroyal had been planning to take. He will go to Toronto.

Chapter 7

"I did tell you they were coming Gareth. You must have forgotten. Old age doesn't come alone, as your mother likes to say."

"I did not forget Rachel. *You* forgot to tell me. Believe me, I'd remember if you had told me that your sister and her husband and their eerily well-behaved teenager were coming for dinner. In about an hour."

"Why? Because you would have come up with some work crisis that meant you had to stay late. On a Friday night?"

"No! Well yes! Maybe. Nick, sorry Nicholas, is OK even if he is an investment wanker and barely says two words but Jocelyn… we just don't see eye to eye."

"You never have Gareth. You think she's a snob and that makes you come over all scrappy working class, like you've just finished a shift and the mine owners are demanding you go back underground for a few more hours."

"I *am* working class. My grandfather was a miner, remember."

"You never let me and the children forget it! But you are a corporate lawyer earning a comfortable salary. You are about as working class as David Cameron lounging around the beaches of Cornwall wearing his Boden shorts." Rachel waves her arms around airily in an expansive gesture that takes in their large house, their leafy garden, the glass of Sancerre they are each holding.

"Don't take the piss out of me Rachel. I've had a tough week. I was looking forward to spending Friday night with my wife and children."

"You're just grumpy because I've given my sister our bedroom."

"And now you're telling me there's no chance of a Friday Fuck!"

When they first met, before they had children, Gareth and Rachel used to celebrate the end of the working week with a leisurely Friday Fuck and then go to the pub. With a house full of children, Friday Fucks are rarely anything other than a fond memory these days.

"My poor deprived husband," Rachel says wrapping her arms around his neck to comfort him. Gareth sighs overdramatically, hanging his shoulders down like the children did when they were little and disappointed.

"They're only here for one night. They'll be on their way to Pembrokeshire by mid-morning tomorrow."

"How come your sister is gracing Wales for the weekend anyway? I thought investment bankers favoured Cornwall along with the Camerons."

"Some friend of theirs just bought a cottage in Newport and invited them. Didn't you know darling? Pembrokeshire is the new Cornwall. Now go hop in the shower and I'll feed Jake quickly and then start getting our supper ready."

"Didn't *you* know love? Here in Wales, supper is two Rich Tea biscuits and a cup of Horlicks before bedtime. Want to come hop in the shower with me? I'll wash your back for you."

"Just go get in the shower, Gareth."

*

Gareth showers and puts on the clothes that Rachel has very unsubtly laid out on the bed for him. There's a pair of linen trousers and a cornflower blue shirt which is Gareth's favourite because Rachel loves it and touches him a lot when he wears it. Still buttoning up the shirt, he hurries back to the garden, looking forward to a second glass of wine before the visitors arrive. He is surprised to find they must have arrived while he was in the shower and are already seated in the garden.

He sees the way Jocelyn looks at his unbuttoned shirt, his bare chest and uncombed hair and tuts. Feeling like an errant schoolboy he does up the rest of his shirt buttons, runs his fingers through his hair, before finding his manners and bending to kiss Jocelyn's proffered cheek, shake Nicholas' hand.

"Welcome, welcome. Good to see you both. Where's my niece?"

"Grace has already been whisked away by Eloise to check out her new bedroom," Jocelyn says.

"Better hope she doesn't come back down with her hair dyed black and a piercing then!"

"I sincerely doubt it," Jocelyn says, primly. "Grace is very particular about the way she looks."

"Takes after her mother then." Gareth claps his hands and then rubs them briskly together, something he does only when feeling very uncomfortable.

Rachel sees the sign and hurries into the kitchen to collect the starter. "Dig in, everyone," she says, placing a large wooden board in the centre of the table, piled high with olives, sun dried tomatoes, mozzarella, Parma ham, melon chunks and fresh, ripe figs. "Lots of ciabatta bread to go with this if you want it."

Jake, who up until this point has been playing quietly in the sandpit, waddles over. He loves olives and hoists himself up on his father's knee to grab a handful from the board.

"Did he wash his hands?" Jocelyn points at Jake.

"On his way between the sandpit and here? Er, no. We're fresh out of bathrooms in the garden." Rachel's irony appears to be lost on Jocelyn.

"Best give the olives a miss, Nicholas," Jocelyn says loudly. Nicholas who is about to pop one into his mouth lowers his hand and looks nervously around for somewhere else to deposit it.

Gareth reaches over, plucks the olive from Nicholas' fingers and puts it in his own mouth. "How about I fetch you and Nicholas a little pot of olives just for the two of you? There's plenty more and I promise to wash my hands. I'll bring us another bottle of wine too, this one is almost empty. Mind yourselves while I'm gone though. Jake loves Parma ham too."

Gareth roots around in the fridge for the oversized plastic tub of olives they always have on the go. He stocks up on these tubs when he and his mother go on their quarterly lunch date to Costco. Gareth and his mother are in their element scouting out bargains at Costco and can spend hours browsing the shelves and cooing at the savings to be had. They are both expert at calculating VAT in their heads.

He ladles olives from the industrial plastic tub into some little terracotta pots his parents brought back as a gift from a holiday in Majorca. They look suitably artisan and authentic and will make Jocelyn and Nicholas think the olives came from a local deli. He also retrieves another bottle of Sancerre from what they affectionately call the cellar, which is their old fridge, pensioned off from food duty due to a tendency to grow mould and stuck in what was once a coal shed. He is about to go back out into the garden when he hears his phone ping, out in the hallway. Ordinarily Gareth ignores his phone on Friday evenings but he is perfectly happy to have a valid excuse to postpone joining the others a bit longer so he checks his messages.

There is an email from Cassandra Taylor.

"Following on from our meeting yesterday, I wonder if you can join me for a series of meetings with potential business associates in London next Tuesday from 9.30am to 6pm. I'm sorry it's such a long day but I have limited time available before I go back to Canada. We could then go out for a spot of dinner if you are free? Let me know."

He starts typing a response immediately.

"Tuesday is good for me and dinner afterwards would be good. Please advise where to meet." His fingers feel thick and clumsy and he checks the message for errors. Before pressing send, he thinks better of it and deletes what he has typed, replaces it with,

"I can make the meetings but will need to get away afterwards, sorry. Let me know where to meet."

Her reply comes straight back.

"Thank you. We can do dinner another time. Meet at Perfect's London office, 12 Bathurst Mews, near Hyde Park, W2 at 9.30am."

He turns his phone to silent and slips it in his pocket. Perfect is a great new client to land and if his client wants him at meetings all day, then he will go to those meetings. But he won't be risking going to dinner with Cassandra Taylor, not next Tuesday, not ever. The way she makes him feel is dangerous and he knows he must not let it take hold. He has always been dismissive when people say that they didn't mean to have an affair and that things just happened and they fell in love. Meeting someone might just happen. Finding them attractive – that can just happen too, as he has recently found out. But after that, it comes down to making conscious decisions – spending time with someone, making arrangements to meet, leading on to secret phone calls and from there to secret sex. A lot of lies. Just as people decide to do these things, they can just as easily decide *not* to do them. Rachel always says that if people put as much effort into their marriages as having an affair requires, divorce lawyers would be a lot less busy. Going to dinner with Cassandra Taylor would be foolish.

"Are you having to crush the grapes for that bottle of wine or what?" He hears Rachel calling from the garden. He gathers up the olives, tucks the bottle of wine under his armpit and hurries out to the garden to top everyone's glasses up.

"Shall I finish making the spaghetti carbonara Rachel? You stay out here and catch up with your sister. It won't take a minute."

"I'll skip on the carbonara thank you Gareth," Jocelyn says, "I'm low carbing at the moment. Could you fix me some scrambled eggs instead?"

"Sure!"

Back in the kitchen Gareth shouts loud enough to be heard in the garden.

"Iris! Can you come downstairs and do me a favour! I need you to pop down the Spar and buy some more eggs. Aunty Jocelyn is on a diet. And ask Nora to come to the kitchen. She can help lay the table."

Seating nine people for dinner is not a problem for the Maddox family. They regularly have people over "for food" as Gareth calls it and their large, battered, pine table can seat up to 14. None of the chairs match but Rachel says that's trendy these days.

"Yeah right, for a collection of antique church chairs maybe," Gareth always teases her, "but not mismatched Ikea."

Twenty minutes later, at Gareth's bellow of "FOOD!" from the bottom of the stairs, Eloise and Grace troop into the kitchen. It is the first time Gareth has seen Grace for some months and he is always uncertain how he should greet his niece now that she is 16 and he can no longer throw her up in the air and give her a big hug. Should he shake hands? Kiss her cheek? Grace looks equally uncertain and at one stage Gareth thinks she may be contemplating a curtsey. Finally he holds up his hand for a high five and Grace lightly taps her fingers against his.

"You're so down with the kids Dad," says eleven-year-old Iris, who is helping her father serve up. She is wearing jeans, a FC Barcelona top and Adidas trainers. Her hair which is the least red of everyone in the family, blonde really, is cropped short. She serves up hearty portions of carbonara for everyone else while Gareth places a plate of (non-organic but don't tell her) scrambled egg in front of Jocelyn. Oscar takes up his usual position under the table to wait for falling scraps.

"Can I have a glass of wine Dad?" Eloise asks.

"If you give Jake his milk and put him to bed after dinner you can." Eloise rolls her eyes but then nods and Gareth pours his daughter a glass of wine.

"What about Grace?" says Eloise, "is she allowed one?"

Gareth looks at Nicholas and Jocelyn.

"Absolutely not," Jocelyn replies, making a face like Gareth is

Count Dracula and is suggesting pouring her daughter a goblet of fresh blood. "She's underage. They're both underage!"

"They're 16 and 17! Don't you remember being that age Jocelyn? Drinking cider down the park with your mates?"

"Drinking cider in the park is not something that happens in Bucks. You obviously had a very different upbringing to Rachel and me."

"Really? I'm surprised. Francesca loves a drink doesn't she? Last time she and Felix were over they'd cracked open the gin and tonic by 5pm most nights."

Gareth feels his wife's heel pressing very deliberately and painfully on his little toe. Skilfully, Gareth changes the subject.

"So, a friend of mine has the opportunity of taking a job in Qatar. Would you recommend life out there?"

Rachel barely conceals a snort of laughter. Jocelyn and Nicholas returned from Doha three years earlier and Jocelyn has still to get over the loss. She likes nothing better than telling Doha stories: how much Nicholas earned there, how the expensive private school Grace went to was better suited for her dazzling academic excellence than anything to be had in the UK and how wonderful it was to have live-in Filipina maids plentifully and cheaply available.

"Absolutely. I only wish we were still there. The quality of life Nicholas and I had was beyond compare. And having a maid to do all the domestic chores meant I had time to get to the gym most days. Of course," Jocelyn says, "to get the best out of the maids, you did have to make sure they knew their place. You never, ever let them call you by your first name. Always insist on Ma'am. Ensures respect."

This is the point in the Doha stories that usually causes Gareth to leave the table and start clearing up but tonight he just smiles and keeps topping up everyone's glass of Sancerre until finally Jocelyn and Nicholas announce they are going up to bed because they've got an early start in the morning.

"You go on up, too," Gareth says to Rachel after they're safely out of earshot. "I've given our Filipina maid the night off so I'll put the first dishwasher load on."

"Thank you. And thank you for making it easy tonight. I know you find them…"

"Money obsessed? Boring? Snobs?"

"Don't spoil all your hard work now! We're in Iris' bed by the way. She's gone in top to toe with Nora."

"Do we get to go top to toe too? If so, I'll leave the dishwasher till the morning. It is Friday after all." Gareth grins, pulling his wife towards him and kissing her hard on the lips.

"You've no chance mate! I haven't been able to see straight since before you opened the third bottle. I'll be asleep the minute my head hits the pillow. Anyway, it's past midnight. The Friday window has closed. Try not to make too much noise when you come up."

Gareth stacks the dishwasher. He should really scrub the carbonara bowls first. The dishwasher is of a similar vintage to the fridge in the coal shed and it doesn't wash egg away, just bakes it rock solid. But he can't be bothered. All he really wants is to clear enough space on the kitchen table so that breakfast can start sooner rather than later and Jocelyn and Nicholas can get on their way. And a fag. He really wants a fag but it's too risky to nip out the garden for a sneaky one. He can still hear people moving around upstairs and they are all so proud of him for having finally given up. But he really deserves a cigarette after the evening he's had.

Oscar! That's it. He'll take Oscar for a walk! Oscar will appreciate a walk and a wee before bed.

Oscar is fast asleep in his basket, his border terrier beard greasy from all his hard work under Jake's high chair clearing up spilled spaghetti carbonara. He opens one eye when Gareth shakes his lead at him but closes it again quickly, pretending to be still asleep. Gareth pretty much has to drag him out the front door. Before they get to the gate, the front door opens again.

"Can I come with you Dad?" It is Eloise. She has her Doc Martens on all ready but her hair is tied back in a ponytail and she has removed all her make-up and jewellery. Gareth feels a twist of joy to see the face of his little girl again.

"What are you still doing up at this time of night?"

"Why are you taking such a reluctant dog out for a walk?"

"Come on then." He sticks the crook of his elbow out towards her and to his surprise Eloise slips her hand inside.

They walk down the hill from their house to the pebbly beach. By now, Oscar is fully awake and rushing around excitedly sniffing late night smells he doesn't normally encounter. The beach is lit by the street lamps but there is only a small sliver of moon and the sea is inky black. Eloise and Gareth stand side by side listening to the waves crash. The late night air is cool on their faces and the beach is empty and peaceful.

"Can I talk to you about something, Dad?"

Gareth steels himself. Is this it? Is his first born about to tell him she is in love? Lost her virginity? Pregnant? On drugs? He gathers himself.

"You can ask me about anything El, you know that."

"It's about Grace."

Gareth tries not to let his sigh of relief be a noisy one.

"What about Grace?"

"She's unhappy Dad. Very unhappy. She didn't say anything to me but I saw the tops of her arms when she was changing into her nightie. She's cutting herself. She's got scars and some new cuts too, all crusty with scabs."

Gareth doesn't say anything. He's not certain what he should say.

"What do you think we should do, Dad?"

"Tell Mum?"

"I knew you'd say that. We can't tell Mum. Auntie Jocelyn is her sister. She'll say she has to tell her."

"But Auntie Jocelyn needs to be told about this!'

66

"No, Grace needs to tell Auntie Jocelyn about it. That's a different thing altogether."

"You're right there. What do you think we should do Eloise?"

"Thing is, I don't really know Grace at all. We only see each other about twice a year when they come to visit us or when we all go to visit Grandma in France. We never stay with them in Buckinghamshire because there's no room for all of us. Our house is always so noisy and Grace is so quiet. We're cousins but we're not friends. Not really. We're not even friends on Facebook. So I don't know what Grace needs. But if it were me I'd need space to think things through."

"That makes sense."

"So... I was thinking I could say to Grace I'd like to spend some time with her, get to know her better, and ask her to stay with us for a couple of weeks. Auntie Jocelyn and Uncle Nicholas could drop her off here on their way back from Pembrokeshire. Grace has got a long holiday now anyway because she's finished her GCSE's and my AS levels are all done and there's only a couple of weeks left in school till the summer holidays, so schoolwork is winding down. If you're OK with it, Mum will be."

"And then what?"

"And then we take it from there and see what happens."

"That means you've got to share your bedroom with her and you love having that space to yourself."

Eloise shrugs. "I'll have it back to myself eventually."

They watch the waves together in silence for a little while.

"Can I ask you a question, now?" Gareth asks.

"Fire away."

"Do you think Iris is gay?"

"What do you think?"

"I think she's Iris. That she's my daughter. That I love her. That's what I think."

"Then you don't need to ask the question because the answer doesn't matter."

"You're a very wise and very observant young woman Eloise Maddox."

"More observant than you think. You can have one of the cigarettes you've got stashed in your pocket, now. I won't tell Mum."

"I don't know what you are talking about. I've given up smoking as you well know."

"Can I have one then?"

"No, you cannot."

On the walk back to the house, Gareth fishes the cigarettes from his pocket and dumps them in the closest bin. Eloise smiles and reaches out her hand to her father and Gareth takes it. They walk the rest of the way home hand in hand.

Chapter 8

Gareth is woken by Rachel curling herself around him, tucking her knees behind his and kissing his back gently.

"Morning, husband," she mumbles through the kisses.

"Morning, you. What a nice way to be woken at…" he glances at Iris' alarm clock, "6am on a Saturday morning."

"Isn't it just," Rachel says, rolling Gareth onto his back to reveal an impressive hard-on. "And I can see that it's going to get better and better."

Afterwards, curled up together in Iris' small bed, Gareth kisses the top of her head.

"We should do that more often. Tell me what I did to deserve it, so I can do it again?"

"You looked hot in that blue shirt last night. You managed not to be rude to my sister the entire evening. You made a mean carbonara."

"Your sister can come for food – sorry supper – whenever she likes if that's the pay off," Gareth grins. "Maybe it could be a new thing for us. The Saturday Shag. It should be a thing for everyone really. It could have its own slot on *Saturday Kitchen*. After the wine review and before the reruns of Keith Floyd."

"Are you going to shut up now and go make me a cup of tea?"

"Your wish is my command, my princess."

"And will you make a start on cooking some bacon for bacon sandwiches?"

"Sandwiches? Jocelyn is low carbing don't you remember?"

"She can just have bacon then. Or nothing. Who goes low carb on a weekend away to Newport, Pembs anyway?

69

"I don't know. They're a funny lot those English people."

"Tea, Gareth! And bring up some milk for Jake. He'll be waking up any minute now. In a cup, not a bottle."

*

Down in the kitchen, Gareth finds that Grace is already curled up on the sofa next to the Aga with Jake sitting very comfortably on her lap drinking a cup of milk. He grins when he sees his dad but makes no move to get off Grace's lap.

"Got yourself a new best friend there, Grace!"

"I heard him crying in his cot. He wasn't wailing or anything. Just crying a bit. And I was awake anyway and you and Auntie Rachel were…erm, not up yet…so I brought him down here. I put his milk in the microwave for 40 seconds like Eloise did last night. I checked it first before giving it to him."

Gareth tries not to think about his niece possibly overhearing the Saturday Shag.

"You're obviously a natural. Thank you for doing that for him."

"I think he's adorable. So giggly and sweet. I like how chunky his legs are." Grace squeezes Jake's legs gently and on cue he giggles. Grace giggles too.

"Would you like a cup of tea?" Gareth asks

"Yes please. Uncle Gareth, did Eloise talk to you last night about me maybe coming to stay for a while?"

"She did and we'd be delighted to have you."

"Thank you, thank you so much. I was wondering if it was OK with you and Auntie Rachel whether I could…"

"Go on."

"If I could get out of going to Pembrokeshire with Mummy and Daddy altogether and just stay here. Their friends are nice and everything but they don't have children so it would just be me and grown-ups and I'd have to hang around while they drink wine and start talking really loudly about business and house prices and how I'm doing at school and stuff and…"

"It's boring for you."

"Very. And if I don't go to Pembroke with them, then Mum and Dad won't have to call back here on Sunday to drop me off." Grace smiles at Gareth, a small, sweet, fleeting smile that says *"And then you won't have to see Jocelyn and Nicholas twice in the same weekend."*

"That is absolutely fine with me, Grace, and it will be with Rachel too. Just need to clear it with your parents. Right. I'm making bacon sandwiches for us all. Want to give me a hand? You can slice the bread. It's in the pantry over there."

Grace disappears into the pantry and emerges after a while looking quizzical and holding two large loaves of crusty white bread.

"I couldn't find any brown bread. Only white. Mummy doesn't eat white bread."

"She isn't eating bread at all, Grace love, so no need to worry about her. Make sure you cut it good and thick now, needs to be able to sustain the weight of the butter."

The smell of frying bacon slowly draws the rest of the inhabitants of the house to the kitchen. Jocelyn and Nicholas readily agree to Eloise's suggestion that Grace come stay for a while and skip the visit to Pembrokeshire.

"It would mean we'd get home sooner on the Sunday which would suit Nicholas as he likes to get into work by 6am on Mondays to get a good start on the week," Jocelyn says.

Gareth notes with satisfaction that she is on her second bacon sandwich – white bread, salty Welsh butter, fried bacon and HP sauce – and hasn't mentioned low carbing once. Nothing like far too much white wine on a Friday night to make a girl not care less about the evils of carbs. "Are you sure you don't mind, Rachel?"

"Positive. It will be lovely for us all to spend time with my only niece."

Once Jocelyn and Nicholas have been waved off, the rest of Saturday is the usual whirl of washing, dog walking and taking Jake to the nearby park where Iris can join in with the never ending football match that is usually being played there. Gareth orders a Chinese takeaway for an early dinner. He orders far too much, the little silver foil and plastic dishes covering most of the kitchen table. They help themselves and take their plates to eat on their laps in the lounge, watching old episodes of *Glee* which is the one thing that everyone is prepared to watch.

Grace keeps an eye on Jake, making sure that the Chinese chicken balls he is eating with such speed don't make him choke. She changes his nappy and fetches his bedtime milk and cuddles him as he drinks it, singing nonsense into his ear till he falls asleep.

"Can I go put him in his cot?" Grace asks Rachel

"Of course you can Gracie, thank you. Sorry. Grace. I know Jocelyn doesn't like pet names.

"I like being called Gracie. It makes me feel like… I don't know really…like I fit in. I'm going to go to bed now, too, and read for a bit, if that's OK."

"Of course it is. I think we'll all be turning in fairly early tonight. We're going to Gareth's parents for lunch tomorrow. They're called Richard and Carol, Nana and Gramps. And there's Grandpa Davey too, Gareth's grandfather. He's 88 now but still sharp and pretty active. Walks by himself to the Naval for a couple of pints every Thursday night without fail. I hope you'll come with us."

"I'd love to. If there's enough food for me too, that is."

"Oh, there'll be plenty enough food, Gracie, don't you worry," says Gareth. "My mother caters on the assumption that a dozen extra people might turn up unexpectedly at any moment."

*

They all drive up to the Rhondda, even Oscar, in the family's seven seater silver VW Transporter.

"Does your dog usually come out for lunch with you?" Grace asks, politely.

"Whenever he's invited, yes. He's a sociable sort is Oscar."

When Grace sees the rows of small terraced houses for the first time, she cannot disguise her surprise.

"The houses are all so tiny."

Rachel groans. "Be careful Grace. You'll set Gareth and his father off talking about King Coal and the industrialisation of the south Wales Valleys."

"I think that sounds quite interesting."

The other children groan.

"Believe me it's not interesting," says Eloise, authoritatively. "Let me spare you from wasting three hours of your life. South Wales used to be agricultural. Then in the 1800's they discovered coal mining and tons of people moved here for work which is why all these rows of terraced houses were built, to house them all. Ordinary people worked for the bosses who owned the mines and got treated badly and were paid poor wages and died in accidents down the pits. There were riots and there was a big strike and everyone hates Winston Churchill but nothing changed and the bosses still kept all the money and got fat and rich on the sweat of the brows of all the ordinary people and built fancy buildings in Cardiff and bought Impressionist paintings and stuff. Then the coal ran out when Dad was little and a horrible lady prime minster called Margaret Thatcher closed down the pits and now it's all nice and green again but no one in the Rhondda has had a job since, except people like Dad who moved away."

"That's not quite how it was Grace. Eloise is being flippant."

"It might have been flippant Dad but it was also flipping short."

"Yes well, we're here now so let's stop discussing coal, shall we, and all have a nice family Sunday dinner together."

Grace follows behind the Maddox family as they troop without knocking into the little house at the very end of the terrace. They march single file right through to the kitchen at the back. It smells deliciously of roasting meat and the windows are steamed up from all the pans boiling on the stove. Carol Maddox is rolling out pastry on her kitchen counter. She has very dark brown hair and is wearing a blue flowered housecoat. She holds out her arms wide, her hands all floury, to greet them.

"Hello my lovely grandchildren. Come and give your Nana a kiss then."

The Maddox children, even Eloise, rush to kiss their grandmother.

"And you must be Grace," Nana says, smiling widely. "How lovely to meet you."

"Thank you for inviting me."

"Not at all lovely girl. You're my grandchildren's cousin. That makes you family too. Do I get a kiss from my son and daughter-in law too? I do! Wonderful. Now, I've just got to finish making these apple tarts but Richard and Davey are out the back already. How about, Gareth and Rachel, you go out and join them and me and the kids will finish up here. Then I'll make a nice Dubonnet and orange for us all."

Rachel lets Gareth go ahead and lingers for a few moments to watch as the children gather quietly round Nana.

"Nice hair, Nana," Eloise says. "Almost the exact same colour as mine."

"Yes, but mine's natural of course whereas yours is out of a bottle. Very lucky we are on my side of the family. We never go grey." Nana pats her dark brown hair and smiles a secret smile at Eloise.

"Now Iris, let me see if I get this right. That's a Manchester United top you're wearing today?"

"Yes, Nana."

"I've got a soft spot for Manchester United. Always rather fancied George Best. Badly behaved, but ever so dishy."

Iris rolls her eyes at her grandmother. "Just finish trimming the apple tarts, Nana, so we can make hedgehogs."

"Yes, sorry Iris, here we go." Carol Maddox expertly twirls the apple tarts round in one hand and trims the excess pastry from the edge. The children swoop on the long ribbons of pastry that fall to the table, even Eloise, and start rolling it into animal shapes.

"Uh, uh, Jake, you can't eat it just yet." Carol manages to stop Jake before the raw pastry hits his mouth. "Here, you get the currants like this…and you poke them into the pastry like this… and it makes a hedgehog. Nana will put them in the oven and you can eat them for your afters. "

Watching the children all playing with pastry, with not an electronic device in sight, it occurs to Rachel not for the first time that her mother-in-law may not be just a retired teacher but very possibly also a white witch.

Leaving them to it, Rachel goes out to the garden where, as she expected, she finds her father-in-law, Richard, and his father, Davey, sitting in a bubbling hot tub. Gareth is perched on the rim of it, a beer in one hand, his socks and shoes discarded, up to his knees in rolling bubbles.

When Carol and Richard had the hot tub installed the previous year, it had come as a shock. The garden – Gwen's garden as it was always known – had always been so very important to this family and Richard and Davey spent hours and hours every year working on it. Then, one Sunday, Carol had led Rachel and Gareth out the back and they found that all the plants and the lawn had been ripped out and replaced by decking. At the bottom, where there had previously been rows of bedraggled, ancient raspberry canes and blackcurrant bushes, there now stood a large, wooden clad, hot tub.

"You didn't expect that, did you!" Carol had clapped her hands in joy at the look on Gareth and Rachel's faces.

"I didn't know you even liked hot tubs, Mam," Gareth had said.

"I love them! Have done ever since your father and I first had a go in one in Tenerife back in 1997. Wanted one ever since and then I saw them on offer at the Royal Welsh. Bargain they were, so I bought one."

"But what about Gwen's garden?" Rachel had not been able to stop herself from asking.

"That bloody garden was a pain in the backside from the day I got married. Never even met the famous Gwen. She died when Richard was 17, just before I met him. My poor mother-in-law, Rosie, she was the one doing the gardening then. Got landed with it, having made some foolish promise to Gwen on her deathbed that she'd keep it going. I spent 50 years of my life watching people work their socks off in this garden – Rosie, Davey, Richard. All so as to grow more veg than they knew what to do with and then having to knock on all the neighbours' doors to get rid of it. Well I always hated gardening and I can buy all the veg we ever want down Morrisons. So I had it decked over and the hot tub put in last week when Richard and Davey were away on a bowling trip."

"What did Gramps make of that?"

"Oh he blew a fuse and he's had a cob on ever since. Keeps moaning that he will miss cutting the grass, even though he'd become a liability with the Flymo and in constant danger of cutting his toes off. He'll come round, you watch."

Come round he did. From refusing to even look at the hot tub, it had taken Carol a matter of weeks to persuade him to give it a try. Turned out, Davey enjoyed a good hot tub even more than Carol and now the difficulty is getting him out of it. Rachel no longer bats an eyelid at the sight of Davey's naked old shoulders, his pale, saggy skin translucent almost, as he boils himself lightly on a Sunday afternoon before lunch.

"Did you bring your bathers, Rachel love?" Davey calls out to her.

"Forgot them yet again, Gramps."

"You'd forget your head if it wasn't stitched on. You never

remember your bathers you don't. You're missing out on a real treat. Nothing better than sitting in lovely hot water with the sun on your face. You know, back in the day my mother used to keep a tin bath hanging on the wall, right there. My father and my grandfather had to walk home from the mine – damp, tired, still covered in coal dust – and wash in that tin bath out here in the garden or in front of the fire. In water that my grandmother had to boil in big pans on the fire. Backbreaking work, she said it was. And even after the pithead baths got put in, and the miners came home clean, she kept that tin bath hanging there, to remind her how lucky they all were. She wouldn't like what Carol has done to her beautiful garden but I reckon she'd be chuffed to bits to see me sitting out in it, aged 88, and up to my neck in hot water that no bugger had to boil."

"I don't know about that Dad," says Richard, taking a swig out his bottle of beer. "Nana didn't take kindly to anyone sitting around doing nothing for very long."

"You're spot on there, son," Davey chuckles.

"Talking of your mother, Gramps, remind me again about the family connection with Canada. I had a meeting this week with a client from Toronto. Made me think about it."

"It's not much of a story and I've told you it already."

"When did having told me a story before stop you telling it again?"

"All right then. My Dad, Tommy, was a twin. An identical twin. His twin was called Idris. The year before I was born, in 1926, not long after the general strike had ended, Idris emigrated to Canada. Flounced off there in a huff my Dad said, because the strike broke and the miners were being starved back to work. It just about broke my grandmother's heart but then I arrived in the nick of time and took her mind off Idris. Which is just as well because he never came back. Not once. Wrote regular letters for a good few years after he went and then the letters just stopped. No one ever heard from him again after that."

"Did anybody ever try to find him?"

"I don't think so. Dad didn't talk about him very much, reckoned he must have died young, maybe killed in the war. "

"How very sad for Gwen," Rachel says, "to never see her son again and not know what happened to him."

"It was a different time," Davey says, matter of factly. "People died young – of disease or hunger or in pit accidents or fighting wars. That's not to say that people didn't love each other the same, just that it was easier to let go back then. To lose touch."

Davey takes a deep swig of his beer, drains the bottle. "I've got some old pictures somewhere. I'll show you after dinner. Now, are you lot going to help me get these old bones out of here or what? I'm about ready for my Dubonnet and orange."

Chapter 9

It does not take Idris long to find work in Toronto and it is every bit as backbreaking as mining. He is a construction worker on the new Union Station, or, more precisely, on the viaduct along Toronto's waterfront that will carry the railway tracks to the new station. The station itself was completed a full six years ago but has yet to open. The building work is hard work and will be harder still as winter approaches but it is above ground and in daylight and the wages are decent. Idris is glad to have it.

A grander building than the new station Idris has never seen. He has learned that the colonnaded porch at the front and the high vaulted ceilings and marble floors of the Grand Hall inside mean that it is built in a Beaux Arts style. He particularly likes the carvings of Canadian place names carved high up in the stone walls. Sault Ste Marie, Vancouver, Halifax. Places in this vast new country of his that he hopes to visit someday.

He has secured lodging at a good house on Fairlawn Ave, a few miles north of the station. It is owned by a married couple, Mr and Mrs Williams, who are from Carmarthen. The first question people ask when they meet new people, here, is where are you from. Idris is often mistaken for Irish or Scots but he doesn't mind. People from the whole of Britain are helpful to him and it was an Irishman who first told him of the Welsh church, Dewi Sant. Not that Idris was ever much of a chapelgoer before coming to Canada, let alone church. He goes because he misses home. It is comforting to hear familiar accents and sing Welsh hymns.

It was at Dewi Sant that he met Mr and Mrs Williams. They

had emigrated to Canada shortly after the end of the Great War, which had taken the life of their only son. Mr Williams had lost his appetite for farming with no son to pass it on to, although he is still involved with farming as he works for Canadian Immigration persuading other British farmers to bring their skills to the Dominion. Idris suspects that his being offered lodging with them owed less to his being Welsh and more to the fact that he is of a similar age to their son when he died. He has a large room all to himself and a bed, a chair and a table at which he can sit and read in the evenings after supper. Mrs Williams is a very good cook – much better than Gwen – and he is fed well. Other men he works with complain bitterly about their cold cramped accommodation and the poor quality of their landladies' dinners. He keeps his own good fortune to himself.

However, he writes to Gwen to tell her of his new job and his new home and she writes back immediately. He has seen no more than a few words of his mother's handwriting in the past and seeing whole pages of it would be strange if everything else about his new life was not already so strange. Gwen writes that she is pleased he is safe and working and has such kind people looking out for him. But mostly she writes about her excitement about becoming a grandmother. For Maggie is pregnant and will have a baby in late spring.

> *"We are all so very pleased at this glad news. We have been more than a little down in the dumps since you departed for Canada and this new baby will be a welcome distraction. Maggie looks very well although she refuses to take things easy. She is the one who has taken over your rabbit traps.*
>
> *I know this part of my letter will not be a surprise to you son but as you expected your father and brother have returned to work at the pit. It pains me to tell you that it is at a lower rate of pay than before the strike and Maggie's hunting, though commented upon unkindly by many as a strange activity for a*

woman, is a necessity. She is much better than me at the process of trading and we now get far more eggs from our neighbours in exchange for a rabbit than we did before."

Idris tries very hard not to think about this baby and how it came about. He could be the father but he seeks to reassure himself that so might Tommy. Maggie's belief that Tommy could not become a father could be wrong. No doctor was consulted. There is every good chance that this baby is nothing more than his nephew which is the way things should be and which absolves him of some of the guilt of betraying his brother.

He tries even harder to block from his mind the image of Maggie striding with strong legs and a growing belly across Clydach Vale mountain. Of how beautiful she is. Of how her skin feels when pressed against his own. He is not very successful in his efforts and it is rare that he wakes of a morning without having dreamed of his brother, Maggie or the baby she is carrying.

He has written too to Jean telling her his address. He thought long and hard about posting the letter to Jean. He remembers the look on her face that last day as they disembarked from the boat and feels uncomfortable at the memory. Jean is still a child and it would be inappropriate for him to give her false hope that her feelings for him are returned. Nevertheless he very much wants to hear about her and Janet's new life and the grand house where they will be in service. In any event he had crossed his heart and hoped to die and he is a man who keeps his word. He finds himself drawing his finger over his chest once more as he pushes the letter to Jean into the letterbox.

It is November by the time he gets a letter in reply. The first snow has already fallen but it is not yet so cold that when he puts his back into his work he does not quickly grow warm.

Dearest Idris

I was so very glad to get your letter. I am very pleased that you have found gainful employment and have a comfortable place to live.

Janet and I arrived safely at the Fairknowe home in Brockville but stayed there only a short while before being allocated our positions.

Regrettably it was not possible to place us together and we find ourselves at separate farms in the Brockville area. Our duties are not solely domestic and include much farm work. I cannot pretend it is not harder work even than I envisaged, but I am glad of the opportunity.

Janet is fortunate in that the family for whom she works have young daughters. By all accounts these girls have taken to Janet and she to them. There are no children at my farm, only Mr and Mrs Barraclough who are not talkative people. Mr Barraclough in particular barely says a word to me.

I thank God daily that Janet and I have a roof over our heads and food on the table and try not to dwell on the fact that the food on Janet's table seems rather more plentiful than mine.

I sincerely hope that our paths will cross again at some point. This hope is strengthened by the knowledge that you too are in Ontario.

With best wishes, Jean.

Jean's letter troubles Idris. He feels her loneliness as she attempts to convey in her letter a strength she does not actually feel. Despite them both being in Ontario, Brockville is more than 200 miles away from Toronto and there is no real danger of their paths crossing again as Jean hopes. But he will write to her often. There can be no harm in writing to her.

Watching Toronto grow is like watching a pan of milk boiling on the stove. There is construction work going on all over the City – hotels and factories and civic buildings. New businesses open all the time as more and more people arrive from all over the world. There is constant dust and noise and movement and a feeling of anticipation, as if the City were on the brink of something. Like the pan of milk is boiling so hard it will soon flow over the top. The Rhondda always seemed full to Idris – of pits and people and houses – but there were always the mountains to escape to. Here in Toronto, there is no getting away from the growing pains of the City.

Despite all the construction work and the enterprise of feeding and housing and transporting Toronto's growing population, there are not enough jobs to go around. Those who have found work are willing to work long hours to keep it and those not in work suffer poverty and homelessness. Idris listens to what the Trades and Labour Congress of Canada has to say about minimum wages and free healthcare and education for all, but he does not join or get involved. The failure of the strike has rubbed the edge off his anger and he has lost faith in trade unionism.

He goes to church a lot. Not because God is filling the gap left by politics but for the social life. Most Welsh families arriving in Toronto find their way to Dewi Sant eventually and there is always something arranged. Choirs and musical evenings and social suppers. The Ontario Temperance Act means that there's no pub by way of alternative entertainment and at Dewi Sant's social occasions there are women his own age and of Welsh origin, some of whom when he glances at them glance back.

There is one woman who does more than glance. Her name is Aeronwen James and she is small and fair, as different a woman from Maggie as there could ever be. Her blonde hair is neatly pinned up and she wears dark fitted jackets cut to her waist and long black skirts that fall to just above her sturdy laced black boots. Keeping warm and sturdy boots are important for both men and women in snowy Toronto and there are no flapper dresses to be seen at Dewi Sant.

He first manages to talk properly to Aeronwen on the evening

83

of a Twmpath Dawns, a folk dancing evening. These evenings are very popular with the younger members of Dewi Sant's audience – they involve set dance steps but also lots of stamping and whirling and changing of partners, an opportunity for the holding of hands and waists, all in plain view and part of the dance. Idris has been to a number of these and he knows the steps by now. He counts the numbers of dancers and their positions and places himself where he is guaranteed of Aeronwen as a partner the most often.

"Good evening, Miss James."

"Noswaith dda, Mr Maddox."

"I'm afraid I don't speak Welsh. My father does – he's from north Wales – but he brought us up as English speaking."

"What a shame! It's what we speak in our family."

"Maybe you should teach me then."

"Maybe I will."

"May I say, Miss James, you look very well this evening."

"I look very sweaty you mean. I love Twmpath Dawns but it doesn't half make you out of puff."

"I thought ladies never sweat, only shine."

"In that case, I'm shining all over." Aeronwen grins at him and Idris grins back and they carry on dancing.

Although Welsh speaking, Aeronwen, the baby of her family, was born in Toronto.

"It's strange," she explains to Idris during a break in the dancing while tea is served, "I am Canadian but I feel every bit as much Welsh as Canadian."

"Whereas I'm Welsh and feel every bit as much Canadian."

"Do you really? Aren't you consumed with longing to go home? See your family? Go to a real Eisteddfod?"

"Not in the slightest. I miss my family – my parents and my brother, of course I do – and the mountains, I miss them too – but I made the choice to come to Canada and this is where I belong now."

84

Idris' life is busy and he has much to write about in his letters to Jean. He tells her how Toronto grows, stretching east and west and north so that there is room in her arms to embrace all the people that arrive to make a new start. He describes the men he works with on the viaduct, the different languages he hears all around him and the foods the men bring with them to work, cooked in the ways of their own countries, strange and delicious. He tells her of Dewi Sant and its social events. Jean's own letters say little about her daily life. She writes only that work is hard but that she prefers that to being cooped up inside by the snow and that she looks forward even more to summer because food will be in less short supply. Jean fills her letters with questions about Idris' life in Toronto, begging for more detail. How high is the viaduct now? How soon till the new station will open? What do pierogi taste like? What dance steps does Welsh folk dancing involve because she thinks it sounds just like a Scottish ceilidh…

Jean does not ask about Aeronwen because Idris has omitted to mention her. In every letter she writes, Jean tells him how important his letters are to her. How they keep her smiling on days that might otherwise be lonely. Idris does not wish to hurt Jean and feels the kindest thing is not to tell her that when he is not working he spends as much time as he possibly can in the company of Aeronwen James.

The winter is long and snow falls most nights. When Idris first steps out of the house on Fairlawn Ave to walk to work in the morning, the ice-cold air punches him in the chest, squeezing all the air out of him. He found it difficult to breathe at first on this journey until he realised that it was because the snot in his nose was freezing and that he needed to wear his scarf up as far as his eyes and to breathe through his mouth into damp, wet wool. The atrocious weather conditions rarely stop work on the viaduct. No work means no pay and the risk of frostbite seems the lesser evil.

Eventually the snow starts to melt and the winter of 1926 slowly becomes the spring of 1927. Even so, there are still a few stubborn patches of snow remaining when a letter from his mother arrives telling him that Maggie's baby has been born safe and sound, a bouncing baby boy, the spit of Tommy, with a big shock of dark hair just like her own boys had when they were born. He is to be christened David but is already being called Davey. He is the apple of the eye of his grandparents and Idris' father is insistent the boy shall call him Taid, like he called his own grandfather, not Tadcu, like they say in south Wales. Gwen writes that her grandson can call her whatever he likes. She really does not mind.

Her words swirl up feelings in Idris that work and church and Aeronwen have managed to keep buried all winter. He imagines Maggie sitting in bed, holding her new-born son, and his brother clucking around them like one of the neighbours' hens, fetching tea and patting Maggie's hand. But the longing, the sadness and the jealousy are washed away by the strongest feeling of all. Relief that when he counts back the months on his fingers, the baby's date of birth in early spring proves that Maggie must have been already pregnant when she asked him to sleep with her and that therefore it must be Tommy, not he, who is the father of the baby. Idris feels like the weight of all the snow of winter has melted from his shoulders. The dreams of Maggie stop.

Lighter and freer, Idris pursues Aeronwen with greater intent. Her father, William James, a hat maker with a small, successful shop in Queen Street, invites Idris to come meet with him there one Saturday afternoon.

"Mr Maddox. It's good to see you are a punctual man. Come through to my office in the back. Would you care for a cup of tea?"

"No thank you sir."

"You seem like a good man, Mr Maddox."

"I hope so, sir."

"A man of honesty and integrity?"

"I am, sir."

"Let me cut to the chase. Aeronwen is my youngest daughter. The others are all married now, which means I have watched this dance you and Aeronwen are doing play out a number of times already. I know my last born very well and I can see she is a willing participant in the dance. I know you very little, yet it seems to me that you are also a willing participant."

Mr James pauses here and Idris realises that some response is expected of him. Not knowing what else to say he holds Mr James' eye and simply says, "Sir."

"What I need to understand from you Mr Maddox is whether your intentions in relation to my daughter are good. That is, that you are not *just* dancing with her?"

"I don't entirely follow you Sir, but I can assure you my intentions in relation to your daughter are honourable and that I'm dancing with her with…er…a view to the longer term."

"Excellent answer. Good. That's what I wanted to hear. Right, now that you're here, how about I fit you for a hat? Something you can wear to the opening ceremony of the Union station. Edward, Prince of Wales is going to cut the ribbon you know. Us Welshmen better look smart for him."

On the morning of 6 August 1927 Idris, Aeronwen, her father and the rest of the James family form part of the large crowd gathered at Front Street to greet His Royal Highness, Edward, the Prince of Wales. There is great excitement amongst the crowd at seeing their future King, accompanied by his brother and sister-in-law the Duke and Duchess of York, British Prime Minister Stanley Baldwin and Canadian Prime Minister William Lyon Mackenzie King. Many of the crowd arrived as soon as it was light that morning to secure the best view, waiting patiently in the summer sunshine which is already hot.

"I don't see what the fuss is all about," Idris grumbles to Aeronwen. "How is he going to be king of this country all the way from over there in London? This is Canada's Diamond Jubilee year for heaven's sake. Why do we even need a king?"

"That's treason that is, Idris," Aeronwen rebukes him, reaching up and tilting his new hat so that it covers his eyes. "You want to watch yourself or else the king's guards will come rushing out of that station and you'll get yourself hung, drawn and quartered. Which would be a grave shame as I've grown really rather fond of you."

Later they read in the papers how the Prince arrived at the station by private train at 10.30am. He walked around the Great Hall for ten minutes or so before using a pair of gold scissors to cut a ribbon, announcing "You build your stations like we build our cathedrals." One paper comments that there was one minute of pomp for every year the construction of the station had taken. All the crowd sees of their future king is the two minutes it takes for him to come out the front of the station, wave a little at his adoring public, before stepping into an automobile and is whisked off to City Hall.

Years later when Prince Edward becomes King Edward VIII and then abdicates within the year, to be with Wallis Simpson, people who were in this crowd will say they could tell even then that Edward didn't have a strong enough sense of public service to be the monarch. But on this day in 1927 the crowd disperses good-naturedly if a little disappointedly and, like Idris and Aeronwen and the rest of the James family, goes in search of somewhere out of the strong summer sun to eat the picnic lunches they have brought with them.

It is after 5pm by the time Idris starts walking home. He hums to himself as he walks. It has been a good day for Toronto. The first thing that people arriving in this City will now see is the wonderful new station, a station whose size and architectural beauty shout loud to all the world that Toronto is investing in itself and its future and will welcome all who arrive. And nothing adds to the enjoyment of a historic day such as this one more than spending it in the company of one so pretty and so much fun as Aeronwen James.

As he approaches the house in Fairlawn Avenue, he sees that Mrs Williams is standing in the window of the front room. When she spots him she hurries out to meet him.

"Idris, thank goodness you're here. I've been a nervous wreck waiting for you to come home. You've got a visitor, a young lady. She arrived about lunchtime in the most awful state – I had to practically carry her inside. She says her name is Jean."

Chapter 10

Carol's white witch skills start wearing off after the apple tart and custard is all eaten.

"Please may I leave the table," Eloise asks. "I've got homework to do."

"You go ahead, love," Carol says. "Front room is nice and quiet and the wifi is great there. The rest of you can go watch television if you like."

Carol and Richard have an enormous 90" television which they claim they need for Davey whose eyesight isn't what it used to be. The children find it absolutely fascinating.

"I'll keep an eye on Jake," Grace says. She unbuckles him from his highchair and he chuckles and reaches his arms up to her. Grace picks him up and swings him onto her hip as if she's been doing it for years.

"Don't turn the telly up all the way though." Carol calls after them. "Next door complain it sets their dogs off howling."

"Shall I go dig out those photos for you then, Gareth?" Davey asks.

"If you tell me where they are, I'll go fetch them Gramps."

"They're in a box on the top shelf of my wardrobe."

It has been a long time since Gareth has been in his grandfather's bedroom. After Nana Rosie's death, his parents decided to move back into the house that Richard's father grew up in so as to keep Davey company. Carol had glossed and laminated and B & Q'd every inch of the house to make it her own except for this room which she was forbidden to touch. It

90

still has the same padded silky orange quilt on the bed, the same framed embroidery above the bed, of a lady in a bonnet and crinoline dress holding a bunch of flowers. It still looks and smells like it did when Nana Rosie was alive and Gareth would stay overnight with his grandparents when his parents went to the Double Diamond club for a night out. Davey would get kicked out to the spare room and Gareth got to sleep next to Nana. She used to wait until he was fast asleep before taking her teeth out but Gareth, who was fascinated by his grandmother's removable teeth, would wake early. He wanted to see what Nana's mouth without teeth looked like. If he saw that she was waking up, he would pretend to be asleep again so she would not know he had been watching her. When he did finally catch sight of her open, toothless mouth it was not a sight he needed to see again.

The box in the wardrobe is wooden, very large and inlaid with mother of pearl. It has different compartments inside that Gareth is familiar with as it is the box in which his grandmother kept precious things, like birthday cards he'd made for her but also her Co-op dividend stamps. As Gareth places the box in front of his grandfather, he can taste the evil, metallic taste of the stamps, feel the thrill of filling an entire book and being allowed to go to the Co-op and spend the divi on sweets.

"All our family history is in this box," Davey says as he rifles through it. "Certificates for births and deaths and marriages. The deeds to this house which have been in the family since 1913, and the amended deeds after Gareth got us our squatters' rights."

Rachel smiles at Gareth. She loves the squatters rights' story, told often by Davey, of how Gwen had gardened the mountainside all around their end of terrace garden for years and years until one night Gwen's husband and son – Davey's father Tommy and grandfather Tom – had gone out in the middle of the night and fenced it all in. Gareth's legal career was launched aged 17, when he discovered that the deeds showed only the original garden and not the additional stolen bits. He had

91

researched adverse possession and drafted all the paperwork needed to acquire title to the land.

Davey finds what he is looking for and pulls out a couple of old black and white photos.

"Right, here we go. This is me with Nana Gwen and Taid."

The photograph shows a couple in their late forties at most. Taid is broad with a chest like a barrel and a quarter of an inch shorter than Gwen who was tall for women of that time. She is wearing a flowered apron and a beaming smile as she holds the baby Davey up to the camera.

"And this, this is my mother Maggie and my dad Tommy and his brother Idris, just before Idris left for Canada."

No one is smiling in this photo. Maggie stands tall and broad shouldered between the two identical men. All three look sullen, unhappy at having their photograph taken.

"Which one is which?" Rachel asks.

Davey consults the back of the photo. "Dad is on the left, Idris on the right."

"You really would not have been able to tell them apart."

"They had very different personalities, my father told me once. Idris was the one who talked back. My father liked a quiet life, hated confrontation, I barely ever heard him raise his voice. My mother is the one I remember shouting at me when I misbehaved as a kid."

"Is that it for Idris?" Gareth asks.

"There's just one more."

This one shows an older Idris, wearing a very dapper three-piece suit and a hat, a Fedora maybe or a Trilby. He has his arm round a pretty blonde lady, a baby in her arms, about the same age as Jake is now from the look of it. It is difficult to tell from the photo whether the child is male or female. They are standing in a garden, in front of a long row of runner bean canes, squinting into the sunshine.

"This must be Idris' wife and child then?" Rachel says.

"I should imagine so, although I don't know for absolute certain. It's definitely Idris because there are photos of my father about this age and he looked just like that, but there's no information about who the woman is or the child."

"And the letters he wrote before losing touch?"

"Must have been thrown away, I imagine."

"But if that is Idris' child that makes him or her your…"

"First cousin."

"And Idris is your great uncle, Gareth, our children's great, great uncle. How weird to think of a Maddox family somewhere in Canada closely related by blood to us, that we know nothing about."

"Like I said…" Davey collects the photos up and puts them back in the box. "It was easy for families to lose touch in those days. To just sort of forget about each other and end up total strangers."

*

Sunday evening is chaotic in the Maddox household, especially when they've been to the Rhondda for lunch. There is a flurry of last minute homework and of locating sports kit that should have been put in the wash but instead has spent the weekend festering in a bag, joyfully abandoned in the hall on Friday evening when Sunday evening seemed such a lovely long time away.

Sunday evening also brings with it the chore of bath time and washing of hair for the younger children. And doing nits.

"You have nits in this family?" Grace looks horrified. The girls of the family are all sitting on Rachel's bed. Rachel is combing Iris' hair with a nit comb and Eloise is doing Nora's hair.

"Non-stop nits. We've had them constantly. Since at least 2001." Rachel says, cheerfully. "I've long since stopped feeling ashamed about it."

"But I thought people with dirty hair got nits."

"Oh they do, and people with clean hair too. It goes round the school like a Mexican wave. As soon as you get rid of them, hello – back round again they come."

"And worse than that, Grace," Eloise says sourly, wiping conditioner flecked with the bodies of lice from the nit comb she is using on Nora, "when they get them, so do I sometimes."

"And so do I," says Rachel. "And a solicitor scratching her head is really not a good look."

"You can shave my hair off if you like, Mum," pipes up Iris. "I would love a number 1 all over."

"I know Iris. One day, maybe."

"I'm never cutting my hair," Nora says, defiantly. "I want it to grow till it reaches my bum. And I want it to turn blonde. Like Saffron Bennett in my class."

Grace shudders. "No one at my school has ever had nits."

"Don't you believe it Grace. Nits aren't classist. They like fee-paying hair just as much as they like state educated hair. It's just that no one will have dared admit to having nits in your school. Anyone ever suddenly get their hair cut short?"

"Yes, now you come to mention it. Pixie cuts were all the rage for a while."

"Ah Ha! There you go! Those pixie cuts? Let me tell you. That was because of nits. Nits!"

"I've had worms too." Iris adds helpfully. "Twice."

Grace goes a little pale and absentmindedly lifts her hand to scratch her hair, revealing thin silver scars on her forearms.

"Do you think you might have nits, Gracie?" Eloise teases. "Want me to check? I'm really good with a nit comb."

Grace smiles. "No thanks! I don't think I've got nits but I've seen with my own eyes that Nora definitely does so I'd prefer to avoid any of your nit combs. I'm going off to bed now. It's been an interesting day, thank you."

"I'll be up soon," says Eloise. "I'll try to not to make any noise if you're already asleep. Right then my little sisters. Toenails and then teeth!"

While Nora and Iris are down the hall in the family bathroom, their electric toothbrushes whining noisily, Rachel pats the bed next to her and invites her eldest daughter to sit down.

"What now, Mum? No I'm not going to have any more piercings in my ears. Yes I really do like my hair this black. No I don't think playing loud music while I'm studying stops me concentrating,"

"It's none of those things."

"Oh, what is it then?"

"Grace."

"What about her."

"I saw the marks on her arms earlier. Cut marks."

"Oh, those."

"You've seen them then?"

"Uh huh."

"Has she talked to you about them?"

"Not yet."

"Do you think she will?"

"Maybe. Maybe not."

"I think I should talk to Grace."

"No Mum, no! That is absolutely not the cool thing to do. And don't talk to Aunty Jocelyn either. "

"Jocelyn is my sister, Grace is her daughter. She has a right to know what her daughter is doing to herself."

"For fuck's sake, Mum, even though Grace wears long sleeves all the time, you've spotted those marks in two days, I saw them on the first night. Either Aunty Jocelyn has already seen them or if she hasn't it's because she isn't looking at Grace at all. I told Dad you'd say you need to talk to Jocelyn."

"You've already discussed this with your father?"

"Yes, Friday night when everyone else was in bed."

"He never said anything to me…"

"Because he's cooler than you."

"Right."

"So, please Mum, don't make a fuss, not just yet. Grace is having a good time with us, she looks way more relaxed than she did. She *loves* Jake, dunno why, because I think he's a monumental pain in the arse, but she does. I've done loads of research online this weekend. The advice all the websites give is to talk with people who are self-harming and be open and honest about it and show that you care about them but we really don't know Grace well enough yet. We've got to help her trust us first – show her we love her – and then we can talk to her about it. I don't think she's cut herself while she's been here. I've been keeping an eye on her. Actually, talking about keeping an eye on her, I'd better go up to bed now."

"OK."

"Really? You're actually going to do what I ask for once?"

"Yes. For now.

"Wow, Mum!"

"Wow indeed. Two more things, Eloise…"

"Yes?"

"You're being an amazing cousin to Grace. And don't use the word fuck in front of me again."

"Fuck off, Mum."

"I love you too Ellie-bellie."

*

With the children all in bed, Rachel hunts around the kitchen till she finds a bottle of wine and carries it and two glasses to the living room where Gareth is collapsed in front of the telly, Oscar spreadeagled on his chest.

"Why didn't you tell me about Grace self-harming and the chat you'd had with Eloise?" she asks, setting the wine and the glasses down on the coffee table and sitting down on the other end of the sofa.

"Don't sound so pissed off Rachel. It's Sunday night. Grace

96

only got here on Friday. We've had a houseful of guests and children round us at all times since. Well apart from a brief, very enjoyable time on Saturday morning when I had other things on my mind. I was going to tell you about it right now but you beat me to it."

"I'm worried about her."

"So am I, but I don't think we should ambush her and start trying to talk about it. Like Eloise says, the best thing we can do for her right now is let her hang with Eloise and with the rest of us. And then we'll take it from there."

"Isn't our daughter wise?"

"Yes, very, just like her mother." Gareth pushes Oscar off his chest so he can pour them a glass of wine each.

Rachel takes a sip. "Kind of makes me feel even sorrier for Idris and Tommy. Losing each other like that. Such a sad story."

"Not really. Brother emigrates and loses touch with family left behind. It was the 1920s. No phones, no internet, no Skype, no Facebook. It must have happened all the time."

"You're right. I'm sure it did. Maybe we should get onto one of those genealogy sites and try to find the Canadian Maddoxes."

"Like we haven't got enough on our hands already, worrying about family members that are alive, let alone dead ones. Like we've got time to research family trees. While we're at it maybe we could get round to emptying the garage of fifteen years' worth of broken bikes and rusty barbecues and all the stuff from the loft that we shoved in there to make room for Eloise's conversion."

"OK, I'll add it to the list of things we're going to do after the kids leave home."

"We'll be about 70 by then Rachel. We can just leave all the crap in the garage and let the kids sort it out when we die."

"I'm glad we didn't have twins. It must be really weird growing up with someone who looks exactly like you. Do you think that Maggie fancied them both?"

"What do you mean?"

97

"Well if she fancied one, she must have fancied the other, mustn't she? They had exactly the same face."

"It's not all about looks though is it? Did you and I get together just because of the way I looked?"

"Pretty much, actually." Rachel smiles. "You like to think it was because you were clever and witty but actually it was because you made me go *phwoar* inside."

"You still make me go *phwoar* inside." Gareth smiles.

Rachel scoots across the sofa to be closer to him. He lifts his arm so she can wedge herself beneath it and rest her head on his shoulder.

"Who's this new client from Canada that got you asking Gramps about your family history anyway?"

"It's a company called Perfect."

"That makes the shirts?"

"That's the one."

"Oh I love Perfect shirts. They're my favourite. I've got three of them. I only buy them in the sales though. They're ridiculously expensive."

"I've never heard you mention liking Perfect clothes."

"Yes, you have. That white shirt you like so much? That's a Perfect shirt."

"That's a great shirt. You look like that woman from *The Good Wife* in that shirt."

"Alicia Florrick. I *feel* like her in that shirt! But I also love the story behind the brand. They are good employers and care for the environment. The shirts cost a lot because they pay a fair price to their employees and they last forever. What are you doing for them?"

"They're thinking of establishing a factory in the Rhondda."

"That would be amazing! Brilliant for Wales and for your beloved Valleys if they did."

"It would be, but we'll see. Early days yet."

"I envy you. That work is so much more interesting than Mr

Cole and Mr Lapthorne and their fabricators and welders. Wish I had the Perfect job instead."

"I don't know if *I've* even got the job yet. I may have to go to London this week to meet with them. I'll keep you in the loop."

"Don't worry about keeping me in the loop. Just remember that if they're handing out any freebies I'm a size 12. "

*

Rachel falls asleep instantly, like she does most nights. Sometimes she even does it mid-sentence. It's a skill that Gareth envies. He has a tendency to run through in his head each night, to a soundtrack of Rachel's snoring, the things he needs to do the following day. The things he should have done that day but has not. But tonight what keeps him awake is a queasy feeling in his stomach. A knot of guilt for having purposefully misled Rachel about the meeting in London, omitting any specific mention of Cassandra Taylor and making out it is only a possibility and not already fixed for Tuesday.

Why did I do that? Gareth asks himself. *I've had lots of female clients in the past. It never bothers Rachel, she's not the jealous type.*

Just before he finally falls asleep, he realises that it is himself he is misleading. Because along with the guilt knotting his stomach, there is excitement at the prospect of seeing Cassandra Taylor again in just a few days.

99

Chapter 11

The 6.24am from Cardiff Central is the train you need to take if you want to be in London in time for a 9.30am meeting. Gareth has meetings in London about once a fortnight, sometimes more, and he has the journey timed to perfection.

He has a shower the night before, lays his clothes out ready on the landing and cleans his teeth downstairs, leaving the house without so much as a cup of tea. This is meant to avoid the rest of the family getting woken up, in particular Jake. Sometimes it works, often it doesn't. Today it does. Gareth shuts the front door behind him very quietly and walks briskly to Penarth train station to get the 6.02am to Cardiff Central. It arrives at 6.13am, giving him plenty of time to cross platforms for the train to London.

He has a first class ticket, costing almost £200. His parents would expect a return flight to Malaga for that but it's an unspoken rule amongst lawyers and accountants taking the train from Cardiff to London that you get a first class ticket. Being spotted in second class is professional suicide – evidence that you must be going bust. This particular train is popular with Welsh business people and Gareth sees a number of people he vaguely knows already seated in the first class carriage.

It's a Pullman service and he fancies a full Welsh breakfast but then he remembers the time he missed his mouth and got egg on his suit trousers. He had had to position his brief case strategically on his lap at all his meetings to conceal the greasy stain. Instead he accepts a complimentary cup of tea from the trolley. Polystyrene cup, hot water, milk in plastic pods, fish out your own tea bag. He recalls that Nora went through a phase of hiding the granola bars from her packed lunch, which she hates, in the various pockets of his brief case. He locates two and a very elderly, brown tangerine, desiccated and rock hard. The granola bars are dry and tasteless and he contemplates dipping them into his tea but decides better of it. He surreptitiously picks oats out of his teeth for the next ten minutes.

The meeting is at Perfect's offices in Bathurst Mews, near Hyde Park. It is not an area of London that Gareth knows very well and he has to check an online map to locate it. He could take the Tube from Paddington – Circle Line two stops to Notting Hill Gate, change to the Central Line and then another two stops to Lancaster Gate – but at this time of year and in the morning rush hour it is quicker and more pleasant to walk.

Mews houses used to be the servants quarters and horses' stables for the grander houses of London. Gareth is delighted to find that in Bathurst Mews there is still a functioning horse stable. Despite the large number of young girls wearing jodhpurs and navy polo shirts hard at work clearing up, the unmistakeable whiff of manure perfumes the air. He walks along the cobbled lane and the pretty brick houses that line it, their front doors are painted shades of sage green, turquoise blue and dove grey. There are no front gardens as such but the owners of these houses have created small garden areas for themselves, with tables and chairs, gas barbecues subtly chained to outside walls, terracotta pots filled with tall purple and white alliums, like pom poms, and stargazer lilies in shades of pink and cream. One or two of the houses even have small trees outside, housed in enormous tubs, festooned with bird feeders.

He finds the number he is looking for. The house has a doorbell not an entry buzzer and when he rings it Cassandra herself opens the door. She is wearing a black trouser suit, high black boots and a bright white shirt. Gareth is flustered to see her.

"Oh hello, I didn't expect that you would open the door!"

101

"Well I did," she smiles. "Come on in. Rupert who does our PR and marketing in Toronto is already here and the London team should be here any minute. Coffee?"

The entire ground floor of the property is one large, light, open space with floor to ceiling windows. It has oak floorboards, a boardroom table big enough to sit 12 people, and a small fitted galley kitchen along one wall with shiny chrome kitchen appliances and a shiny chrome worktop. At the far end of the room is an informal seating area, with two large wheat-coloured sofas, some woollen throws, bookshelves and a small television. On a nest of coffee table next to the sofas Gareth spots a paperback, an empty cup and plate, a tube of Crabtree & Evelyn La Source hand cream.

Cassandra sees him looking.

"We use this place for meetings when we are in London but there are bedrooms upstairs so we stay here too. It's really very comfortable. We bought it ten years ago for what seemed like a fortune at the time but it has turned out to be one of our better investments. Rupert will be down now, he's just getting dressed."

So there it is. Gareth need not have worried. Cassandra has a bloke, he's called Rupert, he does PR and marketing for Perfect in Toronto, and she wasn't flirting with him after all. He feels relief that he is not, after all, going to have to resist temptation. And a disappointment so strong he can taste it in his mouth, like apple seeds when you chew them. Cyanide and marzipan.

"I'm glad you're here a little early as I have a favour to ask of you," Cassandra says as she pours him a coffee from the cafétière already set up at one end of the table. "Would you mind wearing one of our shirts?"

"Excuse me?"

"I'm not saying your shirt isn't a decent shirt, it's just that our shirts are better and I like Perfect's team to be wearing Perfect's product." She hands him a large white box tied with black ribbon and stamped with the Perfect logo. Inside there are three shirts – white, blue and pale pink.

"Collar size 16. Was I right?"

Gareth nods.

"I thought so. I can tell a collar size from ten paces. Hurry up then, pop into the downstairs bathroom and change before the others get here."

As Gareth had suspected and Adrian Matthews had long known, the shirts you wear without ties are not the same as the shirts you used to wear with ties, before ties became unnecessary. He chooses the white and checks himself out in the small mirror above the sink. He looks pretty good. The shirt is far more fitted than his normal ones but he must have lost weight during his morning runs and he is pleased to note that the faint hint of man boob he'd had a few months ago has subsided.

"Look at you!" says a man who must be Rupert as Gareth emerges from the toilet.

"Erm, thank you. And thank you to Perfect. This shirt is way better than mine."

Rupert claps his hands. "Love a duck!" he says in a terrible attempt at a Cockney accent. "I do hope we can come up with a better marketing campaign than that! *Buy Perfect shirts. They're way better than yours.*"

Gareth feels something shift inside his chest, a lightening. On reflection, maybe Rupert is not Cassandra's bloke after all.

The rest of the day is one long round of meetings. PR, marketing, media buyers talking social media campaigns, managed media spend and air time. After a sandwich lunch they meet with buyers from Liberty, John Lewis, and Selfridges. Gareth listens to the pitches, helps with the negotiations, drafts the heads of terms that follow. Cassandra has given him no previous inkling of how she negotiates but he soon works out that she gets what she wants by burying in a long list of demands the thing she really wants. The trick is working out what she is burying and after a while Gareth works out that it's the item she identifies in discussions as "not material." She reluctantly concedes things she never really wanted which makes people feel like they have secured a great deal and hurry to sign off quickly, before she changes her mind.

He starts to play along with her strategy. When she starts to give in on something she doesn't want, he starts interjecting.

"I really can't advise you to accept this amendment, Ms Taylor," he says in his best lawyer's voice. "It is normal commercial practice to include this sort of requirement. Frankly, striking it out puts you in a compromised position."

She instantly twigs what he is doing and plays along too.

"I thank you for your advice Mr Maddox but I choose to ignore it. This is an important deal for us and if compromise is what it takes to make it happen, we'll do it."

When the last meeting finishes it is after 7pm.

"Right, good to meet you Gareth, it was fun to watch you work, but if you'll excuse me I'm out of here." Rupert grabs his jacket. "I'm meeting someone in a bar in Soho. I don't know his name because I haven't met him yet but I just know when I do he's going to be gorgeous. Don't wait up!"

"I won't," Cassandra calls after him but Rupert has already slammed the door behind him.

"Charming! Fancy a quick drink? Just to the pub round the corner. Only one because I've got a dinner engagement later. I'm parched after such a long day."

Gareth doesn't really hesitate. It's been an exhilarating day watching Cassandra Taylor in top speed action. "Just the one then."

"I'm honoured."

"So you should be. It's Tuesday. I normally play squash Tuesday evenings."

They step out of the mews house into a warm July evening that is still sunny. Other residents of Bathurst Mews are home from work and sitting in their garden chairs, suit jackets discarded, bottles of beer in hand. People nod and smile and Gareth and Cassandra nod and smile back.

"Do you know all your neighbours?" he says under his breath.

"Not a soul," she whispers back.

The pub is packed with people, some of whom spill out onto the street to smoke and drink. The sunshine has brought a jaunty feel to the evening, like it's a bank holiday. It is an old fashioned London boozer gussied up a bit for a younger crowd. There's the original long, high, dark mahogany bar with stools, and the original shelves along the back wall lined with optics but the wooden floors have been stripped, the tables and chairs are modern and white and the price list is on an oversized blackboard and lists things as costing 13.5 or 8.5 rather than £13.50 or £8.50. Gareth and Cassandra fight their way to the bar.

"What will you have?" he asks before she can ask him.

"I'll have a Molson if they have it, otherwise any sort of lager. A pint. Those people are leaving right there, I'll go grab their table."

They don't have Molson and so Gareth gets them both a pint of Peroni.

"Well it's not Canadian beer but it's good and cold so will do," says Cassandra, taking a big gulp. "Actually, not bad, thank you."

They are both thirsty after a long day and they drink quickly.

"You were good today," Cassandra congratulates him. "I like the way you understand the sort of person you are dealing with very quickly and change the way you talk to people to get the best out of them."

"I do?"

"Yes you do. Your Welsh accent went up three notches at least when you were talking to the buyer from John Lewis who also had a strong regional accent I couldn't place."

"The Geordie?"

"He was called Jordy? I thought he said his name was Jonathan?"

"He did. He was from Newcastle, in the north east of England. People from there are referred to as Geordies."

"Why?"

105

"I don't really know. Something to do with King George I think. I know my accent gets stronger when I speak to Valleys people. Didn't know I did it with Geordies too."

"Conversely, when you were talking with Hugo from Liberty you had no accent whatsoever and used a lot of really long words."

"He was their in-house lawyer. He understood those long words!"

"As I said, you matched how you spoke to the person you were speaking to."

"That makes me sound shallow."

"It's not shallow. It's a skill. All the best negotiators do it. And you're one of the best negotiators I've seen in action."

"Flattery won't get you a lower bill, you know."

"Worth a try though! So you said when we met in Cardiff that you and your wife had been having children for years. How many children do you actually have?"

"Four."

"Four! More than one wife? Or are you Catholic too?"

"One wife only, and not Catholic, no, although you are not the first person to ask that. They just sort of came along. "

"What flavour?"

"Flavour? Oh, three girls and a boy."

"The boy the last?"

"You got it. Jake – he's just turned one and I've got the bags under my eyes to prove it. But I would have been happy with another girl, they're great and every one is different. I've got a stroppy goth, a tomboy footballer and a soft toy fanatic who wants blonde hair down to her bum."

"They sound fun."

"They are. Rachel and I are very lucky."

"Is that your wife's name, Rachel?"

"Yes. She's a lawyer too."

"Family arguments must be a whole new ball game in your house!"

"It's never dull, shall we say. Do you have children yourself Cassandra?"

She sighs. "No. Lots of long distance travel for work and long-term relationships don't go together very well. Children didn't come my way and I'm having to come to terms with the fact it's probably too late."

She looks down at her glass which is empty, as is his.

"Shall I get us another? One more for the road, as you Brits say?" she asks

He really doesn't want to go. He wants to stay here in this pub near Hyde Park on a summer July evening with a woman he finds fascinating and who is now looking sad. He wants to have another pint of Peroni with her. And then go on somewhere else, somewhere where there is live music playing where they can sit together at a small round table and drink red wine and talk till the sun comes up again.

"I really need to go, I'm sorry Cassandra. Got to catch my train."

"OK, no worries. Another time. I just need to go to the bathroom quickly. Will you wait for me?"

"Of course. I'll be outside."

It's growing dark outside now and it's cooler, quieter, the air a soft blue. Gareth leans on a wall to wait for Cassandra. He feels like a teenager, awkward and needy and excited. Then her face suddenly swings in front of his. He can smell her perfume, see her chest rise and fall as she breathes.

"You know, I thought Rupert was your other half when I arrived this morning," he confesses.

"I know you did. I did that on purpose, to see how you reacted."

"And how did I react?"

"Exactly as I hoped you would."

And she leans in and kisses him. Her mouth is open and her lips are soft and with a speed he has not experienced in a while his cock jumps immediately to attention. He could kiss like this all night. But he's not going to.

He breaks away from the kiss, puts his hand on her shoulder, eases her away gently.

"Good night Cassandra. I've got to go."

"Don't go. Stay for just one more drink. If you do, I'll cancel my dinner engagement tonight. Which is with the charming Adrian Matthews, by the way."

"Don't go for dinner with Adrian, please."

"Why not? It's just a business dinner."

"Tell him something cropped up and you can't make it."

"It felt to me like something already cropped up," she smiles and drops her eyes to look at his crotch. "Stay for just one more and I promise I won't go out for dinner with Adrian Matthews."

"I can't Cassandra. I really can't."

The smile drops from her face. "Suit yourself", she says, briskly. "He's taking me to the Shard. Wants to show me the London skyline. Breathtaking apparently."

Gareth hesitates for a second but she dismisses him with a wave of her hand.

"It's OK, run along home now. There's a good boy."

He texts Rachel from the train.

Sorry not been in touch, hectic day, only now on train, will be late, don't wait up, love you 5.

She texts straight back.

Us 5 love you too x x

Gareth resolves on the journey home not to do any more work for Perfect. He will make some excuse and allocate another lawyer from Maddox Legal to take over from him. Cassandra Taylor stirs feelings in him he'd forgotten. He loves Rachel and he fancies her too and there is no way he is going to put what they have at risk for anything or anyone.

It is at this point that he realises he is going home wearing a brand new Perfect shirt and that the shirt he left home wearing has been left behind at Bathurst Mews.

Chapter 12

When the girls were younger, Rachel found evenings when Gareth was away very difficult. Juggling their various after school activities such as swimming and gymnastics and piano lessons with only one car and driver available. Cooking a decent meal containing at least three of their five a day and then getting them to eat it before bath time. Three lots of story time. By the end of the night she was stressed and grumpy and so were the girls.

Whenever she announced that she was going to be working late and that Gareth was going to be in charge the girls cheered. Evenings on his own never fazed Gareth. He just told the girls they were skipping their after school activities just for this one evening and then took them to Burger King for tea. Not a single one of their five a day but no clearing up either. Back at home, he'd wash their faces with a flannel and they'd all pile into Gareth and Rachel's bed together where he told them made up stories featuring the three of them as princesses, even Eloise who was long past the princess stage. The princesses drove around Wales in a stretch limo visiting castles and beaches where they met all sorts of characters from history. Often when Rachel came home she'd find all the lights on downstairs, no food in the fridge and her family fast asleep in the one bed.

These days Rachel's standards have slipped. She is hosting Book Club tonight and with Gareth at a meeting in London none of her children is going anywhere after school. She needs all hands on deck to tidy up the house before the Book Club girls arrive.

"How come this house is always such a mess?" Rachel mutters

to herself. She is on her hands and knees washing the floor of the downstairs loo. "Does Mrs Morris even clean this toilet floor?"

"No," answers Nora, who is cleaning the sink.

"What do you mean, no?"

"No, she doesn't clean the toilet floor. She says she's too old to go down on her hands and knees for anyone anymore, thank you very much."

Rachel's cleaner, Mrs Morris has been cleaning and babysitting for the family since they first moved to Penarth. She is an entirely useless cleaner with an over fondness for bleach. Many of the family's clothes are decorated with white blobs and streaks thanks to Mrs Morris' habit of putting bleach soaked cleaning cloths into the laundry basket. Rachel is engaged in a number of long running battles with her, none of which she ever wins. These include Mrs Morris' insistence on emptying the entire contents of the bathroom bins into the recycling even though Rachel has repeatedly pointed out that a single empty toilet roll in there does not denote that all the other contents such as dental floss and wet wipes are recyclable, her habit of hiding away any socks for which she cannot find matching companions but forgetting where she put them so that the pairs are never reunited and her mistaken belief that cream cleaner squirted down the toilet and left to solidify is every bit as good as a scrub. Rachel has a theory that Mrs Morris does her job badly on purpose so that Rachel will do the work herself and save Mrs Morris the hassle. She should really get rid of Mrs Morris and get another cleaner but Gareth won't let her. He says Mrs Morris is old and needs the money.

"So, Mrs Morris won't go down on her hands and knees but she expects me to do it?"

"No," replies Nora, who is fond of Mrs Morris and likes to follow her round while she cleans and is therefore the most reliable source of information as to what exactly Mrs Morris actually does. "She thinks Daddy should do it. He's the one who pisses on the floor, she says."

"Don't use that word Nora!"

"I didn't use it. Mrs Morris did."

"That's semantics."

"Is that a swear word too?"

"Just go get a clean towel out of the airing cupboard please – a good one please, right from the bottom of the pile." Mrs Morris doesn't believe in circulating the family's stock of towels either. The towels on the top of the pile are always grey and hard, whereas at the bottom of the pile soft, snowy white towels can be found.

When she's finished the toilet, Rachel tackles the surfaces in the hall and kitchen. Hair brushes, bobbles, loose change, make up bags, junk mail, letters from school: it all gets swept into shopping bags and stashed in the cupboard under the stairs. This is a classic clearing up device of Rachel's. The house looks tidier but the trouble is no one can ever find anything afterwards.

"Girls, put all the bags you've dumped in the hallway into your rooms please. Nora – all these Beanie Boos on the kitchen table, tidy them away please. Eloise – I've bought pizza for tea, put it in the oven please and when it's ready you can all eat it on your laps in the living room.

After forty-five minutes of frantic activity Rachel determines the house will do. Grace offers to start heating the posh nibbles that Rachel has bought from Marks and Spencer, at top speed during her lunch hour, while Rachel puts Jake to bed. When Rachel finally manages to get Jake down, she finds that Grace has been busy in the kitchen. The nibbles are in the oven and she has worked out what has to go in when so that everything is ready at the same time. She has hunted down a couple of large serving platters, some napkins and polished a set of wine glasses that vaguely resemble each other.

"Are you sure you wouldn't want to move in permanently, Grace?" asks Rachel.

Grace smiles. "If you clear it with my mother, I'd be happy to!"

This reminds Rachel that she really should get in touch with her sister to tell her that Grace seems to be enjoying her time in Wales. But over the telephone, Rachel runs the risk of asking Jocelyn how on earth she has failed to notice that her only child is self-harming so she judges it best to send her a text instead.

Grace is a lovely houseguest, very helpful, and she and Jake are getting on like a house on fire.

Jocelyn's text in reply says

I do hope you are not using my daughter like an unpaid au pair.

There you go then, thinks Rachel. Very important to ensure that not only your Filipina maid but also your sister toes the line and shows respect.

Grace reads the text over Rachel's shoulder.

"I'm sorry my mother is such an arse."

Rachel lifts an eyebrow. "I hope you haven't picked up that sort of language from Eloise. If you go home using words like arse your mother will kill me."

Grace laughs. "Don't worry, I won't. I'm good at not letting things slip in front of my mother. What book is your Book Club discussing tonight?"

"*The Goldfinch* by Donna Tartt."

"Oh I loved that!"

"You've read it? I've only managed a few chapters. It's not exactly a fun read is it?"

"Not exactly, no. His mum getting blown up in a museum and then him having to leave New York to live with his father miles away in Las Vegas and then all the drugs he takes with Boris and all the trouble Boris causes. There weren't many jokes no."

"All that happens? Flip. How depressing. I'm glad I didn't finish it. Look, do you fancy joining the Book Club tonight?"

"That would be fun, if you think your friends won't mind."

"They'll be glad to have you join us."

"Does Eloise come along too?"

"Are you kidding? Listen to this." Rachel calls to Eloise who is watching telly in the living room. "Eloise, honey, do you want to join Grace and me at Book Club tonight?"

"I'd rather stick pins behind my fingernails than watch you and your friends drink too much red wine and talk literary nonsense through your red wine teeth," Eloise calls back.

*

Jenny is the first to arrive, a hardback version of *The Goldfinch* clamped under her arm and carrying a large Victoria sponge with cream and strawberries.

"I know, I know," she says as she puts the cake down carefully on the kitchen table. "I'm an angel."

"That looks absolutely gorgeous," Rachel says.

"It will be – so much better than the shop bought rubbish you'd serve left to your own devices."

"You're such a hypocrite, Jenny. One minute you're telling me to stop trying to be superwoman and then the next you're bustling in here like Mary Berry and dissing me for cutting corners and buying cake."

"I'm not a hypocrite at all! Baking cake is part of the slow movement. I can bake cake because I have time. And because I like to eat cake. Whereas you have to buy cake because you don't have time to bake. Are you going to offer me a glass of wine or what?"

"Grace, pass me one of your newly polished glasses will you so I can serve Mrs Berry here a glass of Sauvignon?"

Over the next fifteen minutes or so the other Book Club guests arrive. Eloise reluctantly breaks off from watching telly to open the front door for them and usher them grumpily into the kitchen.

It's a varied group, all women, and made up of friends, neighbours and mums from school. Jenny was the one who got Rachel involved and even though Rachel often fails to finish the allotted book, she enjoys being part of the club. It's a chance once a month to have a good chat with women she otherwise only sees to wave at in the street or at school fêtes and concerts. There is always plenty of wine and Rachel knows that without the incentive of Book Club she wouldn't get round to even starting a book.

When everyone has finished making a fuss of Grace and getting a glass of wine they sit down at Rachel's dining table.

Selecting the books the club reads is done by rota, with the book for the following month's meeting being announced at the end of that month's meeting. The person who selects the book also chairs the meeting. *The Goldfinch* was Jenny's choice.

"OK," Jenny says, bossily, "let's start with a show of hands as to how many of us actually finished the book."

Only Jenny and Grace stick their hands up. Jenny sighs, theatrically.

"Oh come on, Jenny," says Michelle, a recently divorced mum of one who is an executive PA and lives across the road from Rachel. "It was far-fetched and tedious and, more to the point, 900 pages long. The hardback version weighed a ton! Who on earth has time to read a book that long in one month? I think you just picked it to show off how fast you can read."

"I agree that bits of it were turgid," Jenny replies. "But so much of it was brilliant, it made wading through the bad bits worth it. The bits about the antiques that Hobie makes. And Theo's loneliness – how absolutely, utterly, alone he is – and his slide into narcotic addiction. What do you think Grace?"

Grace looks a little uncomfortable at being thrust into the limelight of the discussion but clears her throat.

"Um, I loved this book and I read it in a week." She looks nervously over at Michelle. "I'm not showing off about how fast I can read. It's just I've got time because I'm at school, not working like you. Donna Tartt must have been lonely as a teenager because she knows exactly how it feels."

Discussion of *The Goldfinch* carries on for a while longer round the table but, as the wine bottles empty, the conversation starts to fracture off. Jenny and Grace sitting next to each other at one end of the table continue to animatedly discuss the book but the others have moved on to encouraging Michelle to start dating again.

"I truly can't be bothered," she says. "Dating would involve sex at some point and to be honest, I'm really not that fussed. The last few years with Andrew I would do anything to avoid it. If he tried so much as to kiss me it made me gag. He thought it was sexy to stick his tongue in and out of my mouth as hard and as fast as he could, like it was a little willy. It was disgusting."

"I don't think I'd mind if we never did it again," says Anita, an old friend of Jenny's from school. "Matt and I were all over each other for the first few years, but I think we'd both choose a boxed set and a takeaway over sex these days."

"I think I'd choose *crocheting placemats* over sex any night," says Michelle. "All that fuss and mess and…panting. No thank you."

"You lot should try erotic fiction," says Liz, one of the mums from school, who is married to Nigel, a lawyer at another firm in Cardiff. Nigel is often on the other side of transactions that Rachel is dealing with. "It worked wonders for me and Nigel. We'd gone a bit off the boil in that department. Erotic fiction has perked us both right up. "

"You mean that *Fifty Shades of Grey* rubbish?" asks Anita.

"I don't actually. *Fifty Shades* was the first one I bought because everyone was going on about it, but the story is so ridiculous and badly written. There's a bit on their first date when he kneads her breasts and takes no prisoners or something. It just made me laugh out loud – imagining a jiggly pair of boobs behind bars. Not erotic at all. And the whole sadomasochistic angle didn't sit right with me. But it did get me going, no smuttiness intended. There's loads of feminist erotic fiction out there. I read the stories to myself and then I get Nigel to read the dirty passages out loud to me. Makes us both really hot to trot."

Rachel wonders if she will ever be able to look at Nigel in quite the same way again. Nigel has recently started to wear his hair quite long, very possibly as a result of all this erotic fiction he's been reading. Rachel pushes from her mind the sudden image of a naked Nigel prancing around in his bedroom, shaking his long locks like a stallion might his mane.

"And what would be the point of me getting all, 'hot to trot' as you put it, by myself?" asks Michelle. "What should I do once I am feeling all hot and, er, trotty?"

"Reacquaint yourself with your libido. All by yourself, if you know what I mean."

"Of course I do but I don't really get it. My sister bought me a Rabbit vibrator when the divorce came through, expressing a similar sentiment. That thing looks like a Magimix. Honestly, I'm sure you're meant to use it to whip up a batch of scones, not apply to yourself. It's still in the box."

"Well get yourself something good to read and get it out of the box!" Liz commands. "Believe me, once you've tracked your libido down and restored it to good health, it will drive you frothing at the...well whatever...to Internet dating sites."

"I think I'd really rather my libido just stayed well and truly lost, thank you very much," says Michelle crinkling her nose in disgust.

"I might give erotic fiction a try," says Anita. "I used to enjoy the sex in Jilly Cooper novels at school. Just remembering how I felt back then makes me feel a little friskier."

Liz claps her hands together. "Excellent, because despite what you may think Anita, your husband would almost certainly prefer hot sex to a takeaway and telly. You'll have to tell us how it goes!"

Michelle holds her hand up like a policeman directing traffic. "Anita – do us all a favour. Absolutely on no account tell us how it goes," she says. "But if you've got any good crochet patterns feel free to share."

The women eat and drink and talk and suddenly it is 10.30pm

and they are looking for their handbags and collecting up their copies of *The Goldfinch* and clattering out the door home.

Jenny and Grace have been deep in conversation all night.

"Grace is going to come over to mine later this week, if that's OK?" Jenny says to Rachel. "We enjoyed our conversation and thought it would be fun to continue it."

"Of course, if that's what you would like Grace."

Grace nods eagerly.

"Excellent. Well I've got your mobile number and I'll be in touch, Grace. Goodnight."

Grace helps Rachel clear the plates and glasses and stack the dishwasher.

"Thank you for including me tonight, Auntie Rachel."

"You don't need to thank me, Grace. It was lovely having you with us. Just as well you were here, or else Jenny would have had no one to discuss the book with. You know, you don't need to call me Auntie any more. You can just call me Rachel."

"I like it that you're my Auntie Rachel."

"And I like being your Auntie Rachel." She pulls Grace towards her and hugs her swiftly, kissing her on the forehead.

"Will Uncle Gareth be very late?"

"It'll be after midnight before he gets home. I'm not going to wait up for him. If I'm still awake when he gets in, he likes to talk his head off about whatever it is he has been working on all day in London and asking what I think. I've had far too much wine for that. I'm going to let Oscar out for a wee and then go up to bed."

"Good night then."

"Good night, Gracie."

Before she goes to bed, Rachel stands in front of the bookshelf for a while. Finally, she locates her dog-eared copy of *Riders* and takes it upstairs with her.

*

Gareth is already stripped to the waist when he comes into the bedroom. He is surprised to find Rachel still awake and reading.

"Well hello, husband. You look rather amazing, I must say."

She throws back the duvet and kneels up on the bed to greet him with a kiss. She trails her hand across his bare chest.

"Mm, very nice. You haven't travelled all the way home from London topless have you? What happened to your shirt?"

"Spilled coffee on it on the train on the way home. I've put it in to soak."

"You've put it in to soak? What's come over you? Why not just throw it straight in the washing basket like you usually do? With all the buttons done up so it's a bugger to iron?"

"Ha ha. How come you're still up?"

"I've been waiting up for you. I've been reading the dirty bits from *Riders* again. Read them so often when I was younger the book falls open at all the right places. I'm feeling very horny now."

"Good. Because so am I."

Chapter 13

Jean is waiting for Idris in the Williams' front parlour. It is too small for the heavy wooden furniture that Mr and Mrs Williams shipped over with them to Canada from Carmarthen and dimly lit, because Mrs Williams keeps the heavy lace curtains closed so that the sunlight doesn't fade the silver framed photographs of her son that she keeps in there. It smells of furniture polish and sadness.

Jean is sitting very upright in a tall wooden chair but her eyes are closed and in the dimness Idris thinks at first she must be asleep. Then he sees that her eyes are closed because she has been badly beaten – both her eyes are blackened and swollen and her lip is split.

"What happened to you, Jean?" he kneels down in front of her.

Jean smiles and holds her hands out to him. He takes them and clasps them tight. She has lost so much weight that her collarbone looks like a coat hanger, her skin stretched so tightly it looks like it might poke right through. She is sunburned from outdoor work and her hands when he takes them in his are rough and calloused.

"Did someone do this to you?" he asks, more insistently.

She nods. "It was Mrs Barraclough."

"The lady you've been working for? Why?"

"Because of something I said. Something I told her."

"What? What can you have said to her that would make her beat you like this?"

"I don't like to say."

"Jean, I need you to tell me."

"I can't."

"Please, Jean."

"I told her that Mr Barraclough had been touching me every chance he got and that I'd tried to ignore him, had pushed him off. But that the more I refused the harder he tried. And that finally he had not taken no for an answer and had come into my room in the middle of the night and put his hands around my throat and squeezed so hard I fainted and then forced himself on me. While she lay sleeping down the hall."

Jean does not cry as she tells Idris this. She keeps her eyes down, fixed on her lap.

Idris is silent for a while. He breathes deeply, trying to keep calm. His first reaction is to punch Mrs Williams' oak sideboard until it splinters.

"Do you mean…?"

She nods. "I believe so. When I came to he was gone but there was blood and…other…" She trails off, unable to finish her sentence.

"When did this happen, Jean?"

"Yesterday. I walked straight out, leaving everything I own behind, the trunk the Quarriers gave me, letters from you and Janet, everything. They never paid me any wages the whole time I was there so I begged at the train station for money to buy a ticket to Toronto."

"We should go to the police. Tell them you have been the victim of a terrible crime."

Jean shakes her head, wearily. "No Idris, I am not going to go to the police. 'Little slave child,' Mrs Barraclough used to call me, and tell me that little slaves didn't get to go to school. She said that if I went to the police she would say that I'd been trying to get Mr Barraclough's attention since I arrived, had been throwing myself at him with the intention of blackmailing him, extorting money from him. She said she'd get the farmworkers to say the same thing and that no one would believe a slave. She said I was not the first to make these accusations and I would fare no better than the last girl."

"This is outrageous Jean. These people took you in. They were meant to be responsible for you. They are liars. You can't stand by and not do anything."

"I can and I will Idris. If I go to the police it will be me that is on trial, not them. And I don't ever want to see them again. Not in a courtroom. Not ever. I just want to forget it ever happened."

"We need to get word to Janet. You need to be with her now. You two need to find that big house you talked about, one that will give you both positions as domestic servants, so you can live in the same place."

"Janet has fallen on her feet. The family have taken her in almost as one of their own and she doesn't even have to work anymore, goes to school every day. The children's mother brushes her hair every morning, like she does her own daughters." Jean smiles, sadly.

"But you've been assaulted. If Janet knew that, she would leave so as to be by your side."

"Yes she would, in a heartbeat. And she would also ask her family to take me in and in the process cause them to think less of her. I am not going to ruin Janet's happiness just because mine is ruined."

"So what do we do now?"

"Will you ask Mrs Williams if I can stay here for a few days? Once the black in my eyes has gone and I have rested a little, I will be able to look for a position. I'm going to be 16 very soon."

Idris tells Mrs Williams a very watered down version of the story. That Mrs Barraclough slapped Jean so hard for burning a hole in a damask sheet she was ironing that Jean fell against the hearth.

"I don't know Idris. We only have two bedrooms. I would have to make up a bed for her in my sewing room. It won't be very comfortable. Also, I am not running a boarding house here you know. You are the first lodger Mr Williams and I have taken and I don't imagine there will be another once you go."

"I would be very grateful Mrs Williams. Just for a little while. Until she looks better and I can sort something else out."

"Why is this your problem Idris? The child is no relative of yours, you barely know her."

"Because there is no one else."

"Very well then. It is the Christian thing to do after all. Just a few days mind."

"Thank you, Mrs Williams."

"I'd best get that bed made up then. I've made us cawl for tea – plenty of good neck of lamb, swede, onions and potatoes – that'll help get her back on her feet. Maybe I'll make her an egg custard too, they are delicious and easy to digest."

"You are very kind, Mrs Williams."

"Get away with you boy. You do know you are going to have to consider how you present the news of your visitor to Aeronwen. I am sure you do not need me to tell you that that poor girl Jean is in love with you."

*

Aeronwen is of a sunny disposition. It is one of the reasons Idris has fallen for her. Because she smiles and jokes all the time. Her response the following day after church when he tells her about Jean surprises him. He tells her more than he told Mrs Williams but still not the full picture. He leads Aeronwen to believe that Jean was able to lock Mr Barraclough out of her room that night.

"Why have you never mentioned this girl and her sister to me before Idris? How can someone you have not seen fit to tell me about be so important to you that you must now take care of her? Get rid of her as soon as you can."

"Don't be unreasonable, Roni."

"I am not being unreasonable. And don't call me Roni. Only

my family are permitted to do that. Now you've given me a headache and I shan't be coming for a walk with you."

The few days that Mrs Williams promised pass, but there is no mention of it being time for Jean to move on. Instead Mrs Williams moves her sewing machine out of the third bedroom upstairs and sets it up in the front parlour, pushed up against the pictures of her son, to make more room for Jean upstairs.

When Idris gets home from work the next day, he finds Mrs Williams not in the kitchen where she normally is at that time but busy at her sewing machine. She has opened the net curtains and the sunlight floods in.

"Can't have the poor girl with nothing but the clothes on her back, can we?" she says. "I don't know what I thought I was going to do with all this material I had kept by anyway. No point wasting it."

After tea that night, Mrs Williams presents Jean with a new skirt and blouse.

"You are so very kind, Mrs Williams. You are a talented seamstress and I'm very blessed." It is the first time since she turned up at the house that Idris has seen Jean smile properly.

Aeronwen is not as gracious. When Idris calls on her, she is short with him.

"Is that girl still living under the same roof as you?"

"Yes, for now, at least until she is well enough to find employment."

"It's been almost a week. Surely she's well enough by now!"

"Not exactly Aeronwen. She has been very badly beaten. It will be a little while yet."

"You know what people say about these orphan children from the old country? They say they are children from the gutter. Scum from the slums. How do you know that she wasn't trying to trick that farmer and his wife?"

"Because I just know she didn't."

"Seems to me that you know her rather too well and that there

124

must have been something going on between you on that boat. I've asked you to get rid of her. It displeases me that you have not done so."

"I promise you, Aeronwen, that there was nothing going on between us on the boat. She was 14 years' old for heaven's sake and me a grown man. I will help Jean find a job and accommodation, just as soon as I can. Not because I want to get rid of her, but because I want to help her."

"Very well, Idris. You may leave now. Only call on me again after she has gone." Idris is convinced that as he leaves the room, Aeronwen stamps her foot. Her small, pretty, spiteful foot.

Over the next week, the bruises fade and Jean puts on a little weight. She and Idris play draughts in the evening while Mrs Williams sews and Mr Williams reads the paper.

Jean insists on helping Mrs Williams round the house. Reluctant at first, eventually Mrs Williams relents.

"She's a fine little worker," Mrs Williams tells Idris, "and if that farmer's wife did nothing else for her she taught her very well how to bake bread. I've been asking around, and I've noted down a couple of big houses in this area with vacancies. She's just about ready to start applying. Not that Mr Williams and I want her to leave our house, but I know your Aeronwen is refusing to see you until she does. Rather full of herself your Aeronwen is, if you ask me."

Every afternoon Jean goes off to search for work but returns each night unsuccessful. She remains positive though until finally she is told by one blunt housekeeper why.

"It's because you're a pauper immigrant. Canada is not a dumping ground for children the old country didn't want."

"Perhaps you need to be a little less honest," Mrs Williams advises her. "I'm not suggesting you lie, of course. That would be a sin. Just leave out the Quarriers part of your story. Tell them you've been working for me but have outgrown the job. I'll give you a reference. Anyway, like I keep telling you, dear. There's no rush."

125

But it turns out there is a rush.

Jean creeps down the stairs quietly before Idris leaves for work one morning, before Mr and Mrs Williams are even up.

"I have something I need to tell you."

He knows what it is. It is something he has feared since she arrived at the house in Fairlawn Ave. A fear he did not dare to put into words and one which he had hoped with the passage of time would be unrealised.

"It's my monthly. It has not come."

"Could you possibly be mistaken?"

She shakes her head. "I would rather die than bring that man's child into the world."

"Then there are ways to put this right. I will find them."

This is not a problem he can expect Mr and Mrs Williams to share with him but there is always someone amongst the hundreds of people working on the railway viaduct who knows how to get what a person needs. Within a day of asking, Idris is handed a small piece of paper by one of the Czechoslovakian men who work alongside him. The man says nothing as he hands him the paper. On it there is an address of a physician in Oshawa, some 40 miles west of Toronto. Idris makes his first ever telephone call to arrange an appointment.

The journey by train along Lake Ontario to Oshawa is pleasant. Idris and Jean have almost convinced themselves that the story they have told Mrs Williams of an overnight trip to meet Janet there and celebrate Jean's 16th birthday is true. Idris wears his best trousers and coat. Jean is wearing a pale green dress with long sleeves and a round collar, made by Mrs Williams. They look like a couple on a birthday trip out – not two people on their way to commit an illegal act.

They find the address they have been given easily. It is an ordinary looking, red brick house, with a white painted picket fence and a small porch at the front. The lady on the telephone instructed Idris to go round to the back of the house on arrival and that the back door would be left open for them. Idris pushes the door hesitantly, not sure if he should knock first or call out. He and Jean find themselves in an oak panelled waiting room, with a reception desk and chairs and low tables with copies of *National Geographic* magazine.

"It looks like a proper doctor's waiting room," Jean whispers.

"That's because it *is* a proper doctor's waiting room," a voice says, crisply. "Come right through, you are my only appointment today."

Idris and Jean enter the treatment room. The doctor, who seems young to Idris, no more than in his early thirties, stands up to greet them.

"I'm Dr Abraham. Please, take a seat, and we will complete the paperwork. Now Jean, I understand this pregnancy is in the very early stages, is that correct?"

"Yes, it happened four weeks and two days ago."

Dr Abraham does not seem surprised at Jean's precise recollection.

"In that case, my dear, this will not take long and will be over quickly."

"Will it hurt?"

"A little, yes. Would you like your friend to stay with you?"

"Yes please, very much, if that's possible?"

"It is, he can hold your hand while I undertake the process. Please go to the bathroom to empty your bladder and remove your underclothes."

While Jean is out of the room, Idris attends to the financial part of the transaction. Dr Abraham writes down Jean's name in a large ledger and then places it and the money in a desk drawer which he then locks. Afterwards he washes his hands carefully at the sink, taking a long time over it and scrubbing his fingernails hard.

"I take it you are not the father?" He asks, his back still turned to Idris.

127

"No."

"And that this pregnancy is the result of a non-consensual act."

"It was rape, if that's what you mean."

Dr Abraham finishes washing his hands and turns to face Idris.

"It is an absolute aberration that the law would require this young woman to go through with this pregnancy and that we are all criminals for what we are doing today. This is a therapeutic termination. No one here is a criminal."

"Will it stop her having other children?"

"It shouldn't. She's young, it's being done early, and I'm a good doctor."

When Jean returns to the room the sight of her, pale and frightened, holding her neatly folded underwear to her chest, makes Idris feel a fierce desire to protect her.

"Alright Jean, put your things down on that chair and please go lie on the bed, with your bottom at the very edge of the bed. Lift your skirt and use this sheet to cover yourself. Idris, you should stand by Jean's head and hold her hand."

Jean does as she is instructed. One hand grips the sheet she has placed over her knees and the other grips Idris' hand tightly.

"You will stay with me all the way through, won't you?" she asks him.

He says nothing but with his other hand he draws a cross across his heart. Jean smiles, just a little, and turns her face to the wall.

Idris doesn't know where to look but cannot avoid seeing the tube that Dr Abraham is inserting into Jean. She does not cry out or wince but keeps looking at the wall. Idris sees Dr Abraham pumping vigorously, hears liquid from the tube gush into a bucket on the floor.

Then it is over. Dr Abraham places a cloth over the top of the dark red contents of the bucket.

"I'll leave you for a few moments now Jean, to gather yourself and to get dressed. Take your time. Ideally you should take things very easy over the next few days."

Idris had seen an advertisement at the station for a place called The Homestead, offering Tourists' and Travellers' Rest, on King Street, West. They book in as Mr and Mrs Maddox. The receptionist does not look like she believes them but nor does it look like she cares.

"Why don't you have a lie down for a couple of hours? I'll take myself off for a walk and then when I come back, we can go get something to eat perhaps?"

Jean nods obediently. She lies down on top of the bedclothes, without even taking her shoes off, and closes her eyes. Idris bends down and kisses her on the forehead before leaving.

Oshawa is a thriving industrial city with a growing population due to the number of large industries based there including metal- and steelwork, tanneries and, largest of all, General Motors of Canada. Idris walks around the city, noting the many businesses that serve this growing population – bakers, beauty parlours, stationers, laundries and grocers. There are many advertisements directing tourists to visit Lakeview Park and Idris wonders if Jean may perhaps feel well enough later to go for a short walk.

He wanders around, filling in the time till he can go back to the room and see how Jean is bearing up. He is hungry but he is conserving his money and resists the temptation to call into the Nut-Krust Electric Bakery which advertises bread, buns, cake and pastry that are "Good to the Last Crumb". He finds himself at the entrance to a grand house called Parkwood. There is a job advertisement pinned to the gate inviting applications for domestic staff. He hesitates only a short while before starting to walk up to the house.

He walks round the back of the house to the servants' entrance and rings the bell. A maid opens the door and when he explains the nature of his query, she tells him she will go fetch the head housekeeper.

"Can I help you?" The head housekeeper is a tall lady in her forties, dressed in a black skirt and a white high collared blouse.

"Good afternoon. I am enquiring on behalf of a friend about the positions for domestic staff."

"We have two vacancies for maids. One for assistant cook and another for under-gardener. Which position might your friend be interested in?" She has a Scottish accent. This, Idris thinks hopefully, must surely be an advantage for Jean.

"The position of maid would suit her. She emigrated from Scotland last summer and has been working in a private house in Toronto but would relish the opportunity to work in a beautiful house such as this."

"Then she should apply in writing to me, Mrs Meikle, with references. If she is considered suitable I will arrange an interview."

"We are only here on a short visit, Mrs Meikle, and due to return to Toronto tomorrow. Is there any possibility you might be willing to give her an interview before we leave? It would be greatly appreciated."

Mrs Meikle takes a long look at Idris. He sweeps his fringe of thick dark hair from his eyes, stands up straighter and holds her gaze.

"Tomorrow is Sunday, Mr Maddox."

"I realise that, Mrs Meikle. Could you maybe spare 15 minutes, on your way to church perhaps?"

"Very well. Tell her to be here at 8.30am sharp. I go to early service."

Chapter 14

Grace can hear Jake talking to himself in his bedroom. He isn't crying but that comes next if his loud babbling doesn't prompt someone to come along. Usually Gareth is up by now but he was late home last night and he and Rachel must still be sleeping.

Grace eases herself gently out of bed. She is sleeping on a pull out bed which is perfectly comfortable but takes up virtually all the floor space in Eloise's bedroom. Eloise is still fast asleep in her bed. It has a white wrought iron bedstead which Eloise loved when she was 12 but hates now. She wants to spray it black but her mother won't let her. She is curled up tight in her duvet, like a hot dog, just the top of her head showing. Grace can see the red roots coming through the black hair dye.

Still in her pyjamas, Grace creeps down the spiral staircase and into Jake's room. He beams when he sees her, a wide grin that shows off his two sharp, shiny, bottom teeth.

"Wakey wakey Jakey," she says and lifts him out of the cot. He is compact and plump in his white towelling Babygro, the towelling grown rough from being washed so often. He puts his arms around her neck and drops his head onto her chest and Grace feels what is now becoming a familiar feeling when she cuddles Jake rise up through her. Not just love, but joy.

Downstairs in the kitchen, she warms milk for Jake and opens the backdoor for Oscar. Grace has to poke him to go out for a wee. Reluctantly, he heaves himself off the faded red sofa that Rachel says at least once a day is only fit for the tip but is probably the most used piece of furniture in the house. Grace plops herself down on the sofa and Jake positions himself across her lap to guzzle his milk.

When the kitchen door opens suddenly, Grace jumps, startled.

"Sorry, Grace," Iris apologises. "Did I frighten you? Expected to see my dad."

"Still sleeping, I think."

Iris pours herself a large bowl of Fruit and Fibre and settles herself next to Grace and Jake. Oscar returns from his inspection of the garden and squeezes himself into the gap next to Iris. For a few minutes the only sound is of slurping milk.

"Can I ask you a question?" Iris' mouth is still full of cereal.

"Er, yes."

"Those marks on your arms… Have you been cutting yourself? Only we've been doing it at school and that's what it looks like to me."

Grace immediately yanks the sleeves of her pyjamas down but says nothing.

"Because if you're not happy, and feel like you can't cope, that's normal. You don't even have to have a proper reason for being unhappy, they said at school. Sometimes people just do feel sad. It's because teenagers have lots and lots of feelings…"

"And they've nowhere to go and it gets overwhelming and cutting yourself, making yourself hurt, really hurt, that makes the feelings go somewhere else and gives you something else to feel instead of sad," Grace whispers.

"Is that why you do it?"

"I don't know why I do it. But yes, I think so. It feels outside like I feel inside."

"Oh."

"Does that sound silly?"

"Not silly, no. Just I wish you didn't feel that sad. Or that when you feel sad, there's another way of coping than slicing up your skin. When I feel sad I go out and play football."

132

Grace smiles. "You do that when you are happy too! I don't feel as sad here, actually."

"But you do feel sad in your own house?"

"Yes."

"Why?"

"Because I'm lonely. Because my mother goes on all the time about how she really wants me to get fantastic GCSE results so she can put it on Facebook and brag to all her friends in Qatar that the school I'm at now is every bit as good as the one I went to there. The pressure of it all made me feel sick all through the exams. She totally stressed me out. And when I think about results day I feel sick all over again."

"Bummer."

Grace smiles. "You said it Iris. Bummer."

"Are you hurting yourself here?"

Jake has finished his milk and wriggles off Grace's lap, crawls over to the large tub of toys in the corner of the kitchen. He hoists himself up to a standing position by holding onto the sides of the tub and rummages through it. He discards the things left over from when his sisters were young – the plastic kitchen, the shopping trolley and the dolls – until he finds what he is looking for, towards the bottom of the tub. Small toy cars. He fishes around until he has a pile of them stacked up and then starts to line them up on the floor, bumper to bumper. "Vroom," he says. "Vroom, vroom."

Grace and Iris watch Jake for a while in silence.

"No," Grace says, finally. "I'm not hurting myself here."

"Why do you think that is?"

"Because it's too full on here to be lonely. And too many of you for any one person to be under the microscope. And there's Jake. I never knew I liked babies so much till I met him."

"If you like him so much you can change his nappy. He's doing a poo. I can tell because he's doing that thing he does of going quiet and hiding around the back of the toy box there, so he can do it in peace."

"OK, I'll do it if you fetch me the wipes and a clean nappy."

"Deal."

It takes Grace longer than Rachel to change a nappy but she's much faster now than she was at first. Iris takes the smelly package away and dumps it unceremoniously in the bin.

"You know that thing you said about us not being under the microscope? That's not quite right. You want to try being the one that everyone thinks either wants to be a boy or wants to kiss girls but no one likes to ask."

"Do you want someone to ask?"

"Not really. Well, maybe. Perhaps."

"Do you think you might be gay? Or a boy?"

"I think...I think , what it is, is that I just like to play football. I don't like wearing skirts because I don't like flashing my pants when I play. I get my hair cut short so it doesn't get in my eyes. I hang about with boys because they like playing football too. I don't think I want to *be* a boy but I'd like to be left alone to play football like I was a boy. And I don't fancy any of the girls in my class – I don't much *like* any of them even, all that BFF best friends nonsense, but I don't fancy any of the boys either. Not yet anyway." Iris pauses. "That was an awfully long speech for me. Am I making sense?"

"Perfect sense to me," says Grace. "But then again, you are talking to the girl who keeps a razor blade hidden away in her knicker drawer."

"You really should think about taking up football, Grace. Sheesh – is that the time. You brought Mum and Dad's alarm clock downstairs to give him milk before he went off and now they're going to be late."

*

Gareth's morning is not going well. After the pandemonium of everyone sleeping in and arriving at work later than usual, he is now trying to draft an email to Cassandra Taylor, excusing himself from being her lawyer. He's been at it for almost an hour and has written several versions, none of which he has been convinced by.

> I regret I am about to be heavily engaged on another matter which will not leave sufficient time for me to give Perfect the attention it deserves. Accordingly I will be referring your work to Louise Wallace, one of my partners, who is an excellent corporate lawyer and will take good care of you. There will of course be no charge for any time I have spent to date.
>
> I regret that I have concluded that this area of work is outside my specialism and that you would be better represented by Louise Wallace.
>
> I regret that it appears I fancy you and that gives me a conflict of interest on any number of levels.
>
> I regret that if next time I see Adrian Matthews he tells me that he managed to get you into bed I am liable to beat him to death with my squash racket – no, his squash racket, mine is a good one – and it is better I ditch you as a client than become a murderer.

He is staring glumly at his screen when Celia sashays in, carrying a large gift box. He jumps up guiltily, hurriedly clicks on to another screen so that she can't see what he's written.

"Seems like you were good yesterday…" Celia grins.

Gareth blushes. He has not blushed for years, since first meeting Rachel in fact.

"What do you mean?" he asks, defensively. "I was just doing my job."

Celia looks at him a little puzzled. "And doing it well it seems. This has just been delivered by courier."

She hands him the box with its distinctive Perfect branding and acres of black ribbon. He puts it to one side, looks pointedly

135

at his screen until Celia leaves in a huff, put out that she did not get to see what's inside.

When he's sure Celia's gone he opens the box. Inside are the two shirts Cassandra had given him yesterday and a handwritten note, black ink on thick cream card, subtly embossed with the Perfect branding.

You forgot these. I put the Marks and Spencer rag you had on before in the trash, where it belonged. You should never wear anything else but Perfect shirts. You look great in them.

Sorry that I overstepped the mark. Too much Peroni, not enough food. Very unprofessional of me and I put you in a difficult position. Please don't shove me off to another lawyer. This project needs someone who understands the Rhondda. I promise not to try and make out with you again.

Cassandra

Just reading her name makes his chest feel tight. He thinks about what he should do now, but not for long. He texts her.

Thanks again for the shirts. OK, understood, no blood, no foul. All as before. Strictly professional exchanges from now.

A little while later he gets an email from her advising that she is coming to Wales on Monday to visit the potential site for the factory and attaching a number of documents she requires Gareth to review before then. He stares at his screen for a while, his fingertips pressed together. This is a great transaction for him to be instructed on – high profile work, lucrative, and of particular personal interest to him. No one else at the firm could do as good a job as he would on this deal. But then no one else at the firm has kissed the client outside a pub in London either.

Suddenly he jumps up and grabs his jacket.

"I'm popping out Celia," he shouts. "Got some shopping I need to do."

Celia barely lifts her eyes from her screen. She is ignoring him.

He could drive up to the City Centre or catch the little train that runs between Cardiff Bay and Queen Street but he decides to walk instead. With no time for a run this morning, the exercise will do him good. Within twenty-five minutes he is in John Lewis.

Gareth is good at shopping and not just his quarterly visit to Costco with his mother. He likes to buy Rachel and the girls lovely presents for their birthdays and Christmas and he knows his way around John Lewis very well. He bounds up the escalator to the first floor. He spots the Perfect branding and makes his way over.

"Could you tell me please which is your most popular ladies' shirt?"

"It depends, Sir," the shop assistant replies. He's young, twenty at most, wearing black trousers, a very fitted Perfect shirt and a black waistcoat. "They're all popular."

"Could you tell me which one you sell the most of?"

The shop assistant thinks for a while and then pulls out a shirt from one of the piles on display.

"This one, Sir."

It's a classic ladies' shirt, with single cuffs and mother of pearl buttons.

"No, not that one. Is there one with a wider collar and double cuffs?"

The shop assistant rifles through the displays for a short while.

"Do you mean this style Sir?"

The way he calls Gareth "Sir" makes Gareth feel like a schoolteacher. Or maybe it's because the shop assistant looks young enough to still be in school. The shirt he is holding out has the wide collar and double cuffs that Gareth had in mind and is cut lower at the front. It's the style of shirt that Cassandra had been wearing last night.

"That's the one. Excellent. I'll have two please – one white and one…" Gareth looks at the various colours on display "that colour."

"That's aquamarine, Sir. What size, Sir?"

"12."

"Would you like me to gift wrap them sir?"

"Yes please. Plenty of ribbon. And actually while you're at it I'll have one of the other style, the single cuff. In that purple colour. Size 10."

"The lilac. Also gift wrapped, Sir?"

"Yes please, separate boxes."

"I figured as much, with them being different sizes," the shop assistant says, tapping the side of his nose.

Gareth doesn't bother to explain.

Celia is still sulking when Gareth gets back to the office. As he walks up to her, she keeps her eyes fixed on her screen, exactly as he had done when he wanted to signal to her to leave his room. Celia and he have barely had a disagreement in all the time she has worked for him. Probably because on the odd occasion he has received a case of wine from a client he has always opened it and split the contents with her.

He slides the box containing the size 10 shirt across the desk to her.

"There you go Celia. Every client knows that a lawyer is only ever as good as his PA. And if the client doesn't know it, the lawyer should."

She tries to hide a smile but does not attempt to open the box.

"Aren't you going to open it?"

"Yes, of course, in my own time," she says.. That's him told.

Later on when he gets home and gives Rachel her own box she is delighted.

"I was only kidding about the freebies!"

"I didn't ask for them. They arrived this morning by courier. Two for you and two for me. Look."

He shows her the shirts from Cassandra that had arrived that morning. The handwritten note is now safely locked away in his desk drawer at work, hidden under his tax returns.

"Who sent them?"

"What do you mean, who sent them? The client, of course."

"I know that silly. Who at the client."

""I'm not sure. Rupert, I think, who's head of PR and marketing."

"I just wondered how they knew my size."

"I don't know, maybe they rang Celia."

"Really? Clients don't normally ring their lawyer's secretary to find out the dress size of their lawyer's wife."

"Well maybe clients in the business of making shirts do. It must be second nature. Also Rupert is in touch with his feminine side, if you get my drift."

"Well, whatever, they are beautiful. I love them," she says, already trying the white one on. "This style is amazing. Look! It makes my boobs look great but still totally professional. If you know what I mean."

Gareth knows exactly what she means.

"Looks great on you, love."

Rachel grins. "Try yours on!"

"Later I will. I'm going to squeeze a quick run in now. Missed out this morning."

"Don't go running! There's some wine left over from Book Club. Let's go sit out in the garden and finish it off together."

"I won't be long."

"You're really taking this running seriously, aren't you? I'm going to have to watch you. Getting all fit and slim – you'll be fighting off those eager to please young solicitors with a stick."

"Celia will do that for me I'm sure."

Rachel reaches up and kisses him on the lips quickly. "Talking of shirts, where's the one you put to soak last night?"

"Um, in the kitchen sink, where I left it, I should imagine."

"No, it isn't. I put a whites wash on this morning before I left and I thought I may as well put that one in too while I was at it but I couldn't find it."

"Maybe Mrs Morris moved it."

"It was first thing this morning, Mrs Morris hadn't been."

"Then I haven't got a clue. Not that that's anything new. I never know where anything is in this house."

Gareth runs longer than usual and far harder, pushing himself till his heart pounds. He is running so as not to think about this time last night, when he was being kissed by Cassandra Taylor. And kissing her back. So as not to think about how many lies he has already told today and how each lie he tells – each small lie – leads to more lies to cover the earlier lies. So as not to think about the white Perfect shirt, stained not with coffee but with guilt, that he quickly stuffed into his sports bag last night before going upstairs to have what Rachel had described as the best sex they'd had in a while.

Chapter 15

Eloise refuses to get out of bed the next morning.

"I'm not going in today, Dad," she grunts from under the duvet. Her failure to show up in the kitchen for breakfast has forced Gareth to take the unusual step of climbing the spiral staircase up to her room. Her bedroom door has a panty liner stuck to it on which Eloise has written "Keep Out" in red felt tip pen. The red ink has bled into the panty liner as Eloise fully intended it to. It doesn't deter her father.

"School isn't optional Eloise. You don't get to say if you are going in or not."

Eloise grunts at him "Go away. I'm still sleeping."

"Evidently you're not. Now get out of bed."

Eloise emerges slowly from under her duvet and props herself up on her pillows.

"Leave it out, Dad! I've got just one lesson in English on *The Grapes of Wrath*, which I've already read anyway because you and Mum forced me to last summer when I made the stupid mistake of complaining I was bored in the long holidays. I've finished my AS exams. Just because you were such a good boy at school and never missed a day in your life doesn't mean I've got to be like that too. Anyway, Grace has been invited over to Jenny's later for more erudite discussion about boring books and I am going to walk her over there."

"What does your mother say?"

"She didn't actually say anything because I haven't seen her yet this morning. On account of the fact that I was sleeping till you waded in here in your size tens. But I texted her and she texted me back to say she was fine with it. That I'm growing up and need to get used to planning my own time ready for university."

"That's if you manage to actually get into university, what with all this lounging around in bed."

"It's not even 8am, Dad. Fine! I'll get up now. But I am NOT going into school today." She flings the duvet back angrily and jumps out of bed, scowling at Gareth. "Happy now, dictator!"

She is wearing a pair of pink spotted cotton pyjamas that she has had for years, too short now in the leg and arm. Her hair which she usually has crimped up high has flopped around her face. Gareth feels a deep longing for the way he used to handle her tantrums when she was five which was to pin her down and blow raspberries in her ear, making her squirm and laugh.

"You can stay home on condition that you make tea tonight for everyone. And that does not mean ringing for a takeaway."

"Fine!"

"And there's one more condition."

"What now?"

"Come give your old dad a kiss."

*

Grace watches as Eloise crimps her hair back into its upright position.

"How long does that take you every day?"

"It used to take ages, like an hour, but I can do it in fifteen minutes now."

"That's quite a lot of effort every day?"

"It is, but why on earth would anyone want flat hair?"

"*My* hair is flat."

Eloise pauses slightly. "It is. And that's fine, honestly. Pay no attention to me. I should have said, I like my hair crimped but

142

that's a personal choice. Everyone else is free to have flat hair. Even if it looks…"

"Flat?"

"Precisely."

Once Eloise has finished crimping her hair and loading herself up with eyeliner and silver jewellery, she and Grace set out on the short walk to Jenny and Alastair's house. They cut through the streets of tall Edwardian and Victorian red brick houses and through Penarth town centre.

"It's nice here, isn't it?" Grace says to Eloise. "All these little shops – butchers and bakers and greengrocers and gift shops. A proper high street."

"Penarth is so boring Grace! It's got no place for edgy, urban young people like us to go. Honestly! You talk just like my parents sometimes – shop local, preserve community, blah blah." Eloise punches Grace lightly on the arm to show she is only kidding.

"Ow!" says Grace. "That hurt!'

Eloise looks mortified. "I'm sorry! So sorry! Did I hit you where…"

"Where what?"

"Nothing."

"Where I cut, you mean?"

Eloise looks at Grace through her fringe. "I didn't mean to pry."

"I know you didn't."

"It's just we are sharing a bedroom. It's pretty impossible to miss the state of your arms. I was leaving talking to you about it until you'd settled in a bit more."

"You're OK. Iris beat you to it anyway."

"Iris did?"

"Yes, you're a nosy lot you Maddoxes."

"Do you want to talk about it some more?"

"Have I got any choice? I'm pretty sure that's why Jenny has invited me round. I think she plans on using Theo's loneliness in

143

The Goldfinch as a theme to lead me onto a discussion about self-abuse."

"Fuck! I skipped school and got landed with making tea tonight, all for a therapy session with our local librarian!"

"Don't be mean Eloise. Jenny is cool. And she's nice. You all are. And I'm ready to talk about it. A bit. I think deep down I wanted you all to find out what I've been doing, stopped being so careful to hide my arms like I do from my mother. I think not being so secretive is me starting to face up to my problem."

"Do you want to skip going to Jenny's and go drink cider in the park? I know an off licence that will probably serve us. I find the best kind of therapy is talking about these things when you are off your face."

"Don't tease me, Eloise."

"I wasn't! I meant it. Seriously, Grace, a couple of my friends have had issues. Not cutting like you. Anorexia and bulimia. Anxiety. It's shit feeling like shit, and teenagers are better than anyone at feeling shit about themselves, but it helps to talk about it. We can skip the cider if you prefer."

"I'd actually prefer to go talk to Jenny about *The Goldfinch*."

"You're really weird, you know that, but OK fine. There'll be cake at Jenny's. And, actually, if we ask her nice, she may give us cider too."

"Come in," Jenny shouts when they ring the doorbell. "It's unlocked."

They find her tucked up in a battered, caramel coloured, oversized leather club armchair in the corner of her kitchen, reading.

She doesn't get up to greet them.

"Hello sweet peas, shove the kettle on will you? I made banana bread if you fancy some."

Eloise looks at her, her brows knotted together.

"Keep your jet black hair on! I made chocolate and raspberry brownies too."

"Better!" Eloise says. "Tea everyone?"

While Eloise throws teabags into mugs, Grace stands at the kitchen window, looking out at the garden. It is wildly overgrown, with ivy growing up along the fences and up into a tree at the bottom. The grass is waist high.

"Are you looking at my environmentally friendly wildlife garden?"

"Oh is that why the grass is so long?"

"No, of course not! It's because I can't be fagged doing gardening. I've got better things to do with my time."

"It's…um…interesting."

"It's not interesting. It's a mess. But Daniel likes it. He goes on expeditions down there. Disappears for days on end sometimes. I think perhaps there may be an Amazonian tribe hiding out in there. Comes back happy and smelling of dirt. Alastair moans about it all the time. I tell him if it bugs him that much he should do something about it, but actually he's as lazy as me and never does."

"That sounds fun for Daniel. A company comes in to mow our lawn every week. Mum likes it to be so flat and green you could play bowls on it. Not that anyone ever plays anything at all on it. Mum doesn't like anyone even walking on the grass let alone playing ball games. She likes to keep it nice."

"For whom?" Jenny asks. "Is the Queen coming round for tea soon?"

Grace smiles. "You never know!"

"Well, if the Queen comes round to this house she'll have to wash her own mug out, just like I've had to do with this lot," Eloise announces, as she puts three mugs down on a coffee table next to Jenny's chair. Grace fetches the plate of banana bread and brownies. They pull up two kitchen chairs and sit for a few moments, swigging their tea and eating cake.

Eloise surveys the walls of Jenny's kitchen. Every available space is lined with bookcases and every bookcase is jammed full.

"Ever thought of getting a Kindle?" Eloise asks, through a mouthful of brownie.

"I've got one! It's very handy for travelling or holidays. But it's no substitute for actually owning a book, being able to feel the weight of it in your hands, smooth the page with the tips of your fingers when you read a really good passage."

"That just sounds creepy Jenny!" Eloise wrinkles her nose.

"When I was little, if I'd enjoyed a book, I used to kiss the back of it when I finished it," Grace confesses.

"Ew, you two have got book fetishes. Right! I'll leave you to your deep and meaningful and go out to our delightful little High Street to shop locally for tea. I'm going to go to the butcher's and get some of their lush meatballs and I'll do a load of spaghetti. Easy peasy. I may even get a bag of rocket and some tomatoes to keep Mum happy."

There is a long queue at the butcher's. There always is. Eloise has been coming here with her parents most weekends since she was little. Her father says it's the best butcher in south Wales. She doesn't mind waiting, watching as the butcher and his assistants, their white and green striped overalls stained with blood, sharpen their knives and serve the people in the queue in front of her. They know most people by name.

Eloise sees one of the assistants grinning at her. She recognises him immediately. It is Liam Williams who was a year above her at school and who went off to university last September. He was a good rugby player she remembers. He has thick sandy coloured hair in need of a cut and lots of freckles.

When she gets to the front of the queue, he elbows another assistant away so that he can serve her and gives her a wide smile.

"You're Eloise Maddox, aren't you? Didn't recognise you at first, now you've gone all Emo and...," he stares at her hair and her bangles..."and your hair's turned black. And vertical. Are you mitching from school?"

146

"Ssh, don't talk so loud – not really mitching, only had one lesson of English. *Grapes of Wrath*."

"We did that. I really enjoyed it."

"Yeah, so did I, but don't let on to my parents. They think it was a huge deal I managed to get through it. What you doing back?"

"It's the summer holidays."

"Already?"

"Mad isn't it. A whole three months of summer holiday but no money to go anywhere. Had to come home and work here again."

"Have you worked here before?"

"Er, yes. Every Saturday since I was 16. Served your dad loads of times. Some of those times you were standing right next to him."

"Oh. Where are you studying?"

"Skilful change of subject, right there… London School of Economics. Politics and International Relations."

"Is London amazing?"

"Well yes, I guess. Very big. Lots of people there. I'm glad to be home actually."

"How long are you back?"

"Until the end of September. Till then I'm working here. If I manage to save enough I may go to Greece on holiday for a couple of weeks, otherwise it's Barry Island for me."

Eloise stacks the meatballs she has bought into a canvas shopping bag.

"That's a lot of meatballs. Are you having a party? "

She looks at him disdainfully.

"Sorry, I forgot there are hundreds of you."

"Even more than usual. My cousin Grace is staying for a while."

"I got my lunch break in twenty minutes. Want to come with me for a walk on the pier?"

"Um, sure. OK. I'll go finish the rest of the shopping and come back when I'm done."

147

"Cool. I'll put your meatballs back in the fridge till later so they don't go bad."

Eloise buys the salad stuff she needs and two French sticks. She feels very self-conscious hanging around outside the butcher's waiting for Liam, even more so when he bounds out of the shop door grinning at her. She wishes she hadn't bought the bread as soon as she and Liam start the short walk down the hill to the pier. They stick out the top of the canvas bag and bash against the back of her head as she walks.

"Here, give me your bag," Liam says. He breaks the French sticks in half and shoves them deeper into the bag, then slings it across his shoulder. He brushes her shoulders gently.

"You have breadcrumb dandruff," he explains.

He buys them a can of Coke each at one of the pier kiosks and gets himself a tray of chips.

"Sure you don't want any?"

"Nah! I'm full of chocolate brownie, thanks."

"Just so long as you're not one of those girls who doesn't like to eat in front of people. Or not eat at all. Girls that don't eat freak me out."

They walk past the newly renovated silvery art deco Pier Pavilion which houses art exhibitions, a cinema and a café. It twinkles in the sunlight. At the very end of the Pier they sit down on a bench. It's a bright day and they can see clearly across the Bristol Channel to the islands of Steep Holm and Flat Holm and, further away, the English coast.

"So, what are you doing this summer?" Liam asks her.

"I'm back at school tomorrow but there's a week left then till the end of the term. We're meant to be going on holiday to Tresaith in west Wales for a couple of weeks but we've been going there for years and the place does my head in. Beach, shop, pub. Nothing else. I haven't told my parents yet but I'm not planning on going with them this time. Thinking about going to a festival instead, I've never been to one."

"I've been to loads. I can tell you which ones are the best."

"Cool."

"When did you decide to dye your hair black?"

"Just before sixth form. Wanted to look different for a new start."

"Suits you. So did your red hair, though."

"Thanks, I think."

"Have you ever been on those islands?" Liam asks, pointing in the direction of Steep Holm and Flat Holm.

"No. We went on a boat trip once with school and sailed round the outside but we didn't get off. Aren't they uninhabited?"

"Except for some wardens. And a derelict hospital where seamen arriving in Wales with cholera and bubonic plague used to get isolated. You can go on day trips. A big group of us stayed overnight at Flat Holm a couple of years ago for my dad's 50th. There's a dormitory and you can camp. It was a blast. We could go there together this summer if you like?"

Eloise pauses for a while. "Shall we just try the pictures first? Or going for a pizza? We might not get on. Overnight on an island could be an ordeal."

"Brilliant. Want to go out tonight?"

"I've got to serve meatballs to my enormous family first but I'll be done by 7pm."

"I'll call for you then."

"You'll call for me? What are we? Seven years old? Are you going to ask my Mum if I can come out to play?"

"Trust me Eloise. Your parents will be happier about stuff if I call for you. It's a nice thing to do."

Suddenly and without warning he pulls her towards him and kisses her. He tastes of tomato ketchup and she can smell sunshine on his skin. She doesn't pull away and the kiss goes on and on. When finally they stop kissing, he puts his hand on her cheek and looks into her eyes.

"We're going to get on Eloise," he smiles. "I'm absolutely positive about that."

*

Eloise collects Grace feeling a little giddy.

"What are you smiling about?" Grace asks her. "You normally favour a sarcastic scowl."

Eloise ignores her. "Did you and Jenny have a good time?"

"We did. She gave me a reading list of books she thinks I should read and a load of information about self-harming. And a notebook. She wants me to write everything I feel down. She says I should think about writing a novel and that whenever I feel overwhelmed I should channel it all into writing instead. I'm going to give it a try anyway."

"You're becoming a different person Grace."

"I know. Much more positive."

"You want to watch it. You know what's happening to you, don't you?"

Grace shakes her head.

"I'm sorry to be the one who has to tell you this Grace but the thing is…" She pauses.

"What? What's the thing?" Grace asks worriedly.

"The thing is that it seems likely you are turning Welsh. Next thing you know you'll be calling everyone 'butt' and bursting into song every whipstitch and getting misty-eyed when anyone mentions the Mabinogion. We'll have to get you one of those daffodil hats to wear to rugby games."

Chapter 16

When Idris gets back to their room at the travellers' rest, he finds Jean sitting staring out of the window, perched gingerly on a slim wooden chair. She is pale and there are dark rings round her eyes but she smiles at him.

"You should be resting!"

"I feel fine. I've had a wee nap. It's just like a bad monthly now."

"Oh."

"You did know women have monthlies Idris?"

"Well, yes, of course." Maggie had spoken openly to Idris and Tommy, from the moment her periods started but Idris judges it wise not to tell Jean how he knows of such things.

"That's all it is now. A monthly. And I don't mind the pain at all. I'm glad of it. There was evil growing inside me. Now it's cut out – gone – and I'm clean again. Just me again."

Idris suddenly feels winded at the enormity of what Jean has been through. Not just today but before she even left Scotland.

"Would you like to go for a walk?"

"Very much. It is my 16th birthday after all."

"Come on then. Let's go get a little fresh air together and celebrate what's left of your birthday. "

Idris asks at reception for directions to Lakeview Park.

The girl on reception is making entries in a ledger and barely looks up. "Just keep walking straight down Simcoe Street South till you see Lake Ontario."

It's pleasantly warm in the early evening September sunshine.

151

They find the park and walk around the lakeshore slowly, Jean's arm supported in Idris's.

"It's so very enormous, Lake Ontario," says Jean. "It's difficult to think of it as only a lake and not the sea. It seems every bit as big as the sea we crossed to get to Canada."

"It's bigger than Barry Island, that's for certain," Idris says.

They come to a large property called Barnhart's Pavilion which advertises rooms for campers and lakeshore cottages to rent. There is ice cream on sale and one cent treats like liquorice babies and marshmallow cones.

"Would you like something?" Idris asks. "A birthday ice cream maybe?"

Jean shakes her head. "Not right now. I wouldn't mind a go on that though?"

She points toward a large children's roundabout on the lakeshore beach, pointed like a witch's hat.

"Are you sure?" He gestures vaguely in the general direction of her bottom half.

"I'll be fine!" She smiles.

They position themselves opposite each other on the roundabout and Idris digs his foot into the sand and pushes off gently. The roundabout rises and falls like the waves, dipping and diving as it circles. Jean laughs and lets her head fall back and her hair blow in the breeze, like it did on the boat. Idris pushes the roundabout again and again and they dip and turn like the swell of the sea until Jean notices a small queue of children waiting patiently for their turn and calls to Idris to stop.

Dizzily, she clambers off the roundabout.

"That was great fun," she laughs. "The very best thing to do on your birthday."

They walk back through the park.

"What on earth is that over there?" Jean asks. "Are those cows?"

"Let's go see."

The cows turn out to be buffalo. Six or seven of them, rather scruffy looking, including a calf, staring out forlornly from behind a tall chain link fence.

"They pong a bit don't they?" Jean laughs.

"A little," Idris agrees. "Shall we have a little sit down over there, up-wind of them?"

"Yes please, it's been a long day."

They sit for a while side by side, watching the families with young children and the couples arm in arm strolling by, enjoying the evening sunshine.

"I like it here," Jean says.

"I'm glad. Because you have an interview tomorrow morning for the position of maid at a very grand house not far away. The head housekeeper is Scottish too."

"Oh."

"You sound disappointed? I thought you wanted a position as a maid."

"I do. Very much. But…"

"What is it Jean?"

"I had intended to try for something later, not so soon after…and in Toronto. Somewhere close to Mr and Mrs Williams house, so that I could visit often. Mrs Williams would feel the need of me now."

"She will Jean. And I'm not trying to push you into working while you are still…" he searches for a word "recovering, but I saw the position advertised and the house is beautiful and with lots of servants so there will be companionship."

Idris has never seen Jean cry, not even when she turned up on the Williams' doorstep beaten black and blue, not before or after the pain and humiliation of the process she has undergone without any complaint today. But now she is blinking back tears.

"Jean, have I done the wrong thing?"

"Not at all Idris. You are very kind and thoughtful. Thank you. Let's go back to the room now shall we? I am suddenly very tired and not at all hungry. Perhaps you can eat in the Homestead's dining room while I rest?"

Jean goes straight up to bed when they get back. It is still early, not yet 8pm and Idris is hungry. He takes a seat in the restaurant. Most people are on dessert. The sullen girl from reception has now donned an apron and is the waitress.

"You're very late," she says, grumpily. "I thought I was going to be able to get away. Been working since 7am this morning. Had been hoping no one else was coming and I could start clearing up. If you're going to eat, you'll have to have what's left, no choice left now. I take it your wife isn't eating." She puts an emphasis on the words "your wife" and looks at Idris pointedly when she says them. "She looked peaky when I saw her earlier."

"My wife is a little under the weather and has gone to bed early. Thank you for your concern. So what is left?"

"Soup, baked macaroni cheese with tomatoes, baked apple."

"Macaroni." Idris rolls the word around in his mouth. He has never said the word macaroni before. Never eaten it either. "Sounds delicious."

The food when it comes is surprisingly good. The vegetable soup has some sort of green herb in it that Idris doesn't recognise but it tastes fresh and zesty. The texture of the macaroni he finds odd, although he likes the taste and the full feeling in his belly. The baked apple is stuffed with raisins and honey and is served with ice cream. He eats every scrap.

"You were hungry," the waitress comments as she clears his table. The restaurant is empty now except for Idris.

"I was, very hungry. Not eaten all day."

"Anything else you're hungry for?" With this, the waitress undoes the buttons of her blouse very quickly, revealing her brassiere and the plump, rounded tops of her breasts.

She laughs. "You look shocked sir for a married man. Haven't you ever seen a pair of titties before?"

Idris gets up hurriedly. "If you'll excuse me, I'd best go upstairs to my wife."

"Oh yes, your wife." The waitress does her buttons up slowly.

154

"Pity. You're a looker you are. If you change your mind, I'll be in the kitchen for a while yet."

Idris takes the stairs back to the room two at a time.

Jean has left the door on the latch and for the first time since they checked in, it dawns on Idris that the room, booked for a married couple, has only a double bed. When he pushes the door open gently, he sees that Jean is sleeping as far as possible over onto one side of the bed. Idris kicks off his shoes and lays down fully clothed on the other side of the bed on top of the bedclothes. Even with the excitement at the sight of those splendid breasts running through his mind, he falls asleep immediately.

*

When Idris wakes up the next morning, Jean is already up and dressed, her hair neatly brushed.

"Good morning, Idris," she smiles.

"Good morning, Jean. You're up bright and early."

"I've got an interview, haven't I?"

Idris accompanies Jean on the walk to her interview with Mrs Meikle.

"May I take a walk around the garden while I wait?" he asks the housekeeper.

"By all means. I'll get a message to Mr Wragg, the head gardener, to let him know."

Idris has never before seen anything as beautiful as this house and its gardens. Attached to the house is a large conservatory that Idris can see contains numerous tall palm trees. There are wide manicured lawns and many other smaller greenhouses containing flowers of all sorts that Idris cannot begin to name and does not think that his mother would be able to either. There are secret little corners where two people could sit together and talk and not be overlooked, pools with fountains and waterfalls and a long lily pool completely surrounded by a high, white, lattice fence.

At one end of the pool is a marble sculpture of three naked women and it is while he is contemplating this sculpture and concluding that it reveals more of the naked human form than he has actually seen in the flesh, that Idris encounters Mr Wragg.

"Well there you are. I've been looking for you everywhere since I got the message from Mrs Meikle. I'm Mr Wragg."

"Pleased to meet you sir. I'm Idris Maddox."

"What do you think of my girls then?"

"I beg your pardon, sir?"

"The girls, over there." Mr Wragg motions to the marble sculpture. "They're The Three Graces. A replica of the ones done by Antonio Canova. He did one for Empress Josephine and another for the Duke of Bedford in the 1800s. Glorious aren't they?"

"Glorious," Idris repeats.

"Come, come, it's not the formal gardens that you're interested in. It's the kitchen gardens you'll want to see."

Idris does as he is told and follows Mr Wragg. The kitchen garden is very different to the structured formality of the other parts of the garden and much more familiar to Idris. Like his mother's garden but on a far larger scale, this area is crammed with vegetables and fruit trees. There are greenhouses here too, smaller ones, steamed up inside, in which tomatoes grow and lettuce and beds of cutting flowers.

"So tell me about your gardening experience, then, son."

"I only know what I've learned from my mother. She grows vegetables mostly. Carrots, potatoes, turnips and parsnips. A few roses. Mostly what I know of gardening is digging and weeding."

"Well that's all I really need you to know. Everything else I can teach you. I've got eleven greenhouses and 24 gardeners to look after. I'm most interested in whether a man's arms and back are strong enough and fit enough to do this job and I can see that yours are."

"I'm sorry Mr Wragg but there's been a misunderstanding. I'm not here for the job of under-gardener. I have a job already, on the railway viaduct in Toronto. It's my friend who's here to apply for a position as a maid."

"And what strapping young lad such as yourself would prefer working in smelly, dirty Toronto in the dust and noise of building a viaduct, to working with me in these beautiful gardens, digging the good clean dirt, outside in the fresh air morning till night. You tell me that, eh? And close by his sweetheart too. This is a fine place to work Mr Maddox for a man who's prepared to work hard. What about it then?"

"Jean's not my sweetheart. She's just my friend."

"If you say so, son. If you say so."

"She really is just a friend, Mr Wragg, and one whom I hope will be lucky enough to be working here very soon so that I shall have an excuse to visit your gardens again."

"Well I shan't waste any more of my time on you then, Mr Maddox," Mr Wragg says, not unkindly. "Please take a seat on the bench over there and I'll let your friend know where to find you when she is done."

Within fifteen minutes Jean is walking towards him.

"How did it go?" he asks, as she takes a seat next to him.

"Really well. Mrs Meikle has offered me the job. She doesn't even require references. Says that us Scots need to look out for one another. Even so, I don't think I will be mentioning to anyone that I'm a Quarrier child. That part of my life is forgotten now."

"It's wonderful news, Jean."

"It is, isn't it? I am fortunate, thanks to you. This house belongs to a famous man. Colonel Samuel McLaughlin, the boss of General Motors Canada. Mrs Meikle says that the Colonel and Mrs McLaughlin are kind people to work for and take good care of their staff. They have five talented, much loved daughters, all grown up now, and the youngest recently gone off to finishing school. The house feels a happy one to me."

"I am very glad to hear it. When do you start?"

157

"Today. Right now."

"You won't be coming back on the train with me?" Idris is surprised how very sad the idea of making the journey back to Toronto without Jean makes him.

"I think it will be easier for me this way. I will write Mrs Williams a note – tell her again how very grateful I am to her and to Mr Williams, ask her if she would be so kind as to parcel up the beautiful clothes she has made for me and send them on."

"I'm sure she'll be happy to do that. Mrs Williams is going to miss you, Jean."

"And I am going to miss her." He can hear the emotion in her voice. "But nowhere near as much as I am going to miss you, Idris."

He reaches out and takes her hand in his but does not look at her, keeps his gaze fixed firmly on the lawns ahead.

"I shall miss you too, Jean, very much. We'll see each other again, I promise. Cross my heart and hope to die."

"I do hope so," she says, removing her hand from his. "Goodbye till then, Idris."

*

All the way back to Toronto on the train, Idris can think of nothing else. He knows exactly what he must do. As soon as the train pulls into Union Station, Idris is opening the train door and hurtling himself out before the train has even stopped moving. He runs down the platform and out of the station. If he runs all the way, he should make it to Dewi Sant before the end of evening service. He cannot wait to see Aeronwen's beautiful face again and make everything right between them.

He arrives at church, his shirt sticking to his back with sweat. He is aware that he makes too much noise when he enters the church. Many of the congregation stare at him and he knows he looks a sight in his damp shirt with the sleeves rolled up and that

Mrs Williams will be disappointed in him. But it is worth all the embarrassment to see the look on Aeronwen's face when she sees him. She cannot conceal her delight at seeing him or the look of longing in her eyes. When the service ends some minutes later he waits for her by the door and watches as she elbows her way past her parents and sisters, pushes her way through the other worshippers, patiently filing in a slow, neat row to leave the church. By the time she reaches him, she too is breathing heavily.

"Has she gone? Have you come back to me?"

"Jean has gone, yes. But Aeronwen I never left you. I was trying to help her is all. I was always here. Right here."

Aeronwen throws herself into his arms. She is light and he lifts her easily. He kisses her, full on the mouth, and she kisses him back hard. More than one lady leaving church gasps in shock.

He puts her down gently. "Will you marry me, Aeronwen?"

"You're meant to ask my father first."

"It's not your father I want to marry!"

"You still have to ask his permission."

"And I will. But first I'm asking you. Will you marry me?"

"I will Idris, I will."

Chapter 17

When he met her, on their first day of law school, the thing that had bowled Gareth over about Rachel was how unfamiliar she was to him. The otherness of her. She was uncharted territory and the conquest of her had been thrilling.

He had been attracted to her immediately. Not just the way she looked, in fact not the way she looked at all. All his other girlfriends had been petite and brunette. And Welsh. And here was Rachel, tall and red headed and English and clever. Very clever and not afraid to show that cleverness off either. Teasing him about his Welsh accent and quoting *Under Milk Wood* at him.

"I will knit you a wallet of forget me not blue, for the money to be comfy," she'd said, in a breathy tone, that had made the hair on the back of his neck prickle. It was the first time Dylan Thomas had ever meant anything to him.

He hadn't known when they'd sat next to each other that first day that the seating plan for the remainder of the year was being set in stone. But the next day, without discussing it, everyone sat back down in exactly the same seats as they had the day before and every day after that. Rachel and Gareth, sitting side by side, from September till June the following year.

When she mentioned during that first week that she had a long-standing boyfriend whose name was Will and that she was going to visit him that weekend, for some bizarre reason he'd felt shocked and hurt. Just because he was single following the break up of his last long term relationship in the third year at university, why should she be single? Most of the people at law school were

160

in long-term relationships. Why had he assumed she wasn't? Most probably because of the way she teased him about his accent and laughed at his jokes and caught his eye from time to time in a flirty way, which he had hoped was a reflection of his own attraction for her.

"Good weekend?" he'd asked, nonchalantly, the following Monday.

"Great thanks. You?"

"Very good."

In fact, he'd missed her. Ridiculous. They'd only just met, had only had coffee together round and about lectures, not even been for a drink. And he'd missed her all weekend long.

So he set out to get her, to prise her away from her Will, who had just started training to be a chartered accountant in Southampton. It was hard work training to be a chartered accountant – long days at work during the day, studying at night – and Will was careless and complacent with Rachel's affections. Work and his exams came first and Rachel needed to fit round those two priorities. Gareth put Rachel at the very top of his list and he wooed her fiercely. Weeks of walks in the park and drinks in the pub and long lingering looks while trying hard to beat her at their coursework.

He remembers vividly the first time he saw her naked. Her face freckled but the rest of her body so very pale. Alabaster is how her skin would have been described by poets but to Gareth it was like skimmed milk, so pale it had a bluish tinge. Her pubic hair, fiery red against her skin, had shocked him.

The way she approached sex was also different to anyone he'd met before. Rachel was much more focussed on her own orgasm than anyone else he'd ever slept with.

"Not like that, like this," she'd instructed him in those early, guilty days, when Will had all but lost the battle he didn't even know he was fighting. She'd put her hand over his hand and shown him how she wanted him to move his fingers over her.

161

"Slower, deeper strokes, like this. Don't try to flick me on and off like a light switch."

This had put him off his stride at the beginning. But the things she showed him worked. They always worked. And because they worked for her they worked for him. Rachel had taught him how to make her come within minutes if he wanted. And then he'd come, immediately after her.

Lots of studying and lots of great sex. That's how Gareth remembers law school. Whenever people complained about how awful that year of exams had been and how they would never want to have to live through that ordeal again, all Gareth could do was smile and enjoy the memory. There had been a couple of weekends of tears, over the course of which Will finally got dumped and was considerably more hurt than Rachel had expected him to be. One long night he turned up outside Rachel's flat and called her on the phone, over and over, begging her to come outside and talk to him. Gareth was all up for going out there and talking to him himself until finally Rachel went and sat in Will's car for a while. Gareth watched from the window, his insides turning, coiled tight and ready to rush out and physically fight for Rachel if it was called for. Even though his last fight had been at primary school and he'd lost. He watched while Will pleaded with Rachel and banged his hands down on the steering wheel a few times; Rachel talked calmly to him, shaking her head throughout. Finally Rachel got out of the car and Will drove away and when she came back inside with tears in her eyes Gareth took her by the hand and led her into her bedroom and made love to her till they both felt better.

After that, they hadn't looked back. Gareth and Rachel, side by side, for the rest of that year and every year since. Working hard and raising a family together. Getting the domestic chores done. Laughing and eating and drinking and still having sex. Happy ever after the random act of choosing where to sit in law school.

And now there is no otherness about Rachel any longer. Her body is as familiar to him as his own. How she looks when she is pregnant, or has just given birth. How she looks when she cuts her toenails or cleans her teeth or puts on her tights, the concentrated look on her face as she eases the tights over her calves and then her thighs and finally over her belly button, snapping the elasticated waist with her thumb in satisfaction at having got them on without laddering them.

The steps they each take in the dance of lovemaking. What he does to Rachel and what she does to him. The way she looks at the moment she comes. The exact same look every time.

Rachel and Gareth. Gareth and Rachel. Extensions of each other, parts of the same being. Like the way a person can clap their hands, even in the dead of night, and never miss. They have been together so long that being with Rachel is as instinctive and effortless and as vital to life as breathing.

Cassandra Taylor is other to him, in the way that Rachel once was, so many years ago. Unknown, unexplored, even though Gareth has spent a lot of time today talking on the phone to her or emailing her. She had made the first phone call by 9am.

"Can I ask your advice on something?"

"Of course, that's what you pay me for."

"I'm not expecting to pay you for bouncing ideas off you. I consider that to be one of the added value services which all you lawyers should deliver free of charge."

"Fire away then – at no cost."

"What would you say to Perfect opening its own stores?"

"I'd ask whether you really need your own shops when you have concessions in most of the major department stores."

"Good question. But the amount of space a department store will give us is limited, they are expensive and we can't expand our offering. Our own shops, as you call them, which is a far cuter word than stores by the way, will give us more control."

"So have you looked at rental costs or done any other budgets?"

"Not yet. It's still at the blue sky thinking stage at the moment."

"Well, where do you have in mind?"

"Notting Hill or Chelsea."

"Expensive."

"Very. But I think we'll be able to make it work and achieve more customers and more sales. In-store browsing will also drive up online sales."

"What are the risks? Cost of course. But will you be prejudicing good relationships with the department stores? Biting off more than you can chew at a time when you already have large new projects on the go?"

"One thing you will learn from working with me is that biting off more than I can chew is what I do. I function at my peak when my mouth is too full."

She pauses here and on the other end of the phone Gareth is wondering if she too is thinking about that kiss outside a London pub. He feels himself stiffen again as he had done that night.

"Are you there?"

Gareth gathers himself.

"Yes, just thinking. I suggest you get on to some London agents, get some prices, do some budgets and forecasts of likely sales. When you put your blue sky thinking in terms of cold hard cost it will help you make your mind up."

"I agree. Already on it. I'll get back to you. Thanks for your input. It was constructive."

And so it had gone on all day with phone calls and emails, discussing heads of terms and contractual clauses, negotiations and new ideas, compiling checklists of things they need to discuss while she is in Wales next week doing the site visit, how she wants him to come on the site visit with her given his personal knowledge of the area. Gareth's inbox is full of Cassandra Taylor but his head is even fuller. Despite being able to detach himself enough to do his job, in every single one of his exchanges today with Cassandra Taylor the issues running through his mind on a loop have been *Did you go out for dinner with Adrian? Did you kiss him like you kissed me?*

He even forgot it was Thursday and a squash night until Celia walked into his office and pointed at his squash kit in the corner and then at her watch.

*

When Gareth arrives home after squash, having played worse than he has for years, he pushes open his front door to hear loud laughter coming from the kitchen. He finds something of a party going on there. All of his children and Grace are seated round the table and Rachel, too, who has a virtually empty bottle of red wine in front of her. There is a strange young man sitting at his kitchen table, sitting as close to Eloise as is physically possible without actually sitting on her lap and grinning from ear to ear.

"There you are, at last!" Rachel says. "We've all eaten but there's plenty left in the pan. Might need a minute in the microwave. Do you want a glass of wine? I'll hunt down another bottle, this one's almost done."

"You sound like you've had one glass too many already!" Gareth says as he heaps spaghetti and meatballs into a bowl and shoves it into the microwave. "Who's this?"

"This is Liam. A friend of Eloise's. He was taking her out for a drink but I persuaded them to stay and have a drink with me instead."

"Pleased to meet you, Mr Maddox." Liam gets to his feet.

"Hello Liam. Now if those of you who have finished eating could clear out, I'd like to eat my dinner in peace."

"Of course, shall we go for that drink now, Eloise?"

"It's far too late for her to be going out," Gareth says, tetchily. "She has school tomorrow, you know." He stresses the word school heavily. "And she's not old enough to drink."

Eloise glares at her father and Liam grins. "Fair enough. I'll catch up with you again, Eloise. Goodbye everyone."

As Eloise leaves the table she bends down and whispers in her father's ear.

"You're a total arse, Dad."

"I know. It's what dads do. Now go see Liam out."

"Yes, why *are* you being such a dick, Gareth?" Rachel asks when the other children are all out of earshot.

"The term Eloise used was actually arse."

"Arse. Dick. Ordinarily the difference between those two things is rather important but on this occasion there is no distinction."

"Stop talking like a lawyer at me Rachel. It's been a long day. I didn't want to have to make small talk with some spotty faced kid that my eldest daughter is clearly lusting after."

"Are you for real Gareth? It's Thursday! You've played squash. It doesn't count as a long day if it's only long because you've been out playing squash. You've no need to be so grumpy. Liam is a nice kid. Courteous and well spoken but fun, too."

"Perhaps it's you not Eloise that's lusting after him."

"Now you're just being childish. Anyway, it's about time Eloise fell in love. She's ready for it."

"She may be ready for it but I most certainly am not."

"And so we arrive at the true cause of your being a dick. Or an arse. Take your pick."

"Yes! Maybe! I don't know. Yes I do. I've been a 19 year old boy. I know the sorts of things he's thinking. I don't want him thinking those things about *my* baby girl."

"But she's not a baby Gareth. She's 17. And I've been a 17 year old girl and believe me, she's thinking much the same sort of things he is and has been thinking them for some time by now."

"Well that's made me feel a whole lot better. I'll have that glass of wine now."

"Certainly dear. I'll get it for you now, dear."

Gareth applies himself to his bowl of pasta. Rachel puts a glass of wine down in front of him and kisses the top of his head.

"Better?" she asks

"Sort of," he grunts.

"How was the rest of your day? Pre-squash?"

"Fine. Busy. Tons of drafting."

"On the Perfect deal?"

"Mostly."

"Have they decided on the factory site yet?"

"Not yet. Cassandra Taylor is doing a site visit in the Rhondda on Monday. Maybe there'll be a decision after that."

"Isn't she one of the directors?"

Gareth hesitates. He realises just in time that he has not up until now ever referred to Cassandra by name when talking about Perfect. "Yes, she is."

"Then they must be seriously considering it then, mustn't they. Are you going on the site visit with her?"

"Maybe."

"Well if you go, do the Rhondda a favour and hold back on filling her in on all the sacrifices the miners made."

"What do you mean?"

"You know exactly what I mean. Don't go all Arthur Scargill on her the minute you hit Llantrisant roundabout and start telling her about all the injustices heaped on the struggling workers. Don't try to guilt her into opening her factory in the Rhondda by talking about the past. Focus on the positives of the Valleys and how they can help her business for the future."

"It's not my job to choose the factory site or to try to influence that decision. It would be wholly unprofessional for me to allow my personal interests to cloud my judgement."

"I know that. You know that. But don't delude yourself by thinking you won't try anyway. I'd like to meet her sometime. We could ask her over here to dinner. It's never any fun staying in hotels and eating on your own."

"That would be weird, Rachel!"

"Why? We've invited clients over for dinner plenty of times."

"Only clients we've known for years and who have become friends. Not ones we've only just started working for."

"I was just being nice."

"Well there's no need. Cassandra Taylor doesn't strike me as the type who's the least bit fazed about eating on her own in hotels anyway."

"How would you know? Have you even met her yet?"

"I've spoken on the phone to her numerous times. Right, that's enough talking about work. You go check on the kids. I'll do the dishes. "

"Deal."

As he clears the plates and stacks the dishwasher, Gareth shakes his head at his own stupidity. He could have explained to Rachel any number of times this evening that he had met with Cassandra Taylor twice already. Cassandra is one of the bosses of the company and the person driving this project – of course he has met with her, why would he not have?

He hears in his own head the way Rachel would have applied her trained mind to reply to such questions if posed by anyone else.

You're being coy because you feel guilty and don't want that guilt to show. You're avoiding referring to her in case your body language somehow reveals that you are attracted to her. Doubling back now and admitting to me you've been dealing with Cassandra Taylor all along will cause suspicion because why would you not have put me right on this seemingly unimportant point long before, unless of course there's something to hide.

Rachel has a fine mind and a lawyer's tenacity and she'd be right.

Chapter 18

"Liam is lovely, isn't he?" Grace says. She and Eloise are lying in their beds. They turned the light off thirty minutes ago but neither is asleep yet.

"I don't know if he's lovely or not yet, I've only just met him."

"Yes you do Eloise, you know already he's lovely. He's good looking and he's funny and he's nice to everyone and smiles all the time."

"Sounds as if you fancy him!"

"Well put it like this, if you don't fancy him, let me know."

"Ha ha. Thing is, I do fancy him. A lot. How is that possible? I only met him this afternoon. At the butcher's! This morning when I woke up Liam Williams was absolutely nowhere in my head. And now the *only* thing in my head is Liam Williams. That's just mad!"

"You didn't only just meet him. You knew him at school."

"Not really, I knew who he was, that's different."

"Did you think he was good looking then?"

"No! Not at all. Never even noticed him."

"Well, you're noticing him now! When are you seeing him again?"

"Tomorrow afternoon. After he's finished work, we're going sailing."

"I didn't know you sailed."

"I don't. But Liam's family are all members at Penarth Yacht Club. He says it's good fun."

"Shame."

"What do you mean, shame?"

"Not going to be much snogging action in a boat is there?"

"Shut up Grace and go to sleep."

*

Actually Grace is right. There is no snogging action in the boat. It is great fun though. Liam has been sailing since he was seven, and all Eloise has to do is concentrate on not falling out of the boat.

"It's actually called a dinghy," Liam explains.

"Really? A dinghy is what my father calls the inflatable boats he buys every summer on holiday in Tresaith. A new one every year cos they always spring a leak by the end of the holiday."

"Yep, those are dinghies too. Just a different type. I can tell you why they have the same name if you promise not to call me nerdy."

"Go on then."

"Dinghy is a borrowed word, from similar words in Bengali, Hindu and Urdu, for boat. Lots of Indian words got absorbed into the English language during British rule in India. There's loads of others we use all the time now without realising their origin, like pyjamas and chutney and pundit."

"Hmm, interesting," Eloise says, "if a bit nerdy."

"Oi," Liam says leaning over and cupping seawater in his hand to splash at Eloise. "You promised."

Liam expertly sails the boat from Penarth over into Cardiff Bay. It is a beautiful summer's evening, still sunny, and the water is flat and calm.

"I've never seen the Bay from the water before!" Eloise is thrilled.

"Looks great, doesn't it?"

"Amazing."

Really it is Liam that Eloise thinks looks great. It is fascinating to watch him calmly sailing as if it's second nature, his arms tanned and muscled, his eyes crinkling in the sun.

He catches Eloise looking at him and he smiles at her and the happiness she feels inside spills out of her until she is laughing out loud. Liam starts to laugh too.

"What are we laughing about?" he asks.

"Nothing," Eloise says. "And everything."

The snogging comes later. After the dinghy is put away. After they've had a pint of cider each in the dated Yacht Club Bar which has a red carpet and lots of shiny mahogany furniture and where no one asks Eloise for ID.

"Do you want another drink?" Liam asks.

Eloise shakes her head.

"Want to go for a walk on the beach?"

"Sure."

Liam takes her hand as they stumble along Penarth's loose pebbly beach. He does it in an easy, comfortable way as if they have been holding hands for years. He steers her towards the esplanade wall and they sit down and lean their backs against the wall. Without saying anything he turns his face towards her and kisses her and they carry on kissing until it grows too cold to sit on a windy, pebbly beach any longer.

*

Cassandra Taylor is not someone who stops working at weekends. While Gareth is out running on Saturday morning and Rachel is sitting at the kitchen table enjoying a rare opportunity to read the papers, because Grace has taken Jake to the park, Gareth's phone out in the hallway pings repeatedly.

"Cassandra Taylor is after you love," she calls to him when he gets home. Standing in the hallway, damp with sweat, Gareth feels his skin prickle cold.

He gathers himself. "What does she want?"

"How should I know? I don't read your emails. Got enough of my own to read. I could just see it was her name popping up."

"I'm sorry, love," he apologises.

"Doesn't bother me," she says, not lifting her head, "occupational hazard of this job. Next time I've got a big deal on over a weekend and my phone goes all the time perhaps you won't be so grumpy with me about it."

"I'm going to go jump in the shower and then I need to do a bit of work."

"Okey doke. Make sure you're done by two. I've got to take Nora to a birthday party and Iris needs picking up from football at two-thirty."

Gareth sits on the edge of their bed and scrolls through the emails that Cassandra has sent. Queries about the site visit on Monday, documents from the Welsh government concerning the possible grant funding, terms and conditions from a fabric manufacturer based in Lancashire. The emails keep coming. The last email she sends causes Gareth's heart to pound.

"I've decided I need to come to Cardiff on Sunday if I'm to be sure of being ready for the site visit on Monday. I have so many questions I need answered before then Gareth that I really do think I need a meeting with you before we go to site. I suggest we meet in the Park Plaza at 4pm. I can't imagine it will take longer than a few hours. I will arrange a conference room. Please be ready to respond to all the points raised in my recent emails."

In the shower, Gareth lets the hot water drum on his head and shoulders and thinks about how he should respond to Cassandra. He doesn't have an issue with working at weekends. It is as Rachel noted an occupational hazard of choosing law as a profession and happens all the time. What he does have an issue with is being in a hotel on his own with Cassandra. Just thinking about meeting her, stood here in the shower, he feels excitement tingling through him.

But she is right that they could do with a meeting before the site visit.

By the time Gareth is out of the shower and dressed, he has made up his mind about what he needs to do.

"Hello handsome," Rachel says when he walks into the kitchen. "Want to make some coffee for me?"

Gareth fills the kettle, flicks on the switch. "Cassandra Taylor is coming to Cardiff tomorrow and wants me to meet her tomorrow afternoon before the site meeting on Monday."

"OK. Bit of a pain on a Sunday afternoon, but makes sense."

"And I was thinking, you know you mentioned asking her round for something to eat?"

"Yes. You pooh-poohed it."

"Did I? Well I don't much fancy having to spend my Sunday evening in a hotel conference room. If it's OK with you, I'm going to suggest we have the meeting here and then she can join us for something to eat if she wants."

"Really Gareth? It's chaos here on the weekend. It's not really quiet enough for a meeting is it?"

"It'll be fine. It should keep the meeting short having it here, in the bosom of the family. She and I can sit here at the kitchen table or go into the living room."

"That means I need to tidy-up though. I could do without that."

"Eloise can do the tidying up. She hasn't got out of bed yet after her date with lover boy last night and if she wants to see him again this afternoon, she can bloody well earn it by helping out a bit round the house."

"Don't take it out on Eloise just because you have to work at the weekend and don't like her having a boyfriend."

"I'm not."

"Yes you are and you know it. But fine, Eloise can tidy up the living room a bit and you can spruce up the downstairs loo which isn't that bad anyway because I only just cleaned it for book club. We're having roast chicken and roast potatoes tomorrow and I was doing two chickens anyway so there'll be enough. Grace has already offered to make a big crumble. So go ahead and invite her. Do you think she drinks? Maybe I'll call into Majestic on the way back from Iris' party. Ooh, I'm quite excited to meet her now. Do you think I ought to wear one of my Perfect shirts?"

"No Rachel, that's just weird."

*

Gareth had wondered how Cassandra would take the invite to attend a meeting at his home. The last time he'd seen her they'd kissed. Or at least she'd kissed him and he'd kissed her back. And now here he was playing the devoted family man and inviting her round to meet everyone. When he'd telephoned her on Saturday afternoon to arrange for their meeting to be at his house, she'd agreed with such good grace and enthusiasm it dawned on Gareth that when she'd said their relationship would be entirely professional from now on, she'd actually meant it. Perhaps the kiss had not had the same impact on her as it had had on him.

He insists on picking her up at Cardiff Central from the London train.

"That's very kind Gareth but there's no need. I can hop in a cab."

"Yes you could, of course, but we're a hospitable lot in Wales. I'll pick you up. You can get a cab back from our house to your hotel if you like, that way I can have a glass or two of wine with dinner."

"Well, that's very kind of you."

"It's nothing but I do have a favour to ask of you in return?"

"Fire away."

174

"Would you be able to pretend on Sunday that when I pick you up is the first time we meet in person and that Rupert has sent my wife and I a gift of two Perfect shirts each?"

"Errm, yes, sure, if that's what you need."

"It is."

"You got it."

After he puts the phone down, Gareth thinks that this particular exchange is the most pathetic conversation he may have ever had with anyone in his life, let alone a client.

*

Gareth spots her straight away when he pulls up outside Cardiff station on Sunday afternoon. Cassandra is wearing jeans and an emerald green T-shirt made out of some silky material and her blonde curly hair is tied up in a loose knot on the top of her head. She looks younger than usual. She waves at him and he opens the car door for her to climb in.

"Great timing," she grins at him. "I just this minute arrived."

She smells of something light and fruity. Bits of blonde hair have escaped from the knot and one of them is caught in the corner of her mouth. He feels a sudden urge to reach over and brush it away.

"Do you mind if we get started straight away, while you drive? I've got such a lot to get through."

"Fine with me but you do realise Cardiff is small and we'll be at the house in 20 minutes?"

"Time is money Gareth. You lawyers know that better than anyone."

When they arrive at the house, there is five minutes of clamour while everyone, including Oscar, greets Cassandra. Cassandra and Rachel shake hands and smile and Gareth feels a swell of pride in his wife for being so professional and at the same time welcoming, a swirl of children around her. Rachel ushers them into the relative peace of the living room and there Cassandra and Gareth work solidly for the next two hours until Eloise knocks on the door.

"Mum said to let you know dinner's half an hour off and to bring you a glass of wine. It's a Chablis she said to tell you, Cassandra, but if you'd prefer a soft drink just say."

"Chablis is perfect, thank you."

"Here's your glass, Dad. And, just so you know, Liam's joining us for dinner. Thirty minutes don't forget. " And before Gareth can say anything, Eloise backs out of the living room.

"I guess you didn't know anything about this Liam joining us, eh?" Cassandra says, taking a sip of the Chablis.

"Nope."

"New boyfriend?"

"Yep."

"You don't approve?"

"How can I not approve? He's local, he's a bright lad, studying at the London School of Economics, he's polite and respectful but with a bit of cheek too and he's got himself a job for the summer."

"So your problem is that he's perfect for your daughter."

"Precisely."

They finally call it a day work-wise when their glasses of excellent Chablis are empty. The aroma of garlic and thyme and roast chicken fill the kitchen. Liam is carving, Eloise is dishing up, Grace is popping an enormous tray of crumble into the oven. Rachel is sitting at the table with Jake on her lap, Iris and Nora like bookends each side of her finishing off their homework.

"What a lovely family scene," Cassandra says, sitting down next to Nora. Gareth looks at her quickly from the corner of his eye to check but she is entirely sincere.

Eloise puts plates of chicken and roast potatoes in front of each person and large serving bowls of broccoli and mashed carrot and parsnip in the centre of the table.

Gareth looks down at his plate and up at Liam.

"How come the chicken doesn't look like this when I carve it?

176

This looks like chicken from a restaurant. When I do it, it looks like I've yanked the chicken off the bone with my bare hands."

"All those Saturdays working in the butcher's must have taught me something!" Liam grins.

"I knew I knew you from somewhere," Gareth says. "That's where it was. The butcher's."

Cassandra has already helped herself to vegetables and is tucking in.

"This is delicious. Thank you Rachel."

"Most of it is delicious," Nora says, drily, "except the carrots-n-parsnips." She runs the words together into one. "Those are *disgusting*. Look disgusting and taste disgusting too."

"Don't you like it?" Cassandra says turning to her. "That's my favourite bit. You only ever get it at home. I don't think I've ever seen carrot and parsnip puree in a restaurant ever."

"Poo-ray? That sounds even more disgusting. What's that?" Nora asks.

Cassandra points to the carrots and parsnips.

"That's not poo-ray. That's mash," Nora giggles. "Although it tastes a bit like poo if you ask me."

"That's enough, Nora," Gareth says sternly, but Cassandra is smirking more than Nora is.

"So, Cassandra," says Rachel changing the focus deftly, "what are you hoping to get out of the site visit tomorrow?"

Without missing a beat, Cassandra rolls off her answer, "I'd like to see plenty of factory space which will not need much renovation, a good and speedy transport system, excellent internet speed and a workforce willing to be re-trained and with a realistic salary expectation. Oh…and ideally a large grant cheque already signed by the Welsh government."

Rachel pauses. Cassandra smiles.

"Just kidding. Just some of those things would be great. I'm not expecting a clean sweep."

"Gareth has been really excited about the possibility of Perfect opening a factory in the Rhondda. I really hope you can pull it off."

"Thank you. So do I."

"Did Gareth tell you he might have family somewhere in Canada?"

"He did mention it. A great-uncle wasn't it?"

"Yes, missing Uncle Idris. Last seen in 1926."

"I guess no one missed him enough to go looking then?"

"Seems not."

"But you named one of your daughters after him?"

Rachel looks at her, confused.

"Iris is named after Idris, right? Just without a D?"

"Is that right Mum?" asks Iris. "Did you give me an old man's name?"

"Actually, thinking about it," Gareth answers, "she's not named after Idris as such but there's an obvious connection. Funny how I never thought about it till now. Before you were born Iris, your Mum and I couldn't agree on a name for you. And then Grandpa told us how if he'd been a girl he was going to be called Iris because it was a name his grandmother, Gwen, liked. Your Mum and I thought it was a lovely name."

"Of course!" Rachel says, taking a sip of her wine, "I'd forgotten how we came up with Iris' name but Gwen must've liked the name Iris because it reminded her of her son. How funny it is the way these things come about. You think it's just because someone at some point just liked a certain name but there's history behind it."

Cassandra smiles at Iris. "Well it's your name now Iris and it really suits you,"

Iris keeps her eyes fixed on the table, embarrassed by being the focus of attention all of a sudden. Nora takes advantage of everyone looking at Iris to surreptitiously transfer carrot and parsnip mash from her plate on to Cassandra's.

When everyone is done, Liam helps Eloise clear the plates and Grace serves Cassandra plum crumble with custard.

"I normally don't eat dessert," she says, "but for this I am going to make an exception. It looks delicious. And these plums are an amazing colour. Do you know Grace – I think I'd like to see a Perfect shirt made in just that colour. We don't have anything in our range like it. We've got plenty of lilac and a purple check but nothing like this. It's a lovely dramatic colour, great for a shirt you could wear from daytime in the office through to a function at night. What do you think, Rachel?"

"I think it would look marvellous."

"Just maybe not wear it with a beige corduroy skirt. You wouldn't want to look like an enormous walking crumble," Cassandra whispers to Iris through a mouthful of crumble.

"By the way, Cassandra, I should have said this sooner, thank you so much for the Perfect shirts you sent us. We both love them. I was already a huge fan, but now Gareth is too. And you got our sizes spot on."

"You're very welcome. You can thank Rupert, our VP of Marketing and PR for the shirts. He's great at those sorts of touches and managed to wheedle Gareth's size out of him when they met in London. I'm told he had to do a fair bit of sleuthing round the internet finding pictures of you on your firm's website so as to take a guess at your size."

"Well he got it just right so please pass on my thanks to Rupert. I hope you don't mind my saying this, but there are a couple of design tweaks I think would be great for the working woman's wardrobe…"

"Cassandra stopped working an hour ago, Rachel," Gareth says.

"Ignore him," Cassandra says, "tell me what you are thinking." She fishes out a notebook from her handbag and as Rachel talks of longer length shirts so they stay tucked in to low rise suit trousers and don't flash your back and how she'd like ranges with and without pockets and the choice of longer sleeves. Cassandra makes rough sketches and jots down a few notes.

"Excellent, really good input Rachel. I love that sort of thing –

hearing how real women wear our shirts. It's invaluable. And good food and good company to go with it. I guess you could say it was just, well, Perfect."

"Perfect," Nora says, absent mindedly, staring at Cassandra's largely untouched dessert bowl. "If you're not going to eat that, can I finish off your crumble Cassandra?

"Yes you may. Even though it was absolutely delicious, it seems I helped myself to far too many carrots and parsnips." Cassandra smiles slyly at Nora. "I've had a lovely evening, thank you all very much for the welcome, but I have a big day tomorrow and I need to get an early night. Would someone mind ordering a cab back to the hotel for me?"

"I can drop you into town if you like," Liam offers. "I was driving anyway, and I've got my Dad's car outside."

"That's very kind of you, Liam."

"I'll come and keep you company," says Eloise. "And before you say anything Dad, yes I know I've got school tomorrow and yes Liam will drop me back here before 10pm."

"Glad to hear it. Cassandra, I'll pick you up from your hotel tomorrow at 8am for the drive up to the Rhondda."

"See you tomorrow then, and thanks again both for sharing your family time with me."

"I like her," Rachel says after they've gone. "Easy going but very switched on. It must be great fun working with her."

"It's work, same as any other client."

"How come you always get the best clients? I do exactly the same sort of work as you, and I'm as good as you, too, but you always get the juiciest referrals from the likes of the inward investment team. I would have loved to work on this job with Cassandra. She's clever and sassy and I would have learned a lot from her."

"Just the luck of the draw Rachel. I tell everyone that you're a better lawyer than me. Let's stop talking about Perfect now shall we? Is there any more wine left in that bottle?"

Chapter 19

Idris doesn't understand why any wedding – least of all his own wedding – should take so long to arrange.

"It needs to be at least a year away, Idris," Aeronwen had explained.

"Why? I was thinking next month. Two months at most. I want to be married to you Aeronwen. I don't want to wait any more than we absolutely have to."

"A year's engagement is a respectable length of time. Any more than that will seem like unseemly haste. As if there's a pressing need for us to be married, if you know what I mean."

"Chance would be a fine thing," Idris had mumbled under his breath. Once they were engaged, Aeronwen allowed long lingering kisses and permitted Idris to press himself against her but no more than that. These kissing sessions leave him fit to pop, which Aeronwen is well aware of and seems to enjoy.

"We need at least a year, anyway, to get the arrangements just right. A wonderful wedding day takes time to plan. And with this much notice maybe your family will be able to travel to Canada and attend after all."

"Maybe, we'll see." His mother had written straight back on receiving notice of his engagement to say that much as it pained her not to witness her own son's wedding she did not think they would be able to make the journey. It was too far and too expensive and Davey was still so very young.

Although Aeronwen's father had consented gracefully to Idris' request for his youngest daughter's hand in marriage, he had imposed a condition. Idris must leave his job on construction of the railway viaduct and accept instead a job with Mr James in the hatter business.

"I need someone to take over from me at some point and my other sons-in-law have got good jobs already. Don't take this the wrong way, Idris, but I really don't want my daughter to be engaged to a labourer. You may as well start as soon as possible."

"*I'm a collier not a labourer; she's engaged to a collier,*" Idris had thought to himself but he had not said anything. He did as instructed and gave a week's notice to his foreman. The Ontario Temperance Act having been repealed earlier in the year, he and his fellow workers were able to mark his last day in construction by openly drinking together a few bottles of beer and eating delicious pierogi made by the wives of his Polish workmates.

Idris is not well suited to many of the aspects of the hat-making business. He does not enjoy serving customers in the shop and after a few weeks of trying to instil in Idris the right skills balance of flattery and salesmanship needed to ensure that customers actually buy hats, Aeronwen's father gives up and makes him foreman of his nearby factory. The workforce is small and skilled but Idris proves poor at this job too. His natural inclination is support of the workers not being a boss. He feels again on their behalf the sour taste of anger at injustice.

"You dock their pay by 15 minutes if they are as much as a minute late and pay the women less than the men for the same work. That isn't fair."

"I'm as fair as any other businessman in this City. Being any fairer won't give Aeronwen and my grandchildren the kind of life they are used to. This is how we do things here Idris. You're a bright boy. If you want to keep Aeronwen happy, make sure you learn fast."

Idris swallows the sour taste down and takes refuge in the dusty office rooms above the shop. There amongst discarded stock and old ledger books he does not have to be obsequious to customers or hard on the workers. He concentrates on becoming good at accounts and on dealing with the suppliers, buying the felt and other materials needed to make the hats, keeping the books and organising the wages. It is much easier work than he is used to and for the first time in his life Idris finds he does not fall asleep immediately he gets into bed.

The lengthy preparations for the wedding bore him. He really does not care if the invitations are on white or cream card and what they should serve to their guests at the wedding breakfast. Aeronwen, however, enjoys the shopping and choosing, poring over magazines and discussing every detail with her older sisters.

All in all, it comes as a relief when Mr James suggests that the office rooms above the hat shop could, with a little work and the installation of a bathroom, be a home for Idris and Aeronwen at the start of their married life.

"If you live here for a few years you'll be able to save towards a house. When you clear it out there's more room than you think. There's even an attic room right at the top too. It could serve as a nursery, when the time comes."

Idris does most of the work himself, in the evenings when his day job at the factory is done. He enjoys the physical exertion involved in turning the offices into a home. He has missed feeling his muscles ache at the end of a day, the satisfaction of having done a day's graft. As soon as there is some habitable space he moves out of his lodgings with Mr and Mrs Williams.

"There's no need for you to move out right now, Idris," Mrs Williams points out. "Your wedding is not for some months yet, and you have a comfortable home here with us."

"I do indeed, Mrs Williams, and I shall miss it and your cooking in particular but I'll get more done if I move in now."

"Would you like me to run you up some curtains, then?"

"You are too kind Mrs Williams but Aeronwen has firm views on soft furnishings. I had better leave the issue of curtains to her."

*

From the moment she walked away from Idris that first morning, swallowing so hard to stop the tears coming that her jaw ached as much as the rest of her from the operation, Jean focuses on ensuring she is useful to all at Parkwood.

On her return from church, Mrs Meikle gives her a tour of the grand house and explains its history and that of the family who live in it. It is a speech she has already given many times over her years at Parkwood.

"The house was built between 1915 and 1917 and there are 55 rooms in all," she explains to Jean, "including the servants' rooms on the third floor where you will live. There is an indoor swimming pool, a bowling alley and a games room and a billiard room with specially painted murals that were commissioned just a few years ago."

"That will make the cleaning interesting," Jean comments.

"Just as well, for there is a great deal of it to be done," Mrs Meikle says, drily, "but you should consider it a privilege to work for the McLaughlin family. Colonel Samuel's father owned McLaughlin Carriage Works which at one time was the largest manufacturer of horse-drawn buggies in the British Empire. It was Colonel Sam who made the move into automobiles and established what was then known as the McLaughlin Motor Car Company in 1907. It made the McLaughlin-Buick Model F. Back in the early days, the company made only a couple of hundred automobiles a year. Now as part of General Motors it produces over a million and a half cars a year. That's 44 out of every 100 cars produced in Canada and the United States. This year they have started production of a new car called the La Salle. It is a companion car to the Cadillac and the Colonel says it has set a new record for first year sales of any car in its price class. Are you listening, Jean?"

"Yes I am, Mrs Meikle."

"Good. Automobiles have made this family very wealthy but you will learn that they remain very down to earth and kind people. The Colonel and Mrs Adelaide have been married almost thirty years now. Their five wonderful daughters – Eileen, Mildred, Isabel, Hilda and Eleanor – are all excellent horsewomen and Miss Isabel is an accomplished artist, too, and studied at Ontario College of Art. They are as dear to me as if they were my own. All grown up and moved out, now, but they are frequent visitors, especially the ones with children. The Colonel and Mrs McLaughlin also entertain often, which is something this house and its gardens lend themselves to beautifully. We had Miss Hilda's wedding here just last year and it was one of the most beautiful days I've ever had the privilege to witness. There is never a dull day here, Jean, but nor is there an idle one either."

"It will suit me well, Mrs Meikle, I like to keep busy."

Mrs Meikle has trained up a lot of maids for Parkwood but none have been as quick to learn or as eager to please as Jean.

Every morning, Jean has to be at work by 6am but she gets up earlier than she needs to so as to take a walk round the gardens. Even when winter comes and it is dark and cold out, she finds great joy in the Italian Garden where the Three Graces are to be found but also the Sundial Garden, the Summer House and the Sunken Garden.

"So long as you cause no damage and keep away when there are guests, you can visit whenever you like," Mr Wragg says quietly to her during servants' lunch one day.

Jean is surprised. She didn't think anyone had ever seen her.

"Don't look so shocked. You're not the only early riser in this house you know. It's nice to know my work is appreciated."

"Oh it is, Mr Wragg, very much. The gardens are always so beautiful, even now in winter. I am very fond of them."

"You'll like them even more in the summer. Then the gardens don't just look lovely but they smell lovely too. Lilac and roses but before them, the first flowers of the year are great carpets of

185

lily of the valley. And you wait till you see the chrysanthemums. We grow chrysanthemums that are big as a man's head, ready for Mrs Adelaide's chrysanthemum tea every year. Prize winners they are."

"I shall look forward to it, Mr Wragg."

Mr Wragg was not overstating the position. As the spring of 1928 arrives, so the gardens burst into colour that blazes all summer long. Jean takes to also visiting the garden at the end of her working day with a tray of tea, tracking Mr Wragg down wherever he is so he can tell her in some detail precisely what tasks he and his team of 24 gardeners have carried out that day. She is at her most happy listening to Mr Wragg rattling off lists of flowers deadheaded, bulbs planted, and cuttings taken.

One evening, when her work has kept her inside longer than usual, it is Mr Wragg who finds her rather than the other way round.

"There you are girl, a man could die of thirst waiting for his tea."

"I'm sorry, I'm just finishing, I'll make you some right away."

"I was only teasing you. I have news and I've been wanting to tell you all day. Guess who is coming to visit the gardens tomorrow?"

"I don't know. King George V?"

"No!"

"The prime minister of Canada?"

"No. Mr and Mrs Dunington-Grubb!"

"The landscape designers who designed Parkwood's gardens?"

"Nobody less. And guess who is to serve them tea on the lawn tomorrow when they arrive?" Mr Wragg does not wait for Jean's answer. "You, Jean, you!"

At dinner that evening, Mrs Meikle confirms the arrangements.

"Mr Wragg has specifically requested of the Colonel that you be the one to serve tea to the landscape designers tomorrow."

"So I understand and I'm very honoured, Mrs Meikle."

186

"What a ridiculous name they've got. Dunington-Grubb! Did you know they joined their names together when they got married and emigrated from England to Canada? They took each other's names. How very modern." Jean can tell from the way that Mrs Meikle's face crinkles when she says this that this modern practice is not one she approves of. "Still, I suppose better to be modern than to be called Mrs Grubb for the rest of your life."

The following afternoon is gloriously sunny and Jean is delighted that Mr and Mrs Dunington-Grubb will see the gardens they designed at their most beautiful. As she walks out over the lawns carrying the tea tray, she suddenly feels very nervous at the prospect of meeting the landscape architects but she need not have worried. She is greeted very warmly by the husband and wife team as she serves them and Mrs Adelaide their tea.

"This is Jean, our newest member of staff, all the way from Scotland and mad keen on gardens," Mrs Adelaide says, kindly.

"I'm Lorrie Dunington-Grubb and this is my husband Howard, we're always delighted to meet people who love gardens." She is wearing a very fashionable three quarter length grey silk dress, with large floppy sleeves like the wings of a bat. Jean wonders if that is what she wears when designing gardens or whether the sleeves get in the way.

"Pleased to meet you, Ma'am and Sir."

"Tell me," Mrs Dunington-Grubb asks her, "which is your favourite part of the Parkwood gardens?"

Jean hesitates. "I love it all, of course, but I particularly love the Italian Garden and all the greenhouses. And all the flowers."

"Good choice. Excellent. I designed the Italian Garden. Howard here likes to claim that he helped but mostly it was me." Howard Dunington-Grubb smiles indulgently at his wife.

"So Jean, have you ever considered becoming a landscape architect?"

Jean hesitates before answering politely. "I'm a parlour maid, Ma'am, I don't know anything about gardens."

"Well that's clearly not true is it? You evidently know a great deal, but more importantly you are interested and you care. I realise you may not be able to go to horticultural college but there's nothing stopping you becoming a gardener at Parkwood rather than a parlour maid is there? Is there now, Adelaide?"

Mrs Dunington-Grubb turns to face Adelaide McLaughlin. "You can sort her out with a job with Mr Wragg can't you?"

"We've never had a female gardener before but I don't see why not. Would you like that Jean?"

"I love the gardens, Mrs Adelaide, but I love my parlour maid work, too, and I would not want to let you or Mrs Meikle down."

"Leave it with me, Jean. Let me have a word with Mr Wragg and Mrs Meikle first."

"There you go Jean. It may take some time, but us girls will get to all the same places men do. Eventually."

Jean clears away some of the empty plates and cups and saucers, marvelling at how one afternoon might change the course of your life. Just like that.

*

Maggie's letter is addressed to Idris at Mr and Mrs Williams' house in Fairlawn Avenue. It is picked up from the mat by Rhydian, the Williams' new lodger, a farmer's son who has come to Canada from their hometown Carmarthen. Mrs Williams had found she missed being a landlady and cooking for someone who really appreciated it and Idris' room had lain empty less than a fortnight.

Mrs Williams takes the letter from Rhydian and puts it in her handbag ready to give to Idris on Sunday at church.

"Idris not in church today, Aeronwen fach?" Mrs Williams asks before the service starts.

"No, he said he was in the middle of some plastering that he couldn't really leave."

"That's no excuse not to come to church now is it? It's the Lord's Day."

"Which is what I said to him, Mrs Williams, but he said he'd make it up to the Lord another time."

"Did he indeed? Could you give him this letter that arrived for him? You will see him now before I do. It's come from Wales but it's not his mother's handwriting. I hope nothing is wrong at home."

Aeronwen takes the letter. "Of course, I'll be seeing him later, I'll give it to him then."

Aeronwen knows that letters should only be read by their addressees. But she is curious to know who other than his mother is writing to her betrothed and why. She reasons with herself that the letter must be in some way connected with her – has to be – what else is there to write to Idris about, except their forthcoming wedding? It must in some ways be a letter to her too, and so, during the sermon, Aeronwen quietly opens the letter addressed to Idris.

Dear Idris

Gwen tells us of your wedding plans and of the family you are to marry into and your new job as hat maker. It all sounds very exciting and so very different to being at home here with us in Wales. I hope you shall be very happy.

I know Gwen has already told you no one from the family will be able to come to the wedding. She says it is because Davey is so young but really it is because we could not afford the fare for even one of us to make the journey. That I am sure will come as no surprise to you.

I know Gwen has also told you all about Davey. He means the world to us all and is such a happy, good-natured baby. We all love him dearly. He arrived a month early of which I was glad as no one could then make a connection between his birth and the amount of time you and I spent together before you left for Canada. But he is your son Idris. In case either of us was in doubt, I have not fallen again since, and I know that I will not again. But Tommy and I have Davey and although I would have liked him to have a brother or sister, it is enough that we have him.

I could not bear to say goodbye to you the morning you left. I am sorry. I should have. Then I could have said to you in person what I now say in this letter. Thank you for the gift of my son. Know that I love you, and that I always have and always will, and that I hope for you that your wife loves you even more than I do.

Yours, always,

Maggie

The minister is stopped dead in his tracks. The scream that Aeronwen lets out is so loud that the youngest children in the congregation start to cry. Still screaming she pushes her way past everyone in her pew and tries to run out of church but ends up flopping and fainting around the aisle like a new born lamb trying to find its feet. A great many people try to fuss around her. Her father stands over Aeronwen's slumped body and reads the letter she has dropped. The minister is fairly certain Mr James is cursing and not under his breath either.

The minister has no option but to put his sermon on hold and call an early end to the service. He consoles himself with the idea that he can use the same sermon next week, as he barely got going on it today.

Chapter 20

After years of working in a butcher's shop on a high street, small talk comes easy to Liam.

"What's Toronto like as a place to live?" he asks Cassandra as soon as they drive off.

"I'm biased of course, but I think Toronto is one of the very best places in the world to live. Plenty to do and see and eat, tolerant and diverse, great art galleries, thriving place for business and the best hockey team in the universe."

"The Maple Leafs?"

"That's them."

"I like ice hockey."

"Not ice hockey. Hockey. It's just hockey in Canada. We've got hockey and *you've* got field hockey. Hockey is extremely important to Canadians."

"Gotcha. Toronto sounds really cool."

"It is. You should come see for yourself. I could hook you both up with jobs at Perfect. We always need people in admin support – stuffing envelopes, shredding, making coffee, that sort of thing. Not high level work but international work experience looks good on the resumé, right?"

"It looks great," Eloise agrees. "How about we start next week when school is finished?"

"Why not? Let me talk to Human Resources tomorrow."

"I was just kidding! My Dad is going to go ape when I tell him I'm not coming on holiday with all the family this summer. He'd fizzle and melt like the Wicked Witch of the West under a bucket of water if I suggested going off with a boy I only just met to work on the other side of the Atlantic."

"I don't see why. It would be a great opportunity and it's only for the summer. There's always notices pinned up in the staff room asking for roommates. You guys get working visas easy enough don't you? We've had plenty of British people working with us in the past. No wait, Eloise, you're not 18 yet are you?"

"No, not till next year."

"Too bad. You need to be 18 to get a working holiday visa, I'm sure of it. But hey, you can just come and hang out. I am sure HR can devise some sort of internship programme in return for expenses that the immigration people will be happy with. You guys should think about it. It'd be fun for you. Here, give me your cell numbers and I'll make some enquiries and get back to you."

"Really? That would be fab, thanks so much."

Cassandra taps the numbers that Eloise gives her into her mobile.

"Here you go Cassandra, this is your hotel," Liam announces as they pull up outside.

"Good night both, thanks for the ride. You really should come to Toronto for the summer. It's a great city and greater still in the summer. Gotta warn you though, no hockey till September."

"Is there any point getting excited about this?" Eloise asks on the drive back.

"Not if your Dad's going to melt. I'm working quite hard at keeping on his good side, if you hadn't noticed."

"I thought you were just naturally that smarmy! I'd love to go. It would be such an adventure. Well, so long as you were there it would be." She goes quiet. "I just said that out loud, didn't I?'

Liam laughs. "We could at least think about it I suppose. Depends on the cost of flights and stuff. And how much it pays. But I'm planning on making sure you think every day with me is an adventure."

Eloise feels her cheeks turning pink. "OK, let's look into it this week. But first we've got a full 40 minutes before I've got to be in the house, so let's park up somewhere. Snogging is all I'm suggesting mind, before you get any ideas beyond that. For now anyway."

"Yes Ma'am," Liam lifts his hand to his forehead in an exaggerated salute.

*

Gareth tries to get ready for work the next morning without waking anyone up. He showers in the family bathroom and creeps around the bedroom in the semi-dark getting dressed.

"Make sure you wear one of her shirts," Rachel mumbles, half asleep. "I think she'd be disappointed if you didn't wear one for this site visit."

"Already on it," Gareth whispers as he bends to kiss her goodbye.

"You look great," Rachel says, without even opening her eyes.

When he picks her up at her hotel, Cassandra too is wearing a Perfect shirt and a black trouser suit, this time with high-heeled ankle boots.

"Can you walk OK in those?" he asks, pointing at the boots. "We've got quite a bit of walking to do today."

"Thought of that. I've got some sneakers in my purse."

Gareth looks confused.

"My purse is my handbag. What you guys this side of the Pond call a purse we call a wallet."

"Thanks for the translation. OK, what do you want to work on while we drive?"

"I made a list last night."

They don't get to the bottom of the list in the 45 minutes it takes to drive to the Rhondda and to the location of the industrial estate.

"Here we are, bit early, Mr Griffiths and Mr Alun and Adrian should be arriving very soon."

"Adrian won't be. We've agreed not to work together."

"What happened?"

"Oh nothing. We've been out for dinner together a few times, that's all. We both felt it better not to work together as well."

Jealousy knifes through Gareth, hot and sharp.

"Right, let's get a move on. I've a factory to inspect and some government officials to impress. And some sneakers to put on."

Cassandra walks faster than any woman Gareth has ever met. She whips around the industrial site, making notes in her notebook, identifying units that can be knocked together or knocked down so new units can be built. She fires off questions to Mr Alun and Mr Griffiths. She had requested they set up a meeting for her with some of the former employees of the factory and she insists on meeting these workers privately. When this is all done, she bids goodbye to Mr Alun and Mr Griffiths and turns to Gareth.

"I want you to walk with me up that mountain over there. That way I'll get a proper feel for this place."

"Didn't you already get that from the factory site and all those questions you asked?"

"Not quite, no."

"Fine."

It's been a long time since Gareth climbed the mountain behind his parents' house. He climbed it so often as a child that he thought he knew it like the back of his hand but as he and Cassandra start the steep climb, he realises that it doesn't look quite as he remembered it. He has to lay over the top of his memory the reality of the mountain as it is now, greener, minus pits but with supermarkets. He feels guilty about being home and not calling in to see his parents but has no intention of doing so. He couldn't cope with the possibility of his mother inviting Cassandra to join her in the hot tub and perhaps a stiff Dubonnet and orange or two.

Cassandra stops walking quite so fast a little way into the climb.

"Jeez, this is tough."

"Worth it when we get to the top though."

Both a little out of breath, they climb in silence for the next twenty minutes or so, until finally they reach the top and look out over the valley.

"That view is really something!" Cassandra says once she has her breath back.

"It is, isn't it? Thanks for dragging me up here. It's been ages since I made it up here, might even be years."

"Point out the places you went to growing up."

"Well there's my Mam and Dad's house, and there's my primary school, and over there is where I went to secondary school, and that there, that's the rugby club. Next to a rugby pitch, funnily enough. Not that I played much rugby. I wasn't particularly good at it. But that's where the discos were. And the beer."

"And the girls."

"Those too."

"It's a strong community still, you can still feel it. It's going to be a great place for Perfect." Cassandra looks at him and smiles.

"Seriously? You're going to do it?" Gareth's grin is so wide he can feel it hurting the corners of his mouth.

"Of course we're going to do it. I was almost certain before today, but I was absolutely certain once I'd seen the factory site and spoken to some of the former employees, who I know are going to be great trainers and supervisors of the new talent we bring on. And there was the added bonus of Mr Griffith giving me certain assurances about financial support."

"So you didn't need to climb up here then to get a feel for the place?"

"Not at all."

"Why did you want to come up then?"

"To celebrate."

Gareth knows what she is going to do and he doesn't try to stop her. He lets her put her arms around his neck and lift her face to him and kiss him. He kisses her back greedily. Up there on the mountain, wind whipping their hair, neither of them is put off by thoughts of Rachel or the children or of Sunday dinners and laughter shared around a bashed up kitchen table just the night before.

They almost run back down the mountain, slipping and sliding in their rush to get back to the car. They barely say a word to each other on the journey back down to Cardiff but the whole way to the hotel Cassandra keeps her hand on Gareth's thigh, tantalisingly close to but not quite touching his balls. On the way up in the lift, Cassandra fumbles in her bag for the keycard. As soon as she opens the door of her room, she starts stripping off her clothes, collapsing on the bed dressed only in her bra and pants. All Gareth manages is to kick off his shoes before kneeling over her and kissing her. It is Cassandra who strips off his clothes for him too.

Gareth finds the way she looks and feels so very different to Rachel deeply exciting. Rachel is slim and small chested, her stomach marked with the silver lines of four pregnancies. Cassandra is fuller and curvier and her breasts when he undoes her bra, almost jump into his hands. Her underwear is bubblegum pink and lacy and matching and her pubic hair is just a dark blonde strip down the middle whereas Rachel's is a full shock of red. She makes moaning sounds when he runs his fingers over her nipples that make him grow harder still. The sorts of sounds that Rachel used to make when they first met, before they started to make love quietly so the children didn't hear them. He does to Cassandra the things he does to Rachel and she responds with eagerness before telling him to slow down or he'll make her come. That and the way she says the word come just excites him even more. She makes him turn round so he is lying on his back and kneels over him to pay a great deal of attention to his cock until he too has to tell her to slow down. When he does finally enter her, they both come quickly, together, and fiercely, and then lie, side by side, for a while without talking.

196

"That was amazing," she says, eventually. "You really know how to touch a woman."

"Thank you."

"Tell me when you're ready to go again."

"How about right now?"

Afterwards, they fall asleep. When the alarm on his phone goes off Gareth wakes, startled, and jumps out of the bed.

"I've got to go, that's my alarm. I need to go pick up Nora from gym. Rachel has a partners' meeting tonight."

"No need to explain. You'd better get going then," she says, sleepily. When he's dressed, he stands by the door before opening it.

"Cassandra?"

"I know," she says, face turned into the pillow, "it was a one off, it can't happen ever again, you're sorry, and you'll get another lawyer to act for Perfect."

"Is that the sort of line Adrian Matthews gave you?"

"I only had dinner with Adrian Matthews, not sex."

"I'm relieved to hear it. That wasn't what I was going to say, anyway."

She turns her face away from the pillow and looks at him. "No? What were you going to say then?"

"I was actually going to say stay right where you are. Don't get out of that bed. I'm going to collect Nora and take her home for Eloise or Grace to watch and I'm going to pack an overnight bag quickly and leave a message for Rachel that you need me in London for a late meeting and I won't be home till tomorrow. And then I'm going to come back here and fuck you again."

"Go quickly then. Hurry, so you get back sooner."

*

A few minutes after he's gone, Cassandra gets out of bed and retrieves her phone.

She sends a message to each of Eloise and Liam by text.

197

"Spoken to HR. Jobs waiting for you both. I have a two bed furnished maisonette in the Annex (student quarter, near the University of Toronto) that I rent out that is coming free end of the month. You can have it for the summer with my compliments. Let me know."

And when she's done that, she makes a phone call to her partner, Beverley Allen, in Toronto.

"Is it all going to plan?" her partner asks.

"Yes, I believe so."

"And is Eloise in play?"

"Yes, all in hand."

"Do you think Gareth suspects?"

"Not in the slightest. Hasn't got a clue."

"Good. What are you up to this evening?"

"Oh, nothing much. Might go out for dinner with Adrian Matthews again. He's been a great source of useful information."

"Again? He'll be getting ideas! Or do I have to be worried you might actually like him?"

"Don't be silly Bev. I've not had the slightest interest in men since I met you. I think you can rest assured I'm not going back to cock now."

"Don't be vulgar Cassandra, it doesn't suit you."

"Well don't accuse me of flirting with men, then. You know I'm doing all this for you."

"I know, I know, I'm sorry."

"Forget about it. It's not true anyway. I'm not doing it just for you. I'm doing it for us both. You sound tired. How are you feeling?"

"Not so good, been a rough day today."

"Get some rest. I've got some more meetings so I won't call again today, so as not to disturb you. We'll talk again tomorrow about the next steps."

"OK, I'll try to have a nap now. I love you, Cassandra, and I miss you terribly."

"Me too, Beverley, me too. I'll be home soon."

*

She half expects him not to come back, having thought better of it once he'd got home, but an hour or so later she hears tapping on her door. She opens the door a crack and peeks through to see him leaning on the doorframe, smiling at her. She grabs his shirt and pulls him inside.

Chapter 21

"We're going to have to discuss it with your father, Eloise. You know fine well I am not going to agree to you skipping off to Toronto to live in a total stranger's flat without talking to him about it."

"I know but I'm just so excited about it, I thought I'd get you onside with it first and then we could tackle him together."

"I don't know about that Eloise. You're only 17. You and Liam have only been together five minutes. Your father and I both thought you'd be coming to Tresaith with us again this year. And what about Grace? I thought you wanted to get close to her."

"I'm not coming to Tresaith this year, Mum, even if you stop me going to Toronto. We've been there every summer since I can remember and it's just boring. And Grace and I are close already and she's much more interested in Jake than she is me. Anyway, she's writing her novel now and she loves doing that and she's way happier than she was. Please get Dad to agree. Please."

"Where is he anyway? I'm a bit pissed off with him to be honest. I ask him just for one night to be home on time and get dinner on, and I get home knackered to find you've been dumped with the kids and there's no food in the house."

"I told you Mum. He had to go up to London for a meeting with Cassandra. Says he'll be home tomorrow and he'll call you later if he can but it's likely to be an all-nighter. And he gave me money to order pizza and everyone else has eaten and it's all cleared away with plenty left over for you."

"You've tidied up?"

"Yes, and Grace and I gave them all baths and read them stories and sorted out school uniform for tomorrow."

"My, you really are serious about this Toronto trip aren't you?"

"Yes I am. Wouldn't you be Mum? I really like Liam and I think he really likes me. Cassandra is not a total stranger, she's one of Dad's clients. You like her too, don't pretend you don't. And she's lined us up with jobs in Toronto and somewhere to stay. You always say we need to grab life with both hands. Well that's exactly what I'm trying to do. And it'll look good on my CV."

"Ah, the killer teenager negotiation tactic. I'll look good on my CV! So when you say you really like Liam is that your way of telling me you two are having sex?"

"Omigod, Mum, why do you have to be so upfront and just come out with the question like that? Why can't you be like some of the other mums at school and just tell me you've put something in my bedside cabinet drawer for me and then wink?"

"And what precisely would I be putting in the bedside cabinet drawer?

"What do you think? A big box of condoms."

"Are condoms your preferred choice of birth control?"

"Of course they are! Liam's been at university in London for the past year. I don't know who he might have slept with before. It's not just getting pregnant I'm worried about you know?"

"Very sensible."

"I am sensible Mother."

"But just to be clear, you've not had sex with him as yet?"

"Not yet, no. And just to be clear, for the avoidance of doubt as you like to say, that's all I am prepared to say on the matter now or in the future."

"So do you still want me to put condoms in your bedside drawer?"

Eloise groans through gritted teeth. "Don't worry Mum. I've sorted out my own condoms. Go! Eat your pizza will you?"

Cassandra has ordered room service. Gareth hides in the bathroom while it's being delivered.

"That's a bit unnecessary isn't it? Who's the waiter going to tell?"

"You never know Cassandra. Everyone knows everyone else's business in Cardiff. I'm not joking!"

"Fine, stay in there if you like."

"I fully intend to." He shuts the bathroom door.

Once the food is delivered, Cassandra whistles softly.

"Coast is clear. You can come out now."

They wolf down a burger and chips each and glug cold beers straight out of the bottle.

"All that sex has made me ravenous," Cassandra says, finishing her beer and wiping crumbs off her bathrobe. "Right then lover boy, hurry up and finish eating. I actually do have a meeting in London tomorrow morning and I've got a driver picking me up at 6am. I need some shut-eye. I hope you don't snore."

Gareth does not sleep well, the burger and chips churning noisily in his stomach. He lies listening to Cassandra next to him, breathing gently. Her breathing sounds nothing like Rachel's, which strikes him as odd. Is breathing like a person's voice? Individual to them? He feels guilt washing over him but also waves of excitement and desire. He has always thought he and Rachel have a good and enjoyable sex life but after today it strikes him that it may over the years have become functional and formulaic. Today with Cassandra has been sweaty and messy and joyous too and despite having had more sex today than he possibly has ever had with Rachel in one day, just thinking about it makes his balls ache. And then he remembers the trusting look on Nora's face earlier that afternoon when he'd bundled her in through the front door, calling for Eloise to come downstairs, running upstairs to throw a few things in his bag and barely saying goodbye in his eagerness to get back to Cassandra and he feels guilt land on his chest like a breezeblock.

At some point he falls asleep and wakes up in the pitch dark to find Cassandra whispering in his ear.

"Want to fuck me again?"

He's still half asleep but when she peels the sheet off him, he finds that his body has responded to her whisper and that he really does want to fuck her again, very much indeed.

He sits in bed and watches her as she finishes dressing and packing her bags. She has already pushed back the time of her meeting in London and the driver of her car has been waiting outside for her for over an hour but she seems reluctant to leave him.

"What happens now?" he asks.

"I have no idea. Do you?"

"Not the faintest."

"You're a married man."

"I was a married man before any of this happened. "

"So you were. And my personal life is more complicated than I led you to believe."

"I thought you said you weren't with anyone."

"I said I wasn't married and didn't have kids. That's all true."

"Why didn't you mention your complicated personal life before now?"

"It was none of your business before now."

"Fair enough."

Cassandra's phone pings. "It's the driver. He's saying if we don't leave in the next five minutes, we'll get caught up in heavy traffic going into London. I've got to go." She comes back over to the bed and leans in to kiss him on the cheek.

"You really are fucking gorgeous," she says, running her finger along his jawline.

He smiles. "When can I see you again?"

"I'm flying back to Canada tonight."

"Tonight? You didn't mention that. Can you postpone it?"

"Not really. My girlfriend is expecting me."

"Your *girlfriend?*"

"Uh huh, my girlfriend. Let's just try and compartmentalise shall we? This is, well, whatever it is, and work is work. I'll be in touch on both counts."

As she opens the door of the room and rolls her bag through it, she stops and looks back over her shoulder at him.

"Gareth?"

"Yes."

"Eloise is going to ask you something today. When she does, you really must say yes. Believe me, it's in all our interests."

"What's that supposed to mean?" Gareth asks, but the door is already closing behind her and if she hears him, she doesn't answer him.

*

After such an early start, Gareth is the first in the office. He waits till 7.30am and then calls Rachel.

"Just making sure you're awake," he says, forcing himself to sound cheery.

"Just about. It's much harder when no one brings me a cup of tea in bed. Where are you?"

He has his answer ready for this one. "In the office already. Meeting finished in the early hours and I decided to take up Cassandra's offer of a car to bring me back to Cardiff rather than trying to find a hotel at that time of night. Came straight to the office rather than disturb you."

"You must be shattered!"

"I'll survive. I managed to get a couple of hours sleep in the car. I've had a shower here in the office, which has perked me up a bit. There's a few things I need to get done and then I'm going to come home early, try for a nap."

"Haven't you got squash tonight? It's Tuesday?"

"I'm going to skip squash." Actually Gareth has lost track of the days and hadn't realised it is Tuesday.

"It must have been a heck of a long night then for you to miss squash. I don't think you've missed a game of squash since before Nora was born."

"Very funny, Rachel."

"I'll see you at home later then. Karen is taking Jake to Jo Jingles at the library this afternoon and then picking up Nora after school to go swimming so if you time it right you could have the house to yourself for a couple of hours. Can you put the stuff that's in the washing machine on the line when you get in if it looks like it's not going to rain and have a look in the freezer for something we can have for dinner tonight?"

"OK."

Gareth puts the phone down wearily, suddenly overwhelmed with tiredness and longing for Cassandra Taylor. He checks his watch, then his emails and his text messages. She should have arrived back in London by now but there is nothing from her in his inbox. He deliberates for a while then sends her a text.

What time is your flight? Really need to talk with you before you go.

Twenty minutes later she responds. *Needed to cancel London meetings and go straight to Heathrow. Already in departure lounge.*

He rings her but she doesn't answer. He tries again and this time she picks up.

"Don't go," he says. "Please don't go, not today. I need to talk to you, I need to see you again. Stay there. I'll drive up to Heathrow right now."

"I can't do that Gareth. I'm sorry. I have to get back to Toronto."

"When are you coming back?"

205

"I'm not certain. Not for a little while. I have things I need to attend to. We can work together on the factory project by email, not to worry."

"I wasn't talking about the factory Cassandra. I was talking about you and me."

"That's more complicated. I need to process how I'm feeling. It's all very confusing."

"That's a fucking understatement."

"I've got to go Gareth." She hangs up. When he tries her number again, her phone is switched off.

He tries to work, staring at his computer screen, drinking the coffee that Celia brings him. Finally at lunchtime he gives up.

"I need to push off now Celia," he explains. "Some domestic stuff I need to sort out at home."

"OK," she says, barely looking up from her kiwi fruit. "See you tomorrow."

"See you tomorrow."

As he lets himself into an empty house, it strikes Gareth that he is never home alone. There is always someone or other in the house whenever he gets home from work. And even now the house is not entirely empty. Oscar jumps up off the sofa and rushes out into the hallway, his claws clattering on the tiles, to greet him energetically. He spots Jake's pram and jumps into it, indicating his willingness to go for a walk.

"Not today mate," Gareth says, walking straight past him and up the stairs to the bedroom.

He hesitates for a while by the side of the bed. Just yesterday afternoon he was climbing into bed with Cassandra Taylor for the first time. And now here he is, looking at his wife's side of the bed, at the dent in her pillow her head made while she slept alone last night, thinking he was in a late meeting in London, not knowing he was just across the city, sleeping with someone else. He lies down on his side of the bed. After a few moments he rolls across, pushing his face into Rachel's pillow, breathing in his wife's scent, a mixture of her shampoo and face cream and perfume. Then he rolls back over onto his side, disgusted with himself because this scent, so familiar to him and which smells like home and family and love, is not the perfume he wants to smell right now. He is disgusted and disappointed in himself but these feelings are insignificant compared to how utterly bereft he feels that he is not with Cassandra Taylor.

He must have fallen asleep because Eloise wakes him by knocking on the door.

"You all right Dad? I brought you a cup of tea. Mum said you'd be home early and that if you were in bed to leave you sleep for a while but to wake you up before 5pm and remind you about finding something for dinner in the freezer."

Gareth struggles to sit up, fuzzy in sleep.

"Don't worry. I found some fish fingers and some manky looking oven chips, covered in ice but I think they'll be OK. They'll do for dinner, with a couple of tins of beans. Oh and Mum also said that if you did put out the washing to bring it in because it's raining now, but there's none out there anyway."

Gareth flops gratefully back onto the bed. "Did I ever tell you you're an excellent daughter?"

"Did you speak to Cassandra, Dad?"

For a panicky moment, Gareth thinks that somehow Eloise knows what happened last night, knows that he had so much wanted to speak to Cassandra this morning but that she turned her phone off so he couldn't talk her into staying in London. Then he gathers himself.

"Talk to Cassandra about what?"

"About the jobs for Liam and me in Toronto?"

"I have absolutely no clue what you mean."

"That's funny cos she texted me this morning and said she'd spoken to you and that you were going to be absolutely OK with it."

"Start at the beginning, Eloise."

"Cassandra has arranged for me and Liam to have jobs at Perfect in Toronto for a month and also somewhere for us to stay, starting next week. We really, really want to go and Mum says she's OK with it if you are. Cassandra said in her text this morning that because she had to get back to Canada today, that she needs you to come out to Toronto anyway as soon as possible for meetings and stuff and that she'll organise flights for us all to go over together next week. You'll be able to see for yourself then that Liam and I are settled."

Gareth shakes his head. He feels like there is cotton wool rammed into his ears. Like he can't hear Eloise properly although her words are clear as day.

"Run that past me again. You and Liam have jobs with Cassandra in Toronto and are going for a whole month. And I'm to escort you both out there next week on my way to meetings at Perfect?"

"Yep, that's the gist of it."

Gareth remembers what Cassandra said before she left, only that morning but which already feels like it was days ago. Something about him needing to agree to his daughter's request because it would be in both their interests. He hates the idea of his first born being on the other side of the world, can't even begin to get his head round the fact that she will almost certainly be sleeping with Liam while there, if she is not already, but more than that, he feels his whole body lighten at the prospect of seeing Cassandra again in just a few days.

"I'll have to think about it," he says, gruffly, "and talk to your mother about it."

But he already knows he's going to say yes.

Chapter 22

Idris is high up on a ladder, plastering the ceiling, when Aeronwen's father bursts into the apartment above the shop. He takes one look at his future father-in-law's face and quickly climbs down.

"What's the matter, Mr James?"

Mr James thrusts the letter in front of Idris' nose.

"What do you call this, boy?"

Idris recognises Maggie's handwriting immediately, from years sat next to her in school. He would sit as close as possible to her on one side, Tommy as close as possible to her on the other.

"It's a letter from my sister-in-law I believe."

"Your sister-in-law? Or the mother of your son?"

"Oh."

"So you don't deny it?"

"Deny what Mr James?"

"That you have a son in Wales already? That you were intimate with your own brother's wife?"

"It is my brother that has a son, Mr James. But I can't deny the latter, no."

"You are a disgrace Idris Maddox. An abomination to family values. Don't think for one minute that you shall be marrying my daughter after this. If you can't stay true to your own brother, you are certainly not worthy of my daughter."

Idris feels a familiar heat of anger rising up through him and instinctively curls his hands into fists, but manages to keep calm. "Mr James, you have not as yet afforded me the opportunity to

209

read the letter but I can assure you that the situation is more complicated than it appears. I am not at all a dishonourable man."

"By your own admission, you have dishonoured your brother."

"If you would let me explain Mr James, to you and to Aeronwen, I am sure this can be overcome. I love Aeronwen a great deal, Sir. I will be a good husband to her."

"That you will not Idris. Now get out."

"Get out?"

"Get out of my property before I call the police."

"If that is your wish Mr James, then I will of course comply. But I must speak with Aeronwen. It is her that I am engaged to, not you. If she no longer wishes to marry me, she must tell me herself."

"You can take it from me that she does not wish to marry you."

"I will, if I must, take Aeronwen's word for that, but not yours Mr James."

At this, Aeronwen appears in the doorway from where she has been listening to the conversation. Her face is stained with tears and her voice is low, her throat scraped by tears, but she speaks clearly.

"I do not wish to marry you Idris. I never want to see your deceitful face again, not here, not in church, not anywhere. Get out and don't come back."

"Please let me explain, Aeronwen?"

"There is nothing to explain. I do not want another woman's soiled goods. I do not want to be married to a man who has no morals and might perhaps chance his arm with *my* sisters one day. I should never have taken up with you again after the Jean incident. I should have known that you were common scum like her. Goodbye, Idris."

"You've got fifteen minutes to pack your bags," Mr James says. "I shall stand here and watch you."

It takes even less time than that for Idris to stuff his few possessions into the same suitcase he brought with him from home. He has acquired very little in his time in Canada.

Mr James escorts him out the door. He crumples Maggie's letter into a ball and throws it in Idris' face and then, almost like an afterthought, he whips the hat from off his head.

"You don't deserve anything of mine," he calls after Idris as he walks away.

*

Not knowing what else to do, Idris starts walking to Union Station. He pauses for a while at the site immediately opposite the station where a grand new hotel is being built by the Canadian Pacific Railway. It is to be called the Royal York and Canadian Pacific say it is going to be the largest hotel in the British Commonwealth, with 28 floors and over a 1000 rooms, each one with its own private bathroom. There might be work there for a hard working, strong man with construction experience such as himself. One of his workmates from the railway viaduct will be able to recommend good lodgings. He could come back tomorrow morning when the site is open and make enquiries. Maybe, if he just gave Aeronwen and her family some time, he could fight for her. Woo her until he eventually wins her back. He tarries for a while outside the site, thinking about this possibility, and then he carries on walking.

He enters Union Station and finds a bench in the Great Hall. He sits for a very long time, staring at the arched ceiling and beautiful inlaid tiles and watching people in their Sunday best come and go. He reads over and over again the place names carved high up in the walls of the Great Hall that he has always liked. Some of the place names he is familiar with by now and others he still does not know. Prince Rupert, Edmonton, Saskatoon, Halifax, Quebec, Montreal, Hamilton, Moose Jaw, Calgary, Vancouver.

He could take a train to any of these destinations. The place names sound promising, full of possibility. He has started all over again once already. He can do it again. He found work, a home, a community and love very quickly after arriving in Canada. He need only pick one of these places and then go looking again.

He reads Maggie's letter over and over, each time smoothing the single page out carefully, flattening the creases made by Mr James, before putting it back in his pocket.

It grows dark and the station starts to empty. Soon the last train of the day to any of these places will have gone. But Idris continues to sit, thinking about his family at home in Wales. Each time he reads Maggie's letter he sees again the little house on the side of the hill where he grew up and his mother's stolen garden, crammed full with plants. He hears the tramp of men's feet in the early morning on their way to the pits, his brother and father amongst them. He feels the weight of Gwen's last embrace.

He sees Maggie's beautiful face, the way she looked at him during their last times together before he left for Canada, can picture it as if she were right there in front of him. He conjures up Aeronwen's face instead and when he doesn't feel for her the ache of longing he feels when he thinks of Maggie, he knows he is not going to stay in Toronto and try to woo Aeronwen back.

But Maggie's letter has done more than bring an end to his engagement to Aeronwen and the new life he had created for himself in Toronto. He had chosen to believe that Tommy was Davey's father, conceived before he was persuaded by Maggie to lie with her again on the top of Clydach mountain. And now that Maggie has told him that Davey is definitely his son, he knows he will not go home to Wales again either. He is not a dishonourable man, whatever Aeronwen and her father may think of him, and he will make sure that Tommy and Davey never learn the truth. Of all the places in the world that Idris may travel to, Wales is not and never will be one of them.

Eventually, he digs his thick winter coat out from his suitcase, rolls it up like a pillow and lies down on the bench. He manages to sleep for a few hours till morning. When he wakes up, cold and stiff, he has made a decision about where to go. He takes the first train of the day to Oshawa.

*

As he walks through the gates of the Parkwood Estate, Idris suddenly feels rather foolish. Jean had written to him congratulating him on his engagement and some time after that had sent a postcard of the buffalo at Lakeview Park, informing him that they remained very smelly. He has sent her no word at all in return, only asking Mrs Williams when he sees her at church to add in her letters to Jean his best wishes and fond memories.

As he trudges round the back to the servant's entrance, he is waylaid by Mr Wragg.

"You turned up again then, like the proverbial bad penny. Took you longer than I expected."

"Good morning Mr Wragg. I've come to visit Jean."

"I figured it wasn't me you were coming to see son. Does she know you are coming?"

"She is not expecting me, no."

"Well you won't find her in the house anymore, she works with me now in the gardens. Follow me, I think she's over in the potting shed."

Mr Wragg delivers Idris to the general vicinity of the potting shed and then drops back, saying vaguely that he has things to attend to elsewhere in the garden. Idris stands at the door of the potting shed and peers in. He has never before seen as many clay pots. Hundreds and hundreds of them, all shapes and sizes, stacked up inside each other. The potting shed is long and narrow and dim inside and it takes Idris a little while to spot Jean working inside. She has her back to him and is sorting through the piles of pots, putting those that are cracked to one side. She is wearing an oversized burlap apron and her hair is twisted up on top of her head. There is a pencil behind her ear.

He watches her for a while, humming to herself as she works, methodically but quickly working her way through the pots. She has changed a great deal since he saw her last. Then she had been pale and weak after her operation, childlike. Now she has rounded into a woman, may even be taller than she was, and she is tanned from working outside, her hair lightened by the sun.

"Good morning, Jean," he says, quietly.

Her hands stop moving across the pots. "Idris?" she says, her back to him still and then all of a sudden she is turning around and flinging her arms around his neck and grinning at him. The look of joy on her face suddenly fades.

"What's wrong? Why are you here? Is someone ill? Has something happened to Mr and Mrs Williams?"

"Nothing like that. Nothing bad at all really, depending on how you look at it. Aeronwen has called off our engagement. That leaves me with no job and no home as well as no fiancée so I thought… Well, I thought I'd have a look at Oshawa, see what there is here in terms of opportunity for a collier with some recently acquired business skills. I have one friend here at least, or at least I hope I do."

"Of course I'm your friend, Idris, I always will be," Jean says, softly. "Come, let's go over to the kitchen. It's time for our tea break anyway. Mr Wragg knows everything that is going on in Oshawa, he'll know where there might be vacancies."

"You must apply to General Motors, of course," Mr Wragg says as he sips his tea. "A position can't be guaranteed of course, but Colonel Sam is very fond of our young Jean. She always makes sure that the biggest and reddest strawberries are kept for Sam's breakfast. That will stand you in good stead. One of my boys will be able to recommend good lodgings for the time being, until you two find something more permanent."

"Jean and I are just friends, Mr Wragg."

"As I said to you the last time you were here son, if you say so. If you say so."

214

Idris is taken on at General Motors. He is not popular as a result. The company has recently quashed a series of walkouts by its 3,400 workers demanding better conditions by firing or buying out trade union leaders. Idris has been given a full time position, which is a sore point with many of his fellow workers who are kept underemployed on part time hours.

"It's not fair at all," Idris tells Jean one Sunday as they walk round Lakeview Park, as they do most Sundays. They now know the park is on land originally acquired in 1920 by Colonel Sam's father Robert McLaughlin and his brother George for General Motors and which they later deeded to the Town of Oshawa on condition that the land was used as a public park for its citizens.

"Most of them get so few hours they can't feed their families. No one is allowed to take breaks and if anyone complains they get fired. No wonder people want to join the union."

"Please don't get involved, Idris," says Jean. "It puts me in an impossible position with the Colonel and Mrs Adelaide. "

He does as Jean asks and keeps out of union politics, focussing instead on working hard at General Motors and accepting any overtime that is offered to him. He writes to his mother and tells her of the broken engagement which he describes as being for the best and of his new job and his new address.

It is during one of their walks round Lakeview Park that Idris tells Jean about Maggie and their son. She listens patiently and when he has finished, she asks him.

"Did you do what Maggie asked of you out of love?"

He thinks about this for a while. "Only partly. The other part was selfish. Out of love for myself. I wanted to be with her again before I left."

"That is honest, at least."

After six months at General Motors, and added to the money he saved while working in Toronto, Idris has earned enough to buy a small plot of land, not too far from Lakeview Park. Having proven himself a capable worker when converting the apartment above the hat shop in Toronto, he decides to build his own house. Other emigrants have already done the same on other plots nearby and slowly new streets are growing up around Oshawa. The builders share their experiences, taking turns to help each other out when more than one pair of hands is needed. Even combining forces in this way, without access to lifts or other machinery, all the houses being built are single storey affairs, short and squat.

Idris' house has two bedrooms, an indoor bathroom, a living room, a kitchen and a basement for the furnace. The plot of land is large enough to provide garden space both front and back. He moves in as soon as there are four walls and a roof. The fierce coldness of Ontario winters still takes his breath away but he manages to keep working on the house over the winter of 1928/1929. By the time the last snow is melting in the spring of 1929 the house is all but built.

The last room in the house to be decorated is the kitchen. Idris chooses a wallpaper from Eaton's with a design that mimics blue bricks, with every so often amongst the bricks a repeating pattern in Delft blue featuring a small tree with hanging branches. When he first tried wallpapering he'd been terrible at it, getting wallpaper paste everywhere, hanging the paper poorly and in some cases having to give up and start again with a fresh length of paper. But by the time he reaches the kitchen, the last room of the house, his skills have improved to the point where he can paper without thinking. He finds the work relaxing, soothing almost, and as he papers his mind drifts to the women he has loved.

He doesn't remember falling in love with Maggie. He's not clear when exactly she stopped being the girl that could beat him and his brother at arm wrestling and became the girl he couldn't stop staring at because she was so very pretty. By the time he couldn't stop staring at her, he'd already loved her for years. And so had his brother.

Falling in love with Aeronwen had happened quickly, almost from the moment of meeting her, and he'd fallen hard. Idris liked the way Aeronwen looked and the new life she represented so much, that even when he didn't like her very much, he still found her so attractive he could forget about how nasty and self-centred she could be.

He does however remember the precise moment when he fell in love with Jean. Or more correctly, the precise moment he finished falling in love with her. It was the day at Parkwood when he'd stood in the doorway of the potting shed, watching her work, and she was unaware he was there.

Idris finishes wallpapering the kitchen on schedule. The following Sunday is Jean's eighteenth birthday. He takes her down to the lakeshore for an ice cream and persuades her to take off her shoes and stockings and walk with him barefoot in the sand.

Just like on her sixteenth birthday, he pushes her on the Ocean Wave and as the ride dips and rises he watches how her hair blows in the breeze. He is glad that she has not followed the increasing fashion for short shingled hair and that her hair is still long.

He helps her get off the ride. She is still dizzy. Laughing, she leans against him and he stops and turns towards her.

"Will you marry me, Jean?"

She does not seem surprised at the proposal, but looks at him calmly.

"I have loved you almost from the first day we met and have hoped since you came to Oshawa that you and I might reach this point someday. Hoped it more than anything else in the world. But I must ask you something before I answer. May I?"

"Of course."

"Do you love Maggie, still?"

"A small part of me will always love her, yes, but the rest of me…the rest of me loves only you Jean."

"Are you sure?"

Idris looks in her eyes, slowly lifts his finger and then draws a cross in the air over his heart. "Cross my heart and hope to die."

"In that case Idris, yes. Yes, I will marry you."

Chapter 23

Gareth is glad of all the distraction of preparing for the trip to Toronto. Rachel and Eloise have put together a long list of things that must be done or washed or bought before she goes. The list includes inviting Liam and his parents round for a drink one evening.

"We can't just send our daughter off with their son for a month without meeting them, can we?" Rachel had insisted when Gareth had protested this was unnecessary. "It's just a drink, not a wedding rehearsal supper."

Liam's parents turn out to be as good-natured as their son. The four of them drink a bottle and a half of excellent Rioja between them and agree affably that their offspring are about to have a great adventure together and that yes of course Liam will take good care of Eloise. After they've gone, Rachel and Gareth share the remaining half of the bottle.

"There's a lot of subtext packed into taking good of care her isn't there?" Gareth says.

"Our daughter can take good care of herself, don't you worry." Rachel replies.

Each night before she leaves, Rachel and Eloise stay up late, working their way through the rest of the list and that allows Gareth to slink off and pretend to be asleep already when Rachel comes up to bed. He gets up every morning before she wakes up and goes running, staying out longer than usual so she is already up and dressed by the time he gets back. In this way he is able to limit intimate contact with her. The way Gareth is feeling at the moment if Rachel were to try to make love with him, he knows he would not be able to.

Because all he can think about is making love with Cassandra again. He burns with a lust laced with guilt that leaves him constantly swashing with shame and a desire so strong that he only has to think of her to feel himself stir. For the first day after returning to Canada she ignores his texts. On the second day he sends her a message

I miss you so much I can't sleep. How is that possible when I've only just met you?

This one gets a response

I miss you that much too.

And shortly after that she sends him a photograph of her breasts. She is wearing a black lacy bra. The image excites him so much he has to go have a wank in the bathroom.

He tells her as much by text.

Gareth becomes a secretive texter, taking his phone with him to the bathroom or out on his runs, constantly checking for messages from Cassandra, deleting the messages hastily once he has sent them, his heart still thumping with excitement.

"You're worse than the kids," Rachel comments one evening. "Who are you talking to?"

"Just work." But he is a little more careful after that.

At long last, it is the night before they are leaving very early the next morning. It is time for the little piles of clean, ironed clothes and plastic bags full of purchases from Boots that have been laid out along the landing to be packed away in Eloise's suitcase. For some reason, Rachel has insisted that everyone should gather on the landing to witness this.

"I'm sure that if I should suffer from diarrhoea while I'm in

220

Toronto I'll be able to buy Immodium there Mum. And I haven't taken Calpol since I was 12."

"Better safe than sorry," Rachel mutters, checking items off her list furiously.

Nora has selected one of her favourite Beanie Boos to go to Toronto with Eloise. She pushes a pink striped fox into Eloise's hands.

"Something to remember me by," she says dramatically, gulping down tears.

"Oh but you love this one Nonnie, I can't take it with me, you'll miss it too much."

"I'm going to miss you more."

This makes Eloise cry and, in turn, all the other girls, even Iris who hardly ever cries.

"Good heavens, girls," Gareth says, "she's only going for a month. She's not emigrating for good you know."

"That's easy for you to say," Rachel retorts, angrily. "You get to drop her off and then swan around Toronto for who knows how long afterwards while the rest of us are stuck here. And my mother has announced she and Felix are coming to visit because Grace is here and you're away which means she tells me that they can have our bedroom and I can have Eloise's."

"I would hardly call it swanning around Rachel. Don't pick a fight with me because you're upset Eloise is going away. It's just work."

"Well it's a darn sight more interesting work than I've got on at the moment. Maybe we should all come with you now that school's finished. We could make it our summer holiday and skip Tresaith this year. And it gets us out of a visit from my mother. Grace, you could come with us if you want."

Grace nods eagerly.

"Can we Dad, can we please," begs Nora. "It would be so much fun."

Gareth goes sweaty with panic. He can't think of an answer

221

quick enough that will prevent this idea from gaining steam because it is, after all, exactly the sort of thing that up until a week ago he might have suggested. When he says nothing, Eloise steps in.

"No way! This is my adventure – me and Liam's – it's bad enough Dad's got to tag along for the start of it but there's no bloody way the rest of you are muscling in on things."

Gareth manages to collect himself. "And it won't be any sort of a holiday for me, stuck in meetings all day."

"OK, fine, it was just a thought," Rachel sighs, bending to scoop up Jake who has curled up inside Eloise's suitcase and is trying to hide under a pile of t-shirts. "Right you lot, give Eloise and your Dad a kiss goodnight, they'll be gone in the morning when you wake up."

"Do I get any help packing my suitcase?" Gareth asks.

"No," they all say in unison.

*

At Heathrow airport, Gareth reveals that he has a business class ticket whereas Eloise and Liam are in economy.

"That's just selfish Dad!" Eloise complains.

"I didn't order the tickets, Perfect did. Nothing to do with me. And anyway, you don't want your old Dad sitting in between you and Liam here, getting in the way of love's young dream, do you?"

"If you'd rather spend some quality time with your daughter Mr Maddox, I don't mind swapping seats with you."

"Very gracious of you Liam, I'm sure. And please call me Gareth. It just makes me feel old when you call me Mr Maddox. Why don't you two go find yourselves something to eat? Here's £20. I'm off to the business club lounge to do a bit of work before the flight. I'll see you when we're boarding."

Gareth contemplates accepting the glass of champagne he is offered on entering the lounge but decides it is just too early and

222

goes for a double espresso instead. He logs into the wifi and as his emails download, he spots instantly that there are a number from Cassandra. Most are her responses to emails he has sent her, giving her input on documents he's drafted. One is marked personal.

"I have arranged for the three of you to be picked up by a car at the airport. The car will take Liam and Rachel to the apartment and there'll be someone from the letting agency I use waiting for them there to let them in and show them round. The car will then take you immediately to the Fairmont Royal York where I've booked a room for you. I will meet you there. I can't wait."

Gareth immediately deletes the email in case Celia reads it and adjusts his trousers to accommodate the beginnings of a hard on. He is already feeling rather odd down there. This morning during his early morning shower and already thinking about Cassandra's exciting strip of pubic hair that he will see again soon, he had on a whim grabbed Rachel's razor and given himself for the first time ever a little trim. He had been very impressed with his first attempt at this as he thought it made his dick look bigger. But by now it is a little itchy. It is going to be a long flight.

*

The Annex area of Toronto turns out to be a neighbourhood of tree-lined one-way streets of Edwardian and Victorian houses, mostly red brick with bay windows and tall, pointed, gables.

"It's so lovely round here," Eloise says, as they pull up outside one of these houses.

"It looks an awful lot like Penarth really," Liam comments.

"Possibly. But in Penarth we live with our parents and here we live with each other," Eloise says, smugly. She waits for her father to respond with a groan or a swat across the head but he appears not to have heard.

A smiling letting agency looking person with a clipboard standing on the street waves at the car.

Gareth knows that really he should get out of the car and escort his first-born into the apartment where she is going to be living with her boyfriend for the next month, but he can only think of Cassandra waiting for him at the hotel.

"OK this must be you," he says, curtly. "Out you get. I'll give you a call this evening. Hurry up now. I'm late for my meeting. Have fun settling in."

Before he arrives at the hotel he texts Rachel quickly, so that the job is out the way and he need not think about it while he is with Cassandra.

All arrived, Eloise safely delivered, meeting now, call you tomorrow, love you.

Seconds later his phone pings, delivering a row of kisses. *xxxx*

*

He actually feels a little lightheaded, knocking on the door of the suite in the Fairmont Royal York. Partly jet lag, partly due to having had a hard on stirring for most of the day.

He opens the door with his key card and there she is, lying naked on the bed waiting for him. She says nothing, just puts her finger to her lips signalling to him to keep quiet, and pats the bed next to her.

*

All the time that Gareth has been away from Cassandra, counting down the days until this one, he has been preparing the questions

224

he wants to ask her about her girlfriend. Is it a long-term thing? Has Cassandra always liked both men and women? Which does she prefer?

But while he and Cassandra make love he forgets all about these questions and loses himself in how she feels against him and around him and on top of him.

*

"Wake up, Gareth. You need to start thinking about getting in the shower."

"Uh?" For a moment Gareth thinks he is in his bed at home, dreaming of Cassandra, before he realises he is in a hotel room and that Cassandra is there with him stroking his arm.

"What's happening?"

"We're going over to the apartment in the Annex for drinks with Eloise and Liam."

Now he is wide-awake. "We are absolutely not going to do that." He makes quote marks with his fingers and attempts a female Canadian voice, "*Oh hello Eloise and your boyfriend Liam, you've probably been fucking all afternoon, like me and your dad here.*" He reverts to his own accent. "That's bizarre."

"No more than you having me round for Sunday supper with your family or your daughter and her boyfriend working for me this summer and living in my apartment. Compartmentalise Gareth, please. And you'd better be good at it. My girlfriend is joining us and we're picking her up on the way over. We live just a few blocks away from the apartment."

"What the fuck, Cassandra. That's not just bizarre, that's twisted."

"No it's not. My girlfriend is Beverley Allen, also my business partner in Perfect. She wants to meet this Welsh lawyer I've been emailing so much and meet his daughter."

"Does she know we're sleeping together?"

225

"Of course she fucking doesn't. She thinks that I'm her lesbian girlfriend of twenty years and faithful. She thinks that what you and me have been doing all afternoon is working on legal agreements, not on each other. Remember that."

"I don't want to do this, Cassandra. I think it's a really bad idea."

"Tough shit. You have to. Now come on, let's go get in the shower, I'm going to tidy up that appalling hack job you did on your poor bush – what did you use? A Bic?"

*

The letting agent lady doesn't hang around long. She hands Liam and Eloise a set of keys each and her business card and tells them that there are instructions inside the apartment as to how everything works and to ring her if they have any problems. Then she leaves them to it.

The apartment is on the very top floor of one of the red brick Victorian houses, up two flights of stairs. Liam struggles with the lock for a few seconds until he finds the right pressure to use and then the door opens easily onto an open plan living/kitchen area with large bay windows that let in lots of light. The apartment has parquet wooden floors, white painted woodwork and the walls are painted a soft, dove grey throughout. There is a lot of artwork on the walls – landscapes mostly in bright colours – orange, purple, and greens – more vibrant than real life.

Liam whistles softly. "Nice," he says appreciatively.

"Very nice," Eloise agrees.

They check out the living room that has two large squashy sofas and a low wooden coffee table.

"No telly?" Liam questions.

Eloise opens the door of a French looking white painted armoire revealing a large television and DVD concealed inside.

The kitchen area has a small wooden table that would sit four at a push, covered in a white tablecloth embroidered with small yellow flowers. On it, there is a note from Cassandra.

Welcome to the Annex. I hope you will enjoy your stay here. There are some basic provisions in the refrigerator for you and also the fixings for champagne cocktails because my business partner and I, Beverley, are going to be your first guests in your new place and are coming round for drinks at 7pm. We'll bring Gareth along too. Make yourselves comfortable and see you later.

She has added a smiley, winking face next to her signature.

They rush around opening all the other doors in the apartment. The bathroom has an old-fashioned roll top bath and white tiles with a blue fleur-de-lys pattern. One small bedroom is being used as a study and is lined with bookshelves. It has a large wooden desk and two old fashioned wooden filing cabinets. And there is one large bedroom, containing a modern king-size bed made up with white linen, bedside tables either side with a lamp on each and large wardrobes running all along one wall.

Liam and Eloise hesitate at the door of this one.

"Right then," Eloise says, grinning, "I bagsy this one. You can kip on the sofa."

"I will if you'd like me to," Liam says, gently. "We don't have to share a bed."

"Oh but I want to," Eloise says firmly. "Very much. It's just I don't want to share a bed with you right this very minute, if you know what I mean. It would feel all wrong. And my Dad's coming round for drinks later, apparently…" She fades out.

Liam pulls Eloise towards him and hugs her.

"I agree, all wrong. There's no rush Eloise, we're here for a whole month. I fancy you like mad, you know that, fancied you the whole of my last year in school but you never noticed. But I wasn't actually hoping we'd crack on with having sex the second your dad left. We don't have to do anything. Not until you want to."

Eloise looks visibly relieved. "Are you OK with that?"

"Of course I am. So, how about we go out for a walk and explore? Maybe get an ice cream or something."

"Great idea."

*

In his rush to get to Cassandra, Gareth had paid no attention to the location of the Fairmont Royal York and if anyone had asked him a few hours ago what it looked like he could not have told them. Now while he and Cassandra wait for her car to be brought round to her, and Gareth tries very hard to compartmentalise as instructed, he sees they are directly opposite the train station and that the CN tower is very close by. He cranes his neck up at the hotel, squinting in the afternoon sunshine.

"When was this hotel built? 1930s?"

"Close. It opened in 1929."

"It's impressive now but it must have been something else back then."

"It was indeed. The tallest building in the British Empire when it was built. There's a rooftop garden on the 14th floor where they grow herbs and there are beehives too. Car's here.

"Now don't forget. You're Perfect's lawyer. You're a good lawyer. We spent all afternoon together working. No long looks, no touching, no in-jokes. Just business. Got it?"

"Got it. Don't worry. My daughter's going to be there, too, remember."

"I mean it Gareth. I don't want Beverley to suspect anything. We've been together a very long time, since I first graduated from fashion college and got a job at Perfect as an intern. It was just a start up back then. Beverley was the boss and 15 years older than me and up until I met her I'd only ever been with men and it had never crossed my mind I might fancy a woman. But she – well, she just blew my mind – she was so talented and driven and so very beautiful and she was absolutely determined to have me, even though I was so much younger than her and it wasn't the done thing to sleep with a junior member of staff."

"Why on earth are you sleeping with me then?" A hot spike of jealousy stabs through Gareth.

"Why are *you* sleeping with *me*? It's very obvious that you and Rachel are happily married. Why cheat on her with me?"

"I…I really don't know the answer to that. I've never been unfaithful before. You're the only woman I've met since Rachel that I've fancied. And I just can't stop thinking about you. Not for one second."

"Well for the next few hours, please remember that nothing at all is going on between us."

Chapter 24

Cassandra pulls up outside a house. It's another period property, this one very large, in immaculate condition. It has a turret along one side, three round rooms on top of each other with curved bay windows. The windows get smaller the higher the storey, and the top floor looks like it is wearing a pointy tin hat. There is a porch that wraps around three sides of the ground floor and Gareth spots a wooden swing seat at one end. The lawn at the front is beautifully kept and there's a sprinkler twirling on it, spitting water evenly across the green of the lawn and catching rainbows in the evening sunshine.

"Beautiful house," he says to Cassandra. He swallows down the next sentence that comes into his head. *Rachel would love that house.*

"Thanks," Cassandra replies and beeps her horn.

Gareth watches as a tall lady comes out the door and makes her way to the car. She has blonde hair, cropped short and has a pair of overlarge white sunglasses stuck on top of her head. She is wearing a pale pink blouse, ruffled around the neck, white, wide legged trousers cropped to the ankle and high heeled strappy shoes. Around her neck is a string of enormous pale pink pearls, like sherbet bonbons.

"Good evening," the woman says as she gets in the car. She has a low, deep voice, like she might once have been a twenty-a-day smoker. "Delighted to meet you at last, Gareth. Cassandra tells me you are doing sterling work on behalf of our company."

"Pleasure to meet you, Beverley."

"I'm very much looking forward to this evening. I don't get out as much as I used to. It's going to be fun."

Probably the most bizarre part of the evening is that it does indeed turn out to be fun.

Liam and Eloise have as instructed made champagne cocktails for their arrival.

"Gosh, these are good," Gareth says, draining half a glass in one go. "What's in them?"

"It's a sugar cube soaked in brandy with a drop of angostura bitters and topped up with champagne," Eloise explains.

"These were my mother's absolute favourite," Beverley says in her mellow tones. "She always said champagne cocktails were the very best way to get a party started. And I've started a lot of parties in my time, let me tell you." She winks at Eloise in an exaggerated fashion.

There are canapés too.

"Don't tell me you made these Eloise?" Gareth helps himself to a miniature tortilla omelette. The selection includes king prawns and mango chunks on skewers, fragrant with coriander, miniature hamburgers and duck won tons.

"Did I heck, Dad. A man in a van turned up with them about half an hour ago. Cassandra ordered them. If it was down to me you wouldn't even have had a bowl of Pringles, you know that."

"Have you settled in?" Beverley asks her.

"Really quickly. The apartment is just so lovely. We went for a long walk this afternoon and checked out the area, loads of great bars and coffee houses and independent shops. We're very lucky to have this opportunity to live and work in Canada for a while. And the weather's amazing here, too. Thank you very much."

"Not at all. I'm delighted you like it. This was my first ever apartment, you know. I lived here for quite a few years. I loved being up here on the top floor and looking out over the tops of the trees, especially in the Fall, when all the leaves on the trees turn the most glorious shade of orange. I couldn't bring myself to sell it when I moved on to something bigger. Cassandra looks after it now and always makes sure that only people worthy of it get to live in it."

"Do you know anything about the artwork then?" Eloise asks. "Liam spent ages before you arrived, looking at it all."

"I love it," Liam explains. "But I don't recognise any of it. I really like the style. And the colours. They're loud and they make you look at the landscapes in a different way."

"I'm so glad," Beverley beams. "It's a very well known style in Canada. They're all prints of paintings by the Group of Seven or the Canadian Group of Painters. They were active in the 1920's and 1930's and are best known for their landscape paintings and their love of nature. They had a very strong influence on Canadian art and on cultivating Canadian artistic expression. I've collected them since I was very young and have a number of originals at home."

"And who is this lady?" Eloise asks. "It's the only photograph amongst all the landscapes. She's got such a lovely smile."

"That's Isabel McLaughlin. She was a painter and a former president of the Canadian Group of Painters and also an executive member of the Heliconian Club. That was a club set up for female musicians and painters because they were excluded from joining arts clubs for men. It's still going strong to this day. Some of my favourite paintings hanging here are by Isabel McLaughlin. This is a print of one of hers that I am very proud to have the original of at home." Beverley points out a painting of a garden of white flowers with hedges painted in a luscious, shiny green. "When I look at it, I can almost smell the perfume of the gardenias."

Gareth watches Beverley as she talks. She looks younger than her late fifties, slim and elegant, her blonde hair shot through with caramel highlights. Only her hands, which she waves around a lot when she talks animatedly about the art that she clearly loves so much, show her age. Despite the beautifully manicured nails, the backs of her hands are marked with age spots.

"I'll have to google all this later," Liam says.

"Well if you like the paintings, you should go visit the Art Gallery of Ontario while you are here. They have a fabulous collection from the Group of Seven. Or better still, get yourself up to the McMichael Canadian Art Collection in Kleinburg. Amazing. Can you drive? You are welcome to borrow my car to go there."

"Don't let Beverley bore you too much talking about art," Cassandra interjects. "She can go on about it for hours and hours if you let her."

"Cassandra is a complete philistine when it comes to art, Liam," Beverley says, mock wearily. "If you can't wear it, she's not interested in it."

"Not entirely true,' Cassandra says, laying her hand on Beverley's arm for a second, "but not far off."

Jealousy flashes through Gareth again and he drains the rest of his second cocktail.

"Gosh, you're a thirsty lot you Welsh." Beverley laughs. "You'd better rustle up a few more cocktails, Cassandra for those that aren't driving later."

"Coming up! Eloise, Liam, come help me. Just one more each. We don't want you hungover for your first day of work!"

There is an awkward silence between Gareth and Beverley, but she moves quickly to break it.

"Is this your first time in Canada, Gareth?"

"I came here once before, on a rugby tour when I was in school. It was 30 years ago so I don't think it really counts. I'm paying attention this time!"

"That's good to hear. How do you find the Royal York?"

Gareth's blood freezes for a second. Does Beverley suspect something?

"Cassandra said her PA had booked you in there. At Perfect, we think it's the best hotel in Toronto and we always recommend it to people visiting us. Iconic and historic. And also really central and close to our office too. "

Gareth regains his composure. "It's excellent, thank you. Great location."

"Are things progressing as you would hope on the factory in Wales?"

"They are. There's a lot to do yet, but it is going to plan so far."

"I hope to come to Wales some day and see it in operation. I'm very excited about it all. It means a great deal to us as a company. Ooh look, more champagne cocktails."

"Here you go," Cassandra passes them round. "There wasn't enough time to let the sugar cubes dissolve in the brandy so I had to crush them up a bit with a spoon."

"My mother would not have been impressed." Beverley is teasing.

"I knew you'd say that! Tastes just as good though. Drink up, all!"

Before these cocktails are finished, Beverley, who suddenly looks very tired, brings the evening to a close.

"I've had a very enjoyable evening, thank you all so much, but to my mind champagne cocktails are like boobs. Two is the most a girl really needs. Eloise, I'd like to mentor you during your internship, if that's OK with you."

"That would be completely awesome," Eloise gushes.

"Good, we'll have fun. I'll take you for lunch to the Heliconian one day, too."

"Do you want a lift back to your hotel?' Cassandra asks Gareth. "I can drop you off on the way?"

"Could I walk it from here?"

"Well yes, but it'll take you at least thirty minutes."

"Then I'll walk, I think. It's still quite early and I could do with some fresh air, now that it's cooled down a bit."

"Stay and have another drink with us Gareth?" Liam's invitation is polite but Gareth spots the look of horror on Eloise's face.

"Thanks, but I'll be on my way. Good luck tomorrow."

"Goodnight, Dad…" Eloise kisses him good bye. "And thanks very much again Beverley and Cassandra."

The three of them walk out of the apartment together and make their way down the stairs. Bev walks down the steep stairs in her high heels a little gingerly and instinctively, without thinking, Gareth holds out the crook of his arm to her and she takes it. He walks her to the car.

"You're a gentleman," she says, climbing into the car. "There's not many of those around these days. Goodnight."

Cassandra shuts the passenger door and walks round to the driver side.

"What are the arrangements for tomorrow?" Gareth asks her.

"Can you come to Perfect's offices for about 12pm? No need to come earlier than that. I have a pile of things on my desk I need to sort out first."

Gareth nods. "I'll be there."

"OK, see you tomorrow then. Goodnight."

She gets in the car and she and Beverley drive away. As they pass him, Gareth lifts his arm and waves to them.

Gareth plugs the hotel address into his phone and asks it for directions. He walks fast, wishing he had his running gear and could run instead. Run away from himself and how he feels: jealous and ashamed of himself but more than anything longing for Cassandra.

*

Eloise is watching from the living room window. "Off he goes. Thank God. I thought for a second he was going to take you up in your offer and stay for another drink. What on earth were you thinking! Those cocktail things are so strong and he had at least three. One more of them and he might have ended up kipping on the sofa. With you!"

"I meant it when I said I'd sleep out here if you'd prefer it."

"I wouldn't. Prefer it, that is."

235

"Come on then," he says, reaching his hand out for her to take. "Let's go to bed."

In the end it is Eloise who pushes the pace for them to have sex that night. It is she who fumbles around in her toiletry bag for a condom.

"Are you sure?"

"I'm sure."

"It's a big deal, your first time. It needs to be special."

"We're in Toronto, in a beautiful place we get to call our own for a month, no one can walk in on us, and I'm tiddly on champagne. It couldn't be more special."

"It could be more special."

"No it couldn't."

"For fuck's sake El, stop arguing with me. Yes it could." He pauses for a second and makes her look at him. "I love you, Eloise."

"Oh. I wasn't expecting that. Say it again."

"I love you, Eloise."

"I love you too. You're right, actually, that does make it more special."

*

As Gareth approaches the hotel entrance, Cassandra rings him.

"You OK?" She is speaking very quietly.

"Are you having to whisper because Beverley is asleep in bed next to you?"

"Of course not. She and I don't sleep in the same bed. Are you at the hotel yet?"

"Almost, I think."

"Was that as awful as you thought?"

"Only for as long as I didn't stop to think about what the hell I am doing. Beverley's a nice lady, warm and generous. I'm being a shit to her."

"Its *me* that's being a shit to her actually. You're being a shit to Rachel."

"That doesn't make me feel any better."

"Nor me."

"What are we playing at Cassandra? This is so selfish and destructive. And plain madness. You know I've no reason to be in Toronto, don't you? Everything I need to do on the documents, I'd already done before coming here. I'm completely neglecting my work and my children and my marriage. I ought to go home as soon as possible."

"You can't! Not yet. I need more time with you. I can't give you up just yet."

"The more we do this, the worse it's going to get."

"I know. We should stop. Call a halt to it right now."

"I think that would be the best thing for both of us."

"Is that what you want to do?"

"No. This whole walk home while I've been trying to tell myself how we need to stop doing this, all I've been able to think about is how much I can't wait to see you again."

"Good. Look over to your left."

When Gareth looks up, he sees that Cassandra is standing next to the hotel's doors.

She doesn't end the call. "Want me to leave?"

"No. No I don't."

*

When he wakes up, Cassandra has already left. There's a note on the bedside table.

> *Left at 5am. You were dead to the world and I needed to get home before Beverley woke up. Come to our office by 12pm. You're doing a presentation to the non-executive directors about the Welsh factory project.*

237

Gareth's entire body feels leaden with fatigue from too many champagne cocktails and jet lag and too much sex. It's impossible to tell what time it is because the hotel's thick curtains block out the light. When he checks his phone he sees it is already 10 am and that Rachel has already rung him twice.

He listens to the voicemail she has left. She sounds annoyed.

Hi, it's me. Just wanted to know how you are all are. We're all fine here, just about. My mother and Felix are arriving later and it'll be bloody hard work keeping them fed and watered, as you know. Not that it's your problem out there in Toronto. Where no doubt the sun is shining. It's grey skies here. Call me please.

He takes a deep breath and calls her back.

"Hi," she answers.

"Hi. How are you?"

"Fine, I guess, considering it's the school holidays and I'm managing a full time job and all the kids, all on my own," she answers, in a snippy voice.

"Don't be like that Rachel. You're not on your own are you? You've got Karen, and Grace to help too. And your mother will want to spend some time with the children while she's there."

"You'd think so wouldn't you, but she's already informed me she wants to go to Cowbridge shopping one day because she likes all the swishy fashion shops there and she and Felix have tickets booked for the Welsh National Opera one evening and they're going to the James Sommerin restaurant one evening for the seven course tasting menu because she read all about him in the Good Food Guide. She's not really coming to see us you know, she's coming for a holiday."

"Well she's company at least."

Gareth can hear Rachel breathing in annoyance at him down the phone. He changes the subject.

"Eloise and Liam have got a lovely apartment."

"I know I've seen it."

"You've seen it? How?"

"Our daughter was up and about this morning far earlier than you. She showed the apartment to me on Facetime, turned the phone round and walked me through the rooms. Looks really lovely."

"Ah yes, Facetime. Haven't got the hang of that."

"I don't like it. I could see my own face and it just looked tired and droopy." She pauses. "You're meant to say I'm not tired and droopy at this point, Gareth."

"You're not old and tired my love, you're gorgeous of course."

"I've got to go, I need to finish work early to pick Mum and Felix up from the airport. I don't like them being here and you and Eloise being away. I feel grumpy and put upon. I'm sorry but I'm hanging up now because this conversation is pissing me off. Goodbye."

Gareth sits on the edge of the bed for a while, not certain what to do. He should really book a flight and go straight home, that very day if possible. At the very least he should ring Rachel back and try to lighten the load on her somehow or make her feel better. But all he does is get in the shower quickly before walking over to Perfect's offices.

The high glass fronted office block, the top three floors of which Perfect occupies, has a fantastic view over the waterfront and over to Toronto Islands. Gareth delivers the required presentation to the board members. He is amused to be served coffee by his own daughter, who pretends she doesn't know him.

"Thank you for that," Beverley says to him afterwards. "It was a fantastic presentation. Your enthusiasm really helped to get our message over to the board."

"It's easy to be enthusiastic about such a great project."

Beverley smiles at him.

"I have an appointment out of town later this afternoon. I understand Cassandra has plans to take you to Niagara."

239

"Oh, news to me."

"Don't you want to see our famous Falls?"

"Of course, excuse me, I didn't want to appear rude. I just wasn't aware of the plans."

Chapter 25

Tuesday, 29 October 1929 is a beautiful autumn day and Jean has been dispatched by Mr Wragg to harvest the very largest pumpkins in the patch. They grow all manner of squash at Parkwood – butternut, acorn, carnival and many others – to be used in soups, casseroles and stews throughout the winter months, but the giant pumpkins that Jean is now harvesting are grown specifically to be carved into Jack O'Lanterns for Halloween.

Mrs Meikle excels at carving pumpkins and she and Jean will help the McLaughlin grandchildren with the carving later on. As they carve, Mrs Meikle will tell the story of Stingy Jack in her special, storytelling voice. She will describe how Stingy Jack invited the devil to have a drink with him but was too stingy to pay for his drink so he convinced the Devil to turn himself into a coin that Jack could use to buy their drinks. But instead of buying drinks Jack put the coin in his pocket next to a silver cross so that the Devil could not change back into his original form. Later, Jack releases the Devil on condition that when he dies the Devil does not claim his soul.

When Jack dies, God does not allow him into heaven but nor does the Devil allow him into hell. Instead the Devil sends Jack off into the dark night with a piece of burning coal to light his way. Jack put the coal into a carved out turnip and has been roaming the Earth with his lantern ever since, looking for a home.

Mrs Meikle will tell the children how when she was a child in Scotland where pumpkins do not grow they would carve their Jack O'Lanterns out of turnips and rutabaga, which in Scotland are called neeps and swedes. And at the end of her story she will say as she always does, "So much harder to carve than these pumpkins, I can tell you, our poor wrists would ache all night on Halloween."

The children will put candles in the carved pumpkins and light them to scare away the homeless evil spirits that, like Stingy Jack, roam the Earth.

Jean loves this time of the year, the line between fall and winter. The leaves on the trees are bright orange but not yet fallen and the days are still bright but the evenings darker. She likes the chill in the air and the smell of bonfire as she and the rest of Mr Wragg's gardeners clear the outdoor gardens ready for their winter sleep, although there will still be plenty of work in the greenhouses to keep them busy until spring rolls around again.

On the day the US stock market crashes, a day which will later become known as Black Tuesday and will cause a depression that spreads out into Canada and Britain and other parts of the world, Jean picks through the pumpkin patch, searching for the biggest and best. She thinks about how this time next year she and Idris will be married and she hopes that on the eve of All Saints Days in the future, she will have children of her own for whom she will carve pumpkins and tell the story of Stingy Jack.

*

For the second time in his life, Idris is told he must wait before he can be married. This time it is at the request of Mrs Meikle and Mr Wragg.

"We want to make it a special day for you both, and Sam and Mrs Adelaide want that too, but Miss Billie is to marry Lt. Col Mann next August and everyone's focus is on the family wedding and getting Parkwood and the gardens ready. Your wedding can be after that one. Waiting won't do you any harm anyway, Jean is still only 18," Mrs Meikle explains, briskly.

Idris doesn't follow the logic of why a servant's small-scale wedding needs to come after that of Colonel Sam's youngest daughter, Eleanor, even if she is the favourite. Known as Billie by all, because Sam had been convinced that his fifth child would be a boy whom he would name Billy, she is the best horsewoman of the five daughters and, according to Jean, the one who laughs the most. From what he has heard from Jean, Idris thinks Miss Billie is a fine woman and is sure that her fiancé, Clarence Churchill Mann of the Royal Canadian Dragoons, is similarly fine, but he also thinks that his and Jean's wedding is no business of theirs. Nevertheless, Jean is more than happy to do as she is asked and so, therefore, is he.

While they wait, Idris lives alone in the house that he worked so hard to finish before feeling able to ask Jean to marry him. He has no trouble keeping busy for there is always something to be done – building shelves or re-papering some of the rooms he did first when he was less practiced at the task or digging over the garden back and front – and if there is nothing to do at his own house there is always something to be done at a neighbour's. Of all the houses self-built by immigrants, Idris' house is seen as one of the most competently built and there is regularly a knock at the door from someone who lives locally asking for advice or assistance or just to be shown round.

As Jean only has one day off a week, Idris calls into Parkwood most evenings after work for a cup of tea.

"Don't you be getting in the way of her work, now," Mr Wragg warns.

"She wouldn't let me if I tried, sir," Idris says with a wry smile.

"Exactly what Mrs Wragg says about me," Mr Wragg replies.

On her days off, Jean and he plant the gardens out with plants that Mr Wragg collects for them at Parkwood – cuttings and seeds and divided bulbs. One entire section of the garden is reserved for vegetables.

"Is there anything particular you would like to grow?" Jean asks him.

243

"Some roses would be nice. Pink ones maybe."

Jean brings dozens of cuttings.

"We'll have every shade of pink eventually," she explains. "From the very palest of pinks right through to the deepest cerise. I've taken cuttings from some orange and white ones too. The scent will be gorgeous and we shall have flowers from early summer right through to autumn."

About once a month or so, Idris forces himself to write home. He addresses his letters to all five of the Maddoxes in the Rhondda but only his mother writes back, on behalf of them all. Even with just the one letter needed to cover everyone, he finds the letter writing difficult. Having made the decision that he will never return home to Wales again, not even for a visit, he tries not to think about his parents or the Rhondda. Or about Maggie and Tommy and Davey. When he first arrived in Canada, one of the things he did before falling asleep each night was let his mind roam over the landscape of his old life. He'd walk over Clydach Vale mountain and check out his rabbit traps before looking down across the valley and the pitheads, and then up into the wide expanse of sky. From there he'd walk to his parents' end of terrace house and out into the garden where his mother would be weeding and his father would be sitting on a chair, watching her as she worked, and drinking a mug of tea so strong it is orange, just as Dada likes it. He doesn't do that any more. He misses it all less if he doesn't think about it. The letter writing is hard because it means he has to think about them for a while.

After he writes to his mother telling her of his engagement to be married to Jean, he receives a reply very quickly. His mother must have written back the very same day she received his letter, in the formal style she was taught at school.

My dearest son Idris,

Your father and I send our warmest congratulations to you and Jean on your engagement. We are delighted at the news,

244

as are Tommy and Maggie who also send their very best wishes to you both. I was very sorry at the time when you wrote that you and Aeronwen had decided to end your engagement and I was worried perhaps you were more disappointed about that decision than you were prepared to reveal, but it is clear from what you write in your letters that Jean and you are far better suited. It seems that the two of you were always meant to be together, from the moment you met on the ship. This is a very happy day for the Maddox family!

I only wish that we could travel out to Canada to join you for the wedding for nothing would please me more than to see you again, my son. I see your face most days of course, whenever I see Tommy, but it is not at all the same, just as you and he are not at all the same. Seeing your face in his makes me feel the lack of you more keenly.

I would also dearly love to meet Jean and see for myself the house you have built. Sadly, that is not going to be. Your father has not been well of late – he coughs a lot, from the dust, as many an old miner does, and whilst I do not wish to cast a shadow on your good news, the truth is he will not be able to carry on working underground much longer. Even if he could, we would not be able to afford to make the trip. I wish Tommy could stop working at the pit too, but there is little else in the way of work for men round here, and if wishes were horses, beggars would ride. I shall have to content myself with the hope that one day soon you may bring your family home, if not for good then at least for a visit.

Other than you father's cough, we are all of us keeping well. Davey is thriving and continues to be a delight. He is such a good boy, and bright as a button. He comes to me part of every day while Maggie attends to the rabbit traps and I like nothing better than having him here. I have finally been blessed with a child who enjoys gardening as much as I do. We spend many happy hours together out the back and it is just as well he enjoys

spending time with his grandmother as Maggie is often away
for hours at a time. She loves being up on top of that mountain
almost as much as you did but she is also presently much taken
with going to hear Mrs Elizabeth Andrews speak whenever she
gets the chance. Mrs Andrews is from Ton Pentre and a
member of the Labour party. She is the lady who is
campaigning hard for pithead baths to be installed at every
colliery so that us women can put our tin baths away once and
for all. I too am in support of what Mrs Andrews is fighting
for but I do not feel the need to travel the length and breadth
of these valleys to hear her fighting for it in person.

Maggie is a good daughter-in-law – hardworking, and a
good wife and mother. She and I never have so much as a cross
word. There is a sadness to her though, which I understand. I
only ever fell pregnant the once too, but to the good fortune of
your father and I, there were two of you. For Maggie it seems
there will only ever be Davey. I shall have to look to you and
Jean for more grandchildren, Idris.

Please do write in greater detail about your wedding
arrangements and of the grand house where Jean works and
particularly about the gardens and the greenhouses. I would
dearly love to know more about them. Our windowsill in the
kitchen at home is such a great growing environment for
seedlings, I cannot imagine the impact of an entire room of
glass.

Yours, affectionately,
Mam

*

Despite the coldness of his fellow workers towards him when he
first started at General Motors, or perhaps because of it, Idris gets
promoted at work and is now supervising one section of the plant.
The depression is impacting on sales of the McLaughlin Buick

and the workers are often laid off for weeks at a time, before being called back whenever sales pick up a little and then having to work very long hours and at a backbreaking pace to meet orders. Despite the shame it brings, some families have no option but to claim relief.

Idris hears the workers complain on a daily basis.

"Better because it's Canadian!" he hears them grumble, repeating the company's advertising slogan. "But no good for the Canadians who work for the company, only the ones who bloody own it."

Sometimes when Idris is visiting Jean, the Colonel will summon him up to his study and ask for ten minutes of his time.

"How are the men bearing up, Idris? Is morale good? This recession is tough on them I know."

Each time he is asked this question Idris hesitates for a second, the true answer on the tip of his tongue.

Morale is poor Colonel, he wants to say, *and there is much misery from low and irregular wages and the lack of a collective voice. Whereas here at Parkwood there appears to be no recession at all and you are getting central air conditioning installed ready for Miss Billie's wedding and redecorating throughout.*

But he does not say this because it is not the answer the Colonel wants to hear and because answering truthfully would upset Jean.

"Their workmanship is second to none," is what he actually says. "It's the reason why everyone wants a Dominion built car. Just like your father used to say Colonel – One Grade Only, and that the Best.

Jean and all of Mr Wragg's gardeners are working very long hours getting ready for the wedding, bringing the already impeccable gardens up to an even higher standard. They grow all the wedding flowers in the greenhouses – the flowers for the church, the table settings and for the bouquets and headdresses of the bride and her flower girls. On the day of Miss Billie's wedding in August 1930 Parkwood has never looked more impressive.

Jean is asked if she is willing to put on her parlour maid uniform one last time to help serve the wedding guests with drinks.

"You've never seen anything like it," she tells Idris when it is all over. "I can honestly say I have never seen anyone look as beautiful as Miss Billie looked. She had a long white lace headdress and the train of her dress was as long as you are tall Idris. The other McLaughlin sisters and adult bridesmaids wore white dresses too, all of them of the same design, and large floppy hats while Miss Billie's mischievous little nieces had little bonnets, fitted tight to their heads. Colonel Churchill Mann looked very dashing indeed in full military uniform and he and Miss Billie laughed and smiled at each other all day long. It was just beautiful Idris, so very beautiful. And the gardens could not have looked better – they were exactly as Mr Wragg had planned they would look. "

"I'm glad to hear it," Idris says, "after the amount of work you all put in."

"Do you know Mr Wragg hand picked every single flower for Miss Billie's bouquet, the very best blooms he has ever grown he said they were, and Mrs Wragg was the one who arranged the bouquet and tied it together? It smelled so gorgeous, I could smell the fragrance even when I was serving champagne cocktails."

"Champagne cocktails? What are they then?"

"You take a cube of sugar and soak it in brandy and angostura bitters, then fill the rest of the glass with champagne. They made everyone who had one so giggly, more giggly than even the little bridesmaids."

Idris listens and nods in all the right places. Not that he isn't happy for Miss Eleanor and Colonel Churchill Mann but because his only real focus is counting down the days until his own wedding.

Jean suggests they marry on her nineteenth birthday.

"But that's already a special day," Idris says. "Wouldn't you like a different special date for our wedding?"

"No," Jean says firmly, "It will be three years since we first came to Oshawa and three years since…well, you know, the reason why we came to Oshawa at all. I would like it to be a date with lots of good reasons to celebrate it."

"Then we shall make it so and marry on your birthday," Idris pulls her towards him, wraps his arms tightly around her.

*

Idris is an early riser but he wakes even earlier than usual on his wedding day. He is happy to be greeted by another day of late September sunshine. He takes his cup of tea out into the garden and sits quietly for a while, watching the honey bees visiting the many flowers that Jean selected especially so as to attract bees – lavender, sunflowers and cornflowers and many others that Idris does not know the names of. The early morning sun is warm on his face and on his bare feet and he feels the warmth not only on his skin but in his heart, because today is the last day he will wake up alone in the house he built for Jean.

He arrives far too early at the small Presbyterian church that Mrs Meikle regularly attends and where their wedding is to be held. He has elected not to have a best man.

"You could ask Mr Williams?" Jean had suggested. "Or one of our neighbours? "

"No Jean. It's odd, but even though it's not possible for all sorts of reasons for Dada and Tommy to be here, they are the only two I would want for my best man and in their absence, I'd rather have no one at all."

He sits alone in the front pew of the plain little church and waits for Jean. He hears people arriving, greeting each other and chatting quietly. The church will be full in no time, because Jean and Idris now know many people in Oshawa. Their guest list includes the many neighbours whom Idris has helped and advised on building their homes and who are becoming good friends, the service staff and gardeners from Parkwood and their spouses and children and the very many members of the McLaughlin family, most of whom will be attending. Mr and Mrs Williams have travelled to Oshawa from Toronto to be here and Janet, who is Jean's maid of honour, is bringing her adoptive family from Brockville with her. Idris sits with his head bowed, listening to the people of his new life file into the church behind him and he promises himself to only ever feel grateful for the people who are here rather than missing the ones who are not.

Finally, the organist strikes up and the crowd of people rise to their feet, buzzing gently like the bees had done in the garden earlier that morning, in anticipation of the arrival of his bride. Idris waits for a few moments before turning to watch as Jean completes the walk down the aisle on Mr Wragg's arm. She is wearing a three quarter length cream silk dress that Mrs Williams has made for her, copied from a picture in the Eaton's catalogue that Jean had cut out carefully and posted to her. As is the custom, Jean has refused to allow Idris to see the dress before the wedding day but he knows that the lace at the throat of the dress came from Mrs Williams' own wedding dress. Idris did not see Miss Eleanor McLaughlin on the day of her wedding, but it seems to him that there is no possible way on earth that Miss Billie could have looked a fraction as beautiful or as happy as Jean does walking down the aisle. The bouquet she carries contains some of her favourite flowers – gardenias and white roses– just as for Miss Billie, all grown and selected specially by Mr Wragg and carefully arranged and tied by Mrs Wragg that morning.

As Jean arrives at his side, Idris grins at her.

"Happy birthday," he mouths.

She smiles a small smile at him, looks down shyly at her feet and then back up at Idris. There are tears glistening in her eyes and he instantly feels tears pricking at his own eyes. They both turn to the minister, shaking a little with nerves and excitement, but eager to start their married life together.

*

After the ceremony, the wedding party walk to Parkwood for a celebration tea on the lawn. Miss Adelaide and her daughters help serve the champagne cocktails this time, while Jean and Idris have their picture taken on the stone steps leading up to the house. Janet and her Brockville family shower them with confetti and take dozens of photographs. Janet not only has a Canadian accent now but has taken on the mannerisms and even the look of her adopted sisters.

"She doesn't even talk like me anymore," Jean whispers at one point to Idris, the only point in the day when she seems sad. "She's theirs now, not mine anymore."

"Just like you're mine now, not hers," Idris says, kissing her full on the lips, "and you and I will make a family of our own right here in Oshawa."

When the tea is over, Idris and Jean are driven in one of Colonel Sam's fine McLaughln-Buicks to their house. Before Idris picks Jean up to carry her over the threshold, he stops and takes her hand in his. Gently he takes her finger and without saying a word, he draws a cross with it over his own heart.

Chapter 26

Gareth and Cassandra wait in line with the thousands of other tourists waiting to board the Maid of the Mist. Despite having seen dozens of images of it over the years, Gareth is still impressed by the sheer force of the thundering tons of water, the summer sunshine flashing off it and the deafening roar of the plummeting water.

The sun beats down on their heads. They don't bother with the blue polythene capes emblazoned with images of the boat that they are provided with to shield them from the spray. Instead they stand holding on to the rail of the boat and listen to the stories of the people who went over the falls in barrels or walked over them on tightrope, letting the spray soak them through to the skin.

After they get off the boat, damp now and shivering despite the sun, their hair plastered to their heads, Cassandra leads them to a small grassy park area.

"Let's sit down on the grass here and dry off."

They lie down side by side in the hot sun. After a few moments she props herself up on one elbow and leans over to kiss him. He kisses her back and she hooks one leg over both his. He presses his erection against her thigh and she kisses him harder. He brushes his thumb over her t-shirt and feels her nipple stiffen.

"Come on," she breathes urgently into his ear. "Let's check into one of the love hotels."

"The what?"

"Lots of motels all round the main strip in Niagara. Beverley is staying out of town tonight."

252

The room they are shown to has a heart shaped bed strewn with rose petals. There is a jacuzzi in the bathroom.

"Classy room," Gareth laughs as Cassandra pushes him onto the bed and straddles him, before lifting her arms to take her t-shirt off. She undoes her bra and Gareth reaches up to rub his thumbs over her erect nipples. They both moan. She unzips his trousers and lifts herself on top of him. He holds onto her waist as she moves up and down on top of him. Both of them come, quickly and hard.

"Amazing," she says, collapsing panting onto his chest. "You're fucking amazing. I can't get enough of you."

"I can't get enough of you either," he says, stroking her hair. "You're an addiction."

They venture out later on to the strip, and wander along the street with its tacky tourist shops and Ripley's Believe It or Not! Odditorium. They drink beer and eat chicken wings together in a bar. Then they go back to the hotel and make love again, more slowly this time.

"You're lovely," Cassandra murmurs before falling asleep.

"You're lovely, too," Gareth whispers.

*

Rachel gives herself a stern talking to on the drive to Cardiff International Airport. She knows she is being unreasonable and tells herself that her husband is away earning money for the benefit of the family, her daughter is having an adventure with a very nice boy who clearly thinks the world of her, and her mother and Felix are good company, especially after a gin and tonic or two.

Cardiff airport is small and it only takes twenty minutes or so after a plane lands for the passengers to come through the arrivals lounge. Shortly after the Paris plane lands, Rachel spots her mother and Felix trundling their cases towards the car park ticket machine where Rachel usually waits when she picks her mother up from the airport.

"Hello, Darling," her mother says, kissing Rachel on the cheek. She smells of Chanel No 5 with a faint undertone of tobacco. She is wearing biscuit-coloured tight trousers tucked into brown suede high heeled boots and some sort of poncho thing with a fur trim which to Rachel looks both faintly ridiculous but also impossibly glamorous. After years of buying all her clothes in Marks and Spencer, when her mother met Felix she suddenly became very keen on fashion.

"Hello Mum, Hello Felix."

Felix too kisses Rachel on the cheek. "*Salut, cherie. Ca va?*" He is, as always impeccably dressed, in a grey pullover, dark grey jeans and highly polished black brogues. His skin is tanned and his thick white hair is neatly combed.

"Um, *oui*," she says, in reply. Her French was always rubbish.

Rachel still feels a little awkward around Felix. Not out of loyalty to her father from whom she inherited her red hair but who died after a short fight with bowel cancer when she was four years old and Jocelyn was just two and whom, try as she might, Rachel cannot remember. Francesca grieved for a very long time after his death and became introvert and distant, using the life insurance money to put her daughters in boarding school from the age of eight and buying a run down place in France, the renovation of which took all her energy and time. So far as Rachel and Jocelyn were aware, their mother spent all her time out in France doing DIY and had no interest in meeting anyone else.

Then after so many years of being alone, she met Felix while buying cheese at the local farmers' market. He had asked her which cheese was her favourite and then invited her for a coffee. They fell head over heels in love with each other in what seemed like a matter of days, possibly hours. It was as if someone had found the long lost charger for Francesca and had powered her up. The more time she spent with Felix, the more lively and

254

beautiful and sexy she became. She became a wearer of suede boots and fur-lined ponchos, adopted Felix's liking for smoking and *gin tonique*. And sex.

Jocelyn says it is as if their mother has had a personality transplant.

"It's like we grew up with a Body Snatcher," she complains. Rachel is delighted for her mother that late in life she transformed into a butterfly but does find it all a little unnerving.

"The sex is simply amazing," Francesca had confided in Rachel when she first met Felix. "I don't want to speak ill of your father of course, but it was never like that with him. At least not from what I can remember. It was all so long ago. I can honestly say I could stay in bed with Felix all the live long day. Don't repeat that to Jocelyn though. I don't think she approves of people enjoying sex."

This sexual chemistry between Felix and her mother is not wearing off any with time. On the few occasions they have come to stay in Penarth since meeting, they see no reason to change any of their usual routine, taking long baths together and asking Rachel after lunch if she happens to have any massage oil before going off to bed for the afternoon. Nor do they see any reason to be quiet. The last time they came to visit and the rest of the family were in the living room watching sport on telly one late Saturday afternoon, the noise of their groans had reached the point where Eloise was miming retching and Nora had asked if anyone else could hear a cow mooing.

"Yes, that's a cow all right," Rachel had answered. "It must be in a field nearby. It'll be quiet soon I imagine, when milking's over."

"Good Lord," Gareth had said. "Someone should really tell that farmer about the KitKat quickie."

Rachel had thrown a cushion at him and gone off to the kitchen to start peeling vegetables and Gareth had followed her out and poured them both an enormous glass of wine. When

255

Francesca and Felix came down to the kitchen later in search of an aperitif, they found Rachel and Gareth half sozzled and giggling together like teenagers.

But today Rachel will have to deal with her mother and Felix without Gareth around to help her see the funny side.

"Car's this way," she announces, and she leads the way, Felix and her mother following behind her like puppies.

*

"Glamma, Glamma," Nora says, rushing to the door when they arrive to greet them. "You look beautiful as always."

"Why thank you dear. I do so love it when you call me Glamma. So much less ageing than Granny."

"I'm not going to call you Glamma, Granny" Iris says. "Just because Nora read it on some silly Instagram post. Dad says it's just ridiculous anyway."

"Does he now? Well your father isn't here right now so I'll take that up with him when I see him. Rachel dear, are we in your bedroom as you suggested?"

"As *you* suggested Mum, but yes, you are. Come on through to the kitchen and I'll put the kettle on. Iris, take your grandmother's bag upstairs for her." Rachel is buggered if she is going to refer to her mother as Glamma either.

They find Grace in the kitchen, supervising Jake feeding himself his tea in the company of Jenny and Alastair and Daniel.

"Jenny and Alastair popped in for a cup of tea," Grace explains. "If it's if OK with you Auntie Rachel I thought maybe they'd like to join us for dinner. I've made plenty. Home made caramelised onion and goat's cheese tart with a green salad. Home made sausage rolls for the children."

"Of course it's OK, all sounds marvellous."

Francesca kisses her granddaughter hello. "How very accomplished you are Grace, and how very pretty you look."

256

Grace looks a little embarrassed. "Hello, Granny, lovely to see you, and Felix, you too, of course."

Felix smiles at her. "I have brought some delicious wine from the cellar at home. Shall I pour us all a glass?"

"Yes please," Rachel says.

*

After dinner, when Jake is in bed and the other children dispatched to the living room to watch television, Felix offers to make coffee and stack the dishwasher. The others sit around the battered kitchen table, drinking more of Felix's wine. Felix has insisted that Grace try a glass but she has only taken a few sips.

"That was a fantastic meal." Francesca congratulates Grace.

"Thank you. I've been helping out with the cooking a lot while I've been here. I really enjoy it. I love it when people like what I make and ask for more."

"Jocelyn reckons Rachel has plans to adopt you!"

"That's just a nice way of saying that Jocelyn thinks I'm treating Grace like an unpaid au pair, as she put it." Rachel is tart.

"Oh she's actually said that to your face has she? I thought it was just to me behind your back."

"That's not all Grace has been doing while here," Jenny says proudly. "Why don't you tell them Grace?"

"I don't know…maybe later…"

"Come on now, don't be shy. It's something to be proud of!" Jenny cajoles.

"What is it! Don't keep your grandmother in suspense!" Francesca teases Grace.

"Ok, ok…" Grace is blushing. "Since Jenny and I met at Auntie Rachel's book club—"

Francesca cuts in. "You go to book club Rachel? When did you start doing that?"

"Sh, Mum, ages ago, I told you about it. Go on Grace."

"...well after book club Jenny recommended I should start keeping a journal, which I did, and from there I decided to have a go at writing a novel. And I have had a go and really enjoyed it..." She hesitates.

"We're all on tenterhooks here," Francesca urges.

"And then Jenny suggested I post a couple of chapters of my book up onto Wattpad."

Grace sees the look of confusion on her aunt and grandmother's faces.

"It's an online writing community where you can upload your writing for others to read and comment on," Jenny explains.

"And," the words come tumbling out of Grace, "it's currently top of the What's Hot List and the first chapter's been read 54,000 times!"

"Not only that," Jenny adds, "the online community are posting hundreds of comments that they can't wait for the next chapters."

"It's an amazing achievement," Alastair says. "I'm really enjoying reading it."

"I'm so happy for you," Rachel says, getting up to hug Grace, who looks like she is going to pop with embarrassment and pride. "That's fantastic news."

"Your mother never even mentioned to me you were writing a novel!" Francesca exclaims. "I just spoke to her this morning and she only mentioned the *au pair* thing, not the writing."

"I haven't told Mum, not yet, and please don't say anything, Granny. Not yet. I don't want her to start bragging to all her friends that I'm some sort of junior J K Rowling and about to land a major book deal or something. I'm not. But I'm really enjoying the writing and all the positive feedback, so much so I can even cope with the critical comments."

Felix, who has long since finished stacking the dishwasher, approaches the table with more wine.

"We should toast your success, Grace", he says, topping up everyone's glass. "Félicitations!"

258

"Thank you," she smiles. "But no more wine for me, thank you. I don't really like wine, I'm sorry."

"Well, I love it," Jenny says, leaning over and pouring the rest of Grace's wine into her own glass.

"After all that excitement, I need to go outside and have a cigarette," Francesca declares. "*Tu viens*, Felix?"

He nods.

"Ooh, can I come too and steal one off you?" Jenny asks. "And don't start Alastair! It's just the odd fag every now and then. Just don't let Daniel see me."

"Shut the door behind you!" Rachel calls after them. She and Alastair and Grace continue to sit at the table, watching the others as they smoke. Francesca delicately holding her cigarette away from her body, taking long languorous puffs every now and then, Jenny tucking herself around the corner out of sight and smoking very fast, already patting her pockets down in search of a chewing gum ready for when she finishes.

"You should tell your Mum about your book, Grace. About everything really. How you were feeling before and how you feel now. She loves you very much, you know. Your dad, too."

"I know and I love them, but I'm not ready to say anything and I'm not quite ready to go home yet either."

"You can stay here as long as you like."

"Thank you, Auntie Rachel."

The others troop back in from their fag break, smelling of smoke and fresh air, and in Jenny's case Juicy Fruit chewing gum.

"He's got a keen sense of smell our son." Alastair comments, disapprovingly. "He can tell when you've been smoking you know."

"He's eight and he likes the smell of his own farts!" Jenny replies. "He hasn't got a clue whether I've had a cigarette or not."

"I'm going to put Nora to bed and read her a story and then go on up to bed myself, maybe do some more writing," Grace announces. "Good night all."

259

"We'd best push off too shortly," Alastair says. "I've got work in the morning. I'll go give Daniel a five-minute warning. And you've got a five-minute warning, too, Jenny to finish off your wine."

While he's gone, Jenny tops her glass up. "Ssh, don't tell him. I'll drink fast."

"So what do I need to do to get on this Wattpad thing to read Grace's book?" Rachel asks.

"Just Google it and then register. Takes two ticks."

"Is it very dark? Cathartic?"

Jenny smiles. "Don't worry. She hasn't written about her own life. It's not dark at all. It's set in the future but a bright sunny one, not post-apocalyptic or anything. It's a teenage love story, basically, and the girl character is opinionated and eloquent and is one of a large family that live together in a big house by the sea and bear a very strong resemblance to the members of your family. But it's funny and clever and touchingly romantic. She can really write. I wouldn't say this in front of her, because I wouldn't want to raise her hopes, but I think she might be able to get it published by a mainstream publisher."

They hear the downstairs loo flush and Alastair returns to the kitchen. "Time's up Jenny. Daniel's asleep in front of the telly. I'll have to carry him to the car."

"Good night everyone – lovely evening. See you all soon."

Rachel sees them to the door. When she gets back to the kitchen, Francesca is making peppermint tea using fresh mint and Felix is outside having another cigarette.

"Would you like a cup?"

"Lovely. Where did you find the mint? I didn't know we had any."

"Felix spotted a huge patch of it in the garden earlier. You really need to watch with mint, it can take over if you don't keep pulling it up."

"I haven't got time for gardening, Mum."

"I didn't like to say so, but I can see that for myself, my dear."

"Maybe I should ask Grace to make that her next challenge."

Francesca smiles. "She's obviously very happy here and a great help to you, too, but she does need to go back to Jocelyn and Nick eventually."

"I do know that Mother, I'm not keeping her locked up here against her will."

"I'm not suggesting you were. Jocelyn is my daughter and I love her but I can see her failings the same as anyone else. She goes on about Doha like it was Xanadu when it was nothing of the sort, or at least it wasn't when I visited, and she puts a lot of pressure on Grace because she only has the one child on whom to pin her hopes. Whereas you have lots."

"What are you trying to say, Mum?"

"You need to start sowing the seed with Grace that it's time for her to go home soon."

"It's more complicated than you think."

"Oh, I think I have an idea how complicated it is. Last time I saw Grace she was grey and sad, looking like death warmed up, and here she is now pretty as a picture. You asked Jenny if Grace's book was dark, which said a lot, and I have worked out that Jenny recommended Grace keep a journal in the first place because Grace was struggling in some way. I imagine Jocelyn is unaware what has been going on and is equally unaware how much you and your lovely family are helping Grace. I'm getting old, Rachel, not stupid." She puts her hand over her daughter's. "Here you go, your tea is ready."

Rachel takes the offered tea. The mint leaves smell fresh and tangy. "I'm going to go up to bed, Mum. It's been a busy day."

"Off you go then, I'm going to go back out in the garden and sit with Felix for a while. I do so love being outside under the stars of a summer's night."

Before climbing up to the attic room, Rachel telephones Gareth. It goes immediately to voicemail. She leaves a message.

Sorry I was in a snit. I miss you and love you, we all do. I'm not the best version of me when you're not around. Can't wait to have you home again.

Chapter 27

The Maddox family are spared the hardship of the Dirty Thirties. Idris and Jean read in the newspapers about how the Depression has caused unemployment in Canada to reach 30 per cent and one in five Canadians is forced to claim relief. Wages drop by as much as 60 per cent and after 1931 no commercial or industrial building is built in Toronto. Matters are even worse in the Prairies where a prolonged drought and plagues of grasshoppers cause some people to have to abandon their homes and farms and leave the region for good.

Idris looks at the pictures in the newspapers of the poor, the hungry and the homeless, and feels pity for all the people that he worked with on the viaduct in Toronto. He thinks about the day Aeronwen broke off their engagement and he left Toronto, pausing for a while at the site of the construction of the Royal York hotel and contemplating staying and seeking work there. He wonders what happened to all those men after the hotel was finished and whether they are now amongst the grey-faced, desperate looking men whose pictures appear in the newspaper, lining up at the soup kitchens or being taken in at relief camps.

Idris and Jean know they are lucky and count their blessings. They have good jobs, food on the table and it is a daily source of delight to them both how happy they are to be married to each other and living together in their house. Idris feels a calm contentment when he is with Jean and an ability to just sit quietly and still when she is next to him that he has never experienced before. He likes waking up with her and going to sleep with her, he walks home from work looking forward to seeing her and to working side by side in their garden before sitting down in their kitchen with the Delft blue wallpaper to eat their evening meal, with vegetables they have grown themselves.

Often of an evening and on Sundays they walk together in Lakeview Park, walking along the shore and almost always stopping by to visit the buffalo, until in 1931 the buffalo are removed and relocated to Riverdale Zoo, in Toronto, on account of being just too smelly.

"It's not quite the same without them," Jean says, sadly.

While they walk, Jean tells Parkwood stories.

"The grocer is in Mrs Meikle's bad books," she recounts. "He delivered rancid butter again. The third time in as many months. Mrs Meikle has discontinued his services, which has caused much upset in the kitchen because his delivery boy was handsome and half the girls were sweet on him."

Idris enjoys listening to Jean talk. She has a knack for conjuring up a scene and changing her voice ever so slightly to convey different characters. With the advantage of her own Scottish accent she does a particularly good impression of Mrs Meikle. Idris talks little of his own job. He feels a large debt of gratitude to the McLaughlins but being a boss not a worker does not sit well with him. It is one of the few things he does not discuss with Jean, because she is so very loyal to the McLaughlins and any suggestion from Idris that he does not feel the same way upsets her.

From a slow burn to start, the passion he feels for Jean now burns very bright and the only shadow on their happiness is the fact that despite such passion, Jean does not fall pregnant.

In the dead of one night, tears gathering thickly in her throat, she whispers to him: "Is this our punishment Idris, for ending that other baby's life? Is this God's way of telling us we were wrong?"

"Of course not, my love," he says stroking her hair. "God is merciful."

But as month after month rolls by and there is still no baby, Idris does wonder if perhaps the procedure damaged Jean in some way and left her incapable of conceiving.

And then finally, when they have been married almost four years and are starting to give up hope, Jean shyly announces to Idris that she is pregnant. In May 1935 their daughter Elizabeth Gwendolyn is born. She is blonde haired and blue eyed like her mother and is the most perfect thing that either of them has ever set eyes on.

His mother is delighted to be a grandmother again. Within a week of his letter home announcing the arrival of a daughter, a parcel arrives, wrapped in brown paper, containing a beautifully knitted cardigan and bonnet, white, with embroidered pink roses.

Dear Idris and Jean

We are so very happy to learn of the safe arrival of Elizabeth Gwendolyn. We only wish there was not an ocean between us and that we could be there in person to congratulate you and to meet our granddaughter.

I do hope the cardigan suits her. Maggie did the rosebuds as my eyesight lets me down at close work these days. I am already working on another one for her but wanted to get this one posted the moment it was finished.

Please send a photograph as soon as you are able. I am very touched at the choice of name. It makes me feel part of your lives, even though you are so very far away.

With much affection

Mam

Jean is delighted with the cardigan.

"Just look at the dear little rosebuds, Maggie is so very clever at embroidery." Idris says nothing but when Elizabeth is wearing this cardigan, he often traces his finger over the flowers.

Later that same year, Idris is entrusted with supervising a highly important project at the General Motors Plant. Colonel Sam summons Idris to explain in person what is required.

"We are to build a car for HRH Edward the Prince of Wales himself. He called at the showrooms of our London agent, Lendrum and Hartman in Albemarle Street, and advised Captain Hartman that he wanted to buy a Buick as he did not believe anyone in Britain could build the car the way he wanted it built. We built two cars for him and his brother to use during their Royal Tour here in 1927. Those were beautiful cars all right, with a turquoise strip along the side and tan lizard leather interiors."

"I saw him get in one and drive away, Sam, at the opening ceremony for Union Station in 1927. Blink and I would have missed him. A fine car indeed."

"Well this car is to be even finer. Listen to what he wants – a car that will give two passengers 'luxury and privacy,' and he wants drinks cabinets, vanity mirrors, reading lights, smoking and jewellery cabinets and a radio. We shall make the necessary alterations to a Series 90 limousine. You shall be the one responsible for overseeing the process Idris. What do you think to that?"

"I shall be honoured, Colonel Sam," is what Idris says. In private he says to Jean, "I don't know why everyone is so very excited about this. I didn't think much to this Prince of Wales back in 1927 when he opened Union Station in Toronto and barely showed his face to the waiting crowds."

"Don't be such a misery." Jean teases him. She is playing peekaboo with Elizabeth, a game she loves and that makes her laugh for as long as either of her parents will play it with her. "You may not think it much of an honour but the McLaughlins certainly do."

Idris presides over the process of building the prince's car. It is in gleaming black with beige leather seats, the leather soft and glossy as butter. The luxury fittings ordered by the prince are installed under Idris' watchful eye – silver gilt cigarette boxes, a silver jewellery box, six silver top decanters and two posy holders.

266

"I swear he intends to live in this car rather than at Buckingham Palace," Idris comments to Jean.

The car is commissioned by a prince but when it is shipped and delivered in February 1936 it is to a king. George V dies on 20 January 1936 and Edward, Prince of Wales, aged 42 and a bachelor, becomes King Edward VII.

It is in the McLaughlin-Buick, less than a year later on 10 December 1936, that King Edward VII is driven to Downing Street to advise Prime Minster Baldwin that he is to abdicate the throne to be with Mrs Wallace Simpson, a three times married American.

On 11 December 1936, the former king addresses the nation, telling the people, "*You must believe me when I tell you that I have found it impossible to carry the heavy burden of responsibility and to discharge my duties as king as I would wish to do without the help and support of the woman I love.*" His shy, younger brother, the Duke of York must overcome his stammer and step up to the responsibility of being King George VI. Edward, who now has the title of the Duke of Windsor, slopes off to France with Mrs Simpson. The McLaughlin-Buick on which Idris and the men in Oshawa lavished so much care is loaded onto a warship to make the journey to France too.

Idris and Jean listen to the speech on the evening news on the radio.

"Not that much of a surprise," Idris comments. "I always said he didn't have the makings of a good king, didn't I?"

"Yes, dear," Jean says, not paying a great deal of attention to either Idris or the speech because Elizabeth is fussing, refusing to take her bedtime bottle. "She has a bit of a temperature, I may take her to the doctor's tomorrow if she is not better in the morning."

Elizabeth fusses and cries all night. When in the early hours of the morning her temperature rises even further and she stops fussing and becomes limp in Jean's arms, Idris goes to fetch the doctor.

The doctor examines Elizabeth but it does not take him very long. "I'm afraid it's influenza," he says. "We've seen a number of cases in the past few weeks." The tone of his voice is flat and low.

"But there is medicine to cure that?" Jean asks, hopefully.

"I'm afraid not, Mrs Maddox, I only wish there was."

"So what can we do?" Idris tries to keep his voice calm and positive.

"Try to get some fluids down her. Vicks Vapo-Rub can provide some relief, rubbed into her chest. She is a strong, healthy child. She stands a good chance."

Idris and Jean do as instructed. They take it in turns to stay awake to watch over their daughter. They ease water into her mouth with a teaspoon. They pray. On the third day, Elizabeth's temperature falls a little and she starts to fuss again. They see this as a good sign and for the first time in three days, smile weakly at one another. She is so small and has been in their life for such a very short time but she has been their whole life from the moment she was born.

Her temperature drops further again. Idris holds his daughter in his arms while Jean tries to get a little more water into her mouth. Their baby shudders, just once, and then dies in her father's arms.

They bury her wearing the little white cardigan with the pink rosebuds.

*

Rachel wakes up at 6am. Eloise's bed is comfortable enough and Grace is the quietest sleeper she has ever shared a room with but she can't get back to sleep. She misses Gareth and his being so far away means the last conversation she had with him when she more or less hung up on him weighs heavily on her. She decides she may as well get up. Just as well, because she hears Jake babbling away in his cot the minute she reaches the landing.

She's not used to being up this early. It is usually Gareth who does this first shift with Jake. She scoops him up out of his cot and takes him downstairs to give him his milk. He looks at the cup she hands him disparagingly but then guzzles it down quickly. He scoots his bottom off the battered red sofa the minute he's finished and walks out into the hallway in a purposeful way. She follows, to find him already sitting in his pushchair with Oscar waiting nearby.

"Oh, you two are expecting to go out! Of course."

She pauses to think. All her clothes except the ones for work she laid out on the landing last night are in her bedroom where Felix and her mother are currently fast asleep. But it's fine and sunny outside, a lovely, early August morning. Nobody much will be around to see her. She pulls a navy blue sweatshirt down off the coat rail and finds an old pair of discarded trainers amongst the pile on the floor that she thinks belong to Eloise but will fit her. She, Jake and Oscar go out the door to greet the day.

"Don't expect me to run though," she says to them.

As she walks along the cliff top path, Rachel wonders why she doesn't do this every day. The morning air smells fresh and clean and the sea is flat and calm. She breathes in deeply, and it is as if she is drawing peace into her body along with the seaside air. The few people they pass, also dog walkers and runners, greet the three of them warmly. Nobody seems to notice she is wearing flowery purple pyjama bottoms. She is disappointed when she looks at her watch and realises she should be getting back to get ready to go to work. As she turns the pushchair around Oscar flops to the floor and Jake looks up at her expectantly.

"What's that look for, eh? What usually happens of a morning at this point? Do you normally get a treat each? Well I'm afraid I've nothing for you, sorry, you'll have to wait till we get home.

When they open the front door there are signs of life in the house. Nora is up and watching cartoons.

"Morning Nonnie," Rachel calls.

"Morning Mummy," Nora shouts. "I'm hungry! Will you make me some breakfast?"

"Coming right up," Rachel replies.

She manoeuvres the pushchair into the hallway, which is as usual crowded with discarded shoes and coats. The pram gets marooned thanks to Gareth's sports bag, left in the hallway and no doubt full of sweaty socks and t-shirts stinking the place out. *Lazy bastard*, she thinks, bending down to release Jake from the harness who then toddles off to join Nora in front of the telly.

She unzips the bag and empties the contents out. The sports kit is unused but there is a crumpled white work shirt in there.

"Aha, soaking his shirt, my arse. This is where he must have stuffed that coffee stained shirt when he came home from London."

She shakes the shirt out. It is not stained with coffee at all. It is a Perfect shirt, not one she has seen before. Neither of the shirts that Gareth received from Cassandra Taylor's PA were white.

For some reason, she doesn't know why, she lifts the shirt to her face. When she breathes in she can't smell Imperial Leather. What she can smell, very faintly, is perfume, one she vaguely recognises but can't quite place. An image of Gareth slides unbidden into her mind. He is checking his phone constantly, tilting it towards his body, as if to shield from anyone else what he is reading.

She checks her watch. It is 2.30am in Toronto, the middle of the night. Gareth will be fast asleep. But she goes into the kitchen, retrieves her phone from her handbag on the kitchen counter and calls him anyway. She selects Facetime to make the call.

It takes him a while to answer and when he does, he is disorientated as she had expected him to be, his eyes squinting at the phone. It is dark in the room and he does not register at first that she is using Facetime or that he has already answered the call. She watches him falling back onto the bed, trying to turn the phone off. She sees his face, puffy and slack with sleep, as he jabs at his phone with his finger. Then he drops the phone and the connection is lost. But not before Rachel has seen that there is a woman lying next to him in the bed.

When she tries to call him again his phone is switched off. She does not leave a message. She racks her brain trying to remember the name of the hotel he said he was staying at. This sort of detail has never mattered to her before. If she ever needs him she just rings him on his mobile. She realises he hasn't even said what hotel he is staying at. She tries his mobile again – this time it rings but goes to voicemail – and again she leaves no message. Pressure builds inside her – anger and frustration – she would like to scream at Gareth. To scream and scream at him till her throat hurts.

She already knows the answer to the question that she wants to scream at him. She has seen it with her own eyes.

Chapter 28

The loss of a child can make its parents give up on life, curl into a ball and lie there, waiting for death to finally wash over them and take them away too. And for a while that is how it is for Idris and Jean after Elizabeth dies. The grief sits like a boulder on their chests, pinning them down. They cannot get out from under its weight and they do not really want to. In those first few weeks, Jean in particular wishes the boulder would press down on her even harder, break through her rib cage and stop her heart so it no longer hurts.

Idris frees himself from his own boulder enough to be by her side and keep her strong and eventually, very slowly, the grief starts to loosen its grip on them a little.

They each handle the process of healing differently. When in the April after Elizabeth's death more than 4000 workers at the General Motors Oshawa plant go on strike, demanding better wages and working conditions and recognition for their union, the United Automobile Workers, Idris can no longer keep his principles under wraps.

"I need to resign from General Motors," he announces over their evening meal. "I can't be doing with it any more, being on the side of the bosses while the men are fighting for their rights. Rights they absolutely deserve."

Jean looks at him. There is silence for a few long seconds. "Are you asking me for my permission?" she asks.

"No. Well, yes, in a way. The McLaughlins are like family to you. I don't want to do anything that will impact on that."

"You're my family Idris. If you need to resign, then you must do so. Just please promise me you won't actually join the union or get actively involved in the strike. I couldn't bear it if you were agitating against the Colonel and Miss Adelaide."

"The strike's not against them personally, but against General Motors."

"They're one and the same thing as far as I and the whole of Oshawa is concerned."

"You've no need to worry Jean, it's resigning I wish to do, not become a union leader."

"And find another job, something very different to automobiles, so you can hand in your resignation on the premise you have something else you wish to do. Colonel Sam will find that easier to accept."

"I'll start looking tomorrow morning."

"Even though you don't want to work for the McLaughlins, do you mind if I do? I've been thinking about it for a little while and you've helped me make my mind up. I'd like to go back to work for Mr Wragg if he has a vacancy and he usually does. I was happy to give up working to be a mother. Now I'm no longer one, I would like to work at Parkwood again."

"You'll always be a mother," Idris says, quietly. "Elizabeth having left this world isn't the same as her having never come into it at all."

*

Idris applies for the first job he finds advertised, with the Oshawa Parks Commission, maintaining the gardens at Lakeview Park. He gets it. His explanation of needing a change of career is readily accepted by General Motors and by the McLaughlins who are as sorry to see him leave as they are happy to have Jean back.

"Always said you'd make a good gardener," Mr Wragg says, drily, the next time Idris calls into Parkwood to walk Jean home from work.

273

Being back at work soothes Jean. It keeps her busy and her thoughts occupied by something other than the loss of her daughter. There is comfort in the roll of the seasons and the death and birth cycle of plants and trees. When she sees fresh green shoots push through the earth in spring, it feels to Jean like there is still hope.

When Adelaide McLaughlin becomes ill and Sam requests that a restful white garden be planted at Parkwood, very close to the house so that Adelaide is able to walk there, Jean undertakes most of the design and planting work. Whenever Adelaide feels well enough, Jean drops whatever else she may be doing and walks with the mistress of the house through the gardens, naming the flowers and shrubs she has planted and how she expects them to grow and mature. In this process they both grow stronger. Adelaide makes a full recovery, resuming golf at which she is fiercely competitive and her relentless fundraising for good causes.

The family are very grateful to Jean for her support of Miss Adelaide and present her with a painting by their middle daughter Miss Isabel McLaughlin. It is of the white gardens that Jean created and which the family appreciate so much. Jean loves it and insists Idris hangs it in pride of place in their living room.

Sam tries to persuade Idris to come back to General Motors on more than one occasion, and with particular force in 1939. The company has been commissioned to produce more cars for the Royal Family, this time two McLaughlin-Buicks for the Royal Tour, in May, of King George VI and Queen Elizabeth.

"These two convertibles are going to be maroon, and built specially tall so the King and Queen can fit their ceremonial headgear in. It's the first time a reigning monarch has visited Canada and they're going to visit every province in the country. I could really do with you looking after the production of these two cars, Idris, and it looks almost certain there will be war in Europe very soon. Who knows if this sort of tour will ever happen again."

Sam's powers of persuasion fail.

274

"No thanks, Sir, I appreciate the offer, I really do, but working for the Parks Commission is what I want to do in life. Look at it like this – I may not be taking care of the cars you are building for the British Royals but I am taking care of the park your family gave to the people of Oshawa."

"Then I must content myself with that," Sam replies, good-naturedly.

Idris doesn't want to work in a car plant ever again. He watches with satisfaction as the Canadian region of the United Automobile Workers becomes the Canadian Auto Workers following the strike at General Motors and secures higher wages and pension rights for its members but otherwise he keeps out of politics. He likes working in the park and being outside in the fresh air whatever the season. He goes to the lakeshore most days to eat his sandwiches. He takes off his socks and shoes and digs his toes into the gritty sand of the lakeshore and turns his face to the sun. He is usually very successful at not thinking about his family. Keeping them locked out of his mind also helps lock out homesickness and guilt. But when he eats his lunch in the sunshine, sometimes the image of his brother going underground to the darkness every working day of his life manages to push through his defences and he feels sorry for Tommy.

For some months after Elizabeth's death, he and Jean can do no more than hold each other in bed. Over time, this part of their life also returns and they find comfort here too. Jean says she does not expect to fall pregnant again but Idris continues to hope for a few years, until he too finally accepts they will have no more children.

*

As anticipated by many, Britain and France declare war on the Third Reich on 3 September 1939. A week later, Canada also declares war against Germany. The affection for the British

275

Monarchy stirred up by the visit of King George and Queen Elizabeth to Canada a few months earlier helps secure early support.

Idris has no intention of volunteering for service. Jean needs him at home with her. In any event, Canada is not yet sending troops overseas and its major contribution to the defeat of Germany proves to be the air crew training of thousands of British pilots, navigators, flight engineers, wireless operators and gunners for combat in Europe.

Idris hopes that his family in the Rhondda will be spared by the war. His father is too old to be called up and Davey too young. His brother Tommy works in a reserved industry so will not be conscripted. There is every chance that Idris' entire family will be unaffected.

On 29 April 1941, the small village of Cwmparc in the Rhondda valley is hit by a devastating bomb attack from the Luftwaffe. Afterwards, it is reported that it was probably a get away raid and that the bombers' target was more likely steel producing Port Talbot or the port of Swansea. Harried by anti-aircraft fire, the German bombers likely dumped their bombs so as to lighten their load and make for a speedier escape.

The high explosive bombs tear into the village, devastating a number of houses in Treharne Street and Parc Street.

In total 27 people are killed, including three evacuee children from the same family that had come to the Rhondda from East Ham in London for safety and Tommy's wife, Maggie, who happened to be in Cwmparc that day, visiting an aunt living in Parc Street.

The rescuers manage to free Maggie from some of the rubble until they realise the extent of her internal injuries and appreciate that releasing her completely will only hasten her death.

She remains alive long enough for Tommy and Gwen to get to her. Delirious with pain, she is in a world of her own when they arrive. She isn't making much sense at all.

Tommy lies down on the pile of rubble next to her and takes her hand and puts his face next to hers.

"I'm here Maggie, my lovely girl, I'm right here," he whispers.

"I knew you'd come, Idris," she says, weakly. Her face and lips are covered with dust. Someone has tried to wipe it away for her but there is dust everywhere in the air and a new layer has already fallen.

"It's me love, Tommy, not Idris," Tommy says, wiping her lips with his fingers.

"Where's Idris then? He will get here soon, won't he?"

Tommy looks up at his mother, not knowing what to do. She nods at Tommy and makes a shuffling motion with her fingers that means your wife has not got much time left, you should try to keep her happy.

"Yes of course he will Maggie, he'll be here any minute."

Maggie is weak but she suddenly becomes lucid and animated. "Good. I need to see him. I want to tell him how difficult it was to make the decision between you and him but how I made the right decision choosing you."

"And I'm so glad you chose me Maggie, we've been very happy together."

"And I need to tell him what a good boy Davey is and how glad we are of him, how much we love him."

"Davey loves you too Maggie, very much, and so do I."

"I love you too."

Maggie's eye lids are drooping now, like she is about to fall asleep, and her breathing grows shallower. Tommy holds her hand and strokes her hair, tears rolling down his cheeks. Gwen stands close by, ready to be there for her son.

Maggie opens her eyes wide. "Will you forgive me?" she whispers.

"There's nothing to forgive, my love."

Her breathing is laboured. "I should have come with you. To Canada. Left Tommy behind and brought up your son with you. Had more babies."

"Just leave her now Tommy," Gwen says, briskly. "She's pretty much gone. No point torturing yourself like this."

"Go away, Mam," Tommy shouts. "You know I won't ever leave her."

"She's talking nonsense son, it's the pain."

"She's just telling the truth, Mam."

"Don't talk soft, she doesn't know what she's saying."

"She's not saying anything I didn't already know. Not deep down anyway." He kisses Maggie lightly on the cheek.

"I love you Maggie," he says. She closes her eyes and smiles a little and then stops breathing.

When Gwen writes to Idris to tell him of the tragic death of Maggie, she also tells Idris that it is the last letter she will write to him. There should be no further contact from him with any of them.

Maggie said things before she died. Things she should not have said about you and her. I've discussed it with your father and we have decided it's better for Davey and Tommy that we don't have contact with you anymore. Good-bye, son.

Idris adds more layers of grief onto the loss of Elizabeth. He mourns Maggie whose beautiful face reappears in his dreams again after so many years of being absent. Now that his parents know the truth, he finds he is relieved that there will be no more letters to remind him of what he is missing or to sharpen his guilt.

Jean is practical. "You've said for a while you were never going back to Wales, haven't you?" she asks.

And when Idris nods, she adds: "Well, there you go then, you were never going to see them again, anyway. You and me are a small family Idris, but we're family just the same."

The war continues. Life goes on, as it must.

Miss Bille's husband, now Brigadier General Churchill Mann, plays an instrumental part in the invasion of Normandy and the great Canadian night attack down the Caen-Falaise Road. Less than 48 hours before the attack, the use of bombers to provide fire support is forbidden because of the danger of hitting friendly troops. Miss Billie's husband suggests an artificial bomb line of coloured smoke shells, which he is convinced can be seen from the air at night. The brilliantly successful attack goes ahead.

Finally the war comes to a close. Churchill Mann returns safely, the hero of all who work at Parkwood. He and Miss Billie have two children of their own and later adopt another three. There are always grandchildren visiting Parkwood.

Idris and Jean work and garden and attend Mrs Meikle's church from time to time, although not as often as Mrs Meikle would like. The street where they live and the other streets around it of mostly self-built homes become a community. The people who lent each other a hand when building houses nearby grow to be close friends. Many of them are of Scottish descent like Jean, drawn to seek work in the Manchester of Canada, as Oshawa is sometimes known. Working hard is a given and all the houses and gardens are well maintained. Over the years, they pitch in with each other again to add improvements to their homes, wrap around porches and conservatories.

Idris and Jean attend supper parties at their friends' houses where they play bridge or scrabble. In the summer they are invited to barbecues and family softball games.

Janet marries and settles in Brockville. She stays in contact but is not blessed with children either and although they do not see each other that often, the sisters console each other for their lack of offspring by letter and later by telephone. Idris and Jean's lives are not completely without children. Most of their friends have them and Idris and Jean enjoy helping out from time to time with babysitting, being rewarded with the honorary title of Aunt and Uncle. They watch their friends' children grow and this is a comfort and a joy to them both.

There are picnics at the park and chrysanthemum teas at Parkwood. Later on, there are trips and holidays to other parts of Canada. Idris gets to tick off the names of some of those places inscribed high up in the walls of Union Station.

As she approaches her 45th birthday, Jean thinks her change of life is happening. Her monthlies stop and she gets tired easily. She fears she might perhaps be ill but tries to push this from her mind. She never even considers it might be something else, at her time of life. She grows thicker around the middle and Idris teases her that she needs to cut down on all the teatime cake on offer at Parkwood. And then, one evening, she feels the baby kick.

At first she thinks she must be mistaken. She can't have felt what she thinks she felt. But a trip to the doctor confirms the miraculous news.

The doctors are surprised that a pregnancy so late in life should be complication free. Jean also has an easy birth. After just a few hours of labour, she delivers another girl, healthy and strong and as blonde and blue eyed as her first daughter was.

Idris, who at 51 had been feeling the aches and pains of a lifetime of physical work, stops complaining. They are the age of grandparents not parents but their daughter brings with her a whole new lease of life. They decide to call her Beverley Elizabeth.

When they go to register the birth, Jean has an idea.

"I'd like her to have my maiden name as a middle name. I've got your name now and Janet's got her new family's. I'd like my dad's name to live on in her."

Idris nods.

They both smile proudly as the Registrar writes their daughter's name on her birth certificate in beautiful cursive script before handing it to them.

Beverley Elizabeth Allen Maddox.

Chapter 29

Having managed to disconnect Rachel's call, Gareth is drenched with sweat and wide-awake. He hurriedly switches his phone off and then a minute or so later switches it back on.

He tries to reassure himself.

That was just a mistake, one of the kids playing Crossy Road on Rachel's phone, it was just a voice call, she didn't see anything, everything will be fine.

He switches his phone back on. He goes into recent calls and sees that it was not a voice call but, as he feared, a Facetime call which connected for 12 seconds.

Then he sees Rachel is ringing again. He ignores it and lets it go to voicemail. She doesn't leave a message and for a split second he thinks maybe he has it wrong and that there is nothing to worry about after all. And then a text comes through from Rachel.

Answer your phone, you cheating shit.

He pats Cassandra on the shoulder.

"Cassie, wake up, we need to talk."

She is instantly alert.

"What's up?"

"Rachel knows about us."

"Don't be ridiculous. How could she?"

281

Gareth explains about the Facetime call he answered by mistake.

"Why the hell did you answer it?"

"I didn't mean to."

"She wasn't meant to find out. That's not part of the plan." She sounds scared.

Gareth looks at her. "Correct me if I'm wrong, but I didn't think either of us had a plan."

"You might not have, but we did, Beverley and I. Most of it anyway. This last bit – the sex between you and me – that bit wasn't planned. Oh fuck!" She drops her head in her hands and starts crying.

Gareth gets up, finds a pair of jeans and a t-shirt and pulls them on. It feels wrong, trying to cope with the disaster exploding into his life while stark naked and stinking of sex. He sits in the armchair in the corner of the hotel room. He's never really understood why this chair, the round table next to it, were ever necessary in hotel rooms other than somewhere to throw your clothes. Now he understands.

"Cassandra," he says, coldly, "stop snivelling and tell me what on earth you mean."

"You and I didn't meet by chance," she says.

"Go on."

"Beverley sent me to find you."

"Beverley sent you to find me? I don't understand. Why did Beverley need to find me? D'you mean to work for Perfect? You're the one I've been sleeping with."

"But it was never about me. It was about Beverley. Beverley is related to you. She's the daughter of Idris Maddox and his wife, Jean. She's your great aunt."

Gareth remembers the photos Grandpa Davey showed him just recently, of two identical dark haired young men and a dark haired woman stood between them and the later photograph, taken in a garden, of one of those handsome dark haired men grown older and wearing a hat, a blonde woman with a baby in her arms stood by his side. Of the story Davey told of his father's twin brother Idris leaving the Rhondda in a huff before Davey was born and never coming back. He thinks about the night that Rachel wondered about the possibility of another Maddox family somewhere in Canada.

"That's impossible. My grandfather is 88, his father Tommy has been dead for years. Unless Beverley is some sort of vampire, she can't possibly be my great-aunt. She's not old enough."

"Not everyone breeds as early as your family Gareth. Idris was old when Beverley was born, very old for the time, over 50. Her mother was 45. She was a bit of a miracle baby, apparently."

"I still don't get it though. If Beverley really is my great-aunt, why not just send me an email and introduce herself?"

"You'd think! I did suggest that to her but she said it wouldn't work. The thing is, Beverley worked out that Idris wasn't just her father, he was also Davey's father. She'd been going through her dad's old papers and found some crumpled old letter from Maggie thanking Idris for giving her a baby. Seems Tommy was shooting blanks and she'd asked Idris to step in and do the deed. There was another letter from Gwen, the last one she ever wrote to Idris, because Maggie spilled the beans to Tommy on her deathbed and the family cut off all contact with him after that."

Gareth thinks for a while. He fights the lawyer's urge to get out a pen and a piece of paper and take notes. "It still doesn't make sense. Why not be upfront with me? I don't think that at his time of life Davey is going to mind that his father was actually his uncle and vice versa, he's just chuffed to still be around to enjoy life. I like Beverley! I admire her. I would have been glad to get an email with news of a long lost relative."

"I haven't told you everything yet."

"Get on it with then."

"Beverley didn't want to find you because she needed a bigger family. She wanted to find you because she wants something from you. And she didn't think that just popping up as a long lost member of the Maddox family was going to get her what she wanted in time. So we came up with a plan. A plan where you'd get to know her, get to like her, before you felt any duty or obligation to us. It had to be me who came over to Wales to meet with you and then come up with a plan to get you to come to Toronto."

"Why did it have to be you? Why didn't Beverley come and just leave you out of it?"

"Beverley's not well enough to travel. She's sick. With leukaemia. She urgently needs a bone marrow transplant. She's got no family – parents dead, no surviving siblings, no cousins. I'm not a match and none of our friends who've come forward to be tested are matches either. She thinks there's a chance – only a slim one at that because the family relationship isn't ideally close enough – that one of your family might be a match and might be willing to donate."

Gareth is stunned. He says nothing for a while.

"But why not just ask? Why not just say – your great grandfather is my great grandfather, too, and I would like to meet you as I have a favour to ask."

"She didn't have enough time for family bonding. Be honest Gareth, if you'd got that sort of email from someone you didn't know how much time out of your busy life would you have made available just because you share an ancestor? Beverley's been in business a long time. She knows how lawyers will put themselves out to land instructions on a big deal and earn a fat fee. She knew that the quickest, most direct route to you was to buy your time."

"So the whole factory idea is a fiction? Made up to get to me?"

"A little at first, but not now. We had been considering expanding our manufacturing base into Europe for some time. When we were trying to come up with a reason for reaching out to you, it seemed a good cover. But the more we worked up the idea, the more Beverley liked it and wanted it to actually happen. We both thought her old man would have liked the idea of her opening a factory in the Rhondda."

"You met him?"

"I did. Only a few times. He was 90 something when I first met Beverley. Her mom had not long since died and Idris was refusing to leave his house and move into a senior's home. He was riddled with arthritis and not very mobile but still sharp as a tack, still spoke with a Welsh accent. Beverley employed a couple of nurses to look after him at home and went to see him most weekends but he didn't last too long after Jean had gone. Six months or so. They'd been married 60 years by the time she died. Beverley said that after her mom went he just missed her too much to keep going."

"And you and me, what's that about?"

"This was down to me, nothing to do with Beverley. She knows nothing about it. I wasn't convinced her plan would work so I thought if I engineered a little bit of making out between us that could be a back-up plan. I thought…" Cassandra takes a deep breath, "I thought if it turned out you weren't willing to come forward for any of Beverley's reasons, I could blackmail you a little, by threatening to tell your wife you'd come on to me."

"So you and me – all this," Gareth points at Cassandra and then at himself, "this was all just part of the set-up?"

"No!" Cassandra gets out of the bed and, still naked, walks over to where he is sitting. She tries to put her arms around him. He shrugs her off.

"Right at the very beginning it was. When I was making eyes at you, the first time I met you, that was part of the set-up. I wasn't meant to find you attractive Gareth, I just wanted *you* to find *me* attractive. I hadn't had any interest in men for years. I wasn't meant to enjoy kissing you or to really, really want to sleep with you. Beverley has been sick a long time, she stopped wanting sex a while ago, and I was prepared to accept that, and the thought of cheating on her never crossed my mind. But then after I met you, all I could *think* about was you. Ever since that night outside the pub when we kissed the first time. How I feel about you is very real."

"Am I meant to believe that? You've been telling me lies since I met you, why should I believe you?"

"Because you feel it too! I know you do. When we're together, the connection is as strong for you as it is for me and the sex is off the scale. I can't get enough of you. It has to be like that for you, or else it couldn't possibly feel like that for me."

"I don't know what I feel anymore… Yes I do! I feel disgusted with myself and with you. Ashamed. Dirty. Guilty. All this emotion – this passion – you've been boiling up in me because you wanted a blackmail plan up your sleeve. Oh the irony! Because you can't blackmail me now by threatening to tell my wife because she already fucking knows."

"Well you can blackmail me then, because it will kill Beverley if she knows the truth."

"I'm going out. I need some air."

"It's the middle of the night! Don't believe all you read about Canada being a safe place. People still get mugged here, same as anywhere else."

"Right now, getting mugged is the least of my worries."

*

Rachel gathers herself. There is nothing else she can do. She has three young children in the house, plus her mother and her mother's boyfriend and her teenage niece. Her nanny, Karen, will be arriving for work soon. She can't let go and scream her head off as she'd like to, or smash all the windows in the kitchen or go upstairs and cut all Gareth's suits in half with the garden shears. There are people to feed and things she must do.

So she puts the kettle on to make some tea and she toasts bagels for Nora and Jake. She goes upstairs and showers and cleans her teeth. By the time she goes back downstairs, all ready for work, her mother and Felix are sitting in the kitchen and there is fresh coffee being made. Rachel is surprised that she can still register the lovely smell of the coffee even through the fog of misery wrapped tight around her.

"Are you feeling all right dear," Francesca asks. "You look a little peaky."

"I've got a bit of a headache. Nothing too bad."

"Shall I get you a paracetamol?"

"I'm fine Mum. Don't fuss."

"I wasn't fussing Rachel! Just trying to help. Have you got much on today? Felix and I are popping to Cowbridge for the day but we can be back by 5pm and can take over from Karen if you'd like? Start the evening meal?"

"That'd be a great help, Mum, thank you."

"Right you are then. Felix and I will pop into Waitrose. I do so love Waitrose."

Rachel smiles.

When Karen arrives Rachel quickly runs through with her what activities the children have planned that day and who needs to be where at what time. And then she picks up her jacket and her handbag and car keys and calls goodbye to everyone as she walks out the door. After she gets in the car, she calls work and tell them she has been ill overnight with sickness and diarrhoea and that she won't be in today, probably not tomorrow either. Then she drives round to Jenny's.

"What the fuck has happened to you?" Jenny asks taking one look at Rachel's face.

"Are you working today?"

"No, day off, and Alastair has just taken Daniel round to a friend's house for the day."

"Good because I need you. Gareth is having an affair."

"Don't talk bollocks. Gareth thinks you're made out of chocolate. He'd never cheat on you."

"Well, he is."

"You must be mistaken Rachel. You've got to be."

Rachel tells her what happened that morning.

Jenny sucks air through her teeth. "That does not sound good. Not good at all. Have you tried calling him again?'

"Not for an hour or so."

"Phone him again: now."

She does. It goes straight to voicemail. Jenny grabs the phone out of Rachel's hand and leaves a message

Gareth, this is Jenny. Ring Rachel as soon as you get this message.

"What do I do now, Jenny?"

"You don't know anything for definite yet. You could be wrong. There could be a perfectly legitimate explanation."

"For another woman being asleep next to my husband in bed in his hotel room?"

"I acknowledge it's a long shot. But you're the lawyer. You know better than anyone there's always two sides to every story."

"But he's refusing to talk to me and tell me his side of the story, which suggests to me there really is only one side."

"It's still, like, 4am in the morning there isn't it?

Rachel nods. "If he hasn't contacted me in the meantime, I'm ringing Cassandra Taylor's office as soon as it opens, 2pm our time, 9am theirs. But what the fuck do I do while I wait? Because if I don't do something I am going to have a heart attack or something. For the first time today I understand why Grace and other teenagers cut themselves. I think pain would help right now, give me something to feel which is easier to bear than how absolutely wretched I feel inside. I'm so angry I can't even cry."

"I'm so sorry Rachel. Do you want a glass of gin?"

Rachel shakes her head. "Not just yet. Maybe a bit later. I want to be able to talk straight if and when the lying, fucking cheat rings me back."

"I'll put the kettle on, then."

*

Gareth makes his way down to the Falls. It is just starting to get light. He is wearing only a T-shirt and jeans and he shivers in the cool night air coming off the thundering water. He's glad he is cold and uncomfortable. It is the least he deserves. He leans on the iron railings for a very long time staring at the tons of water, cascading endlessly, and tries to decide what to do.

Finally, he rings Rachel. She answers the phone calmly and coldly.

"Hello, you lying, fucking cheat."

"I take it you can speak then?"

"I'm not in work. Called in sick. I'm at Jenny's. Was that Cassandra Taylor I saw in bed with you?"

"Yes."

"How long have you been sleeping with her?"

"One night before she went back to Toronto and since I've been here."

"Does Eloise know?"

"Of course not. Look, I'm coming home today, as soon as I can get a flight. I need to explain myself in person, not over the phone."

Rachel says nothing.

"Rachel, did you hear what I said? I'm flying home later today."

"I heard you. Bring Eloise with you, she can't stay living in that woman's apartment, working for the bitch. I don't want my daughter having anything to do with her. "

"I'm not bringing Eloise home Rachel. She and Liam are having the time of their lives. The apartment belongs to Cassandra's business partner anyway, Beverley, and it's Beverley that she's interning with."

"I don't care, bring her home."

"I'm not going to do that Rachel. You can't take this away from Eloise just because of what I've done. You can't put your feelings in front of her interests."

"That's fucking rich, coming from you."

"I do realise that. I'll see you later."

Rachel hangs up. "I'll have that glass of gin now, Jen. A big one."

Chapter 30

Gareth walks back to the hotel room, cold to his bones. When he lets himself in, Cassandra is sitting up in the bed, hugging her knees.

"Thank goodness, I was worried about you. Where have you been?" She lifts the bedcovers, inviting him to get back into bed with her. Gareth shakes his head.

"I've been freezing myself down by the Falls, trying to come up with a story that Rachel might buy. Or at least one that she might pretend to buy. I thought perhaps I could tell her she'd been mistaken, that it was dark and all she'd seen was pillows bunched up in bed next to me not a person. Or I could tell her that you'd drunk too much on an empty stomach and been sick in a bar and I'd brought you back to my room to crash on the bed and I'd slept on the floor. I could have made you telephone Rachel and confirm that story. Take a leaf out of your book and blackmail you by threatening to tell Beverley about you and me if you didn't do as I said."

"If that's what you want, then I'll do it. I'll do whatever you say."

"No need. I've already called Rachel. Admitted it was you she saw and that we've been sleeping together."

"Why on earth did you do that?"

"Because after I'd thought about it for all of five minutes, I knew she wouldn't believe me. Even if she really wanted to. She's too clever for that. She would have worried it round in her mind, night after night, like she does when she's got some legal question

291

she needs to resolve, and she would have asked me questions and eventually she would have got it out of me."

"You could have at least tried lying first. There are plenty of relationships out there still going strong because one party decided to turn a blind eye to the truth."

"You might have been able to do that, being, as I've found out to my cost, a liar of Olympic gold medal standard. But I don't want to live like that. However normal I pretended things were, one day, sooner or later, my time would be up. And I wouldn't just be unfaithful but a liar too. I'm glad I didn't try that anyway. She already knew it was you she saw."

"She can't have known for definite. Not 100 per cent. You could have got away with that."

"You clearly don't know me at all and you certainly don't know my wife. I'm going home now to face the music. I'm getting in the shower and when I come out I want you to drive me back to Toronto to fetch my passport and stuff from the hotel. I'll get a cab to the airport."

"If you're sure that's what you want."

"It is. I'll call Eloise from the cab and tell her I got through everything I needed to do here and wanted to get back home. Tell Beverley whatever you need to tell her but I don't want anyone saying anything to Eloise about us being related or leukaemia or anything at all about this whole ridiculous situation. Not yet."

He opens the door to the bathroom. Before he walks in, he pauses: "How on earth did you think this thing was going to turn out, Cassie? When Beverley finally judged it the right time to tell me about the family connection, how did you imagine I was going to react?"

"I wasn't thinking at all, that's the problem, right there. I wanted to be with you so much that I completely ignored reality and just enjoyed the moments. How did you think it was going to turn out? That you'd leave Rachel and your children and we'd ride off into the sunset together?"

"I hadn't quite reached that point yet, but the more time I spent with you, the more I wanted to spend time with you. I don't think it's possible to love two people, to really love them mind, body and soul and yearn to be with them. Not both at the same time. I was falling in love with you Cassandra. I must have been falling out of love with Rachel."

"I was falling in love with you too, but I could never leave Beverley, not after she's been so ill. Can't we carry on as we are? Seeing each other in secret? I can find excuses to be in London on a regular basis, find excuses to get you out here."

"You really do take the biscuit Cassie. I was falling in love with you before I knew the whole thing had started off as a fucking set up. Before I knew the kind of person you really are. That you scheme and you use people. I have no intention of carrying on a transatlantic affair with – let me get this right now – my great aunt's girlfriend – who made me think she fancied me so she could blackmail me. No thanks."

*

Rachel sips at the gin and tonic that Jenny has brought her.

"That doesn't taste anywhere near as nice this time of the morning as it does after work," she informs Jenny.

"Do you want a cup of tea instead?"

"No, it's OK, I'll push through."

They sit for a while together in silence while Rachel takes small sips of gin and Jenny looks on anxiously, her hands wrapped round a mug of tea.

"What did he say?" Jenny asks finally.

"That, as I suspected, he's been sleeping with his client."

"Has it been going on long?"

"Not long, a couple of weeks maybe."

"What are you going to do now?"

"Get drunk. Maybe have a good cry in a bit when I feel less numb."

"I didn't mean what are you going to do right this minute. What are you going to do later on, when Gareth gets home? Can you forgive him?"

"He didn't actually say he wanted to be forgiven. All he said was that he needed to explain himself to me in person."

"He'll want to be forgiven Rachel. Whatever nonsense he's been up to with this woman, she won't hold a candle to you and the children."

"But she must do, mustn't she? Why else put everything we have at risk? She must mean a great deal to him. And he can't have loved us as much as I thought he did to start something with her in the first place."

"Life is long and complicated, Rachel. Even good people do stupid things sometimes."

"You're just being careful not to slag him off in case we stay together."

"Oh didn't I slag him off out loud? Sorry. I think he's a selfish, self-indulgent bastard who's obviously been thinking with nothing but his prick. But for what it's worth, before today I always liked Gareth. And, if I'm honest, thought he was rather cute."

"What's weird is that when I first met Gareth I had this long standing boyfriend called Will and I was cheating on him with Gareth. I knew it wasn't right and that I wasn't being fair, but I was finding it difficult to choose between them."

"So why did you choose Gareth in the end?"

"He wanted me so much more than Will. He fancied me more. He found me more interesting. And he kept telling me as much. And so I eventually dumped Will. How vain is that, when you think about it? Picking my life partner on the basis of how good he made me feel about myself! But right after I dumped Will, I wasn't absolutely certain I was making the right choice and so a couple of times after the big break up – after Gareth and I had become official – I actually snuck back to Will and cheated on Gareth with him, like I was making doubly certain that it was

Gareth I preferred. I've never told anyone that before. That I was once a lying, fucking cheat, too."

"That's not the same thing at all. That was just…a transition period, like keeping your old comfy boots when you get a new pair and wearing them again a few more times afterwards, before you break the new ones in, because your feet are hurting and miss the old pair."

"Interesting analogy, and nice of you Jenny, but it was just plain old fashioned cheating."

"Well it's an entirely different thing to have a bit of post-break up sex with your ex-boyfriend while still in your twenties and not yet married and with no children. I wouldn't beat yourself up about it."

"But I am beating myself up Jenny. Gareth and I were happy. Good jobs, nice house, great kids, still had sex regularly, nice to each other. How could he do this to me?"

"I have no idea. Off his fucking head if you ask me."

"Maybe I should look Will up on Facebook?"

"Don't. He'll probably be bald and fat and have six kids. Or maybe he won't. Either way it's dangerous."

"I feel like all this is happening to someone else and I'm sat here watching it unfold, like it's some sort of television drama. I feel completely dead inside."

"That's shock that does that. I'm afraid it'll start hurting very soon."

"You'd better get me another gin then. And my mother. I really want my mother. Ring my house and ask her to come round. Quick, else she and Felix will have swanned off to Cowbridge for the day, looking continental."

Francesca arrives as Rachel is nearing the end of the second glass.

"My poor baby girl," she says, putting her arms round her daughter. Finally the tears come.

By the time Gareth gets home, late that night, Rachel has long since conked out on gin and tears. The rest of the house is deserted. Round and about keeping Rachel's glass topped up all afternoon, Francesca and Jenny had gone online and found a holiday cottage in Tenby, available to rent immediately. Felix had been instructed by Jenny to pack on behalf of everyone, which he had done willingly but rather nervously, having never either had children of his own or visited west Wales.

"Wellies," Jenny had impressed upon him over the phone. "Don't forget wellies for everyone. And raincoats. And hoodies. Plenty of hoodies. And when you've got all that and the children into the Transporter, come round here to pick up Francesca."

Iris and Nora had accepted without question the explanation Francesca gave them that because their mother needed to work long hours on a big important deal, she and Felix had decided to whisk them all away to the seaside for a lovely few days. Even Oscar.

"There'll be fish and chips and ice cream and long walks on the beach," Francesca promised gaily, as she climbed into the front of the van.

Jenny watched as the van drove away, Felix looking decidedly uncomfortable at the right hand drive wheel, the children and Francesca grinning and waving cheerfully.

"I felt a bit like mothers in the war must have felt, lying to their children when they were being evacuated," she told Alastair later. "Well girls and boys, off you go on your adventure and Mummy and Daddy will be right here, waiting for you when you get home. Only living in separate houses."

"You don't know that for sure, " Alastair had consoled her. "Maybe they'll work something out."

"Maybe."

When the gin was all gone, Jenny had folded a rather floppy

Rachel into her own car, driven her home and put her to bed. She strategically placed a plastic waste paper bin on the floor beside the bed and two pint glasses of water on the bedside table.

The bin is still empty and the glasses full when Gareth gets home and peeks into the bedroom, before climbing into Nora's bed for a sleepless night.

When he hears Rachel get up at 6am and go downstairs, he waits for a while and follows her. He finds her searching through the kitchen drawers for paracetamol.

"I've got a killer hangover," she says. "Put the kettle on, will you?"

For one second, his heart lifts. Perhaps she is just going to pretend as if nothing has happened. Just let the whole sorry situation drift past them without touching them, so their lives together can continue.

Then she sits down at their battered kitchen table, the one they bought when they first moved into this house, marked over the years by their children with felt pens and crayons and forks, the legs chewed by Oscar when he was a puppy.

"Let's hear what you have to say," Rachel says. "And don't try and let yourself off the hook."

He tells it from the beginning.

When he's done, she sighs. "If I didn't have such a thumping head, I'd have another gin about now."

"I'm so very sorry, Rachel. I can't believe how stupid and selfish I've been. I love you very much, you and the children, and I don't want to lose you. Please will you give me a second chance?"

"I've been wondering since yesterday – gosh, was it really only yesterday? – whether you'd be asking me for that or for a divorce. You didn't actually say which it was when we finally spoke on the phone."

"I don't want us to get divorced Rachel. I want to be with you."

"Make your case then."

"What do you mean?"

"You're a frigging lawyer aren't you? Make your case. Why should I give you a second chance?"

"Because I love you and our four children, I can't imagine life without you. I've made a huge mistake for which I'm deeply sorry and it won't happen again."

"Jeez Gareth. That was just terrible. I thought you were meant to be a good lawyer. Surely you've been thinking through all the angles on this since I found out. Try harder. Give me your best shot."

He takes a deep breath.

"OK. If we split up it will be catastrophic not only for you and me to lose what has been a long and happy marriage, it will be catastrophic for our children. Our daughters will be devastated. Eloise could even mess up her A levels or one of them might end up cutting like Grace. Jake is younger and he won't be affected as much right now but later, when he's an unruly teen, he'll tell you that he hates you and wants to live with me all the time. We'll have to share our children – every other weekend. We can barely organise our diaries now when we're all under one roof. Who gets Christmas Day? Birthdays? Results Day? How will we cope when one of us meets someone else? Are you going to be OK if another woman comforts Nora if she wakes up crying during her weekend with me? Or is the person who is around when Iris starts her periods say? We'll have to sell this house so we can each get somewhere smaller. Share out our bed linen and crockery and the paintings, divide up all our photographs – the school ones, the family holidays, the ones we take every Christmas morning of them opening their presents."

"Anything else?"

His voice softens and she can hear tears now thickening his throat. "I want us to celebrate our silver wedding Rachel. I want to go on more family holidays with you and the children, maybe someplace more exotic than Tresaith. I want us to go to their graduation ceremonies together and drive holding hands in the back of fancy cars to their weddings, see you looking beautiful in a lavender mother of the bride outfit and comfort you while you weep during the ceremony. I want to lie by your side every night, your bare skin next to mine, listening to you snore. I want to bring you tea in bed every morning and drink wine in the kitchen with you every Friday night after work. I would miss you every single day of my life if we split up."

"Better."

"Please don't give up on me Rachel."

"I need to think things through Gareth. One of the saddest things about all this – and there are so many sad things – is that I haven't made a single major decision in my life without talking it over with you. I'm sitting here now listening to what you're saying to me and the first, ridiculous thought that jumps into my mind is that I want to talk over with *you* what I should do about *you*. How fucking messed up is that?" She hits her forehead with the heel of her hand as she says this, tears pricking her eyes.

Gareth gets up from his chair and tries to put his arms around her.

"Don't touch me Gareth. Don't you fucking dare touch me. Else I might just break."

He sits back down.

"I just want to hold you."

"And I'm weak enough to actually *want* you to hold me. You! Who's been holding someone else behind my back."

"I didn't mean it to happen, Rach."

"Is that meant to make me feel any better? You didn't *accidentally* cheat on me Gareth. It's not like you tripped and found you had somehow planted your dick inside another woman. You flew half way across the world to do just that for fuck's sake."

Gareth drops his head in shame. "I know. There's nothing I can say in mitigation…"

Rachel stops him in mid-sentence, holding her hand up like a

299

policewoman directing traffic. "If you talk to me like a lawyer, I swear I will cut your cheating dick off."

"You were the one who told me to make my best case!"

"I know I did. I'm entitled to be contrary. Right now, I'm entitled to be inconsistent."

"You are, perfectly entitled. Please can I come over and hug you?"

"No Gareth. I don't trust myself. I don't want to be comforted by you. Have you make me feel better about something that *you* did."

"Is there anything I can do to help make you feel better?"

"Yes you can bugger off to the Rhondda and stay up there tonight. Go tell your parents what a shit you are. That should even things out a bit, given my mother and Felix know, and Jenny and Alastair too."

"I wish you hadn't told anyone. It will be harder for you to give me a second chance when people we care about think less of me."

"Tough. You should have thought of that before you embarked on an affair. As I was saying, you go up to the Rhondda and while you're gone I'll think about what I'm going to do. Don't come back to the house till this time tomorrow."

Chapter 31

Gareth drives up to the Rhondda in a haze. It's a journey he usually loves, always cheering a little, even when he's all on his own in the car, when he passes the sign that says Welcome to Rhondda. He doesn't cheer today. When he pulls up outside the house he grew up in, he feels sick to his stomach at what he has to tell them.

The door is not locked when he pushes it open. It never is.

"Who's that?" his mother calls cheerfully from the kitchen when she hears someone at the door.

"It's me, Mam," Gareth calls from the hallway. "The local axe murderer, come for a spot of killing before going down the Naval for a pint. You really should lock the door you know. It's not safe."

"Course it's safe. We've nothing to nick except the telly and you'd need three people to lift that and they'd need to get past Davey, who'd guard that telly with his life. You coming into the kitchen or what? I'm putting the kettle on. If I'd known you were coming I'd have made a bit of cake. What you doing here anyway? I thought you were away in..." She stops mid-sentence when she sees his face and all the colour drains out of her own.

"Good Lord Gareth, what's happened? Is one of my grandchildren sick?"

"No Mam, nothing like that. Is Dad in? And Davey?"

"Dad's out the back. Davey's at the library with Mrs Roberts from down the street, getting her new books."

"Good. I'll go get Dad."

He finds his father down on his hands and knees, planting out a tray of blue and white flowers into terracotta troughs.

"I thought you were done with gardening, Dad?"

"It's your mother that's done with gardening. I miss it myself. It's just a few pots of lobelia and alyssum. I'm not going to set about ripping up her beloved decking."

"I need to talk to you, Dad. You and Mam together."

Richard wipes his hands on the seat of his trousers and gets to his feet. Without saying anything, he follows his son back into the little kitchen where they find Carol sat at the table, looking worried. Richard slides into the chair next to her and takes her hand.

"Well, get on with it then, son. Put your mother and I out of our misery."

Gareth takes a deep breath. "The past couple of weeks I've been having an affair with a woman I met through work. A client. It was her I was with when I was in Canada. To my shame I was falling for her, really falling for her…"

"This doesn't sound too clever, Gareth," says Richard, gently.

"Not clever at all!" His mother's voice is angry. "Absolutely shameful. And over my dead body are you leaving Rachel and the kids and moving to bloody Canada."

"He's 44, Carol, and a grown man. You can't talk to him like that. Has Rachel found out?"

Gareth nods. "Yes she has, and she's very hurt and angry, as you'd expect and she has every right to be. The affair is over and I really want Rachel to give me a second chance. Cassandra turned out not to be what she seemed to be."

"They never are Gareth. But you men never learn. Always think the grass is greener on the other side,"

"Like I said, Mam, I thought I was falling in love with her."

"So what exactly happened to make you stop?" Carol asks, crisply.

"She told me the truth."

Gareth pauses.

"Go on son," Richard says gently. "Tell us the rest."

"Cassandra was in a long term relationship with an older woman…"

"And that stopped you in your tracks?" Carol cuts in disparagingly. "I didn't raise you to be homophobic! I didn't raise you to be unfaithful either."

"It wasn't that Mam. You didn't let me finish. The older woman is Beverley Allen, her business partner, and the person with whom Eloise is doing work experience over in Toronto. And Beverley belongs to us."

"Belongs? What do you mean?

"Beverley is related to us. She's the daughter of Idris Maddox."

"Blow me down with a feather," Carol says. "But that'd make her around Davey's age wouldn't it? In her eighties?

"Beverley's not that old. Late fifties, maybe. Idris was fifty something when she was born."

"Golly, this is like something off of Jeremy Kyle!" Carol sounds excited by the drama of it all.

"It gets worse, Mam. Beverley claims that Idris isn't only her father but also Davey's. That Davey's father Tommy wasn't able to have children and that before he went out to Canada Davey's mother asked Idris to give her a child."

Carol's mouth sags open and for once she doesn't speak.

"That explains a lot," Richard says quietly, after a while. "Why Idris never came home again. Not once, not even for his parents' funerals. Why Gwen and Tommy didn't like to talk about him and on the rare times they did they always sounded sad. Why Davey was an only child…"

"This doesn't make sense Gareth. I thought you said this woman was a client. Is that how you met her girlfriend? Started cheating not only on your wife but on your…let me see now… your grandfather's sister.

"She's Davey's half-sister Mam. It didn't come about like that.

303

I only found out who Beverley really was two days ago. She's known who I was, who Eloise is, all along. She sent Cassandra to find me. They pretended they needed me as their lawyer. When really what they want is our bone marrow."

"You've lost me now."

Richard and Carol both look confused.

"Beverley needs a bone marrow transplant but hasn't found a match in Canada. She'd thought she'd try her luck over here. In a gene pool related to her. And in case we weren't willing to come forward as donors, Cassandra thought she'd add a little blackmail to the mix by setting me up for an affair."

"You can lead a horse to water Gareth…" his father says, sternly. "This pair of women are not coming out of this story in a good light but you aren't covering yourself in glory either."

"You're right there, Dad. I'm completely ashamed of myself and have put everything I hold dear at stake for—"

"A bit of skirt," Richard finishes the sentence.

"All I can say in my defence is that it felt like much more than that at the time. Much more. I was tricked."

"You should never have been in the market for being tricked in the first place, my boy," Carol points out. "You remember that, when you're begging Rachel to take you back. And you'd better beg hard."

"Your mother's right, Gareth. You must have been off your rocker to risk your family for sex."

"It wasn't like that Dad?"

"Wasn't it?"

Gareth doesn't answer.

"So what happens now?" Richard asks.

"Can I stay here tonight? Rachel wants me to keep away, give her a little time to think. Her mother and Felix have taken the kids away for a few days."

"No," Carol says, coolly.

"No?"

304

"You heard me. You get yourself back down to Cardiff and you grovel to that girl. You've not got a moment to waste."

"But I'm trying to respect her wishes."

"Now's not the time to be doing that. You get yourself down there and if she doesn't let you in, you stay outside all night in the cold and dark until she does. She needs to know you've got sticking power. That you really mean it when you say sorry. That you won't ever, not ever, let her and your children down again. That she is the most important thing in your world and always will be, whatever your John Thomas might have led you to believe for a short, stupid while."

"What you waiting for?" his father asks. "Get going with you."

"But what should we say to Davey? About who his father was and about Beverley?"

"You leave me to worry about that, son. You go and concentrate on what's most important right now. *Your* family. Not Davey's long lost one."

305

Chapter 32

Gareth stops at Tesco on the way back. He buys a couple of bottles of wine and some cheese and biscuits. He hesitates at the bouquets of flowers and the boxes of chocolate but does not buy any. He makes a pact with himself. If Rachel forgives him he will buy her flowers every chance he gets, but tonight he won't kid himself that what he has done can be made even the slightest bit better with supermarket gifts.

He doesn't text her or call to say he is coming and as he pulls up outside their house it suddenly dawns on him that she might have gone out. Or that the house may be full of book club girls, helping Rachel drown her sorrows. He stops at the front door, his keys in his hands, but decides not to let himself in. Instead he rings the doorbell.

"Just a minute," he hears her calling from inside.

"Oh, it's you," she says when she opens it.

"You sound disappointed. Who were you expecting?"

"That bloke with a scythe off Poldark. I rang him and asked him if he fancied a booty call. Said it would take him a couple of hours to drive up from Cornwall but he'd be here by teatime… I'm not expecting anyone. Least of all you. You're meant to be in the Rhondda."

"Can I come in?"

"I'm busy right now doing a major clear up of the kitchen drawers. Did you know we have a tin of chickpeas in the cupboard that turns out to be older than Iris?"

"I didn't know that, no."

306

Rachel doesn't move aside to let him in.

"So can I come in?"

"If you really must."

"I really must."

*

Gareth follows her back to the kitchen and puts the wine bottles on the table.

"You brought wine. At least you're good for something. I was all out."

"Sit down and I'll pour us a glass."

"Make mine a double. It's thirsty work cupboard cleaning. What are you doing here anyway? I asked you to stay away. Did you chicken out of telling your news to your parents?"

"I told them. They are bitterly disappointed and ashamed of me. Although nowhere near as disappointed and ashamed as I am myself."

"Or as I am."

"Or that. I'm here to tell you that I love you. Very much. And the children. And that if you give me a second chance I will never let you down again, not ever."

"But that's one of the worst things about this Gareth. I have never once doubted that you loved me and the children and that you would never let me down. I wouldn't have married you if I didn't feel like that. Wouldn't have stayed married to you if you hadn't made me feel like that every single day of our lives together. Only it turned out I was wrong."

"You weren't wrong Rachel. It's only the past few weeks that I let you down. All the rest of the time it's been like you thought it was."

"So why did things change? I really need to understand that. If I'm to give you a second chance I need to know where we went wrong."

307

"We didn't go wrong Rachel. I did. I found someone else attractive and interesting and I was stupid enough and vain enough to follow it through. Believe me, I've never given anyone else a second look. Not once."

"That just makes it worse. If I've been all you've wanted all these years, she must have been something very special for you to want her instead."

"It wasn't that she was so special, it was just that I stopped seeing how special you are."

"Don't talk crap Gareth. You met someone you fancied more than me. That's correct isn't it?"

"Now you're the one talking like a lawyer."

"Just answer the question."

Gareth pauses. "I didn't fancy her more. But I did fancy her, yes."

"How was the sex?"

"Don't Rachel."

"I want to know!"

"It was good."

"Just good? You risked our marriage for some *good* sex?"

"No. Yes. It was great sex. I risked our marriage for great sex. It felt like when you and I first met Rachel. Do you remember how that felt?"

"Of course I do. But no one can keep that intensity up. Not after four children. Not after just one child! It's not real life!"

"It wasn't real life, that was the point, I think. It was like someone had cloned me and the duplicate me was leading a different, fantasy life."

"Get over yourself Gareth. All you did was have a sordid little affair with someone whose fanny you didn't know as well as mine. One that hadn't pushed out four children. Your children."

"I'm sorry."

"I know you are."

"I want things to go back the way they were."

"Things will never be the way they were."

308

"That makes me sad."

"It makes me sad too."

They are both crying now. Gareth gets up from the chair and goes over to Rachel to comfort her. This time she doesn't push him away. This time she lets him hold her and stroke her hair. Lets him tilt her chin and kiss her. Lets him lead her upstairs.

"You'll have to wear a condom," she says, wiping her nose with the back of her hand. "I don't want to catch anything."

"You won't catch anything!"

"You don't know that!"

"She's been in a relationship with the same woman for years."

"So you say. But she's a scheming liar. Or you are. Either way, use a condom. There's some in my bedside table."

"Why have you got condoms in your bedside table?"

"I bought them for Eloise."

"I'm going to pretend I didn't hear that."

"That makes two of us pretending we didn't hear things we don't want to know then."

*

They fall asleep afterwards and when they wake it is after 9pm. Rachel is lying on her side facing away from Gareth. He strokes her arms and back for a long time.

"Shall I go fetch the wine we didn't drink and the cheese I bought."

"Yes please."

"Anything else you want?"

"Yes, bring up the Scrabble board?"

"You want to play Scrabble?"

"Yes."

"In bed?"

"Yes in bed, while drinking wine with my husband in a house with no children in it."

"OK I'll find the Scrabble. You always beat me at it though."

"I know."

*

They give themselves two days of this. They ring in sick at work, put their out of office on their emails and turn their phones off. There is more wine, more sex and more Scrabble. A lot of tenderness. They go to sleep at night and wake up in the morning curled tight into each other.

But on the third morning, the day the children and Francesca and Felix are due back home, when Gareth wakes up Rachel is already up. He finds her sitting at the kitchen table with a cup of tea.

"More in the pot if you want."

He nods and she pours him a cup, hands it to him. They sip their tea in silence for a while before she puts her cup down and turns to look at him.

"I've reached my decision Gareth."

He smiles and reaches across the table, takes her hands in his. She wriggles her hands away.

"My decision is this. You and I are finished. As a couple anyway. I could take you back – for the sake of the kids, the house, our parents, for an easier life. I could even enjoy it – it turns out, rather surprisingly, that we can still have good sex together, despite your betrayal of me. But I know I'd never forgive you. Not truly forgive you. It would just eat away at me – resentment of you would fester inside me and eventually I'd come to hate you and to hate myself."

"Please, Rachel, don't do this. Everything is still raw. We can make this work. I know we can. We've had twenty good years together. Don't throw them away."

"You did that Gareth, not me."

"But these past few days together have been amazing. So… passionate. What was all that about?"

Rachel answers him in a level voice. "It was about saying goodbye Gareth. It was about giving our marriage a proper send off and finishing things on my terms. It was about making you realise what you had and what you lost."

"Please Rachel, I won't know what to do with myself without you and the children."

"That's not my problem. Take up cycling or something. Join the legions of sad, middle-aged men with skinny legs wearing lycra, zipping around Penarth looking ridiculous of a Sunday morning."

"I'm being serious Rachel."

"So am I Gareth. All these years of being with me and you didn't work even this much out about me. You do not get away with fucking around and I will never be a victim. It's over. Now get out."

*

His mother makes up his old bedroom for him. It's the smallest room in the house and used as a computer room these days but his single bed is still in there. The duvet cover is the same one he had as a teenager – chocolate and caramel stripes, faded now. Gareth has not seen that duvet cover in years and if asked would have been unable to tell you what it looked like but the instant he sees it again a high definition memory pops into his mind, like a memory card being inserted in a computer. He is 16 years old and he and Lynwen Davies spend the whole of one sunny Saturday afternoon pressed tightly together lying on top of this duvet cover, while his parents and Davey are out shopping in Cardiff. It is the first time he ever touches a bare breast. Or inside top as it is referred to at school.

Lynwen lived in the next street down. She was fun and pretty but not particularly academic. She hadn't talked to him again after that afternoon, on account of being asked out by Terry

Pritchard, captain of the local rugby team, who was generally considered by the female teenage population of the Rhondda to be both cool and fit. The last Gareth had heard of either of them they had moved away to live. Swindon, he seems to remember. Or maybe it was Slough? He feels a sudden pang of loss for Lynwen and their afternoon together. The way she had grown impatient with his lack of inclination and lifted up her own shirt for him, confidently taking his hand and plonking it for him on top of her breast.

"I feel like I'm stuck in a bit of a time warp, Mam, back here with you and Dad."

"You and me both son. Don't take this the wrong way because you know you are always welcome, but I'd really rather you didn't have reason to be back."

"Me too, Mam, me too."

"Let's go down to the kitchen and have a cup of tea. Your dad wants to talk to you about this Beverley Allen lady while Davey's out playing bowls."

Gareth sighs and follows his mother down the stairs.

Richard is sitting at the kitchen table. He has been making notes in pencil in one of the small leather bound notebooks his grandchildren buy him every Christmas and birthday. Richard likes to make notes. He has stuck the stub of pencil behind his ear. Gareth recognises this pencil – it is one from his old London law firm, given to his father many years ago. It is now no more than a couple of inches long. Gareth wonders if there are many other people out there who actually use a pencil up, write with it and sharpen it over and over again until it wears down to nothing.

Gareth takes a seat opposite him at the small kitchen table. His mother puts three mugs of tea down and a packet of Jaffa Cakes.

"So," his father begins, in a formal voice Gareth has heard only a handful of times for making toasts at family events, "your mother and I have been talking about this whole sorry situation. We've decided that the right thing to do is say nothing to Davey."

"Dad, the last thing on my mind right now is that lot over in Canada. I've got too much on my plate as it is."

"If you've got too much on your plate, my boy, it's because you were greedy."

"That's unfair," Gareth bristles, "I didn't choose to be misled. That was all their doing."

"Listen now, you're not the innocent party here. Davey is."

"Oh."

"Oh indeed, what with all your recent shenanigans, you appear to have forgotten about your grandfather in all this. And his sister."

"Half-sister," Gareth corrects.

"Same thing. Beverley Maddox. One of us."

"Hardly one of us Dad. Doesn't even use our name. Prefers Allen."

"Gareth, stop being such an arse, as Eloise would say—"

"Good heavens Richard, watch your language," Carol interjects.

"An arse," Richard repeats. "I've been doing some research and Phil Davies from down the Naval has a niece who's a nurse and works with leukaemia patients. Even if Davey were a match, he's past being a donor. His marrow is just too old now."

"You weren't seriously thinking about suggesting to Davey he donate were you?"

"Of course I was. After all this heartbreak, all this distance between a family, don't you want something good to come out of this fiasco? Like saving a life."

Gareth pauses. "I suppose so."

"Right. Talking sense at last. So your mother and I have agreed that we will tell Davey about Beverley having got in contact with the family but not tell him that Idris is his father."

"Don't you think Davey deserves the truth?"

"The truth is powerful stuff. It can hurt people. Who's to say Idris was his father? For all anyone knows it *could* have been

313

Tommy. And even if Idris was biologically his father, Tommy was his dad, just like he was my granddad. Davey's 88, Gareth. He doesn't need his world turned upside down at this stage."

Gareth nods. "OK, Dad."

"But you and I are going to be tested to see if we are a match for Beverley's bone marrow."

"You what?"

"You heard me. Get in touch with Beverley. Sort it out. Quick. Before it's too late for her."

*

When the results come back and neither Richard nor Gareth are matches, Gareth is surprised how disappointed they all are.

"It would have been a redemption, of sorts," he says to Beverley over the telephone.

"Seems to me we were all in the wrong on this," Beverley tells him. "Life's too short to hold a grudge. Mine certainly is."

"I wish Rachel felt the same."

"One day she might. Don't give up."

"I'm not."

"Are you sure you won't come to the wedding?"

"Positive."

The full truth may not have been told in the Rhondda, but it has come tumbling out in Toronto, like a swollen, muddy, river bursting its banks. And far from being crushed by Cassandra's infidelity and betrayal of her, Beverley had instead asked Cassandra to marry her and she had accepted.

Gareth is not having it as easy.

"You are a complete and utter tosser, Dad, and I hate you," Eloise told him. Rachel had insisted Gareth Skype her and tell her the whole story, as close to face to face as possible. "And don't think Liam and I are coming home just because you can't keep it in your trousers."

314

Eloise refuses to talk to Gareth after that. It is Beverley who calls him to break the news that Eloise has insisted on being tested too.

"She's not a match, though."

"I'm sorry Beverley."

"Liam is."

"Liam?"

"He went with Eloise to the hospital to keep her company when she was being tested and he got tested at the same time. Turns out he's a good enough match. And he's agreed to donate."

"That's great news, Beverley," Gareth can feel tears gathering thickly in the back of his throat.

"It is, isn't it? Thank you so much Gareth."

Thanks for what? Gareth thinks. Cheating with your girlfriend? Having Eloise? Bringing her and Liam to you in Toronto? Making a complete and utter balls up of my own life?

315

Chapter 33

Gareth rents a little house in Penarth. It is on a modern estate, a little outside Penarth town centre, a squat, square box with rooms of tiny proportions.

"It's like a dolls' house," Rachel comments whenever she drops the children off.

"Ha, ha," Gareth says. It's got four bedrooms for the children to come stay and it's close to you. It will do."

Rachel refuses to come in, though. And she has changed the locks on their house and not given Gareth a key.

Of the children, it is only Eloise who has not adapted to the new living arrangements. Although she will now at least go with her siblings to visit her father, she refuses to stay overnight with them at the rented house.

"All my stuff is at home and I'm too old for sleep-overs. Anyway, I haven't got time. Too much revision and if I've got any spare time I want to go up to London and see Liam."

Since the bone marrow donation, Liam and Eloise have been closer still. The procedure was a success. Marrow was harvested from the back of both of Liam's hipbones and transferred to Beverley. Liam recovered very quickly and after a week or so he was well enough to leave Toronto. He and Eloise then spent three weeks travelling across Canada on the Trans Canada train, stopping off along the way. Beverley paid for all their tickets and expenses. They flew home from Vancouver, business class, a few weeks before the start of school term.

Eloise had stopped dyeing her hair in Canada and returned

home with redhead roots. It will take a long while yet for the black to grow out completely. Liam is now back at university and they miss each other terribly. Eloise intends to apply to go to university in London too to be near to him but Rachel is not keen.

"You've got to live a little while you're young, have fun, go out with lots of people."

"I only want to go out with Liam, Mum."

"You should spread your wings though. Your father and I got married far too young."

"We're not even contemplating getting married, Mum. We're just happy together. Don't project all your regrets on to me."

Beverley made a good recovery and is now in fairly good health. She still needs to take it easy and has semi-retired from Perfect. Cassandra is now the CEO. Carol, Richard and Davey watched the wedding video on Facebook. The ceremony had taken place at Parkwood, now a National Historic Site of Canada, and a popular wedding venue.

"Looks an absolute fabulous do," Davey had commented. "Pity no one could make it. Those gardens are wonderful. How about we do a couple of grow bags of tomatoes next year, Richard? Just along the decking there. I do miss growing a bit of veg."

The Perfect factory in the Rhondda is due to open very soon. Cassandra has seconded one of her direct reports to live in Wales and oversee the project. He is enjoying the new challenge immensely. It should eventually result in the creation of at least 250 direct jobs in the Rhondda. Training programmes are well underway for the employees who will sew Perfect shirts. The factory and the new jobs it will bring have featured heavily in the media all over the UK and in Canada. Adrian Matthews, now reinstated to the deal, has been seen on telly numerous times talking about the project, looking very dashing in a designer suit and a crisp, Perfect shirt. Whereas Perfect no longer use Gareth's firm as their lawyers.

His fellow partners are miffed at the lost opportunity.

"Best new client to set up in Wales in a very long time and you go and muck it up," one of his partners says tartly when he discloses that Perfect have instructed another firm.

"You win some, you lose some," Gareth shrugs. Adrian has picked up plenty of other new corporate finance work due to the coverage of the Perfect deal and is referring it all to Gareth who will smash his billing target again this year.

His hope is that Rachel will take him back and he still believes there is a chance of that. She is always so pleasant to him for a start, actually looks like she is glad to see him when he knocks on her door with a pizza or a bottle of wine, asking if she fancies some company. She always lets him in, sits in the kitchen with him to share the pizza or the wine, chatting about work, the children, how Iris has been selected for the Welsh regional development women's football squad, how Nora has been nit free for a record seven weeks, the upset of Jake's top two teeth finally coming through, the jagged edges sawing through his tender little gums and causing him pain. She even talks about the Perfect factory opening soon. Smiling and laughing, easy and comfortable with him, as you'd expect from people who've known each other a lifetime. But she always ushers him back out again afterwards and locks the door firmly behind him.

Adrian is keen that Gareth should get back in the dating game.

"I don't know what you were thinking with Cassandra. It was plain as the nose on your face that she was gay. I could tell after just one dinner with her. Zero sexual chemistry. You're a good looking bloke Gar, come out with me on a Saturday night. We can have a game of squash first and then go into town. The good looking divorcees will be all over you like a rash, believe me. Own hair, teeth and car. All the female company you want, no problem."

But Gareth doesn't want this. He wants his wife back, not another woman. He wants to come home of a Friday night with a bottle of good Chablis under each arm and sit next to Rachel in their garden, eating pistachios. Pile up the empty shells in a little heap, pour another glass, and watch as their four lovely children come and go. Take her to bed at the end of the day and hold her close.

Whenever he tries to tell Rachel how he feels, she changes the subject to talk of work or the children or how well Grace is doing back at home in Bucks, having secured not only outstanding results in her GCSEs but an agent for her novel.

"She and Jocelyn and Nick are coming to stay in a couple of weeks. I can't wait. I've really missed Grace being around. Best of all Jocelyn says she hasn't self-harmed in months. How amazing is that? Can't say I'm looking forward quite as much to listening to Jocelyn brag how Grace is going to win a fancy fiction prize some day, but even Jocelyn has been supportive of me since you and I separated. There's something in that old cliché about blood being thicker than water."

Gareth hates this word. Separated. That's how it feels to him. Like Rachel's been torn away from him, his skin ripped raw in the process, like Sellotape he's pressed to his lip and then yanked off, taking little lumps of tender flesh with it.

But eventually there comes a turning point.

It is a Saturday afternoon, his weekend to have the children. His parents have come for a visit and have brought Davey with them. His mother has brought two large bags of shopping.

"Brought a few bits with me, thought I'd make us some corned beef pie for our tea."

Within seconds of arriving, his father and Davey are out in the garden. It is small and square just like the house and completely neglected, the grass knee high, dry and brown.

"How about I go ask a neighbour to borrow a lawnmower and Davey and I will tidy this up a bit. I could even pop down to the garden centre, and buy a couple of trays of winter pansies. Give it some colour for this last little bit of autumn sunshine."

"I don't know any of my neighbours, Dad."

"So? I'll ask nice, don't worry."

319

Iris and Nora seize on the opportunity.

"While Granddad and Davey are doing the garden, how about you take us swimming Dad? To the big pool with the slides?"

"I'm not coming swimming," Eloise says abruptly. "I came for a visit with my grandparents not to sluice around in lukewarm chlorine with half of Cardiff."

"She doesn't need to come, Dad," Iris reasons. "Just you, me and Jake. Please."

"Did you pack your bathers?"

"No, but you could drive home quickly and fetch them for us? It won't take five minutes."

"Oh, ok then."

His younger daughters cheer.

When he gets to the house, the front door is wide open. He knocks and after waiting a while walks in. There is no one downstairs but he hears voices upstairs. He climbs the stairs and finds the landing stacked with brand new bedroom furniture, a king-size mattress still wrapped in plastic, and his bedroom full of book club girls, busily painting the walls.

"Oh – hello you," Rachel says breezily.

"Erm, the front door was open. I've come to pick up the kids' bathers. They cornered me into taking them swimming."

"They should be in their bedrooms somewhere. Or possibly the airing cupboard. Or failing that in a bag dumped in the hall somewhere. While you're here I've got a ton of boxes of your old stuff you can take with you. Including that Oasis T-shirt I wouldn't let you wear, even back in Law School. I don't think you've thrown a single thing out since 1996!"

"What's the story morning glory?" Jenny sticks her head round the bedroom door, breaking off from decorating duties. "Do you want a gin? We're got three different types in here. Delicious."

"No, no thanks," Gareth says, grumpily

"Suit yourself. Another hour or so Rachel and we should be done and we can get on with the next project."

320

"Great."

"What's all the re-decorating in aid of anyway?" Gareth asks

"It was the girls' idea," Rachel replies. Fresh start and all that. I've even got a new duvet and pillows, new bed linen, the lot. Hey, you can have the old one if you want? I've already got spares knocking around and a spare is useful to have – sometimes the children like to take a duvet downstairs to watch films."

"I do know my own children, Rachel."

"Course you do. I know."

"And the next project? What's that?"

"We're trying to persuade her to sign up to a dating agency," Jenny's voice calls from inside the bedroom. "Michelle's met a really nice man online."

"I thought Michelle wasn't interested in men anymore."

"I tracked down my libido in the end!" Michelle's voice now. "With a little help from my friends and my Magimix. Working just fine now, thank you very much."

"Congratulations."

He stands around for a few seconds longer, Rachel looks at him expectantly.

"Hurry up then," she says at last.

"What do you mean?"

"The kids' bathers. Go look for them."

"Oh, yes, ok."

He walks around the house, collecting bathers. Nora's bedroom is the last room he goes to. Her bug-eyed teddies are lined up as usual along her bed in her special order and as usual he takes two of them and switches their places. He knows she will spot it straight away and will then complain about it to Rachel, who will play along with this long-standing joke of his and tell Nora, just like he would, that they must have moved all by themselves when she wasn't looking.

The full weight of his regret kicks him hard in the stomach, winding him.

He goes out to the landing and calls for his wife.

"Rachel!"

She doesn't hear at first, over the clamour of women laughing and painting walls and drinking gin.

He calls again, more urgently.

"Rachel!"

She comes out to the landing.

"OK, ok, whose bathers can't you find?"

"Could we have a word, please? Perhaps in here?"

He walks back into Nora's bedroom and Rachel follows him.

Words gush out of him. "Rachel – I miss you so much I ache. Please let me try again. Let me come back and love you enough that you are able to get past what I did. I can make you happy again, I know I can."

Rachel says nothing, just looks at him. Gareth continues.

"I don't want to fall in love with someone new, however much Adrian tells me that there's wall to wall single women in Cardiff, lining up to meet me. I love you and it's only you I want. I want the chance to make you fall in love with me again. Please say you'll let me try."

"Adrian's right you know. If you re-enter the dating scene, you will be spoiled for choice. You're handsome, good company, got great hair and a well-paid job, you're a hands-on father. All very attractive. And let's not forget that I've trained you to be pretty good in bed too."

"Thanks for the compliments. I think they're compliments anyway. But it's you I want to ask on a date. Will you, please? I love you Rachel, you know I do."

"And I love you too."

Relief floods through Gareth and he grins at Rachel and opens his arms, takes a step towards her to embrace her. But she takes a step backwards.

"But I'm never going to take you back."

The grin on Gareth's face disappears.

"Don't look so upset. I told you this. When it all happened. I don't know what makes you think I would change my mind."

"It's been a few months I was hoping you might be willing to forgive me now. Whenever we've had rows in the past you've always forgiven me within days."

"Gareth! Most of our rows in the past have been about whose turn it is to put the bins out or change a nappy, or who should get up and do a night feed based on who has the most important meeting in the morning. This isn't the same thing at all."

"I know it's not, I know. What I did was selfish and cruel and I betrayed you and our children and I could not be sorrier or more sad. I miss you all so much, miss being home, every second I'm awake. Please Rachel – give me a chance."

"I'm well aware trying again makes more sense. We're stuck with each other for years to come anyway if we're going to raise our children properly. But I want to share my life with someone I trust. Like how I used to trust you."

"You can trust me again, honestly. I warrant, confirm and undertake that you may trust me at all times."

Rachel smiles at the legal language.

"I can't Gareth. You broke my trust, and even if I wanted to forgive you, I couldn't."

He pauses. "So that's it for us. Really it?"

"That's really it, Gareth. Apart from the next eighteen years of co-parenting, followed hopefully by as many years co-grand-parenting. Let's make sure we stay friends for all that, shall we?"

Rachel reaches over and pats him twice, gently on the arm, then walks through the door of her bedroom to re-join the decorating and drinking taking place in there.

Gareth takes a deep breath, bundles the swimming costumes under one arm and walks down the stairs and out the house, closing the door firmly behind him. He hurries to his car. The low, autumn sun is still shining and his children will be waiting for him.

ABOUT HONNO

Honno Welsh Women's Press was set up in 1986 by a group of women who felt strongly that women in Wales needed wider opportunities to see their writing in print and to become involved in the publishing process. Our aim is to develop the writing talents of women in Wales, give them new and exciting opportunities to see their work published and often to give them their first 'break' as a writer. Honno is registered as a community co-operative. Any profit that Honno makes is invested in the publishing programme. Women from Wales and around the world have expressed their support for Honno. Each supporter has a vote at the Annual General Meeting. For more information and to buy our publications, please write to Honno at the address below, or visit our website: www.honno.co.uk

Honno, 14 Creative Units, Aberystwyth Arts Centre
Aberystwyth, Ceredigion SY23 3GL

Honno Friends

We are very grateful for the support of the Honno Friends: Jane Aaron, Annette Ecuyere, Audrey Jones, Gwyneth Tyson Roberts, Beryl Roberts, Jenny Sabine.

For more information on how you can become a Honno Friend, see: http://www.honno.co.uk/friends.php